PEACOCK IN THE SNOW

We gratefully acknowledge the support of the Canada Council for the Arts and the Ontario Arts Council for our publishing program. We also acknowledge the financial support of the Government of Canada.

Cover design: Val Fullard

Peacock in the Snow is a work of fiction. All the characters and situations portrayed in this book are fictitious and any resemblance to persons living or dead is purely coincidental.

Library and Archives Canada Cataloguing in Publication

Mehta, Anubha, 1967-, author
Peacock in the snow / Anubha Mehta.

(Inanna poetry & fiction series)
Issued in print and electronic formats.
ISBN 978-1-77133-557-7 (softcover).-- ISBN 978-1-77133-558-4 (epub).--
ISBN 978-1-77133-559-1 (Kindle).-- ISBN 978-1-77133-560-7 (pdf)

I. Title. II. Series: Inanna poetry and fiction series

PS8626.E372P43 2018 C813'.6 C2018-904366-0
C2018-904367-9

MIX
Paper from
responsible sources
FSC® C004071

Inanna Publications and Education Inc.
210 Founders College, York University
4700 Keele Street, Toronto, Ontario, Canada M3J 1P3
Telephone: (416) 736-5356 Fax: (416) 736-5765
Email: inanna.publications@inanna.ca Website: www.inanna.ca

PEACOCK IN THE SNOW

a novel

Anubha Mehta

INANNA PUBLICATIONS AND EDUCATION INC.
TORONTO, CANADA

For my mother, Molly,
she is the reason that I see.

PART I

THE VAGARIES OF FATE

1. MAYA

THE DARKNESS WAS CHILLING my bones. There was not a single star in the pitch black sky. It must have been past midnight when I tossed in bed one more time, enveloped in an odd uneasiness. The light from the electric lantern that hung in the veranda was dancing on my bedroom door. Wizards, elephants, knights. But none could rescue me from the silent shadows inside. Even the garden crickets were silent, as if in anticipation of my decision.

Finally, exasperated by my lack of sleep, tucking my shoulders snugly under the folds of my shawl, I stepped out onto the lighted veranda. In spite of the heaviness in the air, out of nowhere, a strange wind had picked up. The wind's whispers brought with it the fragrance of jasmine, which was in full bloom between the shrubs.

For a moment only, an insipid moon dribbled from behind a dense cloud. I stretched my hand over the edge of the veranda, where the concrete steps met the garden, to feel for rain. But there was none. I plunged into the cane settee, trying to focus on the winding croton stems, but my concentration was broken by a strong chilly draught flying between the cement grills and heading straight towards the muslin drapes of my open bedroom. Spellbound, I followed it in and lay down.

In the darkness the whispers grew louder. It was a frail, feminine voice, almost an echo, calling out from the dark corners under my bed. I shivered and sat bolt upright.

Was someone there?

I strained my ears and this time I heard the words, distant but clear, "*Mayaaa ... Veeeer.*"

The hair on the back of my neck rose. I did not blink and I could not move. It was definitely the voice of a woman. Within moments she started laughing. Her deep, throaty laugh pulled me into a murky bottomless pit. I couldn't breathe. As I dug my nails into the edges of my bed to keep from falling, its wooden splinters pierced my figures. A heavy blanket of stillness descended from above and with it came a stench of rotten eggs.

And then from the corner of my room, behind the muslin drapes, she rose.

Merely a grey drift. But I saw her.

Her long black hair blew over her beautiful ashen face as her dark eyes looked directly at me. She wore a jade green dress with a peacock feather on her sash.

Oh! I had seen that face before, the colour of her skin, the curve of her jaw, those large doe eyes ... yes, I am sure of it. *But where?*

In a flash she started circling my head, working up to an angry frenzy. Her hair knotted up around her bloodshot eyes and her face turned green like fungus.

I was trapped. I had to get out. Through my tears I saw her reaching for my wrists. My palms were drenched in dark terracotta henna designs of vines and flowers that were to bring luck for the bride, but, instead, their tentacles slithered from the centre of my palm, winding their way around my throat. With the very last breath of life left in me, I moaned, "*Help!*"

Suddenly, the wind died down and I opened my eyelids. A divine smell of sandalwood replaced the earlier vile odour. I sat up. What a terrible nightmare. So real, so close, so sinister.

The night still remained, but the darkest hours seemed to have passed. Slowly my eyelids drooped again. And then somewhere between the heavy state of waking and sleeping, I was once again disturbed by another sound, this time a sharp ringing.

I stumbled for the night lamp and heard Veer's excited voice on the other side of the phone.

"Veer? What? Do you know what time it is?"

"Maya, it is a good time. Wake up!" He sounded like a little boy in a candy shop.

"Maya, do you know this is my last call to you?"

"Eh? Why?" What little sleep had come near me vanished instantly.

"Silly, don't you know that the groom is not supposed to talk to his bride before the wedding?" he laughed.

"Veer ... can we talk about this tomorrow? I..."

"Maya, don't you get it? We are getting married!"

I was silent.

"Maya?" I heard a hint of anxiety in his voice. "Maya ... are you there?" His voice pitched. I could picture the nerve on his forehead throbbing with nervousness.

I had to speak up. "Yes, Veer ... we are getting married."

I heard him breathe again.

I was numb. I sat up without moving. How could I hurt Veer? It had not occurred to him that I might not have accepted this union. Not until just now.

2.

IT WAS MY WEDDING DAY. And I was not ready. Not mentally, not in any way. If I could have run away, I would have. Today was so final. In a few hours I had to walk to the marriage pavilion. Who would have thought that marrying my sweetheart, Veer, would be so terrifying? But then who would have known the dark reason for my hesitancy?

The familiar warmth of my faded silk quilt was somewhat consoling. So were the dancing dust particles in the pale December sunlight. But they were not enough to dispel the storm of doubts that was threatening to drown me.

A sharp chill gripped my fingers and travelled towards my chest. What a coward I was.... I heard my name at the door, "Maya, Maya?"

It was Anita, my childhood friend, my confidante.

"Maya are you still in bed! Get up lazy bones!" Anita plonked herself on the edge of my quilt and slipped her toes under. I extended my cold hand and she cupped it warmly.

"Maya, you'd better soak up this peace before...."

"Yes, I know, Anita..."

But in spite of knowing, our ears could never get used to what followed within minutes: A string of high-pitched screams. Tina and Jiya! The culprits who started it all, who had introduced me to Veer.

"Oh my god Maya! *Uffff*.... Finally getting married.... Well, we always knew,!" Tina shouted. "And to think it seems just like yesterday when we dragged you to watch our school football practice where Veer could not take his eyes off you." Tina sniggered.

They both looked the same as they had in high school, just a little tired, I guessed from their wild party lives and man-hunting.

"Oh yes, if it wasn't for us ... you know ... there would not be a wedding!" Jiya joked.

The image of Veer the first time I saw him flashed before my eyes. Tall and brawny, with shoulders that resembled helipads, his broad forehead tapering into a widow's peak that peeped through a mass of falling hair, his strong angular jaw and *oh!* those hazel eyes dipped in curiosity. As his eyes locked in on mine, they started weaving a spell, pulling me rapidly and effortlessly, and my heart leapt to my throat. On that hot spring day I discovered a feeling I had not known before. I was drawn toward this complete stranger and, in that moment, nothing mattered except him and me.

"Oh, what nonsense," Anita snapped. "These two were destined to be together. I have never seen such bizarre magnetism grow in leaps and bounds with every passing day. Nothing could have kept them apart...."

She had such earnestness in her voice that it made me look up at her. If only I could tell her what had gone wrong. How for the first time, I felt compelled to break our rhythm. If only I could tell her about that weekend that changed everything.

I changed the topic. "There will be two more joining you as bridesmaids—my uncle's half-Canadian daughters from Vancouver, Judy and Ruth. They said that they were happy to be a part of this unwieldy, but extremely striking bridesmaids' group."

"Oh yes, for them, this will probably be a most exotic experience to carry back tales of to the West, and without being too ashamed of their Indian roots either," Anita said acidly.

"So, tell me, does Veer have any *brother-shuthers* ... a few more like him, eh?" Tina asked.

"So, who else is coming Maya?" Jiya chimed.

We all knew how serious Tina and Jiya's questions were.

Anita started giggling and her infectious giggles got to all of us.

They pulled me up to the dressing room. It was ablaze with spotlights to reveal every covert thought, hesitation and sin.

Mother had laid out my ornate bridal gown woven in gold brocade and aquamarine peacock colours, with a blouse that was revealing enough to excite anyone's imagination. There were fresh jasmine flowers for my hair and bronze stilettos with turquoise zircons for my feet.

The door opened once again and in walked two pale girls with suitcases in their hands and confusion on their faces.

"Judy and Ruth, welcome!" I ran to greet them and their frowns turned into smiles.

After an afternoon with the make-up artist, the hairdressers, and intolerable fussing by my crazy bridesmaids, we were ready to step out into the starless night.

"You look stunning!" Ma walked in with a brass tray filled with cups of rice pudding. The room flooded with aromas of jaggery, cinnamon, and cloves.

"Even more stunning than you, Ma?" I teased as she rocked me in the safety of her arms. I had inherited Ma's ethnic features of the Northwest. "I am not going anywhere Ma, I will always be with you," I lied and she sniffed.

"We are not losing you, Maya, we are gaining a son," Ma said somewhat tritely.

Born in Peshwar, and having had to move to Delhi before the India-Pakistan partition, Ma was blessed with a realism that had been so grounding to my flighty teenage views. And today I couldn't have been more thankful for it.

Ma marked a spot behind my ear with a kohl pencil as a century old tradition for warding off evil spirits. I wondered if this little black spot could really shield me against any evil that may be waiting for me.

I looked at my beautiful bridesmaids. Each had matched

their silk gowns to mine with different shades of the peacock's tail. Anita was in an earthy indigo, cloaked in the scent of white magnolias from her hair; Judy was wearing shades of peaceful jade and cobalt blue to match her eyes; and Ruth had balanced Judy with the freshness of violet. Jiya's warm ginger was perfectly synchronized with Tina's passionate burgundy.

Everything was going according to plan. Except a small cautionary voice inside my head had woken up to spar with the cold breeze outside. It was prodding me to open an unpleasant memory buried deep in my subconscious.

Should I stop and listen to it now?

Noooo.

I covered my ears. It was too late for caution. It was too late to turn back.

The cobbled path to the wedding pavilion was lined with silver-rimmed garden lanterns shining with just enough light to conceal my panic. The sweet scent of honeysuckle flew in from the hedges and from nowhere, a stealthy whispering breeze had started rustling through the low hanging branches of the mulberry and jamun trees.

"Ready?" Anita asked me.

I shook my head in denial.

"Maya!" she scolded and nudged me forward.

We started the processional bride's walk.

This was it. From this point onward I would add another world to my life. A new, unknown world of adventure, hope, love. I took a deep breath.

Judy and Ruth entered the marquee first. All eyes turned on us.

I could hear a low buzz of admiration from the crowds. I sensed awe, envy, ovation, curiosity, and pride as we passed each cluster of guests. I had never felt more important in my life.

The daïs was high and carpeted in crimson red with two rickety steps. Veer had already taken his position on it. I was handed a garland of red roses to place around Veer's neck. As

I stretched my arms with the garland to reach up to his neck, he lifted his head even higher.

What was Veer doing?

I looked into his eyes. He winked. A loud sigh escaped from my girlfriends. And then I could no longer feel the ground. Veer had lifted me in his arms. I could reach his neck now. Without wasting another second, I quickly placed the garland of red roses around his neck. He did the same to me and the whole pavilion resounded with loud applause.

But as I feared, the applause only encouraged Veer further. There was no stopping him now. He was already on to the next forbidden sin in our conventional Indian wedding. I felt his warm lips on mine. My heart jumped out of my chest. What was Veer doing? Was he kissing me? *Was he crazy!* This was not allowed in a traditional Indian wedding! Not in front of three hundred gaping guests! Not in front of anyone! The head priest, who was chanting hymns in the corner, stopped momentarily, and shook his head with what I presumed was disgust. Veer's rowdy friends whistled, clapped, and hooted. Tina and Jiya screamed with delight. Ma laughed out loud, Veer's mother looked appalled, his aunts sniggered, and our fathers were completely indifferent.

Everyone threw rose petals at us.

From this moment, the ceremony was a daze, with endless rituals around the holy fire. The priest explained the purpose of marriage and the list of expectations and duties of a good spouse in grave detail in between his Vedic chants. To complete the wedding, he tied a saffron scarf from my wrist to Veer's, connecting us for a lifetime together, for better or for worse.

It was past midnight before the wedding was finally over.

Finally, there was no more waiting to find out what my new life held. I could hear my mother-in-law's sharp voice above all others. She was asking everyone to move toward the waiting cars. It was time to leave. I looked for Veer but couldn't find him.

"Maya, you'd better come and resolve this." Anita pulled me towards the thickest part of the crowd.

Veer was standing in the middle of a small clearing surrounded by my bridesmaids. His face was beetroot red and he seemed to be pleading with them.

"What's happening?" I asked Anita.

"Oh, nothing much, we have his shoes."

"What!"

"Yes, we smuggled them away when he took them off for the prayers while you were busy getting married. And we will only give them back if he gives us what we want..."

"And what is that?"

"Gold rings, one for each of us!"

"Really!" How could I have forgotten one of the most popular Indian wedding traditions! The groom was allowed to take his bride home only after he had bribed the bridesmaids.

I looked at Veer. He was thoroughly enjoying every moment of it.

He dug into the pocket of his ornate *shervani* and pulled out something in his closed fist. The girls started pouncing. So he stood up tall, far above each of them and held his hand high. The crowd had started gathering around. "Judy, start counting," Veer exclaimed.

"One, two, three."

He lowered his hand and opened his palm.

Each girl came away smiling, with a gold-plated ring.

It was really time to leave now. There were no more games, no more rituals left.

My parents were by my side. Suddenly I felt drained. The show was over and I wanted to return to my room. I didn't want to leave. I tried to tell my parents, but the words were stuck in my throat. Ma was wiping her tears and Papa's head was bent in fear of publicly showing his emotions. This was so difficult. It was an unfamiliar quandary, a poignant moment, for I was leaving my parents' house forever.

And then the nudging behind my back grew with stronger hands. I saw a waiting blue Mercedes.

Kitty Auntie explained proudly, "You know, this is a wedding present to you from Veer's late grandfather. He too had brought back Veer's grandmother to his house after their wedding in it. Just like Veer is now. *Hehehe* ... sooo lucky...."

My parents were no longer by my side. I must have left them behind. I could only see a sea of nondescript faces. I called out, "Ma, where are you?" But no one heard me. The noise of the departing band was hurting my head.

Why did I have to leave my home? This was where I belonged. I felt my eyes burn with tears.

3.

"COME ON! Is this the fastest you can drive?" My mother-in-law was shouting at the driver. Her relatives were waiting to complete the rest of the wedding ceremonies at Veer's house. I was sandwiched between my new mother-in-law and my new husband. I could not breathe. I think I had been crying. Our Mercedes Benz was covered with red balloons and white satin ribbons with a caption on a pink cardboard heart: "Forever After."

I looked at Veer hoping for some solace from him, but his face was turned away from mine. Why would he not look at me? Did he have regrets? Did I? I wondered if all young brides in my predicament felt the same.

A chill ran down my legs and settled at the edge of my little toe. I knew I had to face my fears. I opened my mind and let the insidious voice in, finally.

In a flash, I was back to a few weeks ago, when Veer had taken me to meet his parents, Rani and Ranvir Rajsinghania. Veer had never mentioned his parents, so I hadn't known what to expect.

"Maya, make sure you clean behind your ears, pin up that wild hair, wear something decent. And practise several lines about the weather and cricket ... yes, definitely cricket ... that never goes wrong." Anita had advised, having too much fun with my unease.

"Why do I have to meet them, Anita?" I asked the obvious

question, hoping for a less obvious answer.

It was raining heavily when we reached a posh restaurant in the congested Connaught Place circle. As we stepped inside, the smell of re-used oil, possibly from chilli cheese toast and *pakoras,* clogged our nostrils. There were servers balancing teapots on oval trays and navigating through crowds of people waiting to be seated. It took Veer less than a second, amidst the chaos, to spot his parents at the back.

"Mom, Dad, this is Maya, my friend!"

Veer's father was a delicate-looking, well-dressed man. He had the same long face as Veer's but with smaller eyes and a thin moustache. He wore a three-piece cots wool suit and a bow tie with matching suspenders. He held a smoking pipe between his slender fingers and a half-finished glass of whiskey in the other hand. There was a definite air of privilege about him. He immediately threw up his arms and gave me a warm bear hug. "Hello, hello, dear girl!"

And then I turned to see Veer's mother. She was staring at me blankly, silently. I lowered my head and said, "Hello, Mrs. Rajsinghania. It is very nice to meet you." She attempted a pretentious smile but remained silent.

This was an awkward moment, one that I had not expected. Veer felt my distress and gestured to a seat opposite her. There was something about the piercing brazenness of her gaze that made me feel unmasked, as if I had committed a crime without knowing what it was.

To cover up, it seemed, Veer's father started talking loudly: "Very soon you will meet Veer's mother's sisters, Kitty and Minnie."

Much to my relief, Veer sat down next to me and started talking about his win at the last inter-college match.

I stole a sideways glance at his mother. She was a hefty, well-groomed woman with chiselled eyebrows, a sharp nose, and a large cut for a mouth under thin lips. She had specks of grey deliberately arranged within the strands of deep auburn hair that framed her square face, lending it an arrogant sophistication.

Gradually, as Veer unfolded his victory story, his mother stirred a little. And after five minutes she spoke up, chiming into Veer's narrative by interrupting him frequently and twiddling her thumbs. "Oh, that's very nice son. Keep it up. Remember how proud we are of you." Veer smiled and bowed his head in gratitude.

And then to my absolute horror, Veer started talking about my accomplishments, with what I suspected was little hope of acceptance from her. Her approval, I sensed, was important to him. And I could see the pressure he was under to justify choosing me over the other more eligible offers his parents may have entertained. "Do you know, Mom, that Maya plays the sitar and ... and last year she won the award for the best classical music performer of the year at school?"

Veer's mother's face clouded, and I noticed her facial muscles tighten, as if she was restraining an outburst. There was dead silence at our table. It was as if Veer had said something forbidden. Was it about the sitar? Or about my award? When she spoke after a few minutes, it was directly to Veer. "Well, well, you see ... none of us Rajsinghanias feel the need to publicly exhibit ourselves through singing and dancing. There is just no need for such charades."

"Mom! Stop! *What* are you doing?" Veer stood up, rattled. This entire visit was a bad idea. I picked up my bag and was about to follow him out of the restaurant when we heard a couple of shrill voices calling his name: "Veer ... *you hoo*! Veer darling!" Kitty and Minnie had arrived.

"Oh *hella, hella*, our dear handsome buoooy." The taller of the two kissed him on the forehead, and the other smeared her red lipstick on his cheek.

"Well, well, what did we miss?" asked the taller one. She was wearing a revealing red silk blouse over a tight black leather skirt that she kept adjusting clumsily to hide her self-consciousness. Her shorter sister had a fixed grin that lent her a certain forged pleasantness, and she was more at ease in her oversized kurta and terylene pants. Indisputably, both shared the same facial features as Veer's mother.

Veer's father spoke up. "Meet Kitty," he pointed to the taller one, "and this is Minnie, the mini one, *ha, ha, ha*," he said, tickled by his own statement.

I had no choice but to come out of the shadows into the light of the overhanging table lamp to face them. Veer's father gestured toward me. "Meet Veer's special friend, Maya."

"Oh my God!" Kitty's hand flew over her open mouth, her face as white as if she had seen a ghost. She sat down slowly in the chair, her eyes fixed on my face.

Minnie was a bit more restrained in comparison. "Aha *hallo, hallo*. Very nice to meet you," she said, with the same look of surprise on her face.

I did not know what the matter was. Why was everyone in Veer's family behaving so rudely to me? What was wrong with me? I did not want to stay a single moment longer. I did not want to see any of them ever again.

As if reading my mind, Veer blurted, "Well, we were just leaving...."

"What nonsense, you are doing no such thing. We have just arrived." And with that, Kitty pulled Veer into a chair between the two of them. I quietly retreated back into the shadows of the corner chair, hoping to be forgotten. It was much easier watching them from the darkness.

I knew then that I did not belong in Veer's world.

I had made my decision. I was a dearly loved child in my own house and I would never get used to such irrational hostility stemming from no fault of mine.

When we finally got back to my house, I was determined. "Veer it's over," I said firmly. "I don't want to see you anymore. Please go now,"

"You must be crazy, Maya. It can never be over."

Veer was smart enough to guess why I wanted to end it, but

as I had expected, he completely ignored my words. So I shut the door on his face.

The next morning when I woke up, it was raining again. The air was hot and suffocating. I rose and went to my window to open the blinds, and there he was. Drenched and slouching under the jacaranda tree across the street. I noticed that he was wearing the same clothes as last night. Had he even gone home? I sent our housekeeper with an umbrella and then left for university. After dinner, my father answered the doorbell to find a policeman at our doorstep.

"Good evening, Sir. I was on my usual rounds of this area and found a young man camping on the street across your house. Do you know who he is?"

Papa looked at me and I shook my head. "No, I don't know him, Papa." I blatantly lied and then bit my lower lip to numb the pain.

The next morning, he was still there. From my bedroom window, I could see dark hollows around his eyes and the beginning of a little stubble of a beard. It was the second day now. I didn't know if he had eaten, but it seemed like he had definitely been sleeping on the rubble under the tree. His hair was streaked with wet mud, and his clothes were spotted with grime and dirt.

It was a battle of wills now. I was not going to get bullied by Veer. I shut my windows tightly and did not open them till a few days after. It was the fifth day, Friday, and the last day of my class. The rain had passed and the mugginess had lifted. I wanted the sun to soak each damp corner of my room. So I swung open the shutters. Instantly, my eyes went to look at the spot under the jacaranda tree. It was empty.

So, he had left. I sat down on my bed, relieved but gloomy. My heart was heavy, somehow. Why was I sad? This was what I had wanted.

As I was leaving the house an hour later, there was a small crowd in our driveway. I went to see what the commotion was. "Madam, there is a man lying unconscious near your car. Please come and look."

Something exploded in my chest. I did not have to look. I knew who it was. I ran. He was lying on his back and his eyes were closed. I lifted his head and rested it on my lap. I could barely see his face through my tears. Someone brought a glass of water, and I dipped my scarf to dab his face. He looked completely dehydrated. The hollows under his eyes had become deep pits, and the stubble had turned into a short beard.

"Veer, open your eyes. Veer, it's me. You win. Just open your eyes," I cried.

My father had come out now. He was surprised to see me nursing a stranger and weeping.

"Maya, what are you doing? Who is this? Do you know him?" his voice had lost its usual composure.

"Yes Papa, I know him. This is Veer."

***

I was jerked painfully back to the present from my flashback as the driver slammed on the brakes to avoid hitting a cat that was crossing the road.

Our wedding car had turned a corner. We had reached Veer's mansion. Tall wrought iron gates were flung open by a uniformed gatekeeper, who was quick to salute us from under his grey hat. It was a long winding drive. After a few minutes, I noticed a peering crowd that had gathered behind a great colonnade of grandfather trees that lined the road on both sides. Some of them were waving their streamers and others were throwing marigold petals at our moving car. I rolled down the window and took a deep breath of the cool night air. A soft drizzle of velvet marigolds brushed my cheeks. A night heron squawked for its mate somewhere in the branches of the fuchsia bougainvillaea. I guessed that we were nearing the house, as the crowd swelled from the shadows, waving and cheering. I instinctively waved back, and the cheering became louder.

"We Rajsinghanias don't need to wave to the crowd. Roll up the window please." Veer's mother's instructions were swift. I quietly obeyed.

She continued without looking at me. "I have arranged for Sheila, our oldest governess, to take care of you till you settle in. Sheila is also good at explaining the likes and preferences of our family. You will meet her soon."

"Who is Sheila?" I whispered to Veer.

"She was the governess for my grandmother, and she has stayed with our family ever since," Veer replied before he turned his face again, this time for good.

A welcoming silver sheen from a full celestial moon spread itself before us. Large domes over three stone storeys glowed with earthen candles. And in that instant, the sapphire sky burst into streams of fireworks, each climaxing into an ecstasy of colour, perfectly timed with our arrival.

Our car pulled into the circular stone driveway. I looked up and saw the cold, towering walls of the main entrance.

Something stirred inside me. There was a bizarre magnetism in this place. It felt like Veer's mansion had been waiting for me to come home to it. But how could that be? I had never seen Veer's house before. Had I visited this in a dream?

The driver honked ceremoniously to announce our arrival. Instantly, the stone porch came alive with the painted faces of glittering women flashing jewellery and perfumed torsos. The men lingered behind in black tuxedos with gelled hair and neckties, or *shervanis* and tightly-wound turbans.

I wanted to hide.

As the driver held the door open, the intoxicating night jasmine filled my lungs. I took a deep breath and stepped out. But my gown had grown heavier and my heels higher. I fell. And heard laughter. My eyes clouded up with pain from a grazed knee and from the humiliation. And then familiar steady hands quickly pulled me up. I looked into Veer's tender eyes, and that was all that I was thankful for.

The laughter had turned into deliberate commentary: "Oh, how small she is. Very thin, but pretty. Look at the peacocks on her gown! Our poor Veer, he is sooo hooked for life!" More laughter.

I was a bird in a cage.

"Come this way." An army of younger girls ushered me to a flight of stairs. I looked for Veer but he had been escorted to the waiting lounge already.

I entered a palatial living room full of more fashionable people. The chatter was louder than the music, but the noise died down as I entered. I bent my head. Veer was walking a little ahead of me, surrounded by his mother and aunts. There were relatives sitting on both sides of the hall.

As we reached the podium, Kitty excitedly tore into the microphone. "*Hella, hella,* everyone. Our dear nephew Veer has arrived with his bride, and we are ready for the games to begin just as soon as they settle in. So, till then, why don't we all move towards the gardens in the East wing before the bar and the caterers pack up." The hall boomed with an echo of claps and cheers. Veer's mother turned to her sisters. "Before the games begin, take Maya to change into the sari we have selected for this ceremony."

I did not want to leave Veer's side. Everything was new, everyone a stranger. But I didn't have the courage to fuss either. I knew that all eyes were following my every move. So, I meekly followed the aunts towards a long passage.

We entered a breezy veranda that overlooked a dark enchanting garden with tall ashoka and gulmohar trees guarding smaller pomegranate, mango, and lemon trees. The veranda was at play with the garden and the breeze was the referee, sliding in between cement pillars and thick, rubbery branches. But then, as we walked further, the playfulness gave way to tugging and the breeze started pulling at my wedding gown, beckoning me toward the darkness under the branches as it bumped into my chest, talking to me. "*Welcome!*"

I stopped walking. Surely I was hallucinating with the stress of the night. Was I going mad? Wind does not speak, it cannot.

I looked up. I was thankful for the evenly spaced crystal chandeliers on the high ceiling. Their light reflected with prism sharpness and destroyed all darkness. But their piercing glow was making me dizzy. My legs caved in, but before I could drop, I felt a cold bony hand slip under my elbow to steady me. I screamed. But my voice was hijacked by the wind. I turned to face who it was.

A frail old woman was looking directly at me. Her skin was clawed with tales of a life she had endured and survived. There was something melancholy, almost dark about her. Her head was bent, but the sharp eyes that peered from under a pashmina headscarf were alert. She noticed that I was shaking.

Minnie and Kitty had stopped too. They had been walking ahead and constantly whispering in each other's ears. They reached us. "Maya, meet Sheila, our head governess," Kitty introduced us. "She has been with the family since before Veer's grandparents were married. She was Veer's grandmother's governess, and she knows all the family's secrets ... I mean, the family's ways!" She giggled.

Minnie pinched Kitty on her arm to stop her from revealing more information.

"Maya, Sheila will help you settle in." Minnie closed the conversation safely.

I looked at Sheila again and smiled for the first time since I had arrived in Veer's house.

Sheila smiled back. "Welcome," she said.

I had stopped shaking. Yes, maybe, just maybe, with the help of Sheila, I could make this my new home.

4. SHEILA

SINCE RANI MADAM had given me painkillers, my back was not hurting as much as it had last week. Then again, nothing could hurt me today. For today was a special day when happiness would fly in to absorb the gloom.

I had been floating on a cloud since Master Ranvir had gathered all of us staff in the living hall to personally break the news. "A week from now, our son Veer is getting married! And we will rejoice with a celebration that will not be easily forgotten for a long time!"

The pure butter sweets that were handed out to us took me back to the old days of the Master's father's wedding. It was the same season—just before winter set in—and it was the same feeling of happiness.

Yes, yes. I will wear my most expensive pashmina shawl and my old Banarasi sari with pure zari, I thought. It had been given to me by Master Ranvir's father on his wedding day. So what if the *zari* was too bright for my old body? Let those upstart young maids laugh at me, I didn't care. Occasions like this didn't come every day and who knew if I would be alive for the next one.

The wedding guests had already started arriving from out of town.

I had been supervising our head housekeeper, Bahadur, and his team. These days, one can no longer trust the domestic help. Everything had to be personally inspected. There was no sincerity in their work. These no-good village drifters ended up in such houses just to have a good time, nothing else.

Maybe that was the reason Rani Madam called me yesterday to assign special duties to me. "Sheila, I want you to look after Veer's bride till she understands her role in this house."

I felt like history was repeating itself. Once again it has fallen on me to keep the sanity of this new bride. Once again it will be up to me to inform her about the limits of tolerance in this house. I didn't want to do this again. But how could I tell Rani Madam? How could I tell anyone?

Only *she* knew how difficult it was for me when I supervised under *her* time. Only *she* watches over me. I can feel *her* presence lingering in the shadows of a full moon, hear *her* in the swiftness of the wind and the crevasses of the roof beams. Oh, I had to snap out of this mood. In a few hours Master Veer would arrive with his bride. It was time for me to rest a little. I should take a nap on the cane chair in the corner of the kitchen. I should tell Bahadur to wake me up when the old Mercedes Benz arrived.

Yes, the same car. Many decades ago, it was for the same car that I was waiting for when Master Veer's grandfather was to arrive with his bride. *Oh ... I am young again, I have no pain in my body and eyes that can see for miles.*

"Sheila Bai, Sheila Bai, wake up! Come quickly! The bride has arrived." A breathless Bahadur was breathing down onto my face.

I pushed him away, gathered myself slowly, and followed the other staff out into the foyer. The darkness of this starless night had been stabbed by the glitter of the fairy lights trailing down the tall stone walls. Dhiraj, our head driver, was holding the car door open. Any moment now I would see her. My eyes were not as good as they were last year, but today I had rested them to be absolutely ready for this awaited moment.

Ahh haa... There she was. She had stepped out. From the balcony above I could only see her bent head. What a beautiful peacock-coloured gown! She looked so delicate, like a leaf on a branch.

And ... oh no... what just happened? Did the poor girl trip over her wedding gown! Oh my God, she has fallen on the floor. Oh no!

"O Bahadur, Bahadur, run downstairs quickly with the chambermaid and help the bride. Go, will you! Don't just stand there, you imbecile!"

Holding the hand railing, I slowly descended to the main hall. My knees ached, but nothing could stop me.

Madam Rani and her sisters had gathered centre stage to welcome the married couple. The noise had died down. There was a group moving towards the stage. *Oh ho, look at Master Veer! How handsome he looks!* Where was his bride?

Aha ... there she was, trailing behind him.

I wished she would lift her head. I wanted to see her face.

Oh, I got lucky. Then, she lifted her face slowly.

Yes, I could finally see her.

What? Who is this?

I looked at the bride again.

I felt giddy.

This was impossible. Surely this was a trick.

This cannot be! No, *no, no. There has been a mistake. Yes.... Wiping my glasses with the edge of my shawl has always helped. Sometimes the smudges play tricks with my vision. Let me take a better look. Oh no.*

My bones started to stiffen, and my head felt hot.

That beautiful face. I had not forgotten it all these years. After roaming these corridors for years, *she* has walked back to us from the past.

God have mercy. What are you unfolding before my old eyes?

"Sheila! Sheila!" Someone called out to me. "Can you come here please?" I followed Rani Madam's voice in a daze.

"Sheila, take the bride to get dressed for the wedding games."

These were simple instructions. I had to focus. I closed my

eyes to clear these evil thoughts. This was just a young girl born in Master Veer's time. The resemblance was striking, but it was just a resemblance. There was no other explanation. I had to keep this to myself. After all, no one would believe me. There were no photographs of *her* to prove my word, and the last thing I wanted was to be called crazy.

I started out cautiously toward the corridor leading to Master Veer's room. The Madam's sisters were escorting the bride. I increased my pace to catch up. The bride had stopped walking and was propping herself on the pillar for support.

Why had she stopped? Was she okay? I gently slipped my hand under her elbow to support her. She turned. I looked straight into her doe eyes. The same eyes. She smiled. An enigmatic, familiar smile. All earlier reasoning left me in an instant. I was looking at *her* face again. My heart stopped. It started again in a moment, but it was missing a beat. How was this possible?

I caught my breath. While holding her cold elbow, I managed to lead the bride to Master Veer's room. At least the gardener remembered to turn on the lights under the peepal tree to show off the lotus pond. I hadn't looked into her eyes again. As long as I didn't look at her, I was sane.

Kitty Madam had stopped whispering into Minnie's ear.

"Maya sweetie, why don't you sit on this ottoman. Sheila will take off your jewellery," Kitty said. The bride obeyed.

One by one, I slid off the head gear, necklace, earrings, armlets, anklets. I placed everything inside the jewelled box and locked it in the dressing room wardrobe. "Maya Madam, why don't you follow me. There is a changing room at the back," I said, picking up the heavy crimson sari that I had to help her change into.

"Please don't call me *Madam*. You can call me Maya."

This was her first sentence to me. To my surprise, her voice was not like *hers*. It was soft and melodious.

"Oh no, no, I cannot." How could I be free like this generation? I had to maintain some status and decorum.

"Okay then, please think of something that you *can* call me." She looked at me with sparkling eyes.

The door of the changing room was swollen with old moisture and did not latch. The bride took the sari from my hand and went inside to change. I waited outside in case she needed help pleating it around her waist. Through the open door I heard Minnie and Kitty Madam talking.

"So, it has happened. They are finally married," Minnie sighed loudly.

"Yes, they are."

"When I saw her for the first time at the restaurant, oh my gosh, sister, I could have sworn that *she* had come back to haunt us. There is a remarkable resemblance."

"Yes, there is! It was scary at first, and what a coincidence! Our poor sister and bother-in-law..."

"Why are you smiling?", asked Minnie

"Well ... it's poetic justice..."

"What is?"

"I was just thinking about our Veer..."

"What about him?"

"You know the times when 'his mood' comes on."

"*Ya ... ya....*"

"I wonder if Maya knows..."

"She must know. They have known each other since high school, I have heard."

"What are girls coming to these days? In my time we were not allowed to even talk to boys after seven o' clock."

"But we have to admit, she is a beauty ... just like...."

"Oh stop it. You sound as if you are in love with her. What are looks? They will fade in a few years. What matters in the end is how connected her family is and how much money she brings in dowry. And in this case, my dear, I have doubts on both accounts. Besides, are you implying that our Veer had no other choice? Didn't you know that Mr. Khanna had come with a proposal for his daughter Pinky just last week at their dinner?"

"Really!"

What were the Madams doing? I closed my ears and prayed that the new bride hadn't heard from the open door. They did not know the damage they were causing.

What if ... what if *she* had returned as Veer's wife to take her revenge? It was a thought I could not take out of my head. And if so, I feared the Madams would go first.

What was that sound?

The bride had come out. My ... my ... the new bride in her sari looked like a Goddess. But her eyes were drenched in pain. The glow had dimmed, and she was trembling like a leaf.

I feared she had heard everything!

Instinctively I threw a shawl around her frail shoulders.

Now, I knew why God had extended my life. Because its purpose was not over yet. The purpose was to protect this girl. She had no idea what she was dealing with. And, somehow, I also knew that I was not the only one watching over her. *She* was here on every full moon night, when the skies were the darkest, so that the moon could shine uninterrupted. I heard her in the swiftness of the wind, in the crevasses of the roof beams.

I had no control over my tongue. It was distracting her, consoling the new bride. "Madam, I know what I will call you."

She did not reply this time.

I continued, "I will call you 'Beti.'"

Still there was no answer.

"You know why? Because you are the daughter of this family."

I felt her little hand in mine, and, with that, I led her toward the waiting guests.

5. MAYA

THE NIGHT WAS MUCH COOLER as I walked back to the hall, now full of guests pumped up on snacks and drinks. I noticed cocktail glasses in their hands, martini, whiskey, and wine goblets.

The raw pain of Veer's aunts' conversation stung in my chest.

What was wrong with Veer? What did they mean by "his mood?" Who did I resemble? And why was that so frightening?

My heart pounded again. If only Ma were here, I would crawl onto her lap and wrap my arms around. I looked at Sheila, who was leading me back for an exhibition of myself. The calm of her face gave me some solace.

Veer was seated on a throne-like chair with red cushions and gold trims. He was still looking away. I took my designated place next to him. I could feel all eyes glued to me, to my every shudder, every blemish.

Veer's mother cleared her throat and the entire hall fell silent. "Well, hello, hello. Welcome everyone. I am the lucky facilitator of the games for our dear son Veer and his bride, ceremonies that will signal their fate and future together."

Deafening claps boomed within the walls.

Wait! What had she just said? What kind of games were these? Had our fate not already been decided by the wedding?

"Oh, lighten up, dear!" Kitty held up my chin with two fingers as if reading my thoughts. I looked away to hide a tear and felt Sheila's oddly comforting presence somewhere near me.

Veer's mother's voice continued: "The first game is very simple. Veer has to find the first letter of his name, 'V' in his bride's henna design."

It bothered me that she had not referred to by my name. All that seemed to matter to them was that I was *his* bride, *his* new possession.

My palms were lifted toward the zooming cameras. Images of intricate floral vines, criss-cross waves, paisleys, and mango leaves on my hennaed hands were projected on the large white screens in both corners of the hall. Veer came closer, tilted his head, and puffed several times. He was smiling, but I knew that he might lose. Veer does not like losing, not here, not in the soccer field, not ever. And I could not help him. The crowd let out a loud sound of dismay as he gave up. I had won by default.

Our next game was called "Fish the Ring." An enormous oxidized silver bowl with carved handles was brought in and placed on the table before us.

This time it was Minnie's turn to explain: "In this bowl of milk is hidden a small family heirloom, a ring. This ring chooses its owner, and it always tells the truth. The couple have to dip their hands in the opaque milk and find that ring. Do I have to tell you more? Whoever finds the ring is the winner, in the game, and in their life together. They will dominate their partner in making all the important decisions. *Ha, ha...*" Her laugh at the end of her explanation was almost a sneer.

I did not want to play. I would let Veer win, and then everyone would be happy. We dipped our hands up to our elbows in the deep bowl of cold, sticky milk. My plan was not to move my fingers to search for the ring. That way, Veer could find it before me.

But I felt something instantly under my palm as it touched the bottom of the bowl. The unmistakable shape of a cold curve, a thin metallic band. The ring!

I had found it, but no one could know. I moved it quickly toward Veer's searching hand. Endless eyes were peering at our every move. I looked up to see Veer's facial muscles relax and then tighten up again in a smile.

There was cheering, whistling, and clapping as Veer pulled his victorious hand out of the bowl, showing off the ring that he had slipped on his middle finger. This time, Veer was the hero.

Kitty screeched, "So it is a tie! And, dear friends, we all know what this means, eh?"

One of Veer's cousins got up from the crowd and shouted, "Yes, this means that these two will be equally matched throughout life!" And with that the hall was drowned in applause once again.

6.

I WAS GLAD WHEN THE NIGHT drew to an end. Kitty's farewell message instructed the guests to move to the porch to bid the newly-weds goodbye. We were to be driven, accompanied by Kitty and Minnie, to an unknown destination for our wedding night. I was ushered by the same set of girl cousins to a waiting limo, surprised when they too climbed into the car. As the car door closed, I realized that Veer was not with us. I told myself not to panic, though I watched for him anxiously.

A few minutes later, we were driving over the spaghetti junctions and new flyover passes. I saw migrant labourers sleeping under checked sheets on cold stone pavements. We passed shiny skyscrapers with lighted rooftops, and then wide expanses of yellow mustard fields dug up with bulldozers and dump trucks, waiting for more construction. After driving for a couple of hours, our limo started ascending a long driveway that led to a grand marble entrance. Two tired-looking doormen wearing bright red turbans and black suits stood in front of the doors.

"Here you go. We have reached the grandest heritage five-star hotel just recently converted from a Maharaja's palace!" Minnie sounded like a tour guide. I could not help but wonder how perfect this would look to someone from the outside.

There was still no sign of Veer. I hesitated before stepping out of the car.

As if reading my mind again, Kitty taunted, "Looking for your prince, eh?" All the cousins sniggered. I was angry with myself for not being able to speak up and for not having control of my wedding night. I hadn't planned or even known about any of this. I was ushered into the hotel and then up to a large room strewn with rose petals, which formed a trail to a four-poster bed adorned with golden organza drapes. On the bed sheets were more petals the colour of virgin blood.

They left me sitting awkwardly on the bed with some last taunting words: "Good luck! Sweet honey luck!"

After they left, the silence was welcome. My head gravitated to the lacy satin pillow. I closed my eyes, and I was back home playing hopscotch in the sweltering heat in our mango grove. My mother was calling me to come inside from the sun. Her calling grew louder and then turned into a caress.

"Maya ... Maya." I opened my eyes. I was looking straight into Veer's smiling hazel eyes. His earlier strange and aloof demeanour had vanished. I wanted to ask him how he managed to lift the veil of doom that had enveloped him throughout the wedding. Instead I asked, "Where were you?"

Ignoring my question, he said, "Come!"

He took my hand and we stepped out onto the balcony. It was magical. We were overlooking a medieval palace courtyard with intricate stonework columns that had been erected with geometrical precision inside a Mughal garden. Even the gaudy red roses and clipped cypresses lining the walls were organized in straight lines within blossoming bougainvillea bushes and graceful grape vines. The garden was divided by a line of lighted musical fountains in the middle, and, in the glow of the tall boundary spotlights, a sea of turquoise shone. We were in a dream. All my doubts and anxieties seemed inconsequential and petty in front of this magnificence. And then, suddenly, as if riding on my wave of optimism, the darkness was broken by the first ray of pink from the East. We had made it to a new day together.

* * *

It was late afternoon when I woke up. Veer was sipping his coffee on the sun-kissed balcony. He extended his hand and then pulled me onto his lap. Running his fingers through my hair, he said, "Maya, I have a great plan for the day."

"What?"

"There is a grand beach a mile from the palace's boundaries, and I have arranged for two motorbikes to explore the terrain."

If there was a question in his statement, I gave him a hug as my answer. And if this was going to be the reward for a stressful wedding, I was willing to accept it. To leave such a place before exploring it would have been absolutely tragic.

Within an hour, we were riding side by side on an empty road. There were fishermen's huts on the left side and roaring waves on the right.

"Wanna race?" Veer challenged.

Inhaling the toxic bike fumes pumped up my adrenaline. But as the smoke cleared, Veer was nowhere in sight. Where had he gone again?

The hot ruthlessness of the sun was mixed with the nauseating smell of raw fish. A glint of silver caught my eye. It was coming from behind the boulders, where the waves met the sand. My heartbeat picked up. First, I saw the steering wheel, then the tires. It was Veer's bike! What was he doing down there?

The palm-lined road was deserted. I crossed over the stone boundary onto the hot sand and walked towards the rocks. The granules pierced my soles. There was still no sign of Veer. I turned to leave.

"Hey!" His deep voice stopped me. It led me behind the hidden boulder. His face was flushed with the heat, but his eyes were smouldering with an intense emotion that I could not read just yet. He swayed towards me.

"Why did you leave me? I thought we were racing!" I lashed out.

He did not answer. He came closer and pulled me into his arms. The breeze had started blowing my hair in his face, and I could feel his breath on my cheek. He ran the tip of his finger down my back, and I reacted with goose bumps. His breath grew excited, quick, shallow. But anger surged inside me. "Why did you leave me?" I repeated like a child on the verge of a tantrum.

His fingers slid into my hair, steering it off my face, holding my gaze. My back sizzled against the hot rocks and I finally pushed him away. But I could not escape. He pulled me back swiftly and effortlessly. Leaning against my body, he gripped my waist and pressed himself down on me, lean and brawny.

"How can I leave you, you wild, bewitching Maya!" he hissed.

His lips were hot. Between each burning caress, as I gasped for air, he synchronized his next kiss, more urgent than before.

I knew that these kisses would not be enough. His square shoulders caved in as he gently wrapped his muscular arms around me. I stopped protesting. I couldn't restrain him anymore, or myself. My anger had turned into something else. A small murmur escaped my lips. I felt his heart racing. Or was it mine? I couldn't tell us apart. His body scent of musk, sand, and sweat was gripping. And a fresh rush of warm blood filled my cheeks. And then he slid his hand down my blouse and kissed me again. My body ached for him and he did not let go.

Holding hands, we walked straight into the tart beckoning waves. Veer was holding me firmly on the unsteady sand. I stumbled. And before I could fall he scooped me up smoothly in his arms. I pulled his shirt upwards to reveal the firmness beneath the creases of his linen trousers. His hard chest brushed against my breasts, arousing me more. The deep water couldn't cool our sizzling. Then he lifted my legs around his body and pierced me. Painful pleasure filled my soul. We were one. A sword of lightning flashed between the black clouds. We swayed in ecstasy under the elements, the sky, waves, earth, and the wind. We became the elements, laughing and playing till the sultry rising waves had cooled us down. The menacing splinter of desire had made its way deep into our hearts. If this was love, then yes, we were in love, completely and irrevocably. At that moment, I had no doubt.

***

It was a lazy morning. I took my time rising from the crumpled sheets. My mind recalled the wicked temptations of last night. This was a new discovery for me.

I extended my hand to Veer's pillow, but he was not there. The balcony smiled over the lush green garden and the seamless crystal turquoise beyond. The waves were consoled, but the sun was still roasting the shimmering sand below, and the palm leaves were swaying in the mounting, warm breeze.

It was definitely past morning. Just as I dissolved into the enormous goose cushion of the cane settee, Veer entered with a bouquet of red roses. I felt like the luckiest girl in the whole world. My fears and anxieties had been suppressed by a brand-new confidence that we would make it. I wanted to tell him how much I loved him, but he did not give me a chance. His lips were on mine in an instant.

But this time there was something different. His kiss was insistent, urgent, unsure. It was rough, and as the seconds flew it became almost domineering, suffocating. I gasped for breath and pushed him back. "Veer! Stop!"

He sat down on the chair opposite me. The same withdrawn face of our wedding night was back, the same coldness. The rollercoaster of emotions that I was riding was slicing the sky and about to plunge hard on the ground. I was falling. "What is the matter, Veer?"

He didn't answer.

"Okay then, I'm going for a walk."

I wanted to leave him to deal with his thoughts. I had no wish to get into a row with him. I had picked up my hat and slipped on my sneakers when I heard his voice whip across the room.

"Don't go."

"What?"

"Don't go anywhere."

"I just want some fresh air, Veer. I will be back soon."

"No, Maya."

"What's wrong, Veer?'" He walked up to me, took my arm and pressed his figures into my wrist. I could see the redness of his eyes. My arm tingled with numbness.

"Veer, stop. You are hurting me."

"Promise me, you will not walk out on me."

I didn't know what to say. His behaviour was bizarre. His eyes were pleading like that of a child longing for his favourite toy. "Veer, have you gone mad?" This had to be another of his pranks. I shrugged my arm loose from his grip and sat down on the floor to face him.

"Maya, just promise."

"Of course, I will leave you! As soon as I can!" I teased.

"Maya!"

No, this was not one of his pranks. I knew now.

"Say it!"

"Okay, okay, I won't," I blurted and ran out to the balcony with tears streaming down my face.

It took me a few minutes to turn around and look at him again. He was fiddling with the TV remote. He had the look of a child who had just won a tantrum, laughing at something on the screen.

Was this the "mood" that Kitty and Minnie had alluded to?

Everything seemed to be back to normal now. Except my euphoria was over.

7.

"SIR, YOU ARE JUST IN TIME for afternoon tea, Madam is expecting you in the parlour," was Bahadur's way of welcoming us back.

Veer's mother looked up from her pink bone china cup. "All well?" she asked Veer, as we both greeted her with a peck on each cheek. She gestured to the spread of cucumber sandwiches, lemon tarts, and scones served with cream and jam. Sitting next to her was a slightly chubby girl looking out of the stained-glass window.

"Esha! What are you doing here?" Veer exclaimed excitedly. "Maya, come and meet Kitty Auntie's daughter, a brilliant scholar at the Delhi School of Art, and my favourite cousin sister!"

"Oh, you only say that now when there are no other cousins around," Esha teased back. Then her face lit up as she saw me. It was a rare moment to get such a warm reaction from one of Veer's family members, and I was grateful for it. Esha looked much younger than her age, with a high ponytail and round spectacles. She was wearing ankle boots with silver studs over baggy pants and a sweatshirt. It was such a refreshing change in this house where everything always seemed so formal. I remembered seeing Esha in the group of other cousins on our wedding night.

"Hey, Maya, you look cool!"

I hugged her.

"So, what's up, kiddo?" Veer asked.

Esha's eyes glowed with excitement. "Come, Maya and Veer, I want to show you your wedding present." She pulled Veer by his hand toward the open window.

"Noooo, you don't have to give us anything Esha. It's not…" Veer stopped mid-sentence. His back stiffened and I knew that something extraordinary had captivated him. I followed him and froze too.

There, spread out on the hedge, was an outrageously spectacular blue-green tail. His turquoise plumage shimmered in the departing evening rays. "Oh my God! It's a peacock!" I cried.

And trailing in his shadow was his peahen, blissfully camouflaged in his magnificence. As if ready for his performance, the emperor hopped from the short shrub branch onto the ground, the light playing on his vibrant hues: indigo, emerald, gold, scarlet. He opened his fan and strolled out onto the sprawling lawns with his devoted peahen swooning behind him. We quivered in the grandeur of this spectacle.

It was too good to be true. My longing for peacocks had flown from the weaves of my wedding gown to fill our new life with colourful verve. It was as if the coming of the peacocks was symbolic of my welcome into this new life, as if the peacock and I were one.

Esha was by our side now. "Just remember *the joie de vivre* of your life together every time you see these birds."

"And when we see them, we shall always think of you, Esha. Thank you!" I added, as she bade us farewell.

We watched fascinated as the peacocks made their home near the lily pond.

And, for the next few months, Veer was at peace, strutting around like the peacock as long as I hovered around like his peahen, joining him in his little pleasures of feeding the morning birds or playing games with him at night.

Every morning, Bahadur filled a stainless-steel bucket full of fresh seeds and worms for Veer to feed the birds with. And every afternoon, Sheila visited me to make sure that I had everything that I needed. Then she checked with Bahadur whether her instructions about little things like changing the evening sheets, or preparing my jasmine bath, were being carried out properly and on time. And while Veer was at work, I spent long summer afternoons discovering different sections of this huge, cold, and strikingly beautiful mansion, Veer's house and my new home. Every alcove and corner revealed past lives lived in opulence. But most of all I liked sitting under the towering grandfather peepal tree just outside our veranda with a new stack of dusty books borrowed from the East wing library.

Our living area was spacious, indulgent, and quiet. On moonlit nights, we sat on the edge of the shimmering lily pond. Occasionally, a night owl hooted among the tall branches as if conducting an orchestra of chirping crickets. And at night, on good nights, Veer and I goofed around, pretending to be different cartoon characters from our childhood TV shows, Garfield and Jon, Tarzan and Jane, Charlie Brown and Snoopy, Tom and Jerry, Cinderella and Prince Charming, Don Quixote. We ran barefoot on the grass like children till we collapsed out of sheer exhaustion. And on those nights, we made soft, unhurried love. Those nights were magical. Veer's parents were mostly busy with their post-wedding social engagements—"tying up loose ends," as his mother said. And I was grateful for those loose ends.

All the while, I had not stepped outside the gates of the mansion, mainly to keep Veer calm. I spoke to my parents occasionally, reassuring them that I was happy. The peacock colours reminded me of all the promises that life held before me and how indebted I was for those promises. Everything had fallen into an unintentional routine. Until yesterday, when Veer came home from work.

That evening, there was something different about him. He did not talk, and I did not probe. I knew he would tell me when he was ready.

It was after dinner when we were sipping tea on the edge of the lily pond that he looked up. The moon had just risen, and the garden lights from the veranda barely reached his troubled face. "Papa has announced that he would like to retire. This means that I will be attending orientation to pick up more projects from his portfolio ... and this means more time at the office and more travelling."

I exhaled with relief. I thought it was something worse, something like the old Veer coming back.

"Is that all?" I asked.

"What do you mean?"

"I mean, that is not a bad thing that you have an opportunity to grow at work."

He was quiet. I hated his silences. Sometimes he simply withdrew. And this was one of those times.

"Veer!" I nudged. He was looking at the crescent moon peeking from behind a low cloud.

"Maya, one day...." He was quiet again.

"Yes, Veer?"

"One day I will do what has been close to my heart."

I was surprised to hear this. Veer had mentioned that his family business was built around import and export of food commodities and consumer goods. Never before had I caught even a hint that following in his father's footsteps was not what Veer wanted to do.

"And what is close to your heart Veer?" I got up to sit on the arm of his lawn chair. He started stroking my hand.

"One day I will live from the land, grow my own garden, feed everyone with the food I grow, and die in that garden."

Where was this coming from? I had no idea that Veer was attached to the earth, enough for it to satisfy him, or that he had a green thumb. Then I remembered how much time he spent in our garden planting and talking to Ram, our gardener.

"Oh really?" I teased. "And am I a part of your grand plan? "

"Well, while I till our little piece of heaven, you can cook for the whole village." He pulled me onto his lap and started tickling my belly. We burst out laughing.

"You know that I cannot cook at all! And for the whole village! They will banish us for feeding them badly-cooked food!"

"Then I will cook and yes, I will cook for the whole village, Maya, not one person less. For the whole village."

"So we would be living in a village?"

"Yes. We would. Far away. Someday." He was far away.

When he returned, I said, "Until then, my dear, you will have to like what you do."

"You mean what my father likes me to do."

"What is wrong with that, Veer?"

"For starters, I am not creating anything, I am earning empty money. I feel so alienated from what I do. And then it takes me away from you."

"I am not going anywhere," I tried to reassure him. "I will be here when you come back from work."

"You just don't want to spend time with me, do you?"

My heart skipped a beat. The insecure Veer was returning.

"When did I say that?"

"Just now."

"Hey, that's not fair, Veer. Have I left these walls since the day we have been married?"

"You sound resentful, Maya."

And then there was silence. This silence was different. Dense, suffocating. Even the owl and the crickets were not helping. I knew somehow there was more to come. The coldness had crept back into the tips of my fingers and toes.

The evening passed. Then just before bed he spoke again. "Maya, I have been asked to fill in for Papa on a business trip. I have to leave the day after tomorrow. I will be gone for a few weeks."

He spoke without taking a breath, as if getting it off his chest. I sat up next to him and slipped my hand in his. I knew leaving me caused him anxiety. I tried to make light of it.

"You don't have to worry about me. I will be fine, and I will be waiting. Shall I help you pack in the morning?" He did not answer, so I continued, "Do you want me to come to the airport?"

"No."

For some reason, that night, I felt relief. Without admitting it, I was looking forward to Veer going on this trip. I was wrong to feel that way; I did not want to feel that way. But I did. I had come to realize that Veer's presence was too large, too domineering, and sometimes stifling. Sheila had hinted that there were only a few things that I had to restrict myself to in this mansion: keeping myself busy without stepping out of the gates, and waiting for Veer. I knew I could not carry on forever like this. It was a no-win situation. I had no friends in this new home, and the only friend I had kept me locked up.

Yet, I could not leave him. Nor did I want to anger him. Why, I did not know yet. And I suspected, subconsciously and grudgingly, that Veer knew my deepest darkest thoughts. How could he not?

8.

DESPITE MY THOUGHTS of the previous night, each passing stroke of the grandfather clock in the foyer, made me sad. I would miss Veer, without doubt. No more feeding the peacocks in the morning or playing in the evening in the garden with him pretending to be Don Quixote, the blundering Spanish knight rescuing his princess.

I didn't want to be alone in this large, dark mansion either. Veer's parents were out most of the time, and, when they were not, they neither called nor cared to check on me.

And I didn't want to tell Veer, but I had been feeling sick for the past fortnight. A sudden nausea and giddiness enveloped me without warning and then passed as unexpectedly as it had arrived. During these spells, I ran to the washroom and then lay down. If Veer got even a hint of this, he would find his excuse not to go.

The perceptive Sheila had been hovering around like a mother hen. I suspected that she was a mind reader.

The day had slipped by so fast that before we realized, it was dusk, and time for Veer to go. He gave me a long hug and said, "I want to see the same Maya as the one I leave behind, right here when I come back. Promise?"

I wanted to ask him why I would change, and where would I go, but instead I said, "Yes, I promise Veer."

After one last heart-breaking look from his car window, Veer was gone.

With heavy feet, I dragged myself to the lily pond next to the peacocks. As expected, Sheila came by to ask if I would like some tea. She saw my melancholy look and offered me a mango milk shake instead. Nothing was stirring me. So, she said, "Maya-Beti, why don't you go for a walk to the east gardens? The flowers are in full bloom this time of the year, and Ram the gardener can really benefit from some advice on what to plant for the upcoming season." It was simply a suggestion, and, of course, subtly made, but something about the way Sheila said it piqued my curiosity.

"Sheila, why is Ram only planting on the east side? What lies on the west side?" In all my days after marriage, I had only explored the various sections of the east wing. I had neither been introduced to the west wing, nor had I seen any passages leading to that section of the house. Suddenly, this answer was important to me.

Sheila did not answer. A shadow passed over her face and she seemed momentarily deep in thought. And then, with an awkward jerk, she turned her back on me and started hobbling on toward the house. She had totally ignored my question. Without pausing, and with her back still to me, she called out, "If you decide to go for your walk then don't stay out alone too long: soon it will dark and tonight dinner is being served early for the big Madam in the dining hall."

I didn't mind Sheila's rebuff; I knew that was not her intention. But, more importantly, I wondered what she was hiding.

I decided to forgo my walk and go inside instead to look for answers.

From our garden, I climbed up the stairs to the balcony, hoping to slip in unnoticed from the pantry's back door. But I was too late. Sheila was right. Dinner was being served early tonight. Veer's parents were already on their first course of lentil soup and chicken salad. Veer's mother shot me a disinterested glance and rang the bell for one more plate to be placed. Then she asked casually, "Has Veer left?"

I nodded while trying to concentrate on the hot soup. Then I made an effort to be sociable with the safest topic of conversation. "The weather is changing so fast this year, already there seems to be a nip in the air, especially for the peacocks...."

Veer's father listened, but halfway through my sentence, Veer's mother interrupted to speak to him directly, "Do you remember which day is Mrs. Sharma's anniversary dinner? It is their fiftieth, you know." I gulped my soup with my pride and tried not to feel rebuffed.

When she stopped to take her next mouthful, I blurted my main question directly to her: "So, Mom, who lives in the west wing?" She stopped chewing and slowly swallowed the oversized piece of chicken on her fork. With my eyes, I followed the lump of food moving down her gullet. She placed her fork on her plate and shot a look at her husband. I knew that I was on to something. I continued, "Today I was thinking of advising Ram on what to plant for next spring, but then I saw that the west side also needed some gardening. So, I thought of walking down the path to explore the other side. I saw a black key labelled the 'west wing' hanging in the pantry. Maybe tomorrow—"

I was cut short again. Except this time her voice was pitched with anxiety. "Maya, let me tell you this once: no one from our side ventures to the west wing. I forbid it." Then she softened and lowered her voice. "It is uninhabited and crumbling; it is not safe. The key in the pantry does not work. Now that Veer is out of town, we don't want you in any trouble, do we?"

I nodded to her, but I was not listening. I had all the information I needed. My plans were already made.

9. SHEILA

I HAD TO GET AWAY FROM Maya-Beti and her questioning. I was walking too fast and out of breath. It was too much for me to answer.

Why was Maya-Beti asking so many questions? Had she guessed something? I couldn't answer her questions. The look that I saw in Maya-Beti's eyes was not just curiosity, it was determination. Determination to find out more. This is what I had feared since she arrived. *Ahhh ... pressing my palms on my knees helps this grinding pain....*

Many years ago, I saw and felt similar emotions within *her* in the same house.

I knew that Maya-Beti was a different person, different than *her*. But there were many ways in which Maya-Beti was like *her*. They same look, the same free spirit, and the same sense of abandon, and misfortune. And yet, there were many more ways in which Maya-Beti was not like *her* at all. Unlike *her*, Maya-Beti likes our Master Veer, her husband, Maya-Beti 's joyful spirit and laughter lingers in the air long after she has left the room.

For *her*, a silent grudge always followed everywhere. This became *her* misfortune and destroyed this family. I had seen *her* pain, *her* quiet tears, and *her* helplessness. I knew how *she* had suffered.

Suddenly, my throat went dry. That old itch in my gullet was back. Even honey and basil would not cure this.

It felt like *her* long fingers were winding around my throat. I knew *she* was angry with me for not telling *her* secret. *She* wanted me to tell everyone what had happened to her and I had failed her. It was a burden that I had been carrying for a long time. Yes, I had to get rid of this burden before I died. I would have to tell someone, anyone.

Where was my rosary? I had hidden it in the little tin box in the last drawer of the hutch.

The clock struck eight in the foyer. Nothing more could be done tonight. I pulled my aching body to a standing position by holding on to the ledge near the stove. The crispness of cold water from a stainless steel glass cut the itch in my throat and pumped life back into me.

My mind was clear. I knew what I had to do. I had to wait for this dark night to pass and then in the morning I would go straight to Maya-Beti 's room and stop her from entering the west wing. For that, if I had to, I would reveal the dark family secret that I was carrying. And if she still wanted to go, then I wouldn't let her go alone. For god only knew what lay in waiting in the west wing.

Yes, yes ... this was exactly what I had to do.

10. MAYA

THE CRESCENT MOON still peeked from under dark clouds, but I knew it was time to go as the first crack of crimson had already summoned the breaking of dawn. I slipped into an old pair of jeans and faded runners, and grabbed a torch for my back pocket. Thankfully, the nauseating giddiness had not returned. The house was quiet as always. From the garden window, through the mist, I saw the outline of a crouched figure walking toward our bedroom. Or was that just my imagination? I knew that soon Sheila would be back to check on me. I had a nagging suspicion that she had already guessed my plan. But I would not allow anyone to spoil what I was setting out to do. Not even Sheila. So, instead, I snuck out of the dressing room back door. It opened into the cobbled alley near the servant quarters. I followed it to the lawn, climbed over the balcony, and finally reached the pantry. The rusty black iron key that I needed was hanging mutely among the other loud kitchen cabinet keys. I swiftly removed it from the hook, inhaled deeply, and stepped out on to the dark path to explore the forbidden west wing of Veer's mansion.

The path was winding and slippery, choked with thick green moss. A burst of intoxicating fragrances enveloped me. Wild rose bushes crept over obstinate branches of mulberry and mandarin trees, and towering eucalyptus lined up like soldiers guarding the boundary wall. There was a maze of dense flowering creepers growing in untamed patterns and trees that I didn't recognize. The loose red gravel under my feet was noisy, announcing my arrival with every step. I stopped periodically to see if someone was following me. But there was only the sound of a murmuring breeze singing a duet with the rhythm of my feet.

The borders of my path widened into an oval driveway identical to ours in the east wing except that it was covered with dark roots. Two red-stone lion statues guarded a flight of silent, chipped stone stairs at their base. The perfect and daunting symmetry of the guarding lions was strangely balanced by red boulders at the front entrance.

I started my climb to the towering wrought iron door. The wind behind my back swished past my ears, hauling me up.

Come!

Was someone there? I turned again to check. No, I was alone.

The heavy iron key fit perfectly into the dark rusted bolt, but it did not open the door. I hesitated.

I could choose to turn back to the protection of the east wing, to the safety of a confined life, or I could choose to open the door, risk everything that I had taken for granted, and uncover something that had been sealed for a reason, and which perhaps had the power to change my life forever.

What a foolish dramatic thought! How ridiculous of me. Of course, I had to move on. I was a prisoner of my own curiosity no matter what the stakes.

I pushed against the door hard with my shoulder, and it finally creaked open to an opaque darkness. The smell of pungent mildew was overwhelming. I immediately switched on my torch and started walking on a carpet of thick untouched dust stretching beyond the reach of the torch beams.

Suddenly I no longer felt buoyant. An odd and eerie sense enveloped me with the feeling of being a trespasser, of disturbing the peace. This house belonged to another era, and it had been sealed with the aura and emotions of the people who had lived in the house at that time. And from what I could sense, these were not happy sentiments.

The echo of a breeze followed me in and whistled down the corridor into the darkness. My mind no longer buzzed with questions. I felt like an empty vessel waiting to receive whatever came out of the darkness toward me.

Guided only by the beam of my torch, I slowly inched down the corridor. I opened and entered a door on the left. It was a small room mostly occupied by a one-armed reclining divan and a square ottoman at its base. How puzzling. What could possibly have been the purpose of such a room? And then I remembered from a school history lesson. This was a *fainting* room! I had read about these. It was a Victorian tradition and an acquired custom by a few Indian élite. I imagined ladies stopping to quieten their nerves, fuss, gossip, freshen up, and loosen their corsets or petticoats.

A little ahead, the corridor opened up into a large golden hall. Through the carpet of dust, I could see old parquet floors. The walls were carved with antique French *boiseries,* and mantles decorated with oxidized sconces that were mounted over glittering stucco archways. The morning rays streaming through the high windows were igniting the carved gilded panels. A very large crystal chandelier hung from its cathedral ceiling as a crowned centrepiece. I looked up and felt like I had reached heaven. The towering roof was painted in palettes of luminous pale blues, apple greens, aureolin yellows, oranges and pinks, depicting intricate, ornamental patterns, saints with halos, and angels with magnificent wings.

I stood spell-bound in the splendour of this room, and of the entire era. Where had I seen such splendour before? I closed my eyes to think. I suddenly knew. In a picture book about Marie Antoinette, in a ballroom at Versailles. The echo of Mozart's string quartet in *D Major* ribboned through a multitude of dancing gowns that swirled under sparkling lights. My stomach rumbled with the roasted aromas from the grill where dinner was being prepared. I was one with this room and all that it held.

The earlier feeling of gloom had subsided. I was now being pulled by sheer wonder. Wading through the dark with a wobbly torch, I reached an ornate cast-iron staircase with a dusty brass railing in the middle of a rotunda. I couldn't see the ceiling.

My unsatisfied heart did not listen to my head, as always. I had to see more. Dark dust from the cold brass handrail settled on my palm as I clutched it tightly and started climbing the stairs. The interconnected motifs of a faded Persian hall rug were still partially visible as I arrived on the top floor landing.

Where was I? Who had lived here? Who were these people?

I inhaled and then exhaled several times. Deep breaths calmed my heartbeat. I moved on.

The first door creaked open to reveal a replica of the library of our east wing. It had a carved mahogany desk and wall-to-wall bookshelves lined with leather-bound manuscripts, all catalogued to perfection. An empty jewelled ivory photo frame on the desk stared at me. If only it could talk, I would have coaxed it to tell me the story of its missing photograph. A musty aroma hung in mid-air but the padding of the upholstered armchairs was still cushiony. Wait! I heard something. A movement. Was somebody there? Was that an imprint on the cushioned armchair opposite me? A pile of dusty books were scattered in front of a blackened stone fireplace. My hand shook as I picked up the one on the top. I blew off grey dust from its cover, and the title surprised me. *A Farewell to Arms*, by Ernest Hemingway, the very first edition! I lay it down quickly in fear of alarming the owners of this place. I was sure that someone was watching me, whether in person or in spirit. And then my eyes fell on the second book in the pile. *Young India*, by Lala Lajpat Rai. With wobbly fingers, I opened the book and read: *...If the English rule in India meant the canonization of bureaucracy, if it meant perpetual domination and perpetual tutelage, and increasing deadweight* *on the soul of India, it would be a curse to civilization and a blot on humanity....* I scrambled though the rest of the pile and noticed that all the books were published before 1945. I imagined people sitting in front of the fire, with their neatly manicured fingers clutching gin and ale glasses as firmly as their loyalty to their issues and debates. I had just walked through a time machine into a forgotten world, a world that had seen the struggles and turmoil of the great Indian Freedom Movement and the partition of India and Pakistan. The room may have harboured secrets of business meetings, espionage, and war, and other secrets that were waiting to be told through every object that was looking down on me.

I dragged myself out of there and moved on. The dark corridor led to another room, a room like no other. A room of windows! The roof and the walls were made out of glass, open to the sky above and overlooking into the garden below.

So this is what a trapped bird in a cage felt like from the inside.

Something caught my eye. It was an odd shape and covered with a clump of faded fabric. I pulled at the cloth and dry, itchy dust jetted into my nostrils.

I sneezed several times. Between my sneezes, my head turned to see a most unexpected treasure lying in the corner. It was a long-necked tanpura and a large harmonium. Oh my God! These were two magical instruments of the classical Indian music world. Instinctively, my pointer touched the string of the tanpura and I was transported back to my school days when I played something similar, the Sitar. Suddenly I felt connected with the spirit of this room. The edgy sharpness of the tanpura's chords were padded with the sticky grime of decades, but the acoustics of its celestial echo overpowered any gloom that lingered in the air. .

So someone in Veer's family was a musician, but who?

Still thirsty for answers, I tore away from the room and went back into the dark corridor. My torch started flickering. Maybe it was time to turn back. But something was pulling me ahead.

I had the feeling that I was on the brink of a revelation. Something was waiting for me. Between the flickers, I suddenly felt claustrophobic, as if the corridor had narrowed, caving into me. I hit my torch with my palm to steady its beam. And then I could see that there was a wall in front of me. The corridor had ended. A dead end? No, that could not be. My feet kept pulling me ahead in the darkness. I had almost reached the end.... But, it wasn't the end, it was a corner. I turned sideways and faced a pair of tall, prohibiting double doors.

Without a second thought, I tugged at the doors and walked in.

A room of mirrors!

This was a house of surprises. My head spun and the dizziness that I had successfully evaded until that moment started creeping back.

There were mirrored closets that lined the walls of the room.

A cold draught that had been following me from the corridor entered the room and I felt the temperature drop. I shivered. My flickering torch fell from my hand and died. I fumbled for a light switch on the wall, but in vain. The darkness was complete. I was trapped tightly inside it.

I talked to my curiosity. What was this room for?

It had to be a dressing room for the mysterious absentee mistress of the mansion. And then, as if to answer my question, I saw something flash in the darkness Were my eyes playing tricks on me? I was certain I had seen some light ahead. In pitch darkness, I started moving slowly toward this imaginary light.

But the room was empty. I stopped, defeated. I turned around and decided I had to go back.

Then, from the corner of my eye, I saw it again. The flash. I thumped my torch, hoping that would rescue me. Something heard my plea, but it was not my torch. From within the mirrors the room was suddenly softly lighted, like when one holds a candle high up to the ceiling in a dark room. I could see myself standing in the centre of the room looking into the mirrors again. I was smiling. But I didn't remember smiling. I remembered shaking. I looked again. No, here in the mirrors, I was smiling. Something was very wrong here. I looked closer. It was not a very nice smile. It was not a smile I had ever seen on myself before. The smile was sharp and shrewd. I didn't recognize myself. No, this was not me ... this was someone else.

Why was this woman now lying down? There were thick, rough hands with chipped fingernails clasped tightly around her throat. I saw a throbbing vein in the middle of her forehead, just like the vein on Veer's forehead that throbbed when he was distressed. The woman's eyes were wide, as if inviting what was going to happen next. The claw-like grip of those coarse knuckles grew tighter, and her forehead veins were ready to burst. Her mouth curved up at the edges to reveal the depths of her malice.Until she could smile no more. She lay still, very still. He had killed her! I tasted warm salty tears on my lips and came back to the darkness. I was going mad. What had just happened? What had I seen?

I sat down on the cold dusty floor. I didn't care what happened to me anymore. I didn't care if the evil in the room consumed me. I only cared about what happened to the woman in the mirror. Her eyes ... beautiful doe eyes, not in pain, but in hope ... hope of a release... finally being fulfilled ... and then stone-cold evil. I could not get those eyes out of my head.

My mother's voice was calling me, "Maya! Maya, come in from the cold. Veer is here to get you."

Veer's smiling hazel eyes look down on me. I am lying on a rose-strewn pillow and now Sheila's voice: "Maya-Beti, I will help you...."

I felt my face on the floor. The coldness of the ground against my cheeks sent a chill down my entire body. I must have dozed off. I sat up and wiped off the thick layer of dust covering my face, hands, everywhere.

I had definitely napped. It must have been a dream, all nonsense. The exhaustion of the day had gotten to me. There was no one in the house. I was sure of it.

Just then my torch flickered weakly, giving me a bit of light. I wasted no time to prove to myself that I was alone in that room. I quickly moved towards the first mirrored panel. It was empty. Then the second, the third, the fourth. I was right. There was nothing and no one here. There was only one last closet left. It was tucked behind a tattered maroon jacquard drape. I quickly drew the drape and pierced a large spider's web. Behind the drape, the carved ebony closet door creaked under its own heaviness. I recognized the stuffy cedar odour from my grandmother's attic where she stored her heirlooms. More empty shelves.

But it was cold. My fingers stiffened, and the torch fell from my hands. I bent down to pick it up and saw that it was pointing faintly to a deep corner of the bottom shelf. There was something stuck between the seams of the closet walls. I stretched out my hand to pull whatever it was out carefully. It was a piece of torn paper, curved, and jaundice yellow.

Pressing it to the floor, I carefully rolled it out with my fingers. It was a photograph!

My heartbeat stopped once again. It was the same beautiful face looking back at me. It was the lady in the mirror. Peeking out from under her dark waist-length hair were the same brute knuckles, this time clutching her waist firmly. A shimmering sequinned silk gown gracefully accentuated her narrow hips to end just above dainty ankles decorated with silver trinkets. She was holding a conspicuous black-and-white polka dot book. Her wrists caught my attention. They were adorned with the most exquisite pair of gold bracelets, with clasps in the shape of peacock heads! Her head was bowed, but she was looking up just enough to reveal her beauty.

Why did she look so familiar? I knew that I had seen her somewhere, or that I had seen someone who looked like her, but I couldn't remember who that might have been.

There was a movement behind me. It was coming from somewhere close. The torch had once again shut itself off. I stood up in pitch darkness and slipped the photograph into my back pocket.

I could feel a presence right at the nape of my neck. But there were only so many times that unexplained presences could wander in empty rooms. So, this was my opportunity to be brave and dispel any myths I had about such existences. Gathering every ounce of courage, I turned around slowly. Instinctively I aimed my dead torch straight at my target, as if it was a weapon.

To my surprise, the torch flickered again and shone a faint light on a face that I didn't expect to see at all.

Powdered, plump, mascaraed eyelashes under sparkly blue eye shadow and bright red lipstick on full lips. She spoke. Her voice was low and husky. "Hello! Who are you? What are you doing here?" She didn't sound angry.

I attempted an answer: " I ... can we go outside please? It is very dark here."

I saw her turn around to lead the way. In the corridor we had a better look at each other. She was a large voluptuous woman with the air of a pin-up model on calendars sold at bus stations. Her ginger hair was streaked with blonde strands. She was wearing a leopard spotted shirt that opened just enough for you to imagine every fathomable curve. It was tucked into tight white pants over broad hips and pencil stilettos.

I realized I still had not answered her questions. "I live on the other side of the house. I ... I am Veer's wife."

"Holy mother of God!" She dropped her formal tone, threw her hands up into the air, and squeezed me in a hug.

"I am Rosy, Veers father's younger brother's wife. I am Veer's aunt."

"Hello," was all that I could manage.

11.

I DID NOT REMEMBER seeing Rosy at our wedding. Rosy must have known that I was wondering about that. She said, "I ... we could not come to your wedding my dear." She looked away just in time to hide her face. Then she looked back at me, with moist lashes, her gaze gliding over my every contour. It was her turn to study me.

"I see Veer did not do too badly." A hot flash of embarrassment at her directness made me blush. "But ... wait.. You look so very familiar."

"I have a common face."

"No, no, it will come back to me. I never forget a face." And then in the same breath she continued, "Why don't you come around, my place is just across the hall from here."

I hesitated. It was getting late and I didn't want to get into trouble with Veer's mother, who would soon be back from her day's excursions.

"Oh, come on, just a few minutes. I would like you to meet someone."

So I followed her again. She led me to another section of the house, which I would have never discovered on my own. We reached her suite.

It had large windows like the rest of the house, overlooking the garden below. The upholstery and drapes were synchronized in hues of pink, red, and gold, completely matching her personality.

Rosy pulled out a slim Camel cigarette from a gold-plated case, lit it on a cabriole holder, and then rang an indoor brass bell as if to call someone as she exhaled raucously. A few minutes later, a maid entered carrying a bottle of distilled dry gin, tonic, and crackers. Behind her was another figure, a mere shadow. A blue-checked shirt, two sizes too big dropped from scrawny shoulders to cover loose pleated pants out of a 1950's fashion catalogue. The man had a remarkable resemblance to Veer's father, though he was much darker, with a high forehead, a long nose, and eyes set deep into their hollowed sockets.

"Meet Veer's new bride, Maya," she said, pointing at me. "This is my husband, your father-in-law's younger brother, Umang."

I bent down to touch his feet as a traditional mark of respect to elders. He stopped me midway and hugged me instead.

"Well, guess where I found her? In the room!" Her eyes widened as she passed on this piece of information to her husband.

Umang tried to speak but broke into a dry coughing spasm. It lasted for a few minutes. I noticed that Rosy was unmoved. He walked over to the tray and took a sip of tonic, which seemed to soothe his throat.

When he spoke, his words were muffled and hurried: "Welcome to the family, Maya. It is very nice to meet you and our best wishes are with you both."

Now it was my turn and I asked my first question, diplomatically: "It is so nice to meet you both too, but how come you don't visit the east wing?" There is an uncomfortable silence and I instantly regretted the question.

Umang answered. "There are no secrets from you, Maya, as you are now family and will come to know sooner or later. So, I might as well tell you. You see, Rosy came into our life to nurse me from a series of illnesses, from typhoid to jaundice and asthma. Rosy and I grew fond of each other and I proposed to her, and, to my surprise, she graciously accepted." He looked at Rosy and she smiled back languidly.

Then Rosy carried the story: "Just before our wedding, we had to break the news to my new in-laws. They were not happy. They called me many names, and it got worse when they heard that I was the unmarried mother of a toddler suffering from polio and that he lived with my widowed mother in the suburbs of the north. They felt cheated." She paused.

"After marriage, we set up our home in this part of the deserted house, where no one would bother us. I still remember the chill of our first winter in this house. There was a constant draught that crept in from the gaps in the windows and cracks in the walls, reminding us of the family's ill wishes for me, and many before me. My son caught pneumonia and never recovered. The following year my mother also passed away. Since then, we have become the forgotten relatives of the Rajsinghanias of the east wing." There was a distinct bitterness in her tone. I realized that she was talking about Veer's parents. I understood the pain of being unwelcome.

There was a rustle at the curtain of the inner room. An overdressed middle-aged man in a crisp white button-down shirt and a lean cut black jacket with a pretentious red rose pinned to its outer pocket came out from behind the curtain.

"Maya, meet Raju, my business partner and friend." Rosy batted her eyelids at him. "Since Umang was ill most of the time, it was sooo nice of Raju to help me set up my clothing boutique."

Raju waved his hand in the air at me and then dug it into his pocket to take out a cigar. He started adding to the billows of smoke that were already swallowing up the room. Then he slid next to Rosy a little too snugly. Umang shifted uncomfortably in his chair. This was getting awkward. Without thinking, I pulled out the mysterious photograph from my jeans pocket and held it out to Rosy.

"I found this in the room where I met you. Do you know who this is?" Rosy took the photograph from my hand and stiffened. "Where did you say you found it?"

"In the largest closet behind the jacquard drape in the corner."

"Yes," she said distractedly. 'Of course you would find it there. That was *her* closet." I sat up immediately, in anticipation of the information that was about to be revealed. "It is not your fault. How would you know who *she* was? There must not be any pictures of her in that part of the house either."

"Well who is *she*?" I could not contain myself anymore.

"She was Veer's grandmother."

I gasped loudly.

Rosy held the photograph up against the sunlight. She looked at me and then at the photograph. Her jaw dropped. She walked to Raju and pointed to something in the photo. His palm flew to cover his mouth. Umang joined their huddle, and his eyes widened. Something strange was being discussed. What was alarming these people?

I stood up. "What is it?" I blurted out.

"Tell her," Rosy said to Umang.

"What?" I asked again, my eyes darting from one person to the next.

"Don't get startled, Maya, but we just realized why you look so familiar..."

"Why?"

"Well, you see ..."

"Tell me!"

"You are the spitting image of Veer's grandmother!"

"What?"

I froze. No, that couldn't be. These people were delusional. They were making up things. I shouldn't be talking to such people.

I pulled the photo from her hands and looked at it again.

No, they were not delusional. They were right! I was looking back at myself! But how could this be? I sat down trembling. Rosy handed me a glass of the transparent heady liquid and I felt better. Then she came and sat down next to me.

"Don't worry, Maya. It's just a coincidence. Such things

happen, you know..." she said in a tone so unconvincing that even she did not bother to finish her sentence.

I wanted to know more about Veer's grandmother. "What can you tell me about her?" I asked, looking at all three of them. There was a painful silence.

Umang finally spoke: "My mother passed away giving birth to me. This wing of the house was built by my father for her, and it is an addendum to the main premises where you live. Even though I never knew her, I feel her presence here; I feel her in every room. That is the reason I like living in this part. I know that she is close to me. While growing up, I used to come and sit in the mirrored room for hours. Many times, when I lay on the floor there, I could feel her soft caress on my arms. And then I no longer felt like a motherless child. This has been my little secret. Most of this part of the house has not been touched since her time." He stopped to gather his emotions.

Rosy filled in. "One night, I got home late from my friend's party and I had forgotten my keys, so I decided to come in from the door that you used today. It was so dark that night that I couldn't see my own hands. As I passed the mirrored room, I could have sworn I saw her in the mirror trying on her favourite *Jamawar* shawl."

A sharp pain pierced through my head. How would I be able to tell them what *I* saw in the mirror? It was much more sinister than any of what they were telling me. Even I didn't believe what I saw. But after hearing them , maybe, I could believe a little.

Rosy continued, "I know she was a noble woman, a free spirit, like a guardian angel protecting her home and everyone who lives in it. So I am not scared."

There was silence again, this time a little less agonizing. No one said anything for a long time. For once I was thankful for the familiar puffing and dragging sound of Raju's cigar.

"Why did Veer's parents not say anything?" I asked.

"Well, they wouldn't, would they?"

"No, I guess not."

It was all making sense to me. The exaggerated reactions of Veer's mother on seeing me for the first time, the confusing comments of his aunts on the wedding night, Sheila's overprotective behaviour. For some strange reason, now that I understood, I felt a sort of relief that their hostility was not towards me personally, but my resemblance to an unpleasant memory, or at least so I hoped.

I wanted to leave. But before I went, I needed to know more. But how could I tactfully ask such personal questions on such a sensitive subject? The clue had to be in the photo.

"Rosy, is that a book in her hand? With the white polka dotted cover it looks extremely stylish, like the rest of her outfit," I asked pointing to the photo.

"No, it's a diary."

"Was she a writer?"

"No, she was an artist. A musician."

Of course! That explained the sun-kissed room with the tanpura and the harmonium. So she was the mystery musician of this family!

"What was her name?"

"Her name was Gayatri, Gayatri Devi Rathore."

I imprinted that name in my head, repeating it over and over again. It took me a few minutes before I could ask my next question.

"Rosy, how do you know so much if you have never met her?"

Instead of replying, Rosy abruptly got up and went into the adjoining room. Had I exhausted, or worse, annoyed her with my insatiable curiosity? She returned in a few minutes, and in her hands was a black diary with white polka dots! My heart leapt. My defiance and courage for venturing so far had paid off.

"I found this in an old trunk that was given to me with her clothes. It is hers. Here, do you want to take a look?" She held it out to me.

I wanted to jump and grab it, but instead, I took it in my

hands slowly and carefully. It felt much heavier than it looked. The cover was dyed in black homemade ink with batik polka dots on raw silk. The edges were tattered, but the body was still intact, as if the purpose of its life had not yet been fulfilled.

I opened it. The first page had a large dried Banyan leaf, its veins spread out like the map of the Indian North-West Frontier Province. The shrivelled yellow glue had discoloured its edges. I turned the page. And there in the centre of the next page was written: *Gayatri Devi Rathore, 2051 Khyber Road, Peshawar, 1946.*

I stopped. My mother was from Peshawar. Was this a coincidence? Could this be a clue as to why I resembled her? It seems we both belonged to the same ethnic region.

Under this script was a charcoaled stencilled print of a lone resilient tree blowing in the wind, braving the storm and standing steady. My fingers instinctively traced the bent branches and then the bold strokes of the wind. But my hand ached with its weight. Why was it so heavy? I closed the diary and handed it back. But my eyes were glued on it. Rosy noticed.

"You can take it if you want, it is of no use to me." I inhaled sharply. My mind yelled to my heart, *Stay calm.... Don't show how badly you would like to take it, or she may change her mind.*

With the greatest poker face I had ever practiced, I replied, "Are you sure?" She shrugged. My wish had come true. This time, I tightly clutched Gayatri's diary next to my heart. The purpose for my day had been accomplished. All I could think of was how to get quickly back to the east wing.

Rosy and Umang walked me out to the corridor. "Come, I will show you an easier way back to your east wing. We often used this to play hide-n-seek as kids." Umang's eyes were shining. At the edge of the corridor was a flight of rickety winding iron stairs that lead straight into the back of the garden. "Just follow the path and you will recognize your side of the house ."

I should not have felt the pang that I did saying goodbye to

Umang and Rosy, considering the short time that I had spent with these complete strangers. But something so important had just transpired with them that I knew I would carry it with me for the rest of my life.

I ran back. It was almost dark already. I couldn't believe that I had spent the whole day roaming within the walls of the west wing. Now I just wanted the safety of my room. But more than anything, I wanted to read Gayatri's diary.

For once I was glad to enter an empty house. I slipped into my room, bolted it from the inside, and opened the curtains to welcome an early moon in an indigo sky.

There was a knock on the door. Oh no, I didn't want to see anyone—not Veer's mother, not Sheila. There was another knock. I opened the door hesitantly. Thankfully it was only Bahadur.

"Madam, shall I bring your dinner to your room? I thought that you may want it early today since you have been out?"

"Yes, Bahadur, that would be nice. Thank you." I was famished.

Then he paused. "Madam, the big Madam was looking for you." Nervousness gripped me.

"Why? Was she worried?"

Could Veer's mother have known where I was?

"Oh no, they went out for dinner and will be back late. But she asked me to deliver this message to you." He dug into his pocket and handed me a handwritten note: *Cocktails at six in the east lounge tomorrow evening. Dress formal. Be there.*

I crumpled it into a paper ball and aimed for the dustbin in the corner. Bull's eye! Bahadur clapped, and I whistled at my own marksmanship.

"And Sheila came looking for you several times," he said with a half-smile. I knew exactly why he was smiling. I could imagine Sheila fretting loudly to all the maids every time she came to my rooms and did not find me.

A calming chamomile bath soaked my tiredness and drained

the dark grime from my body. Within minutes of eating Bahadur's heart-warming consommé with garlic bread and Caesar salad, I felt energized and ready for the night.

I settled down with Gayatri's diary on the chesterfield, facing the garden and .opened the first brittle page dated 1946. I began to read: *My dear journal, my confidante, and my conscience.* I immersed myself into every word.

I must have dozed off sometime past midnight, for when I awoke there were tiny droplets of dew on the windowsill and a faint brightening of the skyline among chirping morning birds. It was dawn, and with it came a special gift , my giddiness and nausea. With a warm mohair blanket still around my shoulders, I strolled down to the lawn. . The cold wet grass tantalized my toes and brought me back to the present.

The black diary lay mutely next to me on the lawn chair. I distracted myself by trying to feed the peacocks hovering in the garden as a part of their morning routine. The wind through the peepal leaves became stronger, turning their whispers into growls.

My head ached with what the diary had revealed. Gayatri's diary had ended, but I knew that this was not where Gayatri's story ended. I had so many questions, and I knew it was important to find the answers, for me and for Veer. But I did not know why. Not yet.

I sat near the peacocks, and tried to recall her life. It flew back and, at that moment, I felt that I had somehow been a part of all of it.

12. GAYATRI

July 28, 1946

Why is it so hot today? Baba said that it is going to be the hottest and driest summer afternoon in Peshawar. My eyes are full of loose gravel from our courtyard, which blew in with bunches of burnt leaves after dancing round and round in a furious circle. Even before the morning milkman had come, Ma unfurled the musk-scented grass curtains in our open veranda to keep the house cool. Baba said it was to prepare for the fury of the sun as it rose. I was not allowed to play hopscotch with Ashu and Rupa. "Make sure you three sisters don't go out in the heat," Baba had said before leaving for his headmaster's job at our school.

I don't really mind *not* playing with them anymore, as these two are getting more irritating by the day. They are always following me around and asking me questions that I don't want to answer. I will ask Baba tonight if I can sleep in a separate room now that I am big and all.

Today, Ma also decided to stay home instead of going to teach her music class at our school. But that just meant that I had to help her in the kitchen, knead dough, boil rice, and then read to Ashu and help Rupa with her diction. By evening, as the wrath of the sun subsided, I grew restless. All I wanted to do was hit the right notes of the latest raga that Ma had taught me on her tanpura. I need the practise. Ever since Ma had scolded me for not being able to reach the last two high notes, I have wanted to do nothing else but practise under the banyan tree. Its branches spread like that of a protecting eagle, covering our whole courtyard with shade and life. A week ago, a pair of white doves laid eggs on its topmost branches. They have been nesting on this banyan for a year now. I recognize their flutter long before I see them. It is as if they are a part of my day. I've named them Om and Shanti. Their peaceful white sheen brings me luck, soothes my nerves, and gives me confidence before performing. My singing brings our neighbours and some of Baba and Ma's friends to our courtyard. But there is another reason I want to sing. It brings *him*.

September 12, 1946

Something very special happened last evening. I will always remember it. Our courtyard was filled with spectators, more than usual. Baba says that it is because the cool eastern breeze entices everyone to follow the scent of my melodies.

Om and Shanti were perched on their highest branch to bless me with luck. I hit all the right notes, or so I read from Ma's face. I sang into the night, from my selection of evening ragas to night ragas. It was so effortless, and I was in a frenzy to go on. Every time I started a new song, I felt my tongue gliding on a ribbon that lifted me high into the clouds. But then, just before dinner, the air became stuffy, and many people started moving out. I was happy to see that Sachin had stayed on. With a loud sparkling cry, the heavens burst open, sending sheets of happy tears down on the hot tin roofs that received them with gratitude. It was as if the burgeoning rain drops were beating in rhythm to my ragas. But Rupa, Ashu, and Ma started packing up to take shelter inside. I lifted my face to welcome the cold musty drops on my parched lips.

"Don't just stand there, silly girl. Come here and help," came Ma's instructions. She handed me a stack of small hand towels to distribute to the few remaining guests to wipe themselves with. It was getting dark, so I picked up an earthen candle in the other hand. My hair was soaking, and my drenched kurta was sticking to my body like a glove.

As I reached Sachin, the distance between us was just a few inches of the length of the towel I held in my hand. I could feel his warm breath on my cheek. Sachin grabbed the other end of the towel and started pulling me closer to him. His hand touched mine. His voice was deep as a gravel pit and his scent intoxicating. "Thank you, Gayatri."

Something ignited inside me. It was like I was aware of my body coming alive from a slumber. He reached out to shelter my candle from the falling droplets. We stood there in the rain, in the candlelight, soaked to our bones, mesmerized.

"Gaga, what are you doing?" An inquisitive Rupa broke our spell.

"Ohhh, nothing. Just handing out the towels." I ran in to my room to get away. . Ma had laid out dinner.

"Gaga, go get changed," she said without looking up. I was afraid she had seen us. When I came back, to my complete surprise, Sachin was seated at the table with Baba, Ma, and the girls, engrossed in a conversation.

Ma was saying, "So, tomorrow evening, come a little earlier to drop off our glossaries, just before Gayatri starts her practise routine, and I will start with your first lesson...." My ears perked up. What was Ma doing? Had she just invited Sachin for a lesson? But I knew how strict Sachin's father was about his free time. He was only allowed to come here after his daily chores at his father's grocery store. Sachin's father was our local grocery store owner. As a good neighbour, Sachin's father sent Ma a daily supply of green vegetables, lentils, and fresh tea leaves.

"Yes, yes, I will ask for an earlier shift in the store from Papa so that I can arrive on time." He could not contain his excitement. Neither could I. So Sachin was going to come to our house for music lessons every evening. How good could life get?

January 30, 1947

It has been only a few weeks since Sachin had started singing, but it seems that this is what he was born to do. When his deep voice hits the lowest note, or his passion climbs to the highest tempo, I clench my fists tightly, and dig my nails into my palms to avoid being completely sucked in by his sheer magnetism. Oh! How I love him!

Last week Ma asked us to sing together, and the crowds for our evening recital has now started swelling by the day. I overheard Baba tell Ma that he was getting a worried about what, "...being unmarried and singing with a young lad" would do to my reputation. But I did not care. Nothing in the whole world could stop us from the time we spent in heaven, singing together. Our voices synchronize in perfect harmony, our thoughts align, and our souls unite. It is the greatest joy I have ever known. And I pray every night that this time will last forever.

Om and Shanti's eggs hatched last week, and, although I did not see them much, I heard their flutter among the cheerful chirps of their chicks.

I never want anything to change, ever.

June 18, 1947

I spoke too soon. Change has come and jinxed our perfect life. Today was the most cursed day I have ever known. It has changed everything. It was a typical hot June evening until Baba came home after his monthly neighbourhood committee meeting. My music practise had been cancelled as Ashu was running a fever. Ma was oiling my hair when Baba walked in with a worried look. Ma followed him, and they closed the bedroom door behind them. We waited for them to come out for dinner—they didn't—and then waited for them after dinner. Just before bed, the door finally opened and both Ma and Baba came out looking as white as ghosts. We huddled around them, and then Baba gave us the news. His words stayed in my ears for a long time. "There is nothing in life that stays constant, and there is nothing in life that I like more than my homeland and this life with all of you." His voice cracked up and I knew something serious was coming. Baba never spoke like this. Rupa instinctively hugged him, and he held out his hand for Ashu and me. What he told us next changed our life forever.

"The time has come for India to be partitioned into the two sovereign countries of India and Pakistan. Now Ma took over, "We have never stressed about our religion before. We were born in the land of Pathans, and we belong here. However, for the first time, for the sake of our safety, we have to remember that we are Hindus living in a Muslim hamlet. Even though this is the only home we know, we have to leave it now and go where the rest of the Hindus live."

"But why Ma?" Rupa cried.

"How can we not be safe in our own home?" Ashu asked. Instead of answering, she hugged them both tightly.

I did not want to show my weakness, as Ma had taught me, but today I could not stop my tears. I let them flow. Rupa and Ashu clung to me for support, but I could not offer them any.

We have to travel east of the Indus River, all the way to Delhi, where Baba has an old school friend, Ahmed Bilal. Baba assured us that this would only be temporary, only until things quieten down. Then we could return home.

"We have to move before the carnage and painful displacement begins for millions of families like ours. It is inevitable. We leave the day after tomorrow at sunrise," Baba decided.

Why is this happening? Why does it matter which God we pray to? What is so important that we have to abandon the only life we have ever known? The only love I have ever known? Will I ever see Sachin again?

July 30, 1947

If it were not for my parents, I would have rather died than leave my home. This past week has been a daze. I am living in another person's body. My body and soul are left behind with my tanpura under the banyan tree, under the nest of Om and Shanti, and with Sachin.

On that last dark night, I snuck out to see Sachin for the last time. I knew he would be in his room at the back, probably studying under an oil lamp, absolutely clueless about how our lives have been torn apart. I threw some soft pebbles at his window, and, when no one came to see, I slid a note between the cracks of his windowsill. In my note, I told him that we were leaving, that I did not want to be apart from him, and that he should come with us. Then I ran back to my house, slipped under the cold bedsheets and, with each passing hour that Sachin did not come, wept some more.

At the crack of dawn, exactly two days from the evil night that Baba brought the terrible news, we tiptoed out of our courtyard, bolted the main door with an enormous iron lock, and, with our entire life packed in shabby sling bags, boarded a train from Peshawar to eventually reach Delhi.

August 10, 1947

I have never seen such grandeur as in Delhi's Chandni Chowk. Not in Peshawar, not anywhere. But then, we had never been outside of Peshawar. Such broad shopping areas, with colourful stalls of flower vendors, photographers on the sidewalks, and a magnificent clock tower on one end of our street. Ashu and Rupa's eyes widened at the candy stalls, vivid paper kites, and multi-coloured glass bangles. Our mouths watered at the sweet smells of roasted pistachios and carrot cakes at the roadside sweet shops. But what really caught my imagination was a very special hospital, just a few blocks away. It is a bird's hospital. Baba said it is one of its kind in the whole country. They treat all kinds of birds here: pigeons, parrots, sparrows and even peacocks. Nervously, I asked Baba if they also treat white doves, and he said "yes."

My hopes have risen. There is a possibility that Om and

Shanti will pine for me and fall ill, and then they will fly here to the hospital where I will find them, forever. Maybe Sachin will follow too. My heart is full of hope and doubt. Why did Sachin not come to meet me in my last moments in Peshawar? Did he not care? Or did he not get my note? Was he looking for me now? I will never know. No one knew where we were. Unless Baba had told the neighbours. Maybe there was a little hope after all. Hope was all I had for now.

Bilal Uncle's tiny apartment was in a rundown building in a crowded, narrow street. As soon as he opened the door, we immediately recognized a painful and familiar sight. His bags were packed, and his eyes were heavy.

"My wife and I are going to our ancestral town of Karachi, leaving our home in your hands. One day soon we shall return. Till then, my friend, you are most welcome to stay and call our home your home." Within an hour, he and his teary-eyed wife were gone.

August 12, 1947

Life is different here. Life is different everywhere. The whole country is engulfed in flames. The carnage that Baba had anticipated has begun. Baba's radio blasts Gandhi, Nehru, and Jinnah's speeches. I hear the word "freedom" several times among the news of overloaded trains of refugees from either side trying to cross over to *their* side, dodging the violence and the looting. Millions have succumbed, families have been displaced, children orphaned. Once, on a very bad frequency, I thought I heard "Peshawar," and I stopped in my tracks to pick up any word that followed. A reporter was talking about villagers filling their iron rods with gunpowder to explode in the face of the rioters. I prayed every night for them, for Sachin, and for our good fortune that we are all here together safe, with the hope that I will see Sachin again.

Our first few weeks in Chandni Chowk were spent getting our bearings. We needed to be frugal with the limited funds that Baba had been able to take with him from Peshawar.

"Tomorrow I shall follow up on all the calls that I have made. At this point I will take any job that comes first, even if I have to wait tables."

"Didn't that kind man at the wholesale cloth house offer you part time hours? Why don't you start with him first? I will see if I can get a part time job too," Ma pitched in.

"No, you will not look for a job outside. You look after the house and the girls and be my strength. While I am alive and able, there is no need for the women of my family to work."

I did not want to hear any more. This was a very different exchange from the joking carefree conversations that Baba and Ma had in Peshawar. Why did those days have to end?

August 14, 1947

Death visited today, but decided not to stay.

Just as we were starting to succumb to the security of a safe routine, catastrophe struck. Everything was fine until Baba had an urge to eat almond rice pudding. Oh, Baba and his sweet tooth!

"Gaga, why don't you run down to the sweets shop and get five portions?"

"What are we celebrating, Papa?" asked Rupa.

"Just life, my dearest, just life."

But Ma stopped me and scolded Baba: "What are you doing? This is not Peshawar you know, where you can send the girl alone. Wait, I am coming with you."

Ma followed me out along with Ashu and Rupa, latching the main door from the outside.

The trip to the sweets shop was in a more congested part and took longer than expected. Not knowing our way around, we were caught in bottlenecks, and at one point we had to walk in a single file to avoid open drains and live wires hanging down from electric poles. Ma bought five mud containers filled with the rice pudding, one for each of us. Then we headed back.

As we approached our narrow lane, I could have sworn that it looked more crowded than when we had left an hour ago. There was a policeman with a gun on his hip and a stick in his hand, standing at the entrance. Something was not right.

"Are you the woman of house number 1303?" he asked.

"Eh, yes I am." I could hear the nervousness in Ma's voice.

"Come with me."

We all followed him upstairs. Our front door was ajar and the floor was covered with glass splinters from a smashed window. Then I saw the rest.

Baba was lying on a stretcher surrounded by two paramedics who were bandaging his open wounds. His eyes were closed, and he was bleeding from his head through the stained dressing. His white clothes were soiled red with blood. The house was ransacked, and our two suitcases with their measly belongings were gone.

I felt faint. Ma collapsed near Baba's stretcher. The girls started sobbing uncontrollably. Someone brought a glass of water for each of us. That helped. Finding a little of my voice, I asked one of the paramedics what had happened.

"Your father is not regaining consciousness, although we have found his pulse. He has suffered multiple blows to his head, and it is a miracle that he is alive."

The policeman now stepped forward. "This is the work of some neighbourhood goons who mistook this house as belonging to the Muslim family that lived here. You probably forgot to change the name plate on your front door, and the goons mistook you for Muslims. Now that the whole country is engulfed in Hindu-Muslim riots, all such houses are being targeted."

A surge of hatred and anger rose from my stomach and gripped my head. Such small people. For such a petty thing as a name plate, they attacked my Baba. What kind of animals are these people?

Baba was carried away on a stretcher in a waiting ambulance.

Ma went with him too. Ashu, Rupa, and I have been left alone is this sinful place.

August 16, 1947

For once, I do not like having the freedom to lord it over my sisters. I am in charge, but I realize that this is no freedom at all. It is a responsibility. With Ma and Baba gone, I have to manage the house, clean, cook, and feed my sisters.

Earlier, I checked in Ma's small canister where she keeps her loose change for groceries. It had only a few *annas* left. I took the change for our next meal and was latching up the lid when something gleamed from under her torn handkerchief. I gently pulled it out and gasped. There, below a tattered holy book, were two gold bracelets. I have never seen such beautiful engraving before. Their clasps are in the shape of peacock heads, and they are filled with *meenakari* work. I remember seeing them on Ma's wrists at a neighbourhood wedding. The gold was embedded with jewels from the peacock's tail: emerald, ruby, copper, amethyst, and jade. My fingers instinctively glided over the intricate embossment. It is the most beautiful piece of jewellery I have ever touched. I held the bracelets in my hands for a long time. They reminded me of better days and happiness. Then I tucked the peacock bracelets back under her handkerchief and looked at the *annas* again. What can I get with them? Tomorrow morning, I will go down to the market and find out.

August 18, 1947

It must have been midday when I woke up to someone knocking on the front door. Without Ma and Baba, there was no one to wake us up on time. I was almost awake when I opened the door, but it felt like a dream. It was Ma. She was smiling, tired but relieved. Rupa and Ashu were already pulling her in.

"Baba is conscious. He is coming home soon." We hugged her for a long time.

Then Ma took me aside and said, "Baba will not be able to get up from the bed, Gaga. He is paralyzed on the left side. God help us." With Rupa and Ashu not around, Ma let herself go, one tear after another. Ma always relied on me to hold her, to understand her, and to support her. Sometimes I feel it is unfair, but, in times like this, my feelings do not matter. If Baba is disabled, then I have to help Ma pick up the pieces. And for my family, I can do anything.

August 26, 1947

It has been a week since Baba's return. Yesterday he started eating semi-solid food. He looks drained of colour, but he keeps muttering how grateful he is to be back. Ma sold the second last of her gold thread heirloom saris for rations for this week. She has been phoning all of our distant relatives in Delhi, probing for any work opportunities. By evening, defeated and slightly humiliated, she sat down after her last call. I know these are desperate times. I went and sat next to her, and she placed her hand on mine.

I had my journal in my hand. Her glance fell on my journal and then on me. She had just thought of something. I could see it in her eyes.

"Gaga, where did you get this cloth?" She was referring to the polka dotted batik fabric that I had dyed at home to cover my journal. I told her. Her eyes brightened some more. "You always had a flair, my darling, talented child," she said and hugged me. I was quite puzzled by now.

"What is it, Ma?"

"Well, it's just an idea, but if it works, and if we are able to work hard, then it may just be a solution to our problems." Baba and the girls had tuned in now.

"Well?" I probed again.

"You remember the kind-hearted cloth wholesaler who was offering Baba a job? We will go and tell him what has happened and ask him for a loan."

Now Baba chimed in: "A loan for what?"

But that was all Ma was willing to reveal this evening. "Let's talk tomorrow morning, shall we?"

With that, dinner, our only meal of the day, was laid.

October 12, 1947

This morning Ma and I woke up early, before the others, and snuck out of the house. I followed her down the narrow back alley littered with shops and tea stalls that had not opened for business yet. Some were in shambles, with black smoke marks on hollow walls, as if they were tears, witness to the agony of the times. I guessed that these shop owners had been victims of the rioters. In others shops, I could see through the grilled windows. Jewellery, dry fruits, flowers, metal works, cigarettes, shoes. We walked one block after the other. Then finally Ma slowed down. We were standing in front of a cluster of shops that opened for business earlier than all the others.

They were all cloth shops. A spectrum of colours, sizes, and designs hung from hooks on the shanty aluminium shutters. Infant wear, shawls, saris, pyjamas, tunics.

Ma knew exactly which shop to enter. It was a small, stuffy shop with white linen cloth spread on its entire floor, inviting us to sit cross-legged on the ground. An obese but kind-eyed shop keeper greeted us. His lips were stained with betel nut and tobacco, and he had a small glass of tea in one hand. He offered us tea, but Ma dove straight into why she had come to him. He patiently listened to her tale about Baba.

I got up and walked to the back of the shop. It was laden from floor to ceiling with stacks of cloth. Among woollen, machine-made, and handloom fabrics were also loom cotton, silk, and linen. There were separate stacks of synthetics, including nylons, acrylics, and polyesters. A section on natural weaves had intricate *zari* work, and the remaining sections had thread embroidery and block prints. This little shop contained a whole world of fashion.

Soon Ma joined me with a beaming face. I guessed that she had accomplished what she had set out to do. She turned around and said to the storekeeper, "My daughter Gayatri has a flair for design. She will be in charge of selecting the fabric." I looked at her questioningly. "Don't worry, he is loaning the fabrics to us by keeping the last of my gold heirloom saris as collateral. And this *is* my last heirloom. I have to marry you off in it, so I *will* get it back." She smiled confidently. "For now, just pick out twenty pieces of fabrics and ten saris—the ones you like best, Gaga."

I did what I was told gladly. Ma was right. I enjoyed playing with colours, syncing their hues and noticing the harmony in their palettes, as well as feeling the sensual touch of the weaves and the magic of the textures.

With our bundle of treasures, we started on our way back home. It felt like a victory march. For some reason, my step matched the spring in Ma's stride, and somehow I knew this was the end of our bad days.

February 13, 1948

Each side of India's border still sizzles with the embers of a million bodies. Our home in Peshawar now belongs to another country. So does Sachin.

We have been carrying out Ma's brilliant plan for four long winter months. This is how Ma's plan has worked. Every morning Ma calls her distant relatives, especially the ones celebrating a wedding, a christening, birthday or any other occasion. She informs them of her collection of exquisite fabric that she can bring to their doorstep to save them the inconvenience of stepping out. Then both Ma and I lug our bundle to their homes and with god's grace most people like and buy much of what we have to offer. Our feet ache and our backs hurt, but it has worked.

Gradually the word of our flamboyant merchandise spreads, and we start getting more invitations. As Ma predicted, she was able to get her collateral gold heirloom sari back from the shopkeeper. The money that we have earned goes to Baba's medicines, groceries, and buying a bigger stack. We have started having two meals now, and some days Ma even indulges us with ice cream and chocolate. With Ashu and Rupa taking turns, Baba too is looking more like himself. Things have started getting back to some shade of normalcy. There is nothing more that I can ask for. I pray every night.

March 8, 1948

Even though spring has come early this year, the mornings have a crispness that remind me of back home. I have visited the bird's hospital but did not find Om and Shanti. There was a wounded peacock that called out to me from one of the cages. His colours were as brilliant as Ma's gold bracelets. I would have taken him home had it not been for Ma's finicky habit of keeping the house spotlessly clean.

The wedding season has begun, and it is keeping us busy. It was early morning when the phone rang. Thank God for Baba's friend's house phone, for we could never have afforded such a luxury on our own. Usually Ma is pleased after she receives another business call, but today she sat down with a sigh. I went and sat next to her, as always. She placed her hand over mine, as always.

She said, "It was Usha Aunty with an invitation to visit her relatives on Aurangzeb Road. She says that it is one of the richest and most affluent families of Delhi, with big money and all. It is their daughter Nargis's wedding."

"Great! So what's the problem, Ma?"

"I don't think I can go." I instinctively touched her forehead. It was burning up. She continued, "Usha said to take our finest. They are so rich that they will buy the whole stock and many more if they like even half of it. Gaga, go with Rupa."

"No, Ma, let's just tell them we will come when you are better."

"Gaga, their wedding is in a few weeks. Besides, if they pick up the lot, we can take a break for some time. Would you not like that?" Ma always knew how to entice me. Yes, not working for a few days would be a welcome luxury.

As Rupa and I boarded the rickety rickshaw, the silly driver asked us for the address three times, as if doubting our destination. And when we reached it, I understood why he had reacted this way. This was not a house. It was a mansion. A beautiful mansion, in the midst of a lush and verdant garden, the kind I have only read about. A towering gate, a round driveway, stone stairs.

We were ushered into a hall with a crystal chandelier that reflected every colour of the rainbow. We hesitantly sat on the velvet divan, waiting for our buyers to arrive. Rupa had not blinked even once. She was inspecting each corner of the ornate room, which was full of framed portraits and antiques. I elbowed her to break the spell and started spreading out the display. For some reason, I was restless. A few minutes later, a slender girl with two braids, a broad forehead, and a long nose entered the room. She smiled and introduced herself as Nargis. She was not pretty, but pleasant. Behind her was a very frail young woman in a uniform, seemingly younger than me.

"Meet Sheila, my governess."

Nargis's eyes widened as they fell on our treasure. "Such *zari,* such colours! I want it all!" She gestured to Sheila to pick it up. "Do you have more?" she looked from Rupa to me.

I had to be honest. "No, this is all that we have."

"Well then, get more tomorrow," Nargis said.

"I don't have more," I repeated.

"Well, why not?"

"Because we don't have money to buy more. With the money that we will earn for this bundle, we will buy the next one." It felt good laying our boundaries.

"Oh!"

She must have thought I was a very rude person. But then

she probably had never confronted the possibility of not having money.

"Tell you what, I will pay you for everything here now, so you can bring me your next collection tomorrow."

She left the room and Sheila stayed. I could feel Sheila's eyes watching me. Somehow, they were not intimidating. Within a few minutes, Nargis was back with a tall shadow trailing her. The shadow stepped into the light, and I saw that he was a very tall man with a high forehead, and the same long nose as Nargis. He was clenching a stack of rupee bills in his hand.

"This is my elder brother, Prakash."

He did not reply to our greeting. He just stood there and stared. Stared at me. My restlessness grew. I did not feel shy; I did not feel embarrassed. I felt something that I did not recognize. Nargis took the money from his fist and handed it to me. I quickly stood up and pulled at Rupa's sleeve. We made our way out. I was almost running.

"What's the hurry, Gaga? He seemed bowled over by you!" she teased cruelly.

"I don't know, Rupa. I couldn't breathe in there."

In the sunlight, I realized what I had felt. This new, bitter, intolerant emotion. Repulsion. And for the first time I was ashamed of myself.

March 9, 1948

Today, as we returned with our second consignment of fabrics, the door was opened not by the butler, but by Prakash. Rupa smirked, and I almost kicked her under my skirt. He still had yesterday's look, but today he was blinking. I pushed Rupa in front of me so that she could to follow him first into the passage to reach the hall. Without a word, we started opening our display, but he stopped us and held out a fistful of cash.

I was completely disgusted by his crudeness. What did he think of us? Did he find us so desperate for money that we would just take his money without satisfying ourselves that they really liked our goods? We were here to do business, not to sell ourselves. We may be poor but we still had our dignity. I finally lifted my head and said to him, "But you have not even seen the new stock yet!"

"Nargis told me to take the whole lot."

"Without looking? Where is she?" Rupa asked, catching some of my irritation.

He continued, "Nargis has gone for the fitting of her wedding gown. She completely trusts your choice. What can I say?" Then he looked at me directly. "Beauty is an unusual and sacred thing. It comes rarely but surely."

Suddenly I knew he was no longer talking about his sister or the fabric. I felt a shiver down my spine, and my body turned cold. The same feeling from yesterday started returning. I took the money from his extended hand, and, without a word, turned to go.

"Would you like some tea?" he called out as we started to leave.

I did not answer. I did not care if this looked rude or if Rupa followed me or not. I felt claustrophobic inside the mansion's walls and trapped with Prakash.

Rupa was running behind to keep up. "What has gotten into you, Gayatri?" she asked when we reached our cramped, narrow street.

"I don't know. I can't breathe in that house." And I took a deep breath as I entered our small apartment

March 16, 1948

Ma was happy with the money that we had made by adding to Nargis's trousseau. I was happy because I got my much-needed break. But, this morning, my happiness was disturbed when Usha Aunty called once again. This time she told Ma about Nargis's invitation for me to act as her chaperone till her wedding day. She said that Nargis liked my flare for design and wanted my advice on critical fashion decisions leading up to the wedding day. I had to move into the mansion for a week before the wedding. And she would pay handsomely. I immediately suspected that this request was not solely coming from Nargis.

I knew that Ma wanted to say yes to Usha Aunty right away, but she did not. Although I had not revealed how I had felt inside the mansion to Ma and Baba, I suspected that Rupa had mentioned it. Either way, I did not take a chance. I gathered all my courage and told them before they committed on my behalf.

"Ma when I visited the bird hospital, I saw a wounded peacock. Even though he was kept there for his own good, he felt trapped. Well, that is how I felt in the mansion. Please don't make me go there...." My voice cracked.

Baba had wheeled himself into the room. He was strong enough to do that now. Before Ma could say anything, he spoke up on a family matter for the first time after his accident: "No child, you don't have to go." I ran and buried my face in his shoulders in gratitude.

May 18, 1948

Ma and I have been working frenziedly for the past few months, and I am ready for a break again. I am thinking of telling Ma this tomorrow morning. I am sure that with the success we have had with the wedding season, she will welcome a break too.

It was a long day. We left at dawn, and, when we got back, we had a nice surprise waiting for us. Ashu had cooked dinner, and Rupa had bought Baba's favourite pistachio ice cream. I changed into my night clothes and was about to write in my journal when I heard a knock at the door.

"See who it is, Rupa," Ma said from her room.

Rupa opened the door, and we caught the anxiety in her voice. To my utter surprise, it was the same tall shadow from the mansion. It was Prakash. He was wearing a suit and a tie, and was sweating from his temples. He was standing behind a distinguished elderly gentleman wearing an English suit with two shaded cherry brown shoes and carrying a colourful cardboard box on which "*Nathu Sweets*" was written in gold.

Prakash introduced the older man as Lala Yaduveer Rajsinghania, his father.

Baba wheeled himself in. He said that he immediately recognized Lala Rajsinghania from the photographs he had seen in the business section of local newspapers.

I slipped away into my room. I was perplexed and nervous, anticipating something that I feared terribly. It felt like eternity until they left. When Ma came to my room, I still had my eyes shut tight like a child who does not want to know.

"You are a lucky one! Lala Rajsinghani has come to ask for your hand in marriage for their son, Prakash!" I could not open my eyes. I could not speak. Ma continued, "We have until ten o'clock tomorrow morning to give them our decision." She stopped to take a breath.

Baba was in the room now. He put his hand on my head, and I opened my eyes. Tears were gushing down like water in a downspout during the monsoon.

"No, Baba. I cannot do this."

Baba did not say anything. No one said anything after that. We all retired to our beds without speaking and I am certain that no one is sleeping a wink tonight.

May 19, 1948

It must have been a little after six when I went to the kitchen to make morning tea for everyone. Ma and Baba were already up, and I could hear them in the kitchen.

Baba was saying, "We cannot force the poor girl if she is not willing...."

But Ma was not listening to him. She said, "I cannot believe our luck. Imagine Gayatri getting married to the only son, the heir of one of the richest and most elite families of Delhi. They are like royalty here, I have heard. Old money and culture.

It is her good fortune and God's grace that has brought this proposal to our doorstep. In our circumstances, could we ever dream of such a match for our daughter? Besides, see what this will do for her sisters. Ashu and Rupa will also become eligible in the elite circle. God has been so kind to us, this is really a blessing for the whole family."

I cupped my ears with my palms. I had heard enough. Enough to know that this match would alleviate the suffering of my over-burdened mother and my crippled father, and pull my sisters out of poverty and desolation.

I will do anything for my family. And the time has come for me to prove this. How can I be so selfish and think of things like compatibility and love? Yes, I feel Sachin's presence deep in my heart, but I do not know if I will ever see him again. Things like love are for others, not for people in my circumstance.

I walked in and told Ma, "Call up Lala Rajsinghania, I am ready."

Then I put my head on her lap and cried for a long time.

September 12, 1948

This week I was married to Prakash. Ma gave me the last of her heirloom gold saris and her peacock bracelets. I protested, but she joked that it was an investment in my sisters' future. She was sure that in return I would find suitable boys in the Rajsinghania circle for them too. I felt sick the morning of the wedding. I felt sick as I faced Prakash in the stifling Delhi court room. But I was not one to complain, I had wanted a court wedding after all. No fanfare, no rituals, no celebration, just a quiet court arrangement. Prakash was so ecstatic that I had agreed to marry him that I think he would have agreed to anything, even a wedding on a treetop, if I had asked.

Saying goodbye to my family killed me. I did not have the courage to look into their eyes before leaving for fear of having a complete breakdown. Rupa and Ashu clung to me, Baba sobbed openly like a little child, and Ma hugged me for a long time. In return, all that my numb mind could say to them was, "I promise to visit soon. Look after yourselves." But deep inside I knew that was a lie. Somehow, I knew that I would not be allowed to escape the mansion walls.

I was still crying when I reached Prakash's house. He hovered around me possessively, as one does with a newly acquired possession. Now there was no respite—not from him, not from this house, and not from this life.

It was the most painful night I have ever known. Prakash had free rein over my body. There was no stopping him, and his obsession grew stronger each time he penetrated my being and killed a little of my soul. It was endless. The whole night I waited in dread while he took me again and again. After the pain and shock of the first instance died down, I tried to detach my mind from my body to avoid convulsing at his next touch.

These past few days have been overwhelming. Prakash has an ailing mother who needs constant care. Being the wife of the only son, she was quick to delegate the responsibilities of running the house to me. In a way, I welcomed the work as an excuse to avoid Prakash, who seemed to be lingering around corners and passages just for a chance to get his hands on me.

I am happy to see Sheila again. She has helped me note schedules for meals, cleaning, nurses, medicines, grooming, tutors, and entertaining. Most services come to our house, like hair stylists, doctors, tailors, jewellers, and masseuses. So, as I had suspected all along, there is no reason to leave the mansion. But I have discovered this little room hidden under the winding staircase of the rotunda. Its darkness soothes me. I wonder why it is there. But who cares. It is my salvation. I hide there after my day's chores and write in my journal. I can cry, scream, and curse, and no one can hear me.

November 30, 1949

Ma, Baba, and the girls came to meet me on Diwali with sweets and gifts. They heard about my pregnancy. I guess

Prakash told them. They looked well. They said I looked thinner. I dabbed a dollop of face power under my eyes to cover the dark circles and the swelling from crying every night. I wanted to go back with them, but I sensed that there was something distant about them, like a fragile wall of tradition, of societal boundary that kept me apart from them. Maybe they no longer think of me as one of them now. I wanted to scream at them: I am your flesh and blood. I have known no other home, no other parents. I am here because I listened to you, believed you, and obeyed you. And now how can I suddenly belong to others? We just sat awkwardly in the gaudy living room with Prakash and his mother.

Last month, Nargis came to visit. It was like a breath of fresh air to have someone my age to talk to, even if there was nothing important to talk about. She talked about her new family and how much she loved her husband. My mind instinctively drifted, not to Prakash but to Peshawar, to Sachin. It was such a distant memory now.

What does privilege mean for the rich? Was this what Ma and Baba had believed would be good for me? Why do I feel so trapped within these walls, within this life, and with Prakash? Not all women have the freedom to choose their lives. Why should I be any different? Why do I not feel privileged? Why do I feel numb? Especially at night, when I join Prakash in bed. I am afraid Prakash will decode these feelings in my silences, in my disinterest, and in my distant eyes. I am afraid that deep inside Prakash already knows.

December 1, 1949

Ranvir is born. He is beautiful. He has the same milk and honey complexion of those from Peshawar—like Ma, like me. Such perfect fingers, such a mop of hair, such overhanging cheeks, and soulful eyes. All I want to do is hold him tight and rock him in my arms. I don't need anything else in life now. This is enough.

I am exhausted after two days of excruciating pain. Sheila has been an angel, patting my forehead and feet with iced water, massaging my limbs after the delivery. The days slip by in a blink. I have been so preoccupied with the baby that it has made Prakash impatient. Some days he peaks into a kind of frenzy, fixating on me with dilated eyes, as though he is ready to pounce. He does not even hold Ranvir. He would rather embrace me.

The days when I don't pay undivided attention to Prakash, when I am distracted with the baby, he curses me. He reminds me of the favour he did me by pulling me out of the slums and gifting me a life that other women dream of. He repeats how difficult it was for him to convince his father to let him marry me, how much his family had to sacrifice to agree to his wishes. I can see the curl of his lips when my eyes flood up. He enjoys his cruelty. Those days, more than feeling claustrophobic, I feel humiliated and exposed. I feel like I deserve this fate for being poor, for not having any other option but to marry him. I am nothing. On my own, I have no social standing, no money, no privileges. And Prakash makes sure that I know this very well. He remorselessly degrades me, and I suspect that it is his way of taking revenge on me. I suspect he knows there still exists one thing he cannot own: my heart. I don't want to pretend or lie to myself anymore that it will all be okay in the end. With Prakash, I never know how I will be treated tomorrow. Every day is different. In spite of my breathing every moment under his watchful eye, his insane obsession with me is consuming him, and it is growing along with his paranoid suspicions of me. He questions me about every hour of the day now: *What did you do? When did you do it? Why did you do it?* He is waiting for something to fall, for something to go wrong. And this wait is killing him.

Today Prakash told me to be ready to receive some news from him in the evening when he comes back from work. I dread what is coming next.

September 1, 1950

There is no respite from the heat. The dry air has turned sultry, and there is still no rain. I have been nauseous in the mornings for a few months now, and I know this can mean only one thing. But I am not prepared to share this news with anyone yet.

Instead, the news that Prakash gave me a few months ago has had me completely engrossed.

"Gayatri, I want to give you such a present that all women in Delhi will envy you. I will build a west wing, a grand annexe with every possible feature, as a tribute to our life together."

At first I did not know how to react. Then gradually, as the feeling came back into my toes and the numbness subsided, I realized the full consequence of this. The thought of living with him alone stifled me.

"And Gayatri," he continued, "you will help me design it. In fact, I want you to lead the design of it, with your flair. Every alcove and corner, the layout of every room, the colour shading, crystal and chrome accessories, frescoes—whatever you want. I have called the architects for drafting the blueprints."

With some courage, I asked, "Prakash, if we move there, who will look after your parents?"

"Silly Gayatri, the west wing is only an addition to our main house, where you can come and go freely. We shall continue to live here with everyone."

I could breathe again.

And so Prakash and I have started working together. He is like a child, asking my opinion of details such as carvings on doors and the choice of wood and stone for the floor and walls. In this past month, working together with him toward a common purpose, I am seeing a very different Prakash. His ghosts have not visited him. I do not mind him now; he is almost like a friend. Some days I impatiently wait for his return in the evening to discuss the next ideas I have. There is only one section of the west wing remaining now.

Drawing on my courage, I have decided to ask him for my dearest wish. I have been thinking about it ever since the construction began. Tomorrow I will ask him to design a music room. A room like no other, my soul room.

September 8, 1950

Ranvir has started walking early. He now sleeps through the night. I don't know what I would have done without Sheila. She is like a second mother to him, attentive to his every need. She even sleeps in the same room next to his cot.

Meanwhile, my energy is low. My morning sickness is severe, and the bump of my belly has started showing. I had been covering it with loose kurtas and shawls. But it was time to tell Prakash. So I have.

"Really?" he exclaimed. This time he is happy. He took both my hands in his and bent down to put his ear on my belly as if waiting to hear a heartbeat. It is the first time he has shown such fatherly affection.

"I will inform the contractors to get the west wing ready before the baby comes."

I knew this was the only chance I would get. I took a deep breath and asked, "Prakash ... I was just wondering..."

"Yes?"

"Now that there is only one section remaining, I would like to design a special room facing the east."

"What special room?"

"It will be for something I loved to do."

"What?"

"Music."

He was silent.

"Prakash, as a young girl I used to sing every day. It made me very happy."

"Are you not happy now?" It seemed that an invisible wall had risen between us. I think Prakash felt the wall too.

He finally said, "Okay, I will allow your music as long as

you do it in private. I don't want anyone to think that the lady of the Ragsinghania house is on public display."

Riding on my success I pushed my luck a little further: "Prakash, I have been so out of practice that in order to start again after so many years, I would need a trained teacher. Do you mind if I look for one?" Again, Prakash was hesitant. But I think he saw the hope and appeal in my eyes and gave in.

"Just make sure the teacher is from a respectable background, worthy of coming to our house to teach its mistress."

"Yes of course."

I am so excited. For the first time in this house, I have something to look forward to.

September 12, 1950

This pregnancy is different. I feel more carefree with each passing day; I feel a premonition of some release, a *moksha*, waiting for me in the near future. I cannot explain it.

"If it is a boy, I will call him Umang," I said to Sheila as she was tucking Ranvir into bed.

"Yes, yes, it is a good name. What does it mean?"

"It means 'a wish riding on the wave of happiness.'"

"But what if it is a girl?"

"Then I shall call her Diya, 'the eternal lamp that lights our life.'"

Today I started the design of my music room. It will have a roof made of glass opening into the rising sun of the east, and an oil painting of a Banyan tree, like the one in our Peshawar courtyard. It will be sparsely furnished with only mattresses on the floor, again like in our courtyard in Peshawar. Now all that remains is for me to start singing.

December 22, 1950

Last week Prakash announced the completion of the west wing. My music room is perfect. It is filled with golden rays of happiness. It is a room of windows. I can lie down under the roof and pretend that I am flying in the blue sky above. I am still a trapped bird, but every time I look through the windows, I have the hope of freedom. I have started practising on the harmonium. Prakash does not begrudge me this time in the evening because of my involvement with him during the day. But being out of practice for so long, I am not happy with my voice. I have interviewed many music teachers, but none of them sing in Pashto, the dialect of my heart. It was a difficult qualification to find, especially in Delhi.

But luck never announces its arrival. This evening my luck changed. As I ventured into the library and picked up the daily newspaper, there was a news item about a group of Pashto singers who had just arrived in Delhi.

I immediately called for Sheila and asked her to send someone from our staff to find out if any of them would be interested in conducting music classes for me.

December 29, 1950

I am big and clumsy, and the baby kicks constantly in my belly. Everyday chores are a problem now. But I don't mind. My heart has a different beat. I feel freer with each passing day. I don't want to overthink its logic, lest I jinx it.

It has taken less than a week for Sheila to get back with the news. It feels like I have been waiting to exhale all this time. She has lined up three music teachers who sing in Pashto. They are all coming to the mansion this evening.

December 31, 1950

I do not understand God's sense of humour. As a small girl, Baba always told us that a joke is only as good as the person it is played on. But God does not care if we laugh or cry when the joke is on us. At dusk, I was ready for the music teacher interviews. The first woman who walked in sang in perfect Pashto. I wanted to hire her right away, but she could not start till late next year because of family problems. The second person was an old Pathan. He was from my district. He told me that all the Hindus had moved east and that things were edging back to normal. He said he did not sing but recited prose. I wanted to help him with money and anything else that I could offer, but, being a self-respecting Pathan, he refused.

Now I had only one candidate left. I had decided that if this last person did not qualify either, then I would just drop the idea of taking music lessons. I was looking out of the full-length window with the golden rays warming my face. I heard his footsteps first. Blinded by the sunlight, I could not see who was standing in front of me. I gestured for the person to sit. Instead, I sensed the figure approaching me. Startled, I stepped out of the light to focus.

Then I saw him.

Oh my God! The same curly-toed shoes, the same tall broad shoulders, the same brown eyes, the same face I have been yearning to see for what felt like an eternity. On this last day of this fated year, I have found him! My eyes widened and teared up as Sachin approached me. I swayed with this revelation, and his rough hands caught my heavy body in time. We held each other for a long time. Our trance was broken by an evening bird crying in the open sky before taking flight.

He has aged. His hair is grey, his skin is burnt to an unhealthy shade, and the lines on his forehead are deep and final. But I found in his eyes the same boy I had left in Peshawar.

January 18, 1951

"How did you find me, Sachin?"

"I was always looking for you. It was only a matter of time."

"Did you not get my note on the last night?"

"By the time I saw the chit tucked in the window sill, you had already left. I ran to your house, and then waited at the train station for days with the hope that you would return. Hope was all I had."

"Yes, Sachin, hope is all that we had."

"I am glad to see that you are comfortably married. You will no longer be hungry or cold. You will always be looked after. You will have more than I could ever have offered you."

I did not reply to Sachin. I simply smiled. How blind was he? For I am hungry, and I am cold. But now I don't want for anything more. Each day is a blessing. I live for the evening when time stands still. Prakash, now consoled by the renewed interest I have been showing him, has started allowing me the luxury of these music lessons. I feel rejuvenated with every note that syncs with Sachin's, with every song that we sing together. It seems miracles do happen. And then, as if things could not get better, they suddenly did. There was one last remaining gift from heaven: I saw Om and Shanti. They were perched on the peepal in the courtyard of our east wing. I know it was them; it had to be. They had come with Sachin, they had come to the peepal tree, and they had come home to my music, to me.

I pray every night. Life is perfect. There is nothing remaining. Anything can happen now, I do not care. I laugh at many things. Ordinary everyday things. Things that are not funny. I laugh with him.

There is an urgency within us, as if we have snatched this time from our fate. As the grandfather clock chimes eight, Sachin leaves and I get up and go back to my life. I am no longer worried about what Prakash will say. I am not afraid.

February 25, 1951

I could not find my journal this past week. I was sure that I had left it somewhere in the dark room under the stairs, as I always did, but it has disappeared. I frantically searched for it everywhere, turning all the rooms upside down. Then, as a last hope, I took Sheila into my confidence. After a week, Sheila brought it back to me, intact. After a lot of coaxing, she finally told me that the butler had found it in the library. I thought of the possibility of Prakash reading it. But I soon calmed myself, thinking that if Prakash had read it, I would have heard no end of it by now.

I was just happy to have it back—my lifeline, my confidante, my journal.

March 24, 1951

Umang was born at midnight three days ago. He looks more like Prakash—the same tall forehead, long nose, and dark skin. I had a very rough three days. The contractions started earlier than expected, or so our midwife said. Today I feel a little strength returning to my back and legs. Sheila has been taking care of both Umang and Ranvir. She is exhausted too. She keeps a junior maid to help her at night, but during the day she does not let any other maid near them. I heard the midwife say that I have lost a lot of blood. I feel very weak. I drift in and out of sleep. It was on such a sleepless afternoon that Prakash finally came to see the baby and me, after three days.

To my bewilderment, it was a different Prakash whom I met today. His flushed face matched his blood-red eyes. I asked him if he was okay, and then I smelled him. He was swaying and reeking of alcohol. He curled his upper lip, and I knew he was about to say something cruel. But at that very moment the nurse entered for my bath and massage. Before leaving the room, he said to Sheila and the nurse, "I will be back to speak to my wife in the evening at seven. Make sure that she is well rested and waiting for me."

It is almost seven now. I took my bath, played with Ranvir, and fed Umang before I handed him to Sheila for a bath. Then I styled my hair in a high bun with a string of fragrant jasmine around it. I am even wearing Prakash's favourite white Chantilly lace today, the gown that he gave me on our wedding night.

I am curious as to what Prakash has to say this time. Curious, but not nervous anymore. I am ready to receive him. I am ready for anything. I am not troubled. I am free.

13. ANITA

I DIDN'T FEEL GUILTY for leaving my class early. Why should I have? After all, it was time to complete my last courses at the college of social work and step into the real world. That was why the internship was so important for me. I was exhausted after the stringent interview for the internship position. I could not believe that I was selected. Hey, but who's complaining? This time my internship will take me to the heart of rural India, where poor artisans are struggling to organize themselves against the feudal landlords and the local police. This time it was difficult, dangerous. Maybe that was why I was selected for this opportunity: because no one else wanted it.

Today I had a whole afternoon to myself. This was such a luxury. I wondered how I would pass the time. I still liked swinging on the hammock in my room and then landing on the low jute divan. It made me feel like a child again. Yes, childhood. What a wonderful thing it was. Where had our carefree days gone? We all were so busy growing up that we had forgotten to connect with the things and people that mattered.

Maya. Oh my dear lord. Maya. Every time I thought of childhood fun, I thought of her. What a whirlwind she was. What fun. What times we had while growing up. It was always us against the whole world and us, meddling, inquisitive, and always in trouble. We both had an incorrigible nose for mischief and diligently followed its scent.

I took down her wedding album from the top shelf of the

corner bookcase. There we were, dancing without a care to the crazy strokes of her wedding drum; there we were sniggering at the groom being forgotten on his horse by his own guests; there we were whistling at Veer kissing a stunned Maya on the podium; there we were rioting around him for our gold rings. And there she was, looking like a goddess, her flawless features accentuated with peacock shades from her gown, her big eyes flooded with tears as she held on to her mother. I will have to capture all this colour, all this emotion on my canvas somehow, someday. Maybe I will ask her to sit for a portrait this summer. God, I have missed her.

Aha, here it is. Her phone number, I knew I had kept it somewhere. I could not believe that we had not spoken in almost a year. But I did not care. I picked up the phone and dialled. A manservant answered in a formal voice at the other end of the line.

"May I speak to Maya please?" There is a pause. I repeat, "Hello?"

"Yes ... Madam Maya is busy.... We have not seen her...."

That was very strange.

"Then may I speak to Veer please?"

"Master Veer is on a business trip...."

Of course, it made perfect sense now. With Veer away, no wonder no one had seen her around. She would be wandering around at the first excuse. That was Maya. No one could hold her back.

I made up my mind to miss my class and go visit her right away.

***

Reaching Maya's house from mine was worth the long drive in the dark. I left before dawn, to be greeted by the first rays of the rising sun. A half-asleep gatekeeper reluctantly opened the entrance to the Rajsinghania property. I entered into a forest. Tall dark trees, lush velvet grass, mushrooms, and berries sprouting under leafy domes. The lavender flowers of the jacaranda trees mocked the blood-red of the rose bushes. The mature olive branches scolded the bright green younger ones. The melody of an occasional koyal conquered the croaking of morning crows. And the hissing undergrowth played a duet with the swishing of the crisp breeze that blew wildly into my hair. Everything was waking up in complete sundry harmony.

Did Maya live in paradise? I definitely had to paint here and that the next time I would come with my easel and canvas.

As I approached the main entrance, my fiesta died. The stone steps were cold and the towering door, intimidating. It was dark inside.

"Is she expecting you?" a uniformed butler asked in a way that made me think about what I was wearing.

"No. I am here to surprise her."

It seemed a long way as I followed him down broad corridors lined with large doors, each opening into enormous rooms, breezy verandas, and then finally into a more serene side of the house.

"Please follow the path to the lily pond, where you will find Madam Maya. She likes to take her morning tea there."

She was sitting on a lawn chair under one of the grandest peepal trees that I had ever seen. Its roots had sprung out of the ground as if gasping for air and then dived back down again as if being recalled by a spell. She was completely blending in with her surroundings, a woollen blanket around her shoulders, her hair the usual mess, a frown between her brows, and a distant look that I knew only too well. It meant nothing but trouble. She was so engrossed that she did not hear my footsteps on the grass, or even see me approaching her from the corner of her eye. It was not until I was standing directly in front of her that she noticed me. She looked thinner, and, to my surprise, she was white as a sheet. This was a new Maya that I was looking at.

Her eyes lifted and met mine. Then my ears gave way to her fervent screams. The old Maya was back. We danced and hugged and laughed and danced some more.

"You nutcase! How are you here?" she kept repeating breathlessly. I was so glad that I had come. She looked so lonely.

When the frenzy had died down and my legs had collapsed into a cushioned lounge chair, I turned to her and asked, "Maya, what's the matter?" Sometimes I wished that I didn't know her so well.

"What do you mean?" she pretended.

"Maya!"

"Nothing, Anita. I swear."

"Liar."

"Why do I have to tell you anything, Anita?"

"Because you cannot resist telling me, because we are partners in crime, because we live for such moments...."

"Oh really?" she teased, a glimmer of herself coming back into her eyes.

"Yes."

She was quiet again, and I knew she was struggling to keep something back. Whatever it was, it was big. That much I could tell by now.

The butler chose that moment to wheel in the trolley of tea, rescuing her. Hot piping sips inside our bellies did wonders. I spread myself on the soft wet grass, looking up at the overarching branches of the peepal. Then I looked at Maya again. It was rare for her to be so quiet. Yes, there was something different. I could clearly see now. She was pale and subdued. And I did not like it.

My glance fell on something under her blanket. It was a striking cloth print, a black and white polka dotted fabric. Who wore such fabrics these days? But that was no cloth. It held rough sheets of yellowed paper—a diary with a polka-dotted cover! Ah ha! So this was the root of Maya's distraction. I had to look at this diary.

Maya was watching me. She knew what I was going to do. We both sprang at the diary together. Of course, she had the advantage of already holding it. She clung tight as I tugged at it.

"Let go, Anita."

"Why? What is in it, Maya?"

"Nothing important."

"Then show me."

"No."

We were back in kindergarten, playing tug-of-war over a favourite treasure. The diary was really heavy, and my hand gave way. I let go. Maya held on at the other end and fell on the carpet of thick grass. The diary landed in the dew-soaked mud. We both exploded into laughter and simultaneously dove to grab the strewn pages.

Maya got to them first. But when she stood up there was something else in her hand with the diary. This time I was as surprised as she was. The diary had opened up to a hidden cavity under a mass of pages. And from that cavity emerged the most exotic treasure I had ever seen: a pair of glittering gold bracelets with their joints in the shape of peacock heads, embedded in colourful precious gems.

"Oh my God!" Maya screamed. "They are hers!"

"Whose?"

"I saw them on her wrists in the photograph. Now I know why the diary was so heavy all along!"

The glint of the gold from the peacock heads blinded us as the morning rays reflected off them. Maya pulled out a torn black-and-white photograph hidden under the diary's cover and started comparing the bracelets to something in the photo.

"Anita, come, look. They are a match! Anita, surely this is a sign!" She could barely find her voice.

I was utterly confused. Whose diary was it? What did it say? Who did these bracelets belong to? And why was Maya so involved?

Maya sat down at the edge of the pond, staring blankly

at the blooming lotus soaking up the last drops of dew on its rubbery leaves. When she spoke, her voice was calm and steady: "Anita let's go inside. I will tell you a tale like you have never heard before."

14.

NO WONDER MAYA had looked so pale. Now it was my turn to look like a ghost. Maya was right. I had never heard a more intense story. And I could clearly see the effect that this had had on my friend.

There were so many questions that lingered, but the strange part was that the answers were not in the past, but in the present—here, in Maya's world. Why were there no photographs of Veer's beautiful and talented grandmother anywhere in the house with a doting husband like Prakash? Why was her name not printed on Veer's wedding invitation, as was customary in Indian weddings? And, for God's sake, why did Maya resemble Gayatri so much? I told Maya that this was just a coincidence. Lots of people in the world look like unrelated people. I tried to think of some that we knew in school. Maya just laughed at my attempts at making sense of it all. I was glad that I had gone to visit Maya. I think she needed me like never before.

Over some more steaming tea, crisp toast, and fluffy eggs, we hatched a plan for how to uncover the rest of the story. The only person who held the key to this mystery was Sheila, the last living person who had known Gayatri, Prakash, and Sachin. She was our only link, and if anyone knew anything, it was her.

Maya forced me out of my jeans and chappals and into her lemon chiffon dress, much to my dislike, just in time for her mother-in-law's party. It was early evening when we left our rooms to attend cocktails in the east lounge. But before we reached the lounge, we made a stop in the kitchen. On occasions like this, all the servants assembled there waiting for their turn to serve. And this was where we found Sheila.

It was chaotic. There were children running around, dishes clanking, water running, and uniformed bearers bustling in all directions amid the intense fumes from deep fried corn batter.

"There's Sheila." Maya pointed to a crouched figure propped up in the shadows on a three-legged stool. She was shelling fresh green peas with her bent fingers. Her face lit up when she saw Maya.

"Hello Sheila. I want to talk to you. May we go someplace quiet? It is very noisy out here." She took a moment to straighten up. She was very old and wrinkled, but those eyes were sharp as a tack. We followed her through the pantry to the unlit part of the house.

I was sure that Maya was familiar with this part, but to me, as an outsider, it was downright eerie. The long evening shadows from the branches of the peepal drew stretched arms on the walls, as if trying to reach us. The wind had started whispering as we settled in an open atrium of sorts.

Maya did not waste any time. She opened her purse and pulled out Gayatri's conspicuous diary. Sheila stopped breathing. Then, just as I thought she was going to faint, Sheila asked, "Where did you get this?"

"Rosy gave it to me. She found it hidden inside Gayatri's old suitcase full of her clothes."

Sheila was glaring at us intensely, from Maya to me and back. I could feel a storm building inside her, but she still did not open up.

As if completely unaffected by Sheila's reaction, Maya continued, pointing towards me: "Sheila, this is Anita, she is like a sister to me. Whatever you can tell me, you can say before her. Now, tell me. I am looking for Veer's grandmother's music teacher. Do you know where he is?"

Now the colour completely drained from her face. And this time she really stumbled. I extended my hand to lead her to a nearby settee.

"Sheila, please don't be afraid. I am family, and it is important that I know...."

She finally spoke. It was barely a whisper: "Maya-Beti, *why* do you want to know? No good will come out of it."

"It is too late, Sheila. I am too entrenched in this, and you cannot deny me."

There was a long silence. The distant noise from the kitchen seemed so normal, so irrelevant. The sun was setting quickly, and soon it would be dark. The crickets had started chirping, and the night birds were calling occasionally. Seeing that nothing was stirring Sheila, Maya pulled out the last trick from her purse: the peacock-head bracelets.

"And these were hidden inside her diary." When Maya wanted something, I knew how persuasive she could be. Sheila started sobbing. It was the beginning of her breakdown. "Sheila, I am Gayatri's family now, and it is no coincidence that we have met. I am sure Gayatri intended this to happen."

Sheila finally let it flow, her tears, and her tale, but not without some hesitation. "By talking about this," she said, "I shall be breaking the sacred trust of the late Gayatri Madam. I am sure I will be punished by the dead."

Maya placed her hand on Sheila's shoulder, and I went to sit beside her for comfort. "No such thing will happen. You are doing the right thing."

Sheila began: "I still remember the dark moonless night when Gayatri Madam went into labour. In between her contractions, she handed me her diary with instructions to hide it in her suitcase, saying 'I trust no one but you, Sheila.' And that was the last time I spoke to her.

"At the end of the third day of excruciating pain, Gayatri Madam delivered a healthy baby boy, Master Umang. And then she started fading. First her pulse weakened, and then the midwife suspected internal bleeding. We servants found it odd that Master Prakash had not come to see her after the delivery. She needed to be transported to a hospital. Eventually he came, but only after three days. By that time, she was already very frail.

"She sat waiting for the Master, poised on her four-poster bed, looking so grand, wearing a Chantilly lace gown and with white jasmines in her neatly oiled hair. She handed me the baby for his bath. A strange calmness came over her pale face. She looked happy and at peace, despite her condition. I forgot to bring the baby's washcloths, so I entered the room once again, unnoticed. It was a room with mirror panels."

Sheila stopped. Neither Maya nor I disturbed her thoughts. We waited patiently. I remembered Maya telling me about seeing such a room.

It was a long time before Sheila spoke again, this time in a trembling voice: "In the mirror behind the jacquard curtain, I saw Master Prakash standing next to her." Again, silence.

"Yes, Sheila?" Maya nudged.

"Ahh, his large bony hands were on her throat, and it seemed like she was looking directly at him." Sheila had stared sobbing. I handed her my handkerchief. "But what has stayed with me all these years, was not his act. It was her look. A look of salvation, of ecstasy that I saw reflected in the mirror. She was not protesting, she was not afraid. It was as if she was welcoming the Master strangling her. I ran out. I am a coward. I have carried the burden of this secret for decades."

She paused to cry some more, and I put my arms around her shoulder.

Maya was in shock. I knew that she was thinking about the flash of an image she had seen on the same mirrored panel in that room. It all seemed so bizarre. Was this an old woman's imagination?

"I feel lighter by telling you, Maya-Beti, but you do understand that I could not go against the Master. Who would have believed me? And I would have been silenced before I knew it. Besides, no one was there for the children." Sheila took a deep breath and started again. Now she was on a roll, as if the last inhibition had been shed with the revelation of her darkest secret. As if nothing mattered anymore.

"He killed her. He was a savage. Now I had to protect the last remaining wish of hers, her diary. Thinking it was the safest place, I hid her diary under her clothes in the suitcase that she had carried from her mother's house. So you can image the depths of my misery when, a few months later, her suitcase vanished. I have been tormented over how I failed to fulfil her last wish. Today I can go to my grave in peace, knowing now that the diary was not lost and certainly did not end up in the wrong hands." She wiped the tears with the corner of her scarf.

"The entire household came to a standstill. For weeks. After Madam Gayatri passed away, the Master looked devastated. Then, one day, as I was cleaning his room with Ram Kishore, his manservant, a curious letter lying on his bedside table caught our eye. The writing had been slashed violently in pen. Ram Kishore, who could read a little, read it aloud. It was written by Madam in a shaky writing. In it, she confessed to the claustrophobia and misery she had felt before Sachin re-entered her life. We knew that this letter had cut our Master very deep. One evening, during a few hours of drunken weakness, the Master confided in Ram Kishore about how cheated he felt by Gayatri's longing for another man. After that evening, the Master entered a very dark place where he shut down all communication with the outside world. New governesses were hired for the children, and the extended family helped out the best they could. When the Master finally emerged from his quarters, five long months later, his first instructions were to remove all photographs, paintings, and artefacts—anything that reminded him of Madam from the entire house. The west wing, which had Madam in every brick and every corner, could not be salvaged. So it was sealed and forbidden. It was as if she had never existed. For the next few years, the Master entrenched himself deeper into his work, keeping long hours and sometimes not even coming home at night. He drank excessively, and as his business soared, his heart sank irretrievably.

"Then one evening, when the festival of lights, Diwali, was being celebrated in the streets, the Master locked himself in his room with a crate of Johnny Walker and never came out. His ashes were scattered alongside those of the Madam's in the lawns on the west wing, as per his wishes."

Sheila had completed her story. Gayatri's story. She bowed her head and wept. This time we let her. It seemed that the lines on her forehead and her mouth had deepened. Maya was crying too.

Maya found a small voice: "But what happened to the music teacher?"

"I don't know, Beti. He just vanished. You see, after the Madam was gone, Ram Kishore told me that the Master hunted him down, and left him for dead after a good beating by the Master's goons. I thought that this was so unnecessary as he would have left anyway...." Then she hesitated.

"Well? What is it, Sheila? Don't stop now."

"Just a few weeks ago, I heard that a poor old man with perfect Pashto from Peshawar has been employed by the Khanna family's youngest daughter Radha, who is an aspiring singer."

"Have you seen Radha's music teacher?" If anyone could recognize Sachin, it was Sheila.

"No, I have not, but I have heard that he has a small boy with him. A white child."

Both Maya and I were thinking that we might be so lucky as to have found Sachin in our corner. But the child, it did not make sense.

"Did you know that your mother-in-law has invited Radha to perform tonight?"

Sheila was an astute woman and had put the pieces together. The puzzle was falling into place, as if we were all playing a part in a preordained plan directed by forces beyond us. There was a good chance that Radha would come with her teacher. There was a good chance that we would find Sachin.

By the time we were done, the party music had started on the front lawn. The trees, which were adorned with white fairy lights, were swaying in the cool breeze. Their whispering had started again.

Within a short time our worlds had changed irrevocably. It made us extremely uncomfortable, and I could only imagine what Sheila had gone though all these years. It was a hard secret to keep, and now Maya was its custodian.

We escorted Sheila back to the pantry and then entered the decorated section of the house. We had missed the cocktail hour. Maya made a beeline for the section with an open stage with neon lights. We were only interested in Radha's performance. The live band had started, and the crowd was flocking around the barbeque grills. I recognized Veer's mother and her sisters as they headed for the front rows facing the stage. Veer's mother, completely ignoring my presence, said to Maya, "Where were you? A lot of people wanted to see Veer's bride, and, as usual, you...."

Maya smiled politely at her and bent her head. This was a new Maya.

Radha had taken the stage amid loud claps. Kitty was introducing her as a talented and successful TV star. But there was no mention of her music teacher. How typical, I thought. Anyone who is paid a salary is not worthy of respect in the minds of people like this.

Radha sang her first song, then another. Finally, she concluded by reciting prose in Pashto. When she finished, Radha added, "I would like to thank my music teacher, who has taught me so much in such little time. I am also sad to announce that he has decided to return to his native Pakistan. I am heartbroken to see him go, but we wish him well." Radha called out for him. "Please welcome Ustad Sachin."

Maya looked like her heart had stopped. I clenched her hand to shock her back to life. My heart was racing. Maya clutched my palm tightly.

From the shadows of the trees emerged a tall lean man with a dark coat down to his knees, a red Karakul hat over his scruffy peppered hair, and tan leather shoes woven with gold thread that curled up at the tips. And then the light radiated on his face. His square forehead with high cheekbones imparted an instant sophistication to his long face and prominent nose. His chin had a cleft and was covered with the same salty stubble as his hair. In spite of the deep lines around the edges of his eyes, his entire demeanour gave him charisma. He opened his lips to reveal a magnetic smile. I looked around and saw the audience smiling back effortlessly. There was a compelling simplicity about him that made him attractive. The audience instantly warmed to his towering presence with a standing ovation. He thanked them in Urdu, turned around, and without a moment's lapse, fell back into the shadows.

Neither Maya nor I could move. We had just seen Sachin! We were sure of it. Who else could it be? *Ustad Sachin*, she had announced. But we had to find out for sure.

It took us two minutes to come back to life. We raced backstage as quickly as we could. I could feel Veer's mother's prying eyes piercing our backs. Poor Maya! Now I understood what she was up against with Veer's family.

We reached the shadows under the heavy mango trees. He was nowhere to be found. The long driveway to the west wing was deserted but lined by lighted lampposts. Maya sat down on a large boulder and tried to exhale her frenzy. The night had unfolded too quickly. I saw tears flowing down her cheeks. I did not like how deeply she was falling into a story that was not hers.

"Maya, let's go inside. It is very dark here. We will find him tomorrow."

Completely ignoring what I had said, she replied, "Anita,

will you walk with me to the gate at the end of this path?"

It was a long, bitter walk. The shadows were catching up, and not even the crickets challenged the eerie stillness following us from behind the litchi and kul trees. We reached the towering iron gates and walked up to the last cobbled stone before our path greeted the public road ahead. The gates were ajar. A sharp rustle was followed by a strong smell of tobacco.

Squatting on the curb, smoking a cigarette rolled in a dried leaf was Sachin. And next to him was a little boy, white as a sheet. He had blond hair and blue eyes, and the same radiance as Sachin.

Sachin saw Maya. His eyes widened. We both knew then that this was no other than Sachin. Only someone who had known Gayatri could have had this reaction when they first saw Maya.

Not bothering with social niceties, Maya dug into her purse and handed him Gayatri's photo. He took it slowly and gazed at it for a long time. His face did not betray his emotions, whatever they might have been.

"Who are you?" he finally asked Maya.

"I am Maya. I am married to Gayatri's grandson, Veer." The faint light from the tall streetlight fell between them like a shield.

"No, that cannot be. Gayatri does not have a girl of her own. How come you are...?"

Maya finished the sentence for him, "Just like her?"

He looked very perplexed now. The child tugged at his father's arm: "Baba, let's go...."

"Okay, Albert."

Sachin got up to leave. I knew Maya wanted to talk some more. She dug into her purse again and this time she held out Gayatri's bracelets. "I want you to have these," she said. "These were her last parting gift before she died."

His face filled with colour and his fingers caressed each contour of the peacock head. He put the bracelets in his pocket and abruptly turned to leave, with little Albert holding tightly to his fingers.

"Wait, don't go!" He turned back and looked straight at Maya without blinking.

"If your spirit is trapped in these golden walls, then fly. Fly before they catch you and never look back." He turned again. This time Maya did not stop him.

Sachin disappeared into the mist and darkness. The only thing that remained to remind us that this had not been a dream was the lingering aroma of tobacco.

We walked back to the house in heavy silence. We both felt crushed under the weight of these sinister family secrets. Maya looked disturbed. I held her arm as we waded through the dark garden. The guests had gone, and the party was over.

"Anita, stay with me for a few days. Veer is not back for another week, and I cannot stay alone in this ominous house anymore." We had reached the safety of her room.

I could not deny Maya this request, knowing now what I did. But I could not agree to stay with her either. My internship was starting next week, and I had to leave for Chambal Valley fairly soon. I had to persuade Maya to come with me. That was the only way. The trip would take her mind off these matters. We would re-live some of our fun times together. Who knew when we would have such a time again?

"Maya, come away with me."

She looked at me as if I were mad. "Where are you off to?"

"I have one week before I leave for my internship project in Chambal valley. Come away with me for this week. We will have fun, do all the things we used to before." She looked dazed. I repeated myself. She stirred a little.

"I don't know," she finally said.

"Why? What could possibly hold you back here?"

"I am not sure if Veer would like it if I leave in his absence."

This new Maya was timid, reconciling, and totally unrecognizable to me. The old Maya would have jumped at this offer.

What had Veer done to her? What had she done to herself? I had to shake her out of it. "Maya, have you heard yourself? And where is Veer, eh? Is he here to like or dislike anything? Has he not left and gone? Besides, we will be back before he comes home."

Maya still did not respond.

"Okay, I will sleep here tonight, Maya. But tomorrow I leave. And I am hoping that you will come with me."

15. MAYA

HAD TONIGHT BEEN a figment of my imagination? Such menacing secrets had been revealed. And what right did I have to pull Anita into this? Was Sheila telling the truth? Why would she lie? Would one man's obsession, possessiveness, and jealousy escalate to such extremes that he would kill the only person that he lived for? And then kill himself pining for her? Did Veer also carry those genes? Could Veer have the seed of such obsession too? Was that really Veer's grandmother's lover that we met? How did we know for sure? After all, Sachin was a common name. He might have been an impostor, happy to abscond with real gold heirlooms. We would never know now, would we? But I could have sworn that the look that I saw on his face was anything but phoney. Did I really look like Gayatri? I did not feel like Gayatri. I lived in her house, and I lived in her circumstance, but I did not live life with the same feelings. I looked forward to being with Veer, feeding the peacocks, and fooling around. Yes, I could see some madness in Veer's eyes, but only occasionally. And who is not guilty of insanity of one kind or another these days? Were these all coincidences? Or was this all my imagination?

Oh my God. I was going mad. I was spinning in circles. The moon was spread over the lily pond, the peacocks were quiet in the mulberry branches, and Anita's peaceful face was on the pillow next to mine. I felt blessed to have a friend like Anita.

I missed our fun, carefree days together. Maybe she was right to suggest going away with her. If we came back before Veer returned, he would not be angry with me. And how much did it matter to his parents? They were never here themselves. My parents were away, too, on their annual vacation to the Ayurveda retreat in Kerala.

If I didn't go with Anita, would I be able to live here alone till Veer got back? Would I be pulled under by these dark questions? Were there more secrets to uncover? I didn't think I had the capacity to take any more ghastly surprises. Perhaps it made more sense to go with Anita. If I did, then maybe the fatigue that visited me every morning would disappear too. Here were more questions that I did not have answers to.

It was time to step out, get away from this place, and live a little with Anita. I'd made up my mind.

***

When we left the next morning, the house was asleep as always. Except Sheila. She had slept in the next room. And she was up before we left.

"Sheila, I have to go away for a few days with Anita." I was glad that she did not ask me any questions because I myself did not know the answers.

To my surprise she said, "Yes, that will be good."

The warm blood pumping through my veins picked up my circulation and my spirits. Anita and I threw our bags into the back of her car, and climbed into the front. Anita was giddy with excitement. I inhaled from my stomach and filled my lungs with cool morning air.

As the distance from the walls of Veer's mansion increased with each passing mile, so did the lucidity of my mind. Sachin's last words, *Fly and never look back*, were still in my ears. But I had to look back ... and I knew I had to come back. The craziness of what I was doing suddenly hit me. I feared that Veer would be furious.

Anita looked at me and smirked. "From the look on your face, Maya, you would think we were up to something criminal!"

I smiled back at her and tried to calm my uneasiness. Anita was right. I wasn't doing anything wrong. I was enjoying a few days with my friend before she embarked on her next mission. Anita, the eccentric, fervent artiste, her eyes filled with stardust, lived for the work she did in isolated rural communities to help improve the lives of impoverished villagers.

And I realized that before she left, she wanted to ensure that I would be okay. And she was also going to see to that I had a little fun. I let myself sink back into the seat and looked forward to spending the next few days with Anita.

***

What a whirlwind week this had been. These few days snatched from my life had been a gift. A week with this childhood friend had revived my soul.

We had stayed up all night watching old movies, laughing and crying and reminiscing about school pranks, shopping and dining with Tina and Jiya at all kinds of places, from roadside vendors to full course formal dinners with silver cutlery. And in all this time, we had never spoken about the mansion, its story, or its people.

Then as the week drew to an end, I said aloud, a little surprised at my own nervousness, "Veer will be back soon. We should go."

I knew Anita did not approve of my meek demeanour. But I also knew that she trusted my reasons enough to not question me. And for that I was grateful.

I thought about Anita, armed only with hope, conviction and fortitude, who did not think twice about travelling to dangerous regions of the country for a cause she believed in deeply. I was so proud of her. And I was also a little ashamed of myself for all my mistrust and fear of Veer and his family. How inconsequential were my issues compared to the gross realities of life that Anita would be working in, a world in which no one knew what tomorrow held, in which every day counted, and had to be survived. I wished that I could have borrowed some of that resiliency in my life too.

As we climbed into Anita's car to return, a dark and heavy sky descended. By the time we wound down the oval Rajsinghania driveway, everything was smudged under dense sheets of rain. But I could still see that our entrance door was slightly ajar. Veer came out to greet us. My heart leapt as I saw him and Anita waved to him with a big smile on her face. But to my surprise, Veer didn't wave back.

I bade Anita goodbye as I stepped out of the car, and my heart was heavy as tears pricked at my eyelids.

16.

WHEN I SAW VEER'S FACE, I wished that I could have ridden away with Anita. Just as I had dreaded all along, he was angry.

"Where were you?" he lashed out. I did not want to answer to such a tone, so I brushed past him and walked down the dark corridor leading towards our rooms. I heard him follow.

The peacocks were pecking around the lily pond. My head hurt, and I felt weak. But I had to pretend to be strong. So I sat under the shade of the peepal. It was almost midday, and the sun was hot. A flutter on the branches above made me look up. I saw white wings, but then the sun blinded me. Veer was standing in front of me. His arms were crossed, and he was sweating.

He repeated, "Where were you?"

I got up and walked towards the pond. "I went with Anita."

"Where?"

"Why does it matter *where*, Veer? Am I not back now?"

"Maya, I told you not to go anywhere when I am not here."

"Why not? You are not here!"

Our voices were escalating. Bahadur walked toward us with two tall glasses of lemonade with ice. I wanted to drink it so badly. My head had started spinning, my body was burning, and there was a sharp shooting pain in my stomach.

"Maya, do you understand what I am telling you? Mummy told me that you had run away without telling anyone...." Veer did not care who was around. He did not care how I felt. He was shouting at me in front of Bahadur and he was so loud that anyone else lingering in the corridor and overlooking this spectacle would have heard him too. His voice hurt, but his behaviour hurt more.

I had to get out of there. I took one step toward the door to go inside. But my foot flew in the sky and my head landed on the grass instead. For a moment, all I could see was a faded blue and cloudless sky. I was lying on the ground in pain.

***

When I awoke, I was lying on my bed and it was dark outside my window. I could hear Veer on the veranda. "I should check on Maya," he said. "I should not have shouted at her. God knows where she was coming from...."

Veer's mother responded: "She should not have run off like that, you know. I'm sure it's just the heat—you know girls these days...."

Then Veer's father spoke: "I will make an appointment for a medical check-up at Robby's clinic tomorrow. He will look after this."

Veer's mother interrupted him. "Oh ho, let me show you the photos from last week's dinner party at the Shah's. Notice how pretty Ritu Auntie's daughter looks, and see how garish her renovated patio is...."

Veer shook her off. I turned my back, pretending to sleep. I had no wish to talk to him.

The next morning, I was driven to Dr. Robby's posh clinic in West Delhi. It had colourful plastic flowers in ornate vases and big acrylic paintings of half-nude village women carrying urns on their heads. We were ushered into a special room with an ultrasound machine, and I was asked to change into a backless green gown. Dr. Robby entered the room with an eager intern at his side.

"How are you guys?" he asked. Robby was almost our father's

age. Turning to face Veer, he added, "Looking good, old boy. Marriage is treating you well—*ha ha*!" And then he turned to me. "And you, my dear, uh huh ... let's see now ... very pale ... very pale indeed .... Veer, you will have to take better care of this girl," he said, wrapping the blood pressure apparatus around my arm. Then he took a stethoscope to my chest and back. The nurse covered my thighs with a towel and rubbed gel on my abdomen. Then Dr. Robby rolled a transducer over it.

Any second, I expected to see a large ulcer or a tumour. With all the nausea and giddiness it had to be one of those. But on the screen, it all looked like wet mud in marshy waters. Veer reluctantly took a seat behind my head for a full view. The doctor frowned as he concentrated on an area below my stomach. By now, I was sure that the tumour was big and round and malignant.

"Is there something wrong?" Veer asked, baffled. Instead of answering, Robby zoomed in and pressed a button. A white asterisk appeared on the screen over something that was throbbing.

"Do you see that? Do you know what it is?" he asked, smiling.

"A tumour?" I asked. "No, silly! It's a baby! Congratulations! You are going to become parents!"

"What?" I sat bolt upright and knocked the transducer right off my stomach. I turned to Veer, but he was not there! Had he run away?

Then I saw him. He was lying flat on the ground with closed eyes.

Oh my god! He'd fainted! "Oh, please sprinkle some water on his face," I yelled.

Veer opened his eyes and winked.

"Not funny, Veer," I said. I could have killed him. I turned to joke with the doctor, "Why would I need a child when I have a full-grown one right here?" But my humour was wasted on Robby. He was already on his way to call Veer's parents.

On the way back from the hospital, we stopped at my parents' house for some solace. But, instead, we found they were ecstatic.

"No more gallivanting! Veer told us everything last night." My father was rambling, and my mother could not stop smiling.

"But Mom, I am not ready for a baby. You see, I ... I..."

She held her hand up as if I could save whatever I had to say. It did not matter anymore. "Maya, it is time; the correct time is ... *now.*"

17.

THE LAST FEW MONTHS passed languorously. Since the day that we discovered I was pregnant, Veer was a changed person. His anger was a thing of the past and none of the usual triggers, not even his mother's taunts, sent him back into rage, resentment, or insecurity. The new Veer was attentive, affectionate, and relaxed. Day after day, I floated from our room to the shade of the peepal and back. Every morning I looked forward to feeding our peacocks, and every evening I threw out some seed for a group of homing pigeons. Even though my trip to the west wing was a forgotten memory, there were days when I felt someone was watching me through those smudged windowpanes of our forbidden section. But I was growing enormously big by the day to care too much about that right now. By the time the monsoons arrived, there was a whole orchestra inside my tummy during the day, and a football tournament at night.

It was one of those mornings when Veer told me about a party that he had to host for his business clients.

"You don't have to do anything, Maya. It will all be taken care of." I couldn't help but notice that this was the first time Veer had ever bothered to entertain his business clients. Till now, I assumed that there was really no need to appease clients when the family business was doing so well. But then there were nights when he came home stressed from all the recent problems he had been facing at work. Last week, I noticed

Bahadur serving the afternoon tea with a very lean spread at the table. He had muttered something about this being the new reality. I wondered if things were as they seemed in the Rajsinghania household. But of course no one told me these things, least of all his parents, and Veer had only mentioned in passing that the company finances wereat an all time low.

"Veer, even if I wanted to help with your party, I don't think I could do much that would be useful," I laughed and pointed at my big belly.

On the day of the party, our mansion was beautifully lit up when the guests began to arrive. There were fairy lights twisted over flowering gulmohar trees in the peacock garden. Every corner was exposed, illuminated. Today, the mansion looked like it housed no secrets for people who were blissfully unaware. I looked up to the grand peepal under a full new moon. The lilies were sparkling in a silent pond under its smile. A turquoise spotlight accentuated each contour of the peepal's grainy bark, giving it an aura of eternity. I could feel nothing but the soothing touch of love here.

A low whispering breeze had picked up and I shivered. I strained my ears to listen to its moans but there was none. Suddenly, the murmuring was invaded by sharp voices at the entrance.

Who was that? I looked for Veer. He was smiling behind me.

Surprise!

I instantly recognized Rony, goalie of Veer's school soccer team, despite his weight. He handed me the most exquisite bouquet of blue iris, orange tulips, and carnations. Close at his heel and inseparable as always was Sam, Veer's centre back. They made a beeline for the bar. Behind them were Tina and Jiya.

My pupils dilated with excitement and my face was flushed. I couldn't find my voice. Veer bent over and kissed me. Oh, how I loved him!

Then entered more friends from high school with feathered hats over sparkling masks and revealing dresses. Except for a few inches on their waistlines, they all looked the same. To complete their *Moulin Rouge* effect, they carried streamers, helium balloons, and plastic whistles.

And just behind them walked in Anita.

This evening was now complete.

"Hey Maya, you look like a queen in that black chiffon gown," Tina's figures stroked the *zari* trim to feel for its genuineness.

Anita hugged me and we clung to each other for moment, happy to be together.

"So, have you thought of a name yet?" Jiya always popped the most predictable question.

"Yes," I replied smugly.

"Well?" Tina nudged. "Tell us!"

"Diya. Her name will be Diya."

Anita gasped. She knew, she remembered. I had decided on the same name as Gayatri had chosen for her baby if it had been a girl.

I could hear Anita's internal voice persuading me to change my mind. But before she could say anything out loud, Jiya was already on her next question. "How do you know it's a girl Maya? Have you found out?"

"No, I haven't found out. I don't need to. I know," I said and walked away looking for Veer.

An enormous black forest cake sat on the table outside, surrounded by glasses filled with sparkling champagne. Veer made a toast for our upcoming baby and for many such nights with friends. Glasses clinked and everyone clapped as we started to cut the cake.

As plates were passed, loud music from large speakers hidden in the bushes began to play. An outdoor wooden dance floor came alive with flashing multi-coloured disco ball and artificial fog. Veer had thought of everything. In a matter of seconds we had moved from the Garden of Eden to a swinging teenager party zone.

The women had started lining up to form a circle. I was told to clasp the waist of the person in front, forming some sort of a train. The volume of the music was turned up and we started moving forward, cheering, whistling and circling the boundary of the endless yard.

I was so happy that I was terrified something would jinx my joy. Nothing mattered to me but this moment. I wanted this night to last forever. I freed my swollen feet from my shoes and danced barefoot on the cold grass. My bulky body didn't stop me from swaying and swirling to the beat of the music. Hoarse from all the loud singing, I was about to collapse into my usual lawn chair under the peepal, when I felt a cold hand clasp my arm.

I turned around, thinking it was another crazy friend. Except, it was anyone but a friend. It was the last person I wanted to see. I was looking directly into her eyes. Veer's mother's eyes. My breath left my body.

I was barefoot, grimy, and sweaty with the ear-splitting singing and frenzied dancing. My hair was tangled strewn over my hot face and my chiffon gown stained with tell-tale marks of candy floss and *tandoori masala*.

The music stopped and silence fell. Our friends huddled around me in anticipation of what would transpire.

Veer's mother's voice was like a whip across my face. "Maya you will have to immediately pack up this charade, your crude display of uninhibited self-indulgence. Look at you. Should you be behaving so hysterically in such a state? Your actions bring nothing but disgrace to our family." Her forehead was soaked with sweat even though it was a cool night, her nostrils were flared under narrow eyes, her hands were on her waist, and her feet were pulled apart.

My head swirled, my eyes blackened. I was so faint that I felt like vomiting. I had done nothing wrong but it felt that as though I had done something terrible. I had never been spoken to so harshly by anyone before. Tears were rolling down my cheeks liberally.

Veer was by my side. She looked at him. He lowered his head, as if in shame. We were humiliated in front of all our friends.

She said to Veer in a sharp voice, "What a fool you are to be under her spell this way.... If you continue like this, very soon she will be dominating everything in this household with her carefree, hippie ways. Is this why I brought you up? To witness this day, this shame fall upon our family?" Her voice choked up in sympathy—for herself.

An eerie stillness that had descended over us like a dark omen. Not even the breeze gave way. Veer did not say a word. His head continued to be lowered.

Suddenly we noticed a frail figure stepping out of the shadows. It was Veer's father. Looking embarrassed at this public outburst, he tried to salvage whatever was left of this situation. "Calm down dear, the children meant no disrespect. They were simply having some fun. We have our own parties all the time, don't we?"

Veer's mother shot her husband a look that completely destroyed whatever courage he had. Then she turned her back and stomped out of the lawn towards the house.

Veer's father placed his hand on my drooping shoulders, gently kissed my forehead and left after her.

Our party was over. Anita was by my side, but I was too numb to talk. Our friends wanted to stay to ensure that we were okay but Veer asked them politely to leave.

And then suddenly a surge of anger gripped me. Livid and mortified, not caring who was around to hear me, I asked, "Veer, why didn't you tell your mother that this wasn't my idea?"

But before he could answer, I felt like an elastic band had popped within my stomach. I knew it was time. I screamed. And between hospital lights, stretchers, and incredible pain, all the rest was a blur.

***

Everything was dark. I was falling in a bottomless pit. There was nothing to hold, no one to catch me. I gasped for air. Opaque shadows were suffocating me. There was nothing to look forward to. I was alone in this pain. No one understood. No one liked me in my new house. I was not worthy of this new family. I had brought shame to their family name. Veer was disappointed in me too or else he would have spoken up in front of his mother. I don't want to live anymore. I had no strength to get up from this strange bed. Where was I?

There was a rustle in the darkness and a warm familiar hand cupped mine. Ma! I wanted to go back home with her. "Congratulations Maya. We have a beautiful granddaughter!"

Diya had arrived.

"Why don't I remember anything Ma?"

"We had to sedate you. And you had to have a caesarean."

I tried to prop myself up but my lower abdomen hurt.

"Don't try to get up just yet," she said. "Your incision is still fresh and I am sure it hurts." She started stroking my head gently and it felt good to let myself relax under her fingers.

There was a knock at the door. The nurse walked in with a small bundle. She handed it to me.

The bundle stirred and then I saw her. That upturned nose, the soft, rosy cheeks, the long, dark eyelashes, the tiny and dainty fingers and toes. She was perfect. She was mine. I was complete.

The door opened again and a euphoric Veer entered the room with soggy eyes and a bouquet of red roses.

"Do you want to hold her?" I asked, my voice low and unsure.

He didn't wait to answer. He took Diya into his arms and he was transformed. He radiated love and gratitude and I realized I had been holding my breath.

I looked away. Why did I feel so different? What was happening to me? I looked at Ma, at my husband and the tiny infant in his arms, and I realized that something strange was pulling me down into a sinister place.

18. SHEILA

WHY WAS MAYA-BETI SO QUIET? She didn't speak, she hardly ate, and she no longer sat near her peacocks. It has been three long months since she returned from the hospital. I was worried.

The only time her eyes lit up were when she held little Diya. I tried to tell the big Madam yesterday, but she did not listen. Master Veer was also silent, except when he held Diya. I asked God to bless this young family and protect them from the darkness of this house.

Last week, I went to oversee Diya's new nanny when I heard Master Veer's raised voice. "Why don't you speak to me? What is wrong? Why are you unhappy?"

This was how things always started. I knew it too well now. My worst fears were surfacing. I worried that Maya-Beti was not able to come out of this spell, just as Madam Gayatri had not been able to. I was unaware of Gayatri Madam's suffering then, and I didn't want to make the same mistake again. I had to do something.

I thought about this for a while. It would be best for them to leave this house and go far away. I knew that somehow I would have to talk to Master Veer and convince him. Somehow. Yes, maybe a trip away would help.

I sat at the pantry window. I could see the dining room from that spot. I decided to wait for Bahadur to clear the dinner table and I would catch Master Veer before he left the room.

Bahadur was picking up the sweets. The last course. I pulled myself up and started walking so that I could arrive on time.

When I finally arrived, the dining hall looked bigger than I remembered from when I used to wait there on my Madam. I thought perhaps some furniture was missing, but that worry was for another day. Master Veer had settled on the couch under the lamp. He was reading the paper and he looked peaceful. It was a good time to talk.

Just then the elder Master entered and sat next to his son. "Veer, I want to talk to you."

I quickly turned around to face the table and pretended to be clearing the last of the dishes with Bahadur's team.

"Veer, it is time to venture out. You know how bad business has been in the past few years. I would like you to personally oversee the expansion of the international wing of business."

"But Papa, it will entail a lot of travelling—for days and even months. You know I don't want to leave Maya, who is not in the best of health."

I hobbled over to to the kitchen. I didn't want it to be obvious that I was listening. I suddenly understood why the room seemed bigger, why little privileges had vanished for us servants too. So, the rumours were correct after all. The Rajsinghania business was going down.

The first time I noticed something was when little Malti, Bahadur's youngest daughter, came from the village to live with him. She came to sleep in my room. "Why? Don't you have space in your father's quarters?" I asked.

"No, father has to share his room with three of the junior helpers."

"Really? Why? What happened to their own quarters?"

"Well, they have been rented out by the big Madam for a few months."

Also, the lavish spreads after tea of fruit cake, chicken sandwiches, and coconut macaroons, had gradually diminished over the year, leaving less and less to be returned to us in the kitchen. And then I was told that the junior maids had been let go, and I was requested by the big Madam to come and help out in the kitchen during parties. Even Maya-Beti had only a part-time nanny for her newborn. This was something never seen before in this family.

With the running water and the clatter of the dishes, I couldn't hear anything. So I had to go back to clear the rest of the table.

The senior Master was leaving. "Think about it. I want your decision by tomorrow evening, Veer. I hope you will consider your duty to this family."

Master Veer was deep in thought. This was my only chance. He looked up and smiled as I approached him cautiously. "Oh, hello Shelia. How are you?"

"I am well, Master Veer, thanks to the family's blessings. You keep me well. Only good things should come to families like this."

"Well, thank you, Sheila." He turned his head back to the newspaper he was reading.

I carried on without shame: "I was referring to the little light that has come into our lives, our little Diya."

"Uh huh," he nodded absentmindedly without lifting his head.

"But Maya-Beti, not so much...."

Master Veer then abruptly lifted his head to look at me. "What do you mean, Sheila?"

"I mean that she is not very bright these days, Master Veer. She's not her usual self."

"Yes, I know. Dr. Robby says it is the exhaustion of childbirth. He has prescribed some pills."

"It is not my place to be so bold, Master Veer, but this should not last for so many months, don't you think? Master Veer was silent. "You see, Master Veer, in situations like this, often a little change of scenery does wonders. She will revive herself in new surroundings, even if it is only for a few days."

There was silence all around us. Master Veer's head was bent, but he was not reading the paper. That was all I could do, but

I think it was enough. I knew that I had planted the seed in his head. I turned and walked away. I slept well that night.

***

My hands were still cold in the morning mist as I entered Maya-Beti's room to check on the new maid. Both mother and daughter were sleeping soundly. Such a heavenly sight they were. Master Veer was staring out the window at the neglected peacocks. He seemed distraught and did not respond to my greeting.

Instead, he asked, "Sheila, what you said last night about a change of scenery..." I eagerly encouraged him to go on. "I think it is good advice. I think I shall take it." I nodded and smiled.

19. MAYA

TIME WAS A GREAT HEALER. I felt better as the days passed. Today was an especially a good day. I felt like I had just emerged from a deep slumber. The words of Veer's mother no longer rang in my ears. And I no longer lived among the ghosts of this house's past. There were no long shadows following me, and Gayatri's tragedy was inconsequential when I looked into Diya's eyes. I felt like the old me. Where had the year slipped by? Diya walked a few steps now, all too quickly, to fall *plonk* on her rear. And I was always ready to catch her before she fell.

Sheila laughed. "Our Diya is running before she can walk. She will take you far."

Whatever little time Veer could spare in the evening, he joined in to play. But he kept long hours at work now. And that is why I was so surprised to see him in the middle of the afternoon. He smiled as I came to greet him in the peacock garden. "You look happy today, Maya."

"And aren't you happy, Veer?"

He thought a little before he replied. "Maya, you know what will really make us happy?"

"What?"

"Going away."

I was surprised.

"Papa wants me to open a branch in the West. This means that I will either have to travel for long periods of time or simply live there till the expansion is well established."

I could not believe what I was hearing. Did that mean that I had to live without Veer in this mansion? I felt my fear returning.

Veer continued. "Maya, I have been thinking. This may be a blessing in disguise. We can leave together and start a new life."

At first I couldn't focus on what he was saying, but he repeated himself several times, saying the same thing in different ways. It finally sank in.

His gaze was piercing. I was stunned. Just the thought of leaving my country, my parents and friends ... leaving everything I had ever known ... was overwhelming. I did not speak. But I knew Veer was reading my mind.

He said, "We can go for a couple of years and then we can decide if we'd like to stay on or come back."

My head started to hurt. I was falling into the darkness again. I didn't give him an answer right away.

I walked back into the house and I immediately called my parents. I could hear the same anxiety in my mother's contrived tone and ruptured exhales. I knew it was taking her all her strength to carefully sculpt sentences of consolation.

I called Anita. She listened intently to what I said. "Maya, what do you have to lose?" Anita said. "Imagine discovering a new land, something magical in each city, something insane in every new person's story. It's like being born again ... when you have all the possibilities at your feet to take any path leading to any unknown destination. Maya fly ... fly away from the ill wishes of Veer's mother, away from the evil secrets of the past. It is time to move on, Maya, for you, for Veer, and for your daughter, Diya. Embrace it...."

Why did Anita have a way of making anyone look forward to the hardest of decisions?

I didn't like it. I wanted at least one person to indulge me, and agree that we should not leave. That night I lay awake thinking about all that had transpired since my wedding day. Was this really a blessing in disguise? Was this really a way to fly away as even Sachin had suggested? And what did I have to lose, as Anita said? Was this an opportunity for me to gather some of the courage that I had so admired in Anita?

And then there was Diya. Maybe her fate was away from the curses of this mansion. How could I deny her a clean slate, a life that had every possibility, good and bad? And then there was Veer. I would have to endure his possessive behaviour in a new land. But then maybe he would cease to be so insecure and grant me a little understanding, a little space. Perhaps, away from his mother, he would have more courage, more confidence. Yes, the possibilities were endless. For once, I was not going to be a coward. I was going to take up this challenge head on.

***

Months had flown by since that fated day when Veer had spoken about leaving for another land. Over the year, Veer spoke only once more about a possibility of us moving to Canada. In the meantime, I had gone on the internet to see what Canada looked like. Except for the long Canadian winters, there were many good things posted about this quiet and polite northern neighbour of the United States.

Life was moving fast whether we liked it or not. Diya was another year older and talked continuously. Anita had had to dig into some of her own optimism when she was faced with the hard decision of settling down with someone she had met on one of her internships and had fallen for head over heels. Ajay was an Assistant Commissioner of Police who had been placed in one of the rural districts where she was leading a grassroots artisan project.

I still remember the hot spring morning when an excited Bahadur brought with him the telephone receiver along with my morning mango shake. Anita was always someone I looked forward to talking to.

“Where have you been, girl?’ I asked her, breathless with excitement.

"Why, you should ask! I have called you so many times and you have never returned a call."

"When? I didn't get a single message from you."

"Oh!"

There was silence.

"Anita, who did you speak to?"

"The first time I spoke to Veer's mother, and then some other lady ... I think she said Kitten or Kitty or something like that."

I did not want to know more. I changed the subject.

"I'm so sorry, Anita. I would have been so happy to talk to you. So, what's up?"

Anita's voice cheered up. "Maya, I'm getting married!"

My heart jumped. "What? *Really?* Oh my God. Our grand Anita has finally succumbed and is now indulging in the acts of us common mortals!" I teased.

"Yes, it was a hard decision for me." Her tone was serious. "You know that my work takes me for months on end to no man's lands deep in the country. So how can someone like me think of settling down to a domesticated life if I have to be apart from my family for so long? But Ajay explained this to me in a way that made perfect sense. You see, I can only work in one district at a time. Ajay's next posting is in the North West at the base of the Himalayas, in a small town called Udalguri in Assam. Here, for the first time, I will get to work with the tribal people on the tea plantations. Since each of his postings is for a minimum of five years, this gives me ample time to understand and support these folk and rural tribes that are barely eking out a living. With Ajay's support and connections, we will have access to resources and networks for them."

She was breathless. Her excitement was palpable and I was thrilled for her.

"Yes, Maya. I thought about it long and hard," she sighed. And that's why I called you so many times. But it's a boon in disguise that we didn't talk, because now I will not have anyone to blame if things go wrong."

"Anita, why would anything go wrong? Remember what you told me? What do any of us have to lose when we decide to move on?"

"Maya, my eternal optimist. So I gather you have thought about moving away with Veer?"

"Yes, Anita. I have thought about it."

***

It happened fast. Once the decision was made that we were leaving our life in India, there was not enough time to reconsider, to regret. Our school friends were surprised but not particularly moved by our decision. Veer's relatives had been visiting in droves, mainly out of curiosity. My parents were respectful of our decision but I knew they were distressed to see me go. Then they sped up their plans to renovate to their summer cottage in Kasauli. And our peacock had shed his entire tail this season, as if in protest.

I had stopped thinking about how I felt. I had started packing a few things to take with me and parcelling other belongings that would be given away.

And, as I packed, I found once again, the conspicuous polka-dotted diary of trouble—Gayatri's diary. I did not want to take it, and I did not want to leave it. What if it got discarded and ended up in the hands of scrap paper collectors, and eventfully got pulped in a large iron machine? Gayatri would be lost forever. But I wasn't sure I wanted to be its *de facto* custodian. It would mean carrying the grisly past with me. And would that not defeat the entire purpose of my leaving this place?

As I contemplated this, I heard Sheila call for me. "Maya-Beti, Maya-Beti, come quickly. See what Diya is up to!"

I absentmindedly tucked Gayatri's diary into the bottom of my suitcase, away from all prying eyes, thinking I could make a decision about its fate the following day when the house was quiet.

I walked into the living room where Diya was fiddling with the phone receiver, pretending to speak to her imaginary friend. We both laughed at her antics as she continued to babble into the phone. Sheila had been hanging around us like a protective shield. She had been sleeping in Diya's room in order to wake up early and help me pack.

I wanted to give away everything I wasn't taking with me. There were many things that I thought others might find useful and who needed them more than our waiting empty rooms did.

Of course, Sheila did not agree with me. There were labelled boxes everywhere. Our soul collection of music was going to Veer's favourite cousin, Esha, whose gift of the peacocks had made our mornings magical; our clothes and books were stacked in piles for donation; our cutlery and the best of the china were for Veer's aunties; our cell phones and cars were to be left behind for family use; and our freedom was still with us.

"Maya-Beti, I will seal your room till you come back. It will be covered and locked," Sheila said to me after putting Diya down for her afternoon nap and joining me in the garden outside. In a flash, my mind was back in the west wing, in Gayatri's mirrored room with the jacquard drape. I shivered. The last thing I wanted was a waiting mausoleum.

"No, Sheila, please don't do that. I want these rooms to be living, happy spaces, alive with people—where you have parties, where you have house guests." Sheila's expressive eyes narrowed with disapproval. "And Sheila, have you ever thought of the possibility that we may never come back?" I teased.

What Sheila said next shook me out of my carefree mood.

Shaking her head with conviction, Sheila said, "But here's the truth, Maya-Beti: even though I don't wish it, even though I wish you to go away to live your life in peace, I know that you *shall* return. I just know."

She hobbled to the edge of our lily pond and picked up the lone peacock feather that had been left behind by the gardener while clearing the leaves this morning. She straightened its tassels and caressed its crescent. I could have sworn that she was talking to this feather, as if casting a spell. Then she hobbled back to me and stretched out her hand. I took the brilliant blue-green stalk in my hand. I felt Sheila watching me intently. "Maya-Beti," she said, "please take this peacock feather with you and return it to me as a sign that you are well and happy. But, mind you, remember to return it. For, I will only die in peace when I see it back in my hands—not before." Sheila was upsetting me. She was being so melodramatic, but somehow what she said also sunk deep inside my heart.

I tried to laugh it off. "So Sheila, does that mean that you cannot die until I bring this feather back to you?"

This time she laughed with me. "Okay then, Maya-Beti, it is settled. You will have to come back to return it!" She had won her point. I had conceded to coming back just as she had originally wanted.

As she turned to go back inside, I walked over to the peepal tree. As I stood there stroking this eye-tailed feather, I wondering if the peepal had witnessed what had just happened. I had been bound by a pledge to return even before I had left.

***

It was our last day at home. It was past the breakfast hour, the smell of the porridge and burnt toast still lingered on the veranda outside the pantry. In the study, the fierce sun was penetrating our transparent drapes to smoulder every corner and crevasse with angst. Sheila and Bahadur had promised to look after our peacocks. Veer's mother did not mind having these exotic birds around as they were an impressive showpiece for her evening parties.

We did not want to say goodbye. We were not leaving, only visiting another exciting place for some time. Denial was a wonderful thing. Besides avoiding the immediacy of the problem, it also always gave room to retreat. We would come back home whenever we wanted.

As our time to leave came closer, all I wanted to do was slip away quietly. A long cold bath did wonders to soothe my nerves. I dressed in a "western" outfit that Anita helped me buy: long leather boots with a tweed skirt and a matching suede coat with tassels. Gathering every ounce of courage and faith that I could muster, I stepped into the living room to face the family. Veer's parents were standing next to his mother's two inseparable sisters, who were with their husbands. My parents were sitting quietly on the edge of the sofa. Diya was playing in a dimly lit corner with Sheila, who was singing her a lullaby and occasionally wiping her tears. Ma picked up Diya to cuddle her for the last time. We checked our meagre belongings and zipped up our suitcases. I had coached myself for this moment for weeks. I was brave and showed no obvious signs of weakness.

I looked at my mother. She had the same face that I was trying to emulate. Papa placed his hand across my shoulders.

"It will be okay. Just be true to yourself and never bend down to anything that does not seem right to you...." His voice cracked. Being such a practical man, his presence had always calmed me, and his words had always grounded me in a pragmatism that only a few possessed. But not today. I nodded vigorously, more to convince myself than him. A sneaky tear absconded from the edge of my lashes, but I quickly brushed it off.

Veer was tightly sandwiched between his mother and aunts, who were holding his hands, one on each side. Their exaggerated gestures of wiping imaginary tears with a succession of tissues in between loud sniffles almost made me laugh. Veer's mother had not spoken a word to anyone, implying that the spectacle and occasion of her son's going away took precedence over all other things that day.

And away is where we were going. .

I suddenly wanted to crumble. My mind started protesting, and my heart began to sink. But it was too late for this indulgence. We were about to leave.

Our bags were loaded in to the car, and our driver started revving the engine to tune it. The strands of hair at the back of my neck stiffened. I tried the poker face that I had been practising for days. With Diya in my arms and Veer by my side, with folded hands, one by one, we said goodbye and descended the stone staircase to our waiting car.

I turned to give my parents one last look. My mother had her arms open. I ran back to her, up the stairs, and into her arms. She held me tight and let me cry.

After a few satisfying moments, she said, "Maya, stand up." There was strength in her voice.

Gathering some of her spirit, I walked straight to the open car door and didn't look back again.

PART II

PEACOCK IN THE SNOW

20. MAYA

IT WAS A LONG JOURNEY. I tried to grab as much sleep as I could with Diya in my arms clinging to any part of my clothes or my body that she could grab. It was very uncomfortable. It was not till we stepped off the plane that it dawned on me: *What have we done*? A sense of loss hit me hard, and it hurt like nothing had before. I didn't know if Veer felt the same.

We stepped into the airport lobby and were greeted by a group of dark-skinned people under a banner with a large red maple leaf. "Welcome to Canada! Please come this way." This group lacked the typical North American twang; instead their accent seemed to hint at a tropical language. Diya was grumpy and tired. I was expecting a tantrum at any time, so I unbuckled her from the stroller to give her some air. As our attention was caught up in filling the long forms that were presented to us at Customs, Diya saw her opportunity. She wiggled out of her stroller and ran towards the thickest part of waiting passengers.

Thud!

We all looked up. She was lying face down. She had tripped over the suitcase of a passenger and had hit her face on the ground. I ran to scoop her in my arms. The irritated passenger scolded me. "How do you people let your children loose at an airport?"

Diya's tiny nose was swelling up, and she had started crying loudly.

But inside my head, the only sound that I could hear was the one from the group that had greeted us: "Welcome to Canada."

Veer was looking out for someone in the waiting crowd. His mother had arranged for her distant cousin to pick us up.

"It is all taken care of," she had said. "Gautam Uncle will put you up in his house until you find your own place, and he will help you settle. We have done a lot for his family in the past, and I trust him." She had handed Veer a photograph of his uncle so that he would be recognized when we arrived.

I watched as Veer started waving. Gautam was a stocky and short middle-aged man in a khaki safari suit with large pockets on the chest. He had small beady eyes under bushy eyebrows, a broad nose, and spiked, oily hair parted in the middle. We finished the paperwork and made our way over to him. He hugged us with enthusiasm and then pulled Diya's cheek with affection. She started bawling again.

On the way to Gautam's house, I rolled down the window to let in Toronto's surprisingly cold April air. The streets were sparkling clean, and the roadside evergreens were swaying under a spotless blue sky. There was not a single person on the street. Where were the people? In India, there was not an inch of uninhabited space. Here, the cars were fast and the traffic so organized. Everyone stopped at red lights and obeyed the lords of the road: the pedestrians. We inhaled the sterile crispness and braced ourselves for what lay ahead.

We landed in Gautam's small townhouse in the suburbs. It was a neatly organized block of closely-built housing units. They were identical expect for small differences in the potted plants on their porches and the colour of their front doors.

We entered his house and were assaulted with the smell of stale curry and synthetic air freshener. He proudly showed us each scantily furnished tiny room and then the balcony overlooking the highway. "With a lot of immigrants coming to Toronto in this recent years, the value of my house has really gone up, you know."

And with that singular statement, we were successfully filed in the category of "new immigrants."

He piled our small suitcases in the corner of a large bedroom. They were the only evidence of our previous life. I tucked Diya in for the night and then joined Veer and Gautam in the dining room.

Veer was anxious to get started the next morning, and search for an office space before looking for a house. Gautam assured him that he had already lined up some showings for tomorrow. Veer had not smiled since we had arrived. His enthusiasm about this trip was a past memory. He was talking in monosyllables, and his facial muscles were tense.

My eyes were heavy with exhaustion. I took my leave and went to lie down next to Diya. But sleep was the last thing that visited me. Veer came in and lay down quietly beside me without switching on the light. I held his hand in the dark. It was cold. Veer's hands were never cold. He patted my palm, and then turned his back on me.

I could not sleep. I was hot and thirsty. After tossing and turning in the cramped new bed between Veer and Diya, I finally got up to get a drink of water. I went down the stairs and walked toward what I thought was the kitchen. But I took a wrong turn and found myself in a room with couches.

I could hear the muffled voice of a man speaking to someone. As I came into hearing range, I realized that Gautam was on the phone. I did not want to disturb him so I tiptoed around looking for the kitchen. It was dark and I could still hear Gautam speaking to someone.

"Ya, *yaar* ... listen ... I will bring them to you in the morning. No, no, they don't know that you are my friend. Remember, our deal is that I get a twenty-five percent cut from the sale. *Ha ha* ... yes, we will cover our cut with the hike in price.... No, no, how will they know? They just came from India. You know the family is very rich and they trust me...."

I had reached the kitchen. I took a glass from the cabinet and then opened the fridge to look for a jug of water. There was none. So I turned on the tap and filled the glass to the brim. I heard a sound behind me. I turned to see Gautam in his pyjamas. His lips were stretched in the pretence of a smile. "You should have called me, I would have brought water for you."

"No, no, it is no trouble really."

"Oh, so Veer did not come down with you?"

I could have sworn that he exhaled a breath of relief. He tried to avoid looking into my eyes. Did he suspect that I had overheard him? Even if he did, my overhearing him somehow did not bother him as much as the prospect of Veer's overhearing him.

He came toward me and reached for my glass, brushing his hairy hand across mine very deliberately. And then he grabbed my wrist with his other hand. Startled, I looked up. His eyes red and watery and his smile had turned into a leer. His breath smelled. Repulsed, I immediately pulled myself away and ran upstairs without looking back. I could still hear him whistling when I reached the safety of our bed. I was shaking, but I calmed myself eventually by placing my hand over a sleeping Diya. And this was our first night in Canada.

***

The next morning, we all were disoriented and jet-lagged. I wanted to tell Veer everything about last night, but when I saw his face I knew that he was as eager to move out of this house as I was. If I told Veer about Gautam, I also knew he would instantly break all ties with the only person in this new land that could possibly or supposedly help us. So, I decided that this information would have to wait for now.

Diya cried constantly, asking for her room, her toys, and for Sheila. She wanted everything that we did not have. I was terribly homesick too. I missed my parents, the peacocks, and Anita. I prayed that the deep emptiness I felt would gradually wean away.

Veer had left with Gautam right after breakfast to look for office spaces, but didn't return with him in the evening.

"Where is Veer?" I asked and headed to make some tea.

Gautam followed me into the kitchen. "I left Veer with the property dealer to finish up the paperwork."

I had more questions for Gautam but I did not want to be trapped in the kitchen again. Diya was holding my finger tightly. I think she sensed my tension. Before he could come closer, I changed my mind about tea and went straight up to our room. I locked the door and waited for Veer.

The next few hours dragged. I read to Diya, fed her some crackers that I had saved from the plane, and then put her to bed. I did not risk going down to the kitchen again. The watch on the mantle showed that it was ten at night. Where was Veer? I would have to go down to look. I could no longer stay cooped up in the room. So I slipped silently down the stairs and out the main door onto the street . Gautam did not hear me because of the TV in the other room.

A few speckled stars shone from behind passing clouds. I could smell sweet roast on charcoal. Maybe someone was barbequing in their backyard nearby. I did not know where Veer was or who to call. Was he not worried about leaving us alone in this new place? He had not spoken to me since we had arrived.

Wrapped up in my brooding, I did not notice Veer's shadow moving up the path until he was almost next to me. I could not see his face. It was dark. I opened my lips to say something about how worried I was, but just then the moon fell at an angle on his face, and I saw what I least expected. He was smiling. It was an expression he had not had since our last happy time together, in another land, and now only a distant memory. My heart beat faster.

"What is it?" I asked.

He was silent.

"Tell me." I pulled his arm.

"Well ..." he hesitated.

"Well what?" I asked.

"I have just bought our office, and a new car. Maya, this is the beginning of our new life here. I will take you and Diya for a spin in it soon."

I knew then that we would be staying here for some time. This would be our new home, for better or for worse. Veer explained how much it had all cost and how much we had left to survive on until the business picked up. I briefly thought of telling him about Gautam, but once again I decided against it. Even though I was not listening to Veer's words, I heard him. I knew that we would never look at money the same way as we had in the past. Money would buy us a life, safety, a reason to stay on—things that we had taken for granted in India. I now understood why everyone counted their pennies in the West.

And today, we had joined them.

21.

WHEN WE RETURNED, Gautam was waiting at the dining room table with a glossy binder, alphabetically-organized, showing houses for sale in the Greater Toronto area. He was beaming with excitement, and I knew then that he had already received his commission from his crooked friend for selling Veer the office space. Now he was looking forward to his next kill: finding us an overpriced house. He had our names printed on the listing sheets. There were no secrets from him. He knew our bank balance and our potential capacity to secure the remaining difference from India. He was our guarantor and our point of reference in this new city. He spent the next few hours calculating how much the deposit on our home would be. He knew exactly the kind of house we could afford. Gradually we found ourselves surrendering to his counsel on every matter from the choice of neighbourhood to the kind of house he thought we should buy.

The next day, we drove with Gautam to look at houses in the neighbourhood. There was a house on the next street that had just come up for sale. Gautam told us that this was one of the most sought-after areas, so if we were lucky to find something for sale, we should buy it without question.

We entered a broad street lined with open drains and mature trees. The houses were made of faded bricks and aluminium siding. They were all built in the same style, and Gautam explained that these were post-war construction, subsidized by the government for war widows.

We parked in the broad driveway of one of the older looking homes and followed him through the main door, into a dark room. He fumbled for the light switch but could not find one. So he opened his bag and pulled out a torch, which I was certain that he kept for such occasions. It was a very cold, dim, and damp house with a pungent smell. There were bamboo blinds covered with green mildew. The worn wooden floor creaked with loose planks, and the broken buffet table was strewn with flaking speckles of paint. There were sparks coming from the next room with open wires.

"Look Mama, it has so many legs ... one, two, four, six ... so many ...." I immediately picked up Diya in my arms before she could touch the centipede that scuttled by.

"Who lived here?" I asked Gautam.

He answered that the previous owner had been a war widow who passed away recently, leaving no children behind. She had lived alone. I walked out of the house.

Once in the car, Gautam asked, "Ahem ... so, would you like me to draw the paperwork for this house?"

"But it's in shambles!" I blurted.

"It is a good neighbourhood, and we can get it fixed for a little more cost."

"But Gautam Uncle, the house has water damage...."

Gautam interrupted: "To get a house in this neighbourhood is very lucky. I don't think you should think twice. I am telling you...."

We were both quiet. And he eventually started the car and drove us to the second house he had earmarked for us. It took a long while to get there as we had to drive across the city, first on the highway and then through some inner winding streets.

"This is another good area, going up in price due to the money coming in from Chinese immigrants."

The houses were so closely built that their owners could

probably hear each other talk through the walls. We passed a crowded strip plaza with large dragon lanterns. There were all kinds of cars cramped closely together, fighting for every inch of the tight parking space. The noise and bustle of the place reminded me of a market in India, not in Canada.

We entered a driveway that smelled like a roadside Chinese restaurant. The door was opened by a older Chinese man with grey hair and spectacles. He did not respond to our greeting; instead, he turned his head inside and shouted in a singsong language, possibly Mandarin. Then a younger version of him came to the door to meet us. Gautam handed the young man his business card, and we were ushered inside. The deep-fried smell that had greeted us grew more pungent as we walked down the hallway and entered the living room. It was cluttered and strewn with toys, cushions, diapers, and plastic bags with things spilling out on the floor. There were three children sitting close to each other, their eyes glued to a Chinese channel on the television. There was an older woman pouring oil in a decanter at the corner table, and there was a very pale and thin younger woman feeding a toddler a bowl of noodles on his high chair. All these people were crowded into the main living room together. We followed Gautam from one overcrowded and dingy room to another.

I found this way of looking for houses very strange. I was glad to be out of there.

"Well, what do you think?" Gautam asked as we got into the car.

This time neither Veer nor I replied.

Instead, Veer said, "Let us take you for dinner, Gautam Uncle, for all your hospitality and help. Which is the most expensive restaurant here?"

"No, no. Why eat out when we can have fresh Indian cooking at home?" Gautam said, looking pointedly at me.

Veer tried again. "Maya must be tired too, and Indian food takes a long time to cook from scratch. So how about it?"

"No, it is not too late. We will be home in thirty minutes and then Maya can start right away." I gestured discreetly to Veer to keep quiet. The fuss was not worth it.

"Sure, Gautam Uncle. Whatever you want."

I was a bad cook. But for some reason I was not supposed to be a bad cook since I was woman from India. Why did he not understand that we did not cook? At Veer's home, we had cooks!

I hesitantly asked Gautam to show me where the ingredients were stored.

It was as if he had been waiting to get me into the kitchen. He brushed against me as he reached for one of the upper cabinet doors. Then he pushed past me several times, each time leaning some part of his body against mine, each time with a different excuse about an ingredient.

Just before leaving the kitchen, he said unashamedly, "Oho, dear Maya, my advice to you is to buy the house that I have shown you—the one in the next lane. You can cook for me every evening like this! *Ha, ha, ha.*"

I shuddered and fought the urge to hit him on his face and then march into the living room and tell Veer, no matter the consequences. Yes, Veer would be livid, and then we would have to walk out. Of course, I would be blamed by Veer's mother for everything, including seducing this repulsive man. Was I prepared for all this drama at this time? But Gautam was getting bolder, and I would have to be cautious. The sooner we left his house, the safer it would be for Diya and me.

I struggled for a few hours in the kitchen while Veer played with Diya. Finally, I was able to serve a simple meal of yellow lentils, okra, and rice. My poor cooking skills were a blessing in disguise. The look on Gautam's face as he sat there chewing suggested that I would not be requested to cook again.

While I put the dishes away, Veer stood in the kitchen by me. I was grateful to God for this. As Gautam entered the kitchen, Veer said to him, "Gautam Uncle, we would like to see a few more houses before deciding which is the one."

"Yes, of course, dear son Veer. Yes, of course. Whatever you want," he replied in an oily voice, almost bowing with sleaziness.

After washing the utensils, mopping the kitchen floors, and tucking Diya into bed right next to us, both Veer and I lay awake. He did not speak, nor did I, but we were connected in the same thought. After a few restless hours, we picked up Diya, strapped her in the car seat, and reversed out of Gautam's driveway. The sky was opening up slowly to reveal a ripe pink belly. But it was still too early for dawn. Armed with just a map of Toronto's suburbs, and with no knowledge of which direction to take, we set out.

22.

THE ROADS TOWARD THE EAST looked easy to follow, broad, and clean. As we left the city behind, the spaces between one house and another started growing. Weak morning rays sneaked from the sky to gently kiss the highway, and soon we could see without the help of the street lights. Veer took a random exit, and we were suddenly in a beautiful enclave with colossal houses, high domed roofs, towering gates, sprawling, manicured gardens, and trees tall enough to spread their branches over the entire breadth of the road.

We both gasped. What flamboyance, what affluence. And then I thought, maybe this is what people thought about us in Delhi.

We had almost reached the lake.

At the end of the street there was one lone house standing apart from the exuberance of the rest. It was a corner house with a sign that was hidden with overgrown dandelions; it read, "Open House." We picked up a sleeping Diya and stepped out of the car.

The small wooden gate creaked at the hinges as we rang the doorbell. Nothing stirred. So we rang again. We heard a latch on the other side, and then the door was flung open by a plump, olive-skinned man with a big nose over a square and friendly face.

"Hello, we were just passing and saw your sign for the open house." Veer extended his hand.

"Oh, that was two days ago. I think the agent forgot to take the sign off."

"Who is it, Mario?" said a woman's sharp voice from inside.

The man turned his head. "Don't worry, Mama. I am looking after this." And then to us he added, "Come in. I can show you around."

Veer hesitated. We knew that we should not go in without Gautam's counsel, but this was our only chance, the chance that we were waiting for. If we liked this house we could move out of Gautam's immediately.

"Veer, let's see," I nudged.

The man introduced himself as Mario Biasatti, and led us into the house. Once my eyes became used to the dark room, I spotted a small bent figure in the corner. She had a colourful scarf on her head and the same prominent nose as Mario. She stopped her knitting momentarily and looked straight at us. Her cheeks had deep wrinkles that looked like gashes and her fingers were bent inwardly as if they had no bones inside them.

"This is my mother, Mama Biasatti," said Mario.

"Hello." We dipped our heads in respect.

She did not greet us back. Instead, she looked at Mario and said something sharply in what must have been Italian. Her bowed fingers left the knitting needles and waved at Mario. Her voice rose. It was obvious that we were not welcome.

Veer whispered, "Let's go!"

We turned around to leave, but Mario stopped us. "Let me show you our home. It's a very magnificent house."

We were a little perplexed by what was going on. We were certain that we were not welcome by Mama, but her son seemed eager to sell the house, probably against her wishes.

We followed him inside. It was an old house built on different levels. There were cobwebs in the corners and thick layers of dust on the counters. The walls were painted sunshine yellow with blue windowsills—the colours of the Mediterranean.

Nothing enticed us until we stepped outside.

It was a deep, unkempt garden with wild creepers growing around grandfather trees. And then there was the endless blue expanse. The soft sound of the waves crashing against the shore was hypnotic. The water shimmered in the morning sun and touched the sky for miles.

In the middle of the overgrown sprawl, there was a tiny pond underneath a fountain flowing from a life-size stone angel sculpture. The angel's wings were spread, and his hands were raised towards the sky as his head bowed to look down upon us.

I was mesmerized by the wild grandeur and tranquillity of this space. I wanted to move here immediately. It reminded me of our house in Delhi, somehow. But this was a house that the elders were not ready to part with. So, until we had Mama Biasatti's blessing, we could not buy it.

I made my way back to her. Mama Biasatti was sitting in the same pose as we had left her. She started coughing. I lay a sleeping Diya down on her couch and fetched the elderly woman a glass of water from the kitchen sink. She took a few sips and stopped coughing. Then she looked up at me curiously.

"I am sorry—I should have asked before laying my daughter on your couch." I went to pick her up.

She said, "No, leave the child. She is sleeping."

I quietly sat down on the dining chair next to her, and she let me. She started her knitting again. A complete, thick silence enveloped us. She saw that I was not fidgeting, or asking her for anything. She relaxed. "What is your name?" she finally asked.

"Maya." I paused before adding, "I really like your house."

"Why?" she looked up suspiciously, her eyes skewed and her lips a thin line.

"It is a beautiful old home."

She let her guard down a tiny bit. "Yes, it is."

"How long have you lived here?"

"All my life."

"Really?"

"My husband and I bought it from a police officer who was

moving west to Vancouver. We had just come from Italy, and my sons were only three and five years old ... my beautiful children. We had a good life here until...." She sank into her thoughts.

"Well, it is very lucky for you and your husband to have your children still around you..."

She cut my sentence short. "No, my husband left for Italy."

"Ohh ... and you? You did not go?"

She spoke after what seemed like a very long few minutes: "How could I leave my children here and go?"

"Yes, I understand. My husband has come from India to set up his office here. I too could have decided to stay back in the comfort of my own country."

"But you did not stay."

"No, I did not stay behind. I came with my husband, for better or for worse, whichever part of the world he is in, even if it is difficult."

"But what about the hardships for your child?"

"What about them? My Diya will be happy when both her parents are together. And once she is grown, she will have to find her own life. She will leave her nest, no matter which part of the world we live in. That is the way of nature. That is what we have done with our parents and that is what our children will do."

She bent down to pick up the ball of wool that had dropped from her lap. I was sure I had said something to offend her. I feared that I sounded preachy. This was a different kind of silence. I started to rise, intending to pick Diya up and tom-look for Veer.

She put her needles on the table and asked, "Do you want some coffee?"

"No, no, we should be going now."

But she had started walking slowly to the kitchen and switched on the coffee machine. Within seconds, the whole living room was enveloped in the rich, warm aroma of freshly roasted coffee beans. She walked in with two frothy, steaming cups and a plate full of chocolate-covered almond biscotti.

Between gulps of the piping hot brew and chocolate butter crumble, Mama picked up the conversation again. "My whole life..." she began, "I have lived in this house, brought up my children. How can I just leave and go? I will not be a good mother."

I could feel her internal struggle. I said gently, "Joining your husband may not make you a bad mother. You have devoted your life to your children."

Diya stirred and woke up. She rubbed her large eyes, looking for me. Then, before she started crying, I lifted her in my arms. A smiling Veer walked in with Mario on his heel. We thanked them for letting us in to their home.

Much to my surprise, Mama came to see us off at the door. Before stepping out of the door, I instinctively gave her a hug and said goodbye. And, to my utmost surprise, she hugged me back.

On the way back, Veer was excited. "Maya, I like that house. Let's talk to Gautam and see if it will work."

I kept quiet. I kept thinking of Mama Biasatti. I did not want to go into a house where someone was being forced to move out. I knew that meant bad luck. I shared Mama's story with Veer. But he just brushed me off. "Maya, your problem is that you get into too many unnecessary details with people. If the house is on sale, and if we can afford it, then we should buy it."

"No, Veer. I don't want the house if Mama Biasatti is not happy giving it to us."

"For God's sake, Maya, you don't even know her. At this rate, we will be homeless." Veer was distressed.

When we returned, Gautam had already prepared some paperwork for the houses he had shown us earlier. Veer told him about the house we had seen.

Gautam was upset. "What is wrong with the houses I have showed you?" he asked. "You will regret it later on," he said and looked sharply at me. I knew that he thought that I was behind this. In a way I was. Only he and I knew why I wanted to buy a house that would be as far away from him as possible, and he did not like it.

"Gautam Uncle, don't worry. We have not spoken to any agent. We will still go through you," Veer consoled him.

Gautam puffed up again. "Okay, okay. If you really would like me to help, then it can be arranged. Let me see what I can do."

Gautam was trying to salvage a slipping opportunity. Immediately, he called the Biasatti's agent to negotiate a deal, and within an hour he had the paperwork ready for us to sign. The only problem was that I was not ready to sign the deal yet.

"I would like to visit the house again before I sign," I managed to say aloud.

"Maya, just sign the goddamn papers," Gautam scolded loudly. Veer looked up sharply at Gautam for speaking to me like that.

"I would like to visit first," I insisted, standing my ground. Gautam was getting more aggravated.

"Maya, you do not have a choice now—the deal is done," he said.

I wished he had not said that. Something inside me snapped. "If there is anything I have left, it is the freedom to make my own choices, Uncle Gautam."

I stood up and walked away. I wanted to pack my bags. I did not want to stay there anymore, no matter what blame might be hurled at me. After all, I was not asking for anything unreasonable. Veer spoke up: "Gautam Uncle, why don't we visit the house tomorrow? We were to do that in any case after the signing." He was mediating, but I recognized from the edge in his tone that he was on the verge of losing his patience too.

Gautam banged the door on his way out.

***

I almost stepped on some unopened mail lying on the doormat

when Mario opened the front door for us. Before handing it to Mario, I noticed that it was from Canada Pension and it was addressed to Mrs. Sophia Biasatti.

Mama Biasatti came to greet us, this time with a smile that spoke for itself. I extended my hand to give her the envelope, but Mario intervened and snatched it midway. A dark shadow engulfed Mama as she withdrew back into her dimly lit chair.

It did not take me long to understand what was happening: Mario was taking her pension earnings. So this was the underlying pain that she was trying to come to terms with: To give up everything for your children, only to be controlled by them in old age. How humiliating and hurtful for a mother.

I sat down in the same chair I had taken the day before. Gautam and Veer were talking to Mario and following him around.

"What do you want, girl?'" Mama Biasatti finally asked. Her voice was gentle.

"I don't want your house if you don't want to give it."

"Why does it matter?"

"It matters to me. This is your home. And ... I want this house to bring good luck to my family."

She looked at me for a long moment. "You are a strange person." What she said next completely surprised me. "You have wisdom far beyond your years. After you left I started thinking about what you said to me, and I have made a decision. I have decided to join my husband in Italy. I leave next month." She was smiling.

"Just like that?" I asked

"No, it sounds sudden, but, my child, it has been coming for some time. I was a fool to hold on to the past."

There are very few moments in life when you feel that life just falls into place. This was one of those moments. I was grateful to her, to God, to everyone.

I blurted out, "So you will bless us to take over your house?"

"Yes, I bless you. Make it your home. You have all my best

wishes. And thank you for your message. The angel spoke through you...." I immediately thought of the stone angel in the backyard.

She opened my palm and placed something in it. A pair of small white ceramic doves. "They will guide you and bring peace," she said.

Now, this was a sign that I did not expect. Were these Gayatri's Om and Shanti returning to me through Mama Biasatti? I did not have time to ponder. Gautam had entered the room and was looking at me angrily. "I am ready to sign the papers now, Gautam Uncle," I said demurely.

His anger subsided immediately. "But don't you want to see the house again?" Gautam asked suspiciously.

"No, I don't need to." He looked perplexed.

"What she means is that since you and I have gone through it, that is good enough for her." Veer came to the rescue again.

"Oh," he nodded, not convinced still, but happy that his deal was going through.

The next week we moved into our first home in Canada. As we unloaded the car, Veer did a very traditional thing. He held out the keys to me and told me to step in first. When I opened the main door, I saw a vase full of puffed rice centred in front of the door. I toppled the rice vase with my big toe, stepped over the strewn grains and walked inside. In my palm, I held Mama Biasatti's white doves.

I was touched by Veer's gesture. He had remembered an age-old Indian tradition in which the woman of the house crosses the threshold and steps over rice as a symbol of the prosperity and luck the family will enjoy in the new home. Yes, there were some traditions that I would retain and pass on to Diya. And as for others, we would interpret and customize as they made sense to us in our new life.

The possibilities were endless and so was our joy.

23.

IT DID NOT TAKE US LONG to unpack our life from our suitcases. First, I unfolded Diya's clothes and toys. She was thrilled to get her Raggedy Ann doll and her yellow birdie back. Running from one room to another, with the doll on her left hip and the giant yellow bird on her right, she talked to them about the wonders of the open, lighted rooms. Yes, she had inherited some of our foolish spirit— she was not afraid of new places, as long as she knew that she could return to the safety of my arms. How innocent and resilient was childhood, how uncomplicated and trusting.

I went to check if Veer needed my help, but he was already unpacked and fast asleep in the dusty armchair. I quietly slipped off his shoes and covered him with a blanket.

Now it was my turn to unpack. The upper layers of my suitcase were filled with things that Sheila thought that I would need in a cold country: a hot water bottle, warm socks, my Jamawar shawl, and herbal hair oil. I piled up the essentials at the back of the wardrobe and started digging deeper to unpack my clothes. My hand hit something square and hard. I pulled it out. Black dye over white polka dots. Oh my god! Gayatri's diary! My eyes froze at the sight. I remembered how I had hidden it on the last day, hoping to make a decision on where to leave it. And then the next day I had forgotten all about it. I should have just left it in Sheila's safekeeping, or even returned it to Umang and Rosy. What had I done? Had I just carried the sinister past with me into our new life? It was only a matter of time before I would know.

The next morning, I decided to clean this large, dilapidated house. I spent more time discovering hidden nooks and dusty corners than doing anything useful with the dustpan. Imagining that there was a cleaning route, like the great silk route of ancient China, which wound through all the rooms and eventually led to the backyard, I picked up my enthusiasm and tried again. Reaching the backyard was my goal, and sipping iced tea under the stone angel statue was my prize. But soon I discovered that I was not too good at cleaning either. I was no good at any housework. I wish I could have borrowed Bahadur. Even a new chamber maid would do. I had to get out, I thought. Perhaps I would be better out of the house than inside it.

Diya was also edging to play with other children, and constantly asked me, "Mama can I get some friends for Ann and Birdie?" She was at the age that, had we been in India, she would be in school full-time.

I decided to speak to Veer about getting a part-time job. I was sure he would not deny me such a small indulgence.

I did not hear Veer calling out to us when he came back in the evening. Diya and I were engrossed under the angel statue. I was throwing seeds for the evening birds sitting on the stone bench, and Diya was talking to her imaginary friends. Veer called out again, and Diya ran into his lap. Her tiny face glowed, her wavy hair caught the sparkle of the late evening sun, and her hands were coated in mud.

Veer lifted her high and threw her up like a little ball. She giggled loudly, then she ran to bring her only two friends in the world to him. "See Papa ... Ann and Birdie ... see Papa."

"Hello, Ann and Birdie. Did you have fun today?" Diya bent her head, looking at her toes. Her lower lip hung as it did when she was on the verge of a tantrum. Veer repeated his question.

"No!" She stomped her feet, one after the other.

"Well, why not, Diya?"

"Because they want to play in the park." I had joined them on the deck. Veer looked up at me.

I smiled reassuringly and said to Diya, "Yes, we will take them to the park tomorrow." She liked that. She picked up her friends and ran off while talking to them about the park.

Veer waded through the tall grass to sit on our chipped stone bench under the statue of the angel. He chose the exact spot where I had just been sitting and started sprinkling bird seed around absentmindedly. Within minutes, our garden was flooded with cooing and pecking doves: grey, olive, and beige. I got up to call Diya, but Veer held me back.

"Wait, you must not go till you see ... aha ... there they are." He was pointing to them.

A pair of white doves, heavenly and pure, had landed in the middle of the garden. I could not believe our luck. The first dove hurriedly pecked at the bounty, but the second looked alertly over her shoulders. I moved closer to Veer, and the dove looked at me but did not flap its wings.

"No, don't come here, Maya. You will scare them." The dove was startled by his voice and fluttered. Her mate took the cue and together, without a moment's hesitation, they flew off into the dusk.

I sat down next to him with an unexplained sense of calm. My heart was beating fast but this time not out of anxiety. It was what I had been waiting for—it was hope. Mama Biasatti's lucky white doves had visited our new home. Veer held my hand and we walked back to the deck.

Once we had settled with a hot cup of coffee, he asked me, "What was Diya's little tantrum all about?"

"Veer, I think I will need to figure out what to do during the day. I mean, we cannot just stay in this house all the time."

"What did you have in mind?" he asked without looking at me.

"For one, I will explore the neighbourhood to see if Diya can join a play group or if she is not too young for kindergarten here."

"Yes, that seems like a good idea." I heard relief in his voice.

"And then, while Diya is away, I would like to find out more about this place."

"How?"

"I will go to the nearby mall, the one we saw on the corner, and then I can look for something part-time."

"Something part-time?" he repeated.

"Yes, like a part-time job."

"For what? You don't need to work."

"Veer, what will I do at home the whole day?"

"You have plenty to do."

"You know I am no good with housework," I laughed.

"No, you are not," he laughed with me, but I knew he was getting nervous about my moving out of the house. The old Veer was returning, and, before that could happen, I decided to change the topic.

"Okay, who wants to play Pied Piper?" I picked up an imaginary magic flute, and Veer tucked his palms on my waist at the back. Diya came running and started leading the way.

We closed the sliding glass door on the cold outside and went inside. If I could, I would have led us all the way home, to our real home, Delhi.

That night, it occurred to me that the white doves may not have belonged to Mama Biasatti at all. What if they belonged to someone from the past? What if they indeed were Om and Shanti? No, that was not possible. I had a very vivid imagination.

24.

IT WAS A WHOLE YEAR of *firsts* in this new house. As the days became longer, so did Diya's restlessness to get out of the house and play with real children who matched her in age and size. "When can I go to the park to play mama?" she would whine constantly.

"Soon," I would reply. Most days this answer would satisfy her.

We both had fallen into a summer routine. Every morning as Diya potted around our large unkept backyard with her two stuffed friends, I tried to hone my culinary skills. The television became my best friend and if I could have the TV remote set on speed dial to all the cooking shows, I would have. Then by early afternoon, I would pack some sandwiches and lemonade to take down to the edge of the lake where Diya splashed to her heart's content and returned to refuel her energy with a quick nap. Every afternoon, I battled with a choice of reading a book or cleaning a new corner of the house. I always succumbed to the easiest option: reading. I had some remorse at the end of each day for my terrible housework skills, but that guilt passed when I was able to show off my "dish of the day" at dinner time.

Summer flew by and when it came to an end, I was ready to take Diya to the neighbourhood kindergarten. Diya was very excited and took to school like a fish to water. Unlike the other children, she didn't fuss or cling. She would hug me at the school entrance and then run in at the first bell. I always felt a pang to see her go, but I was happy to start this new phase of our lives. I had hope that our past pains were going to vanish like the falling golden leaves.

Our first winter in this old house by the lake was brutal. No matter how many layers I wore, the tips of my toes were always cold. Diya and I stayed mainly indoors, except for our trips to her school and back. The icy draughts that blew in through the rickety windows made the old heating system completely ineffective. I was very thankful for our living room fireplace and Veer's ability to always have a stack of chopped logs available to keep it burning during the coldest parts of the day and night. Veer left early every day and came home in the evenings tired.

It had taken Veer a few months to establish his business and although he sometimes discussed his problems and challenges, I could tell that he was not unhappy with the progress he had made with his company. One evening, he came home in an unusually good mood.

"Maya we have closed our first quarter of the year with good overall profits. And this weekend I would like to buy you a car".

I was a little surprised at this indulgence.

"Why? What is the need Veer?"

"Diya would be starting school next year and you would need this... "

"Diya's school is not far,Veer. We can walk-"

"No, Maya, this is something I would like to do"

I wanted to continue my protests as a second car would be a significant expense, but then I thought of the mobility it would give me during the day to pursue and explore opportunities outside the home. "Well, okay then, Veer. Thank you," I said with a big smile on my face. And I saw that he too in that moment was happy.

Finally, the days started brightening up and I started getting restless once again.

And, this time, I decided that once Diya started school, I would make my trip to the neighbourhood mall for a part-time job. I knew Veer would not be happy but it was a risk that I was willing to take.

***

It was a crisp fall morning and I had kissed an excited Diya goodbye at her school's doorstep with a promise to be waiting under the grand willow tree as always. As I watched her two bouncy pigtails tied with multi-coloured pompoms disappear into the corridor, I made up my mind that today was the day that I would venture in search of a job.

I drove around the block and then parked the car in an empty mall. I realized that as a result of being cooped up in the house, I had not even bothered to buy myself some more western clothing that would help me blend in with the rest of the people here, and would also be suited for work.

I entered the quiet mall though automatic glass doors. The shops were still closed. I looked into one display window after another, examining the fashionable mannequins dressed in warm tweed coats in pumpkin shades, glamorous stoles, leather bags and purses, and sparkling pendants. When I reached the food court, I saw a middle-aged woman in a candy-striped dress cleaning the counter of an ice cream parlour. Suddenly I longed for a cool, creamy cone. I decided to give the woman a few minutes before I approached her shop, so I looked the other way. That was when I noticed a shop that seemed different from the rest of the shops in the mall. It was a fashion boutique. It had fancy bronze doors, and the mannequins in the display were draped with unstitched cloth in different weaves of earth colours.

It was open. I walked inside and while browsing through the aisles, I heard what sounded like someone hammering on a keyboard. It was the store manager. "Aarrgh ... I lost all my data! Christ!" She was talking to herself.

I was from India, the Mecca of computer geeks, and had learned a few troubleshooting tricks in school. Without hesitating, I approached the woman and said, "Let me see."

She seemed desperate for help, as she let me sit in front of her screen. She looked surprised, but also relieved. I fiddled with the general keyboard functions, and the screen showed some life. A spreadsheet popped back up. The manager started jumping with joy and gave me a high five. And, just like that, we started chatting.

"Hello, I'm Lucy." She extended her hand. "Thank you so much for your help! Have you looked around the shop? Is there something in our store that you might like?" she asked.

"Like something? I like everything!"

She laughed. "Are you looking for something special?" she asked.

"Yes, I am looking for your most fashionable clothes, something I can wear when I get a job."

She laughed even louder. "Does your job require you to wear 'fashionable' clothes? I felt foolish. Perhaps I was not able to explain properly. I had used the term fashionable because I found all the designs in this boutique very chic, whether they were meant for daily wear or not. I tried to explain again. "I need some appropriate clothes so that I can go to job interviews and be suitably dressed."

"Yes, of course." She was still laughing and studying me closely. Something about me amused her. I did not particularly like being laughed at, so I thanked her and started walking out.

I heard her voice again: "Would you like to work here?" I stopped and turned around to face her. I did not expect that. My heart cried "yes!" but my head stood its ground.

"To do what exactly? To fix computer glitches?" I asked as politely as I could.

"No, no. I am looking for someone to work here, someone who is able to cover some shifts when I have to run to the other store locations. I haven't advertised the position yet, but, if you agree, I won't have to. We pay a reasonable hourly rate, and we offer merchandise from our store as a commission on sales. Our clothing, you must know, is among the best in the country."

I did not know what to say. I was looking for a job, but I hadn't expected anything like this.

"Okay, let me go to the ice cream parlour first." She did not even pretend to hide her laughter. She burst into a roar. I could not understand why.

The ice cream lady in candy stripes smiled as she piled an extra dollop of chocolate over vanilla. As the sugar hit my blood, my mind cleared up a little. So, a job was falling into my lap, and it was near the house. But I would have to be there for Diya and how would I handle Veer?

After five minutes of licking my cone, I made my decision. I walked back, and she smiled knowingly. "So, you could not resist? You will take it?"

"Well, only if you agree to let me go in the afternoon to pick up my daughter from her school."

She chuckled. "Do you always dictate terms to your employers?"

"Well, frankly, you are my first." This time it was my turn to smile. I saw her jaw drop.

I completed the paperwork, and confirmed the start time for the next day.

It was a different Maya who walked out of the mall. I had a spring in my step, and a tune on my lips. The truth was that she had me at the offer of a "merchandise bonus." That appealed to me. I decided to start small and work for fun. I promised myself not to get dependent on the puny money that came in, although I already knew that promise would be difficult to keep.

***

Over dinner, I told Veer about Lucy's job offer. "Will you take it?" was all that he asked.

"Yes, I would like to. It will not affect our routine, and I will only go during the day when Diya is in school."

He picked up his dinner plate and loaded it in the dishwasher. Then he went to his room and shut the door for the night.

The next morning, after waving goodbye to Diya, I arrived to find Lucy waiting anxiously at the door.

"Hello, Maya, I was afraid that you wouldn't come. I'm so happy to see you!"

"Hello, Lucy."

"I have called Brenda from our other location for your orientation. I have to run to a meeting at our head office. Our Annual Fashion Show date has just been announced. I will bring back more news soon." She said all this in one breath and ran out of the door.

Brenda was in her late thirties, with kind brown eyes and auburn hair. Her tall tan boots matched her leather jacket that she was wearing over a lacy fawn-coloured shirt and brown, pencil-thin skirt. She was stylish and efficient. Her tone was soothing, and she had a lot of patience with my practise repetitions behind the cash register. The hours slipped by, and before I left I visited the chirpy candy-striped ice cream lady to pick up a tub of caramel praline for Diya.

That night over dinner Veer did not ask, nor did I volunteer, to tell him about my day. He had decided to disengage with anything about my life that he did not like, and I was grateful that he had found a way of coping with it, however temporary. But Veer was irritable. He snapped at me for his dinner being too hot. I could feel a storm brewing. That night before I went to sleep, I closed my eyes, folded my hands, and prayed.

25.

A ROUTINE DID WONDERS for my anxiety. As the novelty of the new schedule wore off, so did its associated nervousness. Work gave me something to look forward to.

But Veer had become withdrawn and quiet. The more I tried talking to him, the more he lashed out about something or other, but he never addressed the elephant in the room. I was not doing anything wrong and I could not understand Veer's need to control and possess every minute of my life.

Every night I stroked Diya's hair and sang to her. She sang with me, and she sang beautifully. After all, music was in her genes. "What's wrong, Mama?" she asked one night, her hand pressing mine.

It was uncanny how children always knew. Every night I prayed for a better dawn, and some nights I drew solace from the cold seams of the stone bench under the angel statue. On many of those nights, I heard the wind laughing and sometimes whimpering. But I was not afraid of the wind anymore. I was not afraid of anything.

I simply didn't know how to answer Diya's question and it pained me to think that she might be worried or afraid. I'd tried my best to reassure her that everything was fine.

As the months went by, Lucy had started entrusting me with more work. Then one day when I arrived at work, she was waiting at the door. "Maya, have you ever been involved in a fashion show?"

My pulse quickened as I shook my head.

"Well, get ready then. William, our Production Director, is here from head office to orient you and other staff on our upcoming show next month. For the next few days, he will be with us to go over every detail."

With that, she left for her daily site visit to the other showrooms across town. I returned behind the cash register and I was so engrossed in what I was doing that I did not notice someone standing behind me.

"Hello, Maya." It was a deep and soothing voice.

I was startled and turned around abruptly. I found myself staring into the bluest eyes I had ever seen.

"Hello, I am William." He extended his hand. His grip was warm and firm, his smile radiant.

"Hello, William."

William was a tall, well-groomed man, almost debonair. He reminded me of Cary Grant in *An Affair to Remember*, except that he was a modern version. He was wearing a beige Polo shirt under a well-fitted blue suit jacket, over crisp blue-jeans, a blend of formal and casual. He had a lean jawline with an attractive cleft. His hair, a golden brown, was combed to the side, showing his widow's peak. There was an unmistakeable athletic grace and sophistication about him.

Behind him was his young blonde assistant, attentive to his every word and radiating with a glow that only youth brings. She had a peaches and cream complexion, and her golden hair cascaded from her high forehead to the nape of her neck.

They were both so beautiful.

He was still holding my hand. I pulled it back, gently. His blue eyes were spellbinding, and he was staring at me without blinking. I looked away quickly.

"And this is Samantha." We shook hands too. Her handshake was soft, brief, and supple.

Then William dove straight into work talk. Samantha pulled out the blueprints of the stage set up, and William started explaining each detail with the marked precision of someone who had been doing this for a long time and was very good at it.

That night, over dinner, I told Veer about the upcoming fashion show and how I might be asked to work some extra hours. For a moment, he seemed to have stopped breathing and he did not lift his head up from his plate. With the hope of appeasing him, I rattled on. "Veer, you don't need to worry about anything. I have it all figured out. I have arranged with Norma, the woman who lives a few houses down, to babysit while I am away. And I will always be back in time to make dinner." He still did not stir. I also wanted to tell him about William, Samantha, and all the other exciting things that were happening at work, but thought I would save it for another day, when he felt like my friend again. I was waiting anxiously for the day when I could share my life with him again. For now, it seemed we both were living in different worlds.

26.

THE PAST MONTHS HAD BEEN nothing but a countdown for today, the day of the fashion show. The auditorium was booming with amazing acoustics, fashion critics had been pampered and ushered to their centre seats, and the rest of the spaces were filled with event managers, casting directors, and staff from stores and boutiques across the province. The front rows were reserved for international guests and the press.

As I sat backstage in the shadows of the wings, I was captivated with the fashion models. Their tall immaculate lines, slender grace and seductive gait, their perfectly matched hairdos and makeup. The angled lighting further accentuated each dimension of their flawless figures.

William was sitting in front, taking notes and talking into Samantha's ear, making her chuckle repeatedly. I enjoyed looking at William and Samantha. They made me curious. They sparked my imagination about a world that was free and easy, so different from mine, a restricted world in which I felt I was always trespassing.

I was thrilled to have gotten one of the best jobs a stage-shy girl in a fashion show can ask for: to assist one of the models, Rosita.

Each of the staff members had been given one free ticket to invite a friend or family member. I, of course, had invited Veer. He had not refused, he had not shouted, he had just replied with his silence. So I had left the ticket near his wallet that afternoon before walking out the door.

The music started and the curtains lifted. After a few announcements in English and French, the show began with loud applause.

I was in the dressing room helping Rosita with last-minute touches. She was to walk in about twenty minutes. She was displaying the "Northern Weave"—the celebrated showstopper of the show. But just as I unstrapped her bolero, she flinched.

"I need to go to the washroom. I won't be long..." she said and bolted for the door.

Five minutes led to ten, and Rosita had not come out. I started fidgeting. I walked to the washroom and knocked gently on her door. I heard sniffles. "Rosita ... are you okay?"

"No," came the flat answer.

"What is the matter, Rosita?"

"I can't tell you. Can you call someone? *Please* ...?"

I panicked and ran into the adjoining dark corridor, which led to a brightly-lit room at the other end. Inside, Lucy was talking to William, but she stopped as soon as she saw the look on my face. They both ran back to knock on Rosita's washroom door. The door opened slightly and Lucy was let in, leaving me waiting uneasily with William. When Lucy came out, her face was beetroot red with worry.

"I am afraid that Rosita is sick ... some kind of a stomach bug. She will not be able to walk tonight."

"What?" William exclaimed. "She's supposed to model the best outfit in the show!"

"I know!" Lucy shouted and then said, "Well, do we have any backups?"

"No."

William was pacing with one hand over his forehead, thinking.

"What are we to do Bill?" Lucy asked, the worry in her voice palpable.

"Don't worry Lucy, I will figure something out," William replied, still pacing.

As I sank quietly on the corner couch watching William, I realized then that in the midst of this he was consoling Lucy and trying to find a solution. The power of those two words, "Don't worry," sank in. They built a bridge between all who were facing this crisis. I had not heard those words from Veer ever since we had arrived, although we both shared the same circumstance of trying to settle in a new world. I realized it didn't have to be this way. Why couldn't we share our pain and our dilemmas? Why was something so simple so difficult to do? When I turned to look at William, he had already come up with a solution.

"We will make an announcement and place Rosita's walk at the end of the show. I will have Nicole pulled out of the line up to replace Rosita. Altering the outfit to her size won't take long for Louis as they are almost the same size, and then Jon will have forty-five minutes to coach her. He had said this without stopping to breathe. I admired William's creativity and resilience. It had taken him less than ten minutes to come out on top.

"Okay William, I trust your judgement. Let's do it!" I could feel how emotionally exhausted and desperate Lucy was.

I was not sure if my services were needed anymore since Rosita was no longer in the line up. I picked up my bag and started looking for a paper to write an exit note. It was time for me to return home and face my crisis there. If wished I could borrow some of William's ingenuity on how to come out strong in tough situations

A petite, somewhat effeminate man entered the room. He was sporting a Salvador Dali moustache, a big bottle of frothing Dom Perignon Champagne, five crystal glasses on a tray, and a broad smile.

"Hey, Jon!" William waved to him.

I didn't know where Lucy had disappeared to, so I turned to face William. "I don't suppose I am needed now, so I would like to go."

William walked towards me and placed his hands on my shoulders. "Of course, you are needed, Maya." His tone was so warm.

I could smell his cologne. "But Rosita is no longer in the line-up," I stuttered.

"Yes, but I need you ... I mean, I need you for Nicole'.

"Of course," I nodded,

Jon offered me a glass of champagne. "Take a sip. This is to calm us all." Jon wore black-and-white striped pants that deliberately wedged every curve of his shapely legs and a crimson beret. His smile was genial and kind, and I gladly accepted the glass he had handed me.

Just then Nicole had walked in. She was a little frazzled. Jon didn't waste any time. He chuckled in a high pitch and snapped the tips of his fingers as he walked over to her. "Chop, chop. We don't have all day. Imagine you are a trapeze artist walking on a synthetic string some twenty feet above the ground. Now imagine you have a glass of water on your head. And now you are walking that line..."

The next fifteen minutes flew by. Jon and I helped Nicole into her outfit that fit her like a second skin. William and I walked her to the stage wings.

"Nicole, anytime now the emcee will announce your piece. That is your cue. Think of yourself walking into the night with no one watching you, as though you are going for a swim in a deserted lake with only your bathing suit on."

I wondered if I would ever be able to walk through life with no one watching and living in any way that I wanted to live? Like William did. I looked up to see William smiling. He was obviously happy with his last-minute solution. With one hand in his trouser pocket, he extended his other over my shoulder. I did not pull away. "Well Maya? Are you having fun?"

I looked back at him and smiled. Quite unexpectedly, I had had fun tonight.

There was a resounding applause that filled the auditorium,

and then the curtain fell. An army of models were already lined up, ready to make their closing curtain call. William and Nicole joined the back of the line, and, then they all walked on to the runway to take a bow.

It was over. The models were rushing to get some cocktails and go to the press shoots in the lounge, but I just wanted to get out of there. I kept thinking about Diya. I quickly changed back into my cardigan and slacks and picked up my handbag to head out. As I was leaving my dressing room, I heard a familiar voice call my name.

It was a voice that I had not expected to hear this evening.

Veer! He was standing there in his loafers and faded jeans, a blue-and-white checked shirt tucked neatly into his pants. I ran into his arms. But I did not feel his arms wrapping around me. I felt cold. Then I looked up to see his face. His brows were drawn, the nerve on his forehead throbbed. "So this is what you do here? This is your new job?" he spat out. I was taken aback by his anger.

"What do you mean?"

"Don't pretend, Maya, I saw you standing there in the dark with that man."

"So Veer?"

"So, Maya? He had his arms around you!"

"No, it is not what it seems..." I tried in vain to explain.

He walked out before I could finish. I ran after him, fury surging inside me. He was already in the car. I managed to climb in before he pulled away from the street, He drove straight to our house and we did not exhange a word the entire way.

We entered a dark house. Diya was asleep. I paid Norma the babysitter and went to kiss Diya's forehead. As I was coming out of her room, the phone rang. Who could be calling this late at night?

"Hello?" There was a pause.

Then a familiar, displeased voice said, "Hello."

"Hello, Mom! How are you?" I said to Veer's mother.

"I am okay. Is Veer there?"

"Yes, he is. One moment, please." I ran to Veer and handed over the receiver. "It's your mother!"

He took the receiver and walked away from me. I finished eating my sandwich in the kitchen and took one to the living room for Veer. He was cupping the speaker with his palm and whispering into it. I caught a fleeting line, "... And then I saw her backstage in the dark with a tall, blond man. She is one of them now."

What was Veer doing? Was he talking about me to his mother? Is that what her phone call was all about?

Veer had turned me into an outcast. I had not listened to him; I had not allowed myself to be trapped in this house day in and day out. He did not care if I did not have any friends or family in this new country; he did not care how I was to survive within these walls, as long as I did not go outside them. I had no right to jump at the opportunities life was presenting to me. I had adapted more quickly to this new land than I should have, than he had. And now I was to be punished.

I felt dizzy. My head started throbbing. My eyes burnt from falling tears, and my whole body ached from exhaustion. I felt something new and different, something that had not visited me before. It was a feeling of betrayal. I was being betrayed by Veer, not for another woman, but for the woman I had been in the past.

I got up and threw Veer's sandwich in the garbage. As I entered the kitchen, I heard Veer call out, "Where is my sandwich?"

"I threw it out," I replied, wiping my tears.

"Why?"

"Because you don't like my sandwiches." Another tear fell.

"I'm hungry."

"I don't care, Veer."

It came out harsher than I wanted it to. I followed him to the living room couch. He collapsed on to it. In the shadow of the lamp, his crouched figure looked even bigger than his already large physique. Why did I see Veer as a little boy trapped in a big body who needed help to escape the darkness inside him? Why was I cursed with this empathy for Veer when the easier thing to do was walk away?

I forgot my hurt and anger. I ran toward him without thinking. I put my hands in his. His palms were damp, and I realized then that maybe he had also been crying. Or maybe they were my tears on his hands. I could not tell them apart.

"Veer, we both are just trying to keep our heads up in this new country. We are in a different world now. But I don't want to live in a different world with you while under the same roof. I know we have not found our way yet, but we will soon. Whether that way leads us deeper into Canada or back to India only time will tell."

With that, I left him to go up to our room, which faced the lake. A harsh screeching wind thrashed our rickety shutters open. I went to close them and glanced out at the garden. The stone angel was looking up to the sky as rain slashed down in sheets over his eyes, becoming tears. I latched the window tightly and lay down on a cold pillow. I did not know what tomorrow held. But I did know that tomorrow I would be applying for a new job.

27.

"VEER, I HAVE DECIDED to leave my job." He lifted his head from the newspaper and stopped chewing his breakfast.

"Oh, really?" I expected this sarcastic reaction.

"Yes, really."

"What will you do then? Won't staying at home stifle you?" I hated his sarcasm.

"I was hoping that I could help you out in the office. That way I can be flexible with my day as well." He dropped his head back into the folds of the newpaper and did not say anything.

"Veer?"

"No, Maya. That is not possible."

"Well, why not?"

"Because I already have someone helping me." That was an answer I had not expected.

"Who?"

"Her name is Suzy." He picked up his bowl of cereal and left the kitchen.

I stared at the wall for some time. What had just happened? Did Veer say that I was not welcome in his life outside the house? And who was this Suzy? Livid, I followed him out to the deck. "Who is Suzy?"

"She is my secretary. Mummy referred her as a trustworthy person, the daughter of one of her friends."

His mother. Of course she had. Visions of the oily Gautam

flashed before my eyes, another trustworthy referral from the same source. I wanted to ask him why I could not come to help, with or without Suzy in his office. But instead I swallowed my pride and decided to go back to Lucy's job.

When I arrived, Brenda excitedly took me to the back room and gave me a card with my name written on it. I opened it slowly, guessing who it might be from. It was dated and signed, *To the tiniest pistol backstage. Thanks for deciding to stay on, William.*

That afternoon after work, I decided to walk to pick up Diya from school. The cool air brushed against my cheeks and cleared my mind. I felt better. In spite of our differences, I had faith that Veer loved me and no one could come between us.

Diya had not yet returned from her school field trip to the eco-camp in High Park, so I waited in the school corridor, looking at the broad tree-lined street outside. The door opened, and a skinny, blonde woman in tight sweatpants and an equally tight T-shirt walked in. Her green eyes were kind, and she smiled at me. "Hello, I'm Jill. My daughter Bella is in the same class as your daughter."

I wondered how she knew who my daughter was. Then I realized that Diya was probably the only brown girl in her class.

"Hello, I am Maya." We shook hands. She took a seat next to me but did not gaze out of the window.

"So where do you live, Maya?"

"Oh, just a few blocks away on Frazer Street."

"That is a beautiful street. Have you lived there long?"

"A few years. We came from New Delhi ... you know ... the capital of India." Her eyes lit up with interest.

"Well then, how do you like Canada?"

"I am still getting used to it. It is a lonely life."

"No, of course, you wouldn't like it here. In the city, I mean. If you really want to get to know Canada, then you need to go to the countryside." I listened intently as she continued. "My mother lives on a fifty-six-acre farm northeast of here, just a four-hour drive. We are going there for Easter. Why don't you join us?"

I found this very strange. I did not even know this woman, and she was already inviting us to join her for Easter.

Just then the school bus pulled into the driveway, which gave me an excuse not to answer her question. Diya jumped out, red-faced and sulky. I knew something was the matter instantly. I gathered her quickly and started for home. Once on the sidewalk, I heard someone beep from behind. It was Jill.

She opened her car door and said, "Come on, pop in! I will drop you." Before I could stop her, Diya instantly slipped into the back seat next to Bella.

"Well, thank you, this is kind of you." I got in the car and closed the door. The car jerked and then screeched forward.

"Before dropping you, I just have to make a quick stop home to pick up my grocery list. I forgot it on my fridge door." At once I regretted getting into the car with her.

Jill's house was large, in a spacious green neighbourhood. "Would you like to come in?"

"No, I am sorry, we have to get going...."

"Okay, then, no problem."

The children were already running toward the open side door, which lead to what looked like a large backyard. For the sake of their smiling faces, I dragged myself inside. Jill had a pot of tea going by the time I reached her kitchen.

"No, please don't bother with tea. I really have to be going." I went to call Diya. She was climbing a tree fort and then diving down into the sand box. "Come on, Diya. We have to go now!"

"Noooo, just five minutes, Mama!" she pleaded.

Jill was standing behind me with two mugs of steaming black tea. I gave in and thanked her. We sat on her deck under the chirping evening birds.

"So what do you do for a living?" she asked as we settled down. I had long ago understood that in this country, one's job defined their identity.

"I work part-time in a fashion boutique in the mall

"Oh, that must be so exciting. More exciting than massaging clients the whole day."

"Massaging?"

"I am a massage therapist, and my husband works on the Ford Motor's assembly line. We are blessed for his steady factory job and salary. They have good worker compensation you know."

What an equalizing country, I thought. Even blue-collar workers lived in luxury. We chatted about school and the children. And then she wanted to know about me, about us, our life in India. It was such an unexpected and pleasant evening.

Before dropping us home, Jill mentioned her mother's farm again. "Well, please think about it," she said. "Maybe you all can drive down with us some time?'

"Yes, Jill, thank you, I shall think about it."

Finally, I was back to the only place I wanted to be: my home.

***

We returned to a dark and cold house. Veer had not returned yet. But I no longer expected him to return so soon. He had expanded his business since we had arrived, and that meant long work hours. Still, my heart hoped and longed to spend some time with him after our fight that morning.

Diya switched on every lamp in the house on the way to her room. I heated some butternut squash soup, sweet potatoes, and roast duck, and laid out three mats, one candle, and the wine decanter on the table. I tossed Diya's favourite Caesar salad with extra croutons and parmesan. And then we waited.

At eight, when there was still no sign of Veer, Diya emerged from her room. "Mama I'm hungry."

"Yes, why don't you eat. You have a long day tomorrow."

"Won't you eat, Mama?"

"No, I will wait for Papa."

With that, Diya devoured her dinner and excused herself

from the table. Within an hour, she was asleep. I tucked her in with an extra blanket and closed her window to keep the room warm. Then I settled on the settee in the living room in front of the TV. The phone rang, and I jumped. It had to be Veer, so I ran to pick it up.

"Maya!" Her sweet voice filled the room and beyond. It was Ma from India. "We miss you so much. Our house is so quiet now." I could taste the salt from my tears on my lips.

"I miss you too, Ma."

"How is our little granddaughter?"

"Diya is growing up fast. It is a school night so she is sound asleep. Although she is not even in second grade yet, Diya might be placed in a special music program in elementary school. "

"Send us lots of pictures, Maya. And how is Veer? Papa and I would like to say hello to him as well."

"Oh, Veer is still at work," I said. "He has to work long days because of the expanding business."

She cut me short: "What's wrong, Maya?" Ma could always tell when things were not right.

"Nothing's wrong, Ma. All is well," I lied.

"Are you sure?"

"Yes, I'm sure, Ma."

"Maya, we called to tell you that our renovations went well and now we have decided to move to our cottage in Kasauli permanently. The commute to the hills each time has become very strenuous, and we think it is best that we stay in one place now.

"That sounds wonderful."

"Come to visit us soon with Veer and Diya. It is not the same without you. "

"Yes, Ma. I will some soon. How is Anita?"

"She and Ajay have moved to Darjeeling—I think the hills of *Mim* tea estate—for their next posting."

Everyone I loved in India seemed to be happy and at peace. I could not help but wonder how our life would have been if we had not left. It was almost midnight now. I dragged a blanket from our bedroom and spread it over my legs. I didn't remember when I fell asleep, but I was woken by the sound of our front yard gate opening with its usual squeal.

I ran to the French window and peered through the curtain. A car had stopped outside our gate. It was not Veer's car, but it was Veer's silhouette that got out of it. Whose car was it? My question was answered the next minute. A softer outline, that of a woman, came out from the driver's side. She moved toward Veer, who was gripping onto the car door for support. She placed a shoulder under his arm, and then they started walking to the door.

Before they could reach the doorbell, I flung open the door. I switched on the porch light to get a better look at the woman with my husband. She was a tall and well-built Indian woman with wiry shoulder-length hair and a very large chest. She had a wide red-lipsticked mouth and large brown eyes under short heavily mascaraed lashes and pencil-thin eyebrows. Her entire appearance was that of a very measured and planned person.

She was still propping Veer up, who seemed to be swaying horizontally.

I stepped forward and said, "Thank you for bringing him home. I will take it from here." She reluctantly handed him over, and we hobbled inside. He was reeking of alcohol. I turned around to look at the woman one last time. "Hello, I am Maya. I am his wife."

"I am Suzy. He and I work closely together." What an interesting choice of words, I thought.

"Thank you again," I said, shutting the door while she was still standing there and staring at me without blinking.

Veer laid down under my blanket on the living room settee. I switched off the TV, blew out our dinner candle, and left the sorry remains of our cold dinner on the table. Today, for the first time, I doubted Veer's will power. For many dark hours,

I found solace on the cold bench under the angel's wings and I welcomed the mocking wind that rose from the lake and threatened to take me with it.

28.

I DID NOT FUNCTION WELL the next morning. I stared at our roof beams over our bed for many hours after waking up. Thankfully, it was the weekend and I did not have to drop Diya or go to work. I could hear her singing in her room. Veer's pillow was still untouched. I was angry.

When I crawled out of bed and made my way to the kitchen, I saw from the window that Veer was sitting under the stone angel feeding the birds. The white doves were not there.

"Veer!" I called as I walked out onto the deck. He looked up at me and then looked down at the ground again. Barefoot, I waded through the grass and sat next to him. And then he surprised me.

"I am sorry, Maya." He said it in a soft voice, not a tone that I could snap a retort to.

"Sorry?"

"Yes, Maya. I am sorry for dragging you here, and I am sorry for my behaviour. I really don't know what comes over me. I get these frenzies in my head, these voices, dark untrusting thoughts ... and then I cannot control myself."

I felt his pain, his helplessness.

The wind suddenly picked up from nowhere. It blew in from the lake, crisp and bitter. In a flash, I understood what was happening. Gayati's story flashed before my eyes. I remembered her narrative about Veer's grandfather's behaviour. Veer had to know. I had to share the secret. Maybe then he would understand why these voices started in his head.

"Veer, do you know about your grandfather?" A dark shadow crossed his face.

"Yes, Mummy told me."

"Well, what did she tell you?"

"Only that he was cheated by his wife who was beautiful, and cruel." I gasped. How menacing and damaging was his mother's interpretation of events.

"No. No, Veer. You have it all wrong. You see, I know about her. This is not the truth."

Veer was looking at me strangely. "How do *you* know?"

"I found her diary."

"Her what?"

"Your grandmother used to write in a journal every day. It will make you understand her tragic life, her passion, her pain, her joy. No Veer, she was not cruel."

"Maya, you have gone mad. You are always meddling in things that do not concern you."

"But you see, it *does* concern us, in ways that are deep and disturbing."

"What do you mean?"

"She writes about how your grandfather had the same voices in his head that made him want to control her, hurt her. So now that we know, we can find a cure. We can cure you." I was breathless with a child's excitement who has just divulged something important.

Veer became completely still. "And where is this diary?" he finally asked.

"Wait here." I ran in to fetch the book.

When I returned, he had not moved. He was still staring at the same ground near his feet, and the vein in his forehead was throbbing furiously.

"Here. See." I handed him the diary.

"So you brought this here, into our new life, into our new home?" I was taken aback by his superstition. This had crossed my mind too, but when Veer put it so directly there was no escaping what I had done.

He opened it and something fell out. I should have hidden the photo. How silly of me.

He instantly picked it up, and his eyes gave him away. They became alert and enlarged. His body stiffened. I tried to take the photo back from his hand, but he stood up. He was so much taller than me, and I could not reach it anymore.

"Who is this? She looks a lot like you."

"You should know."

"Why?"

"Because I was told this was your grandmother."

He sat down slowly, gravely. His back was as straight as a stick, and sweat gathered on his temples. Nervously I started flipping the pages, and something else fell out. Something that I had forgotten about. Something more auspicious and bright. A short peacock feather. A token from Sheila on our last day. I suddenly remembered that I promised I would return it to her as an assurance of our happiness. A salty, sneaky tear edged out of the side of my eye and rolled down my cheek. I wanted things to change, to be different, so that I could go and tell Sheila how happy we were after escaping the walls of the mansion.

"Veer, look at this." I showed him the feather

"Veer, does it not remind you of warm nights in our peacock garden over a shimmering lotus pond?"

He did not answer, but sat silently with the photograph clenched in his fist.

I tried to explain my resemblance to Gayatri, from what I had understood.

"Oh, that is a mere coincidence. My mother was from the same town of Peshawar as your grandmother. So we carry the same ethnic semblance of the North West, it happens a lot in the world you know..."

Veer didn't respond, but I sensed then that Veer knew more

about his grandparents than he admitted to me.

"No, it doesn't." Veer's voice was shaky. He started moving towards the house.

"Veer!" I called out. He turned around, his eyes red.

"Don't you see what is happening here, Maya?"

"What?"

"*We are them.* We are trapped in their misfortune. We cannot escape it wherever we go.... We are doomed together."

I sat on the cold bench, barefoot and shaken. For a long time. Veer was going mad and he was pulling me with him in a downward spiral. Something inside me didn't agree with Veer. It was a stubborn compulsiveness that believed in a better day. It was hope.

***

At eight when the doorbell rang, I thought Veer had returned from work. Instead, I opened the door to a face that I never wished to see.

"Oho, hello, hello, Maya ji. How are you?" It was Gautam. He had eyeliner around his eyes and the stench of his hair oil was making me queasy.

"Veer is not here. Please come another time."

"What is the hurry, my dear, eh? I mean, I know that Veer is not here. Don't you want to ask me how I know?" I pressed my lips tight. "Okay, dear girl, I will tell you. I visited him at the office. You see he wants to buy another business property, and..." I knew more was coming. And it was not pleasant. "Well, well, so we signed the papers today. Wait, did he not tell you? Ohoo, then maybe he forgot in all the celebrations in the office."

"What celebrations?"

"Now I am speaking out of place, Maya ji. That new exciting Suzy had a big cake, music, and drinks.... You not invited?"

I tried to hide my emotions but I could no longer keep up the facade. I did not care if I broke down. Before I knew it,

Gautam was sitting next to me on the couch with one hand on my back and another slowly edging to my thigh. Diya walked in. Gautam looked up at her slowly.

"Oho, so who is this beauty?"

And just like that my spell was broken. What was I doing? In my weakness, I had let my guard down? How was this lecherous man sitting next to us in our home?

I stood up.

"Please leave right now."

He was shocked at my sudden rudeness. But he sensed his limits. "You will regret this. No wonder Rani aunty says you are a witch. Now I know...."

I shut the door and locked it. Diya held me for a long time. She knew not to ask questions, questions that only would only lead to more hurt. She was perceptive and far wiser than her years.

Eventually she went back to her practising. In the midst of her high notes I did not hear the phone ring. When she stopped abruptly, I finally heard it and ran to pick it up, thinking it might be Veer.

"Gosh, Maya, I have been trying to call you forever."

"William! Hello..."

"Is this a good time?"

"Yes, yes. Is everything okay?"

"Well, I wanted to talk to you about an Eastern line of apparel that we have started developing."

"No, William, I can not model for you."

He laughed warmly. "I know I cannot be that lucky! " There was an ease about talking to William. "I wanted to ask you something else, though I haven't worked out all the details yet. But, I would like you to be involved in this project."

"What do you mean?"

"I mean, I would like you to work with me in a small team and I will personally train you over the months to choose and develop the merchandise."

"You mean like an apprentice?"

"Do you really have to call it that, Maya? All I need is your willingness to learn and time."

"Why me, William? Surely you have an abundance of trained personnel at your disposal?"

"Yes. But when I am building a team and starting a new line, then I need people whom I have worked with and I can trust."

"William, you know I have a daughter to pick up after school and look after when she gets home?"

"Yes, I do. Whatever she does at home, we can set up a space for her here. Who knows, this exposure may just spark something in her."

"You really have thought of everything." I was familiar with William's persistence when he wanted something.

"No, not everything, Maya."

"What do you mean?"

"You did not mention your husband. From what I heard, he was not too happy the last time I caught a glimpse of him."

I was quiet. Gossip travelled fast. It was an awkward moment between us. And William bridged it with ease. "Just say yes."

I was quiet.

"Maya?"

"Yes, William, I will work with you."

"You have made me a very happy man. Thank you."

And I did not feel like crying anymore. I wanted to thank him too, but I decided not to.

29.

VEER DIDN'T COME HOME that night. The next morning we went about our routine as if nothing was amiss. When we returned that evening the phone light was flashing with messages.

"Hello, Mrs. Rajas ...sa...nia. This is Mrs. Hodge from Wellsworth school. Please call me back at this number. It is regarding your daughter, Diya."

Diya was standing behind me. She had heard the message. "Mama, I don't like Mrs. Hodge. Please don't call her...."

"Why don't you go and change. I will warm up dinner, and then we can talk."

I switched on the burner and heated up some fried chicken from the other night. This time I laid only two plates at the table. Then I dialled the number. "Hello, this is Maya, Diya's mother. I believe you wanted to speak to me."

"Oh yes. I am glad you called me. I wanted to tell you before it got worse. You see it is a matter that we don't take lightly in this country."

My heart started beating faster. "What happened?"

"This morning, at recess, I caught your daughter Diya bullying another child—a boy, Chris."

"Bullying?"

"Yes, bullying."

"She had grabbed Chris by his collar and was saying something to him which frightened Chris."

"Well, I am sorry to hear that, Mrs. Hodge. Did you find out what the reason was? It is not in Diya's nature to do this kind of a thing."

"What is there to find out? Being caught in the act of bullying speaks for itself."

"There must have been a reason, Mrs. Hodge. I apologize on her behalf. I will talk to her tonight."

"You see, Mrs. Raaas ... ania, when people come to our country, they bring with them certain values and customs that are 'un-Canadian.' They will try to spread them around if we don't nip such practices in the bud."

I immediately resented the patronizing undertone and the negativity of the past few days finally descended on me. "I am sorry but I don't quite understand you. What are you saying? Are you implying that I am teaching Diya to bully? And how would you define people like us? How do you define 'un-Canadian'?"

She was taken aback by my outspokenness and it took her a moment to answer. She retreated. "Well, well. It is in the principal's hands now. I will let her know tomorrow that I had counselled you with, as I had expected, not much success."

I sat down at the table. Was this all my fault? Was I responsible for Diya's pent up anger, which led her to bullying other children simply because I did not agree to all that Veer wanted in our relationship? Was this the price I had to pay to stand on my own feet? No. If Diya was affected by the troubles between us, it did not matter whose fault it was, or what the reason was. It simply had to stop.

The next morning, Diya and I set out early for school. I decided to walk in the falling snow, with bulky snow boots, jackets, hats, mitts, knapsack and all. "Diya, I am going to meet your principal. If someone has been bad then that person will be punished, so tell me what happened," I prodded gently.

"I don't want to," came Diya's answer.

"Well, then you will be punished, but not by me."

"I don't care." I knew she was telling the truth. She really didn't care.

"Diya!"

"I was just scaring Chris, and then Mrs. Hodge came and heard what I was saying to Chris. She was very angry with me.."

"Why were you scaring Chris, Diya?" We had stopped walking.

"Chris was saying rude things...."

"Like what?"

"He called me a liar and told me to go back to where we came from, back to India."

My heart was breaking. But I needed to hear the whole story. "Why was Chris calling you a liar?"

"'Cause I lied to Mrs. Hodge."

"Why?"

"Because Mrs. Hodge would not let me skate on ice. Bella and I both forgot our skates, but she gave Bella another pair. When I asked, she said, '*No.*' There were many spare skates on the shelf, so I picked up a pair and told her that they were mine." Diya's face was red, her fists clenched.

"Diya did Mrs. Hodge hear what Chris said to you?"

Diya nodded with her head bent. "When Chris said those things to me, Mrs. Hodge was standing behind him."

Now I was furious, both at Mrs. Hodge and at Diya. We had almost reached the school compound. Diya kissed me goodbye and ran off in the direction of her class.

The principal was already in her office. She was a large, handsome woman with thick chestnut hair tied tightly in a knot at the nape of her neck. She reminded me of a very efficient matron, but with the tenderness of a grandmother. I found myself drawn to her immediately. She got up and closed the door. "I have sent for Diya from her class, but before we talk to her I wanted to chat with you for a bit." She paused and smiled at me again. I wanted to believe that she liked me. But I had to confront her about what had transpired, even at the cost of my supposed popularity with her.

"So, Mrs. Raajaa..."

"Call me Maya."

"Call me Mrs. Lucas."

"So Maya, how long have you been in Canada?" That was not a question I was expecting from her.

"Not long enough." Her face betrayed her. I think she picked up on my sarcasm. "And does it really matter how long I've been here? The real issue is how long does it take one to be accepted?" I stopped talking. I sounded bitter even to myself.

Mrs. Lucas was smiling. "Mrs. Hodge briefed me about what happened in the school yard between Diya and Chris and then her subsequent conversation with you last evening."

I told her everything Diya had said to me earlier. "Is Diya in trouble?" I asked.

She took a deep breath before answering. "Yes, Diya will be punished and counselled for this act, just to ensure that she makes better choices in similar situations in the future. But Chris will be punished too for his hateful and inflammatory remarks to Diya. We will ensure that Diya learns the importance of telling the truth and continues to stand up for herself in difficult times, but using other more peaceful ways."

I was right about the principal. She was effective, wise, and kind. And whatever trust I had lost overnight in the Canadian education system was restored that very minute.

There was still one matter remaining, that of Mrs. Hodge's comments to me. I knew I had to address this. So, I added, "Don't give my child special treatment, Mrs. Lucas, but don't discriminate either. Is that too much to ask for? I know you as educators deal with a lot, but remember not to place everyone in the same stereotypical boxes by calling them 'un-Canadian' as Mrs. Hodge did with me."

"Yes, I will have to have a word with Mrs. Hodge as well," she nodded. "I am glad you were able to speak your mind Maya."

"I have been accused of doing worse!" We laughed.

"Well Maya," she continued, "Diya is special. As you know that she is being considered for placement in a special music program. Well, I have some good news. She was auditioned by our music teacher and she is now slated to join our elementary school choir. In her next school year, she will be ready to attend a special session in our downtown rehearsal hall to give her first her 'grown-up'expreience."

My heart filled with joy.

Just then the door opened and Diya walked in, followed by Mrs. Hodge. The principal took her aside and started speaking to her in a soft voice. I saw her nodding, and Diya's face was no longer angry.

Spontaneously, I asked, "Mrs. Lucas, it has been a few rough days for us at home. Would you allow me to take Diya back home with me?. I would also like to talk to her while this issue is still fresh in her mind."

I saw the principal hesitate at first. But then she finally said, "Yes, you may. Enjoy the day"

And, just like that, the two of us walked out the same way we had walked in an hour ago. Except, something was different now. A weight had been lifted. On our way out, we saw a small red-haired boy and his mother sitting on the edge of the same couch that I had occupied in the waiting room. I smiled at the mother, who looked away angrily.

The morning air was still fresh on our way back. I was happy to have gained this one unplanned day from our lives to live.

As Diya opened the front gate, she shouted with joy: "Mama, Papa is back!"

***

I did not want to see Veer. We had been managing without him. Why had he come back now? Where had he been for two days? Who had he been with?

I walked into the house, hung up my jacket, and avoided the kitchen and living room. The morning sun was surprisingly warm through our bedroom window. I called my work to inform them that I was taking some time off, and then I stepped into a hot shower to let the tension of the morning slip away.

When I came out, Veer was lying on the bed. He was smiling. I looked away immediately. He got up and threw his arms around me.

"Stop!" I almost screamed at him. He was a little taken aback.

"What's wrong, Maya?"

"What's wrong? I cannot believe you are saying that!" He looked absolutely dumbstruck. "Where were you, Veer? Two days? Not a phone call, not a single message...?"

"Wait, what are you saying? Did Suzy not tell you?"

"Tell me what?"

"I told her to let you know that I had to travel to Alberta to inspect one of our shipments that was being held at the port there. I would have called myself, except it was an emergency and I had to rush."

I sat down on the edge of the bed. "No, Veer, your Suzy did not tell me." He sat down with me. "Veer, why did you storm out the way you did? I did not know what to think. I even called your office."

But he was not listening to me anymore. His lips were on mine, stroking my hair and my back. I gave in. The old Veer was back, the good Veer. My rollercoaster was heading to the sky. "I have taken a few days off," he murmured. "Let's go for a drive."

Diya entered the room. "Yes, Papa, let's go. Let's! Bella's parents are driving to her grandma's house. I really want to go. Papa, please...?"

Veer looked at me. I shrugged.

Diya ran to the phone to call Bella before we changed our minds.

30.

WITHIN AN HOUR, we were packed and following Jill's van on the highway, and within a few minutes, we were gliding through the outskirts of the city. The tall buildings had given way to lush green open fields speckled with splintered barns, ebony horses, and rusting iron ploughs. The four-lane highway with multi-layered spaghetti junctions was now a narrow one-lane road with spruces and pines instead of streetlights. It had been an exceptionally warm winter and though there was still a few scattered patches of snow, the evergreens trees were still a beautiful dark green, and the promise of spring was in the air.

After driving for a few hours, we reached a small subdivision with lofty Gothic churches that had large parlour windows and that towered over stone houses and backyards with no boundaries. The road dipped and soared until we reached a valley within another hamlet. A rickety footbridge led straight to the private driveway of one of the most spectacular country homes I had ever seen.

Jill spilled out of the van with Bella and her husband, Brian. Brian was a tall scraggly man, with uncombed brown hair, a matching moustache, printed pyjamas under snow boots, and a broad friendly smile. He gestured for us to follow him inside the house. Diya had already bounded after Bella and gone inside.

Jill's mother had the same green eyes as her daughter, and her flaming, carrot-coloured hair complemented her natural flamboyance. "Hello, I am Edith," she said and extended her cheek for a quick peck. She smelled of cinnamon and warm spice. Her cheeks were firm and bony, and her hands cold. She was my mother's age, so I felt odd calling her Edith without using a respectful title like "aunty."

We entered a room made out of pine and teak. It had a stone fireplace with freshly piled logs. I opened my small attaché and got out a present that I had packed in a hurry before leaving. It was one of the few things my mother had given me before I left Delhi.

Edith thanked me and then absentmindedly left the gift-wrapped box on the side table as she gestured for us to make ourselves comfortable on the couch. "I hope you don't mind meeting my Thursday afternoon knitting group. We were just finishing up some last-minute pieces for the orphan charity fundraiser."

Then, turning to Jill, she added, "You know, it's our special "dress-up Thursday" party, when we all have to dress like we did thirty years ago, except for the host of course. Thank God for that! Wait until you see what everyone is wearing, Jill. And Uncle Andy is dying to finally see you again...."

Jill's face lit up. "How nice, Mother! All feathers and nets! And did Uncle Andy bring his fiddle?"

"Come and see for yourself!"

Veer looked relaxed and held my hand occasionally. I prayed inwardly for these moments to last. I knew that this was borrowed time.

The next room opened onto a view of an enormous and verdant forest that seemed to almost enter the room through the large glass windows that faced it. The smooth wooden planks creaked under our feet and led us down the hall to a flight of grey stone stairs. We descended into a room below that smelled of cigars and smoked meat. There was a large round table set under an antique stained-glass ceiling lamp, like in old churches. At the table, sat Edith's knitting group with their balls of wool and needles sparring to a feverish pitch. Seated near a roaring fire were a few men busily smoking and talking. They were all plump and red-faced with receding hairlines, round paunches, and happy faces.

"Hello, Uncle Andy!" Jill exclaimed.

The largest of the men, with a bow tie and suspenders, waved to her.

Edith introduced us to all of them one by one. I tried hard to remember their names, Judy, Kate, Jane, Mary, Jeanne, Rose ... and John, James, Mike, Andy. We politely shook hands. The women all wore glamorous hats with magical shapes, edges that pointed to the ceiling, or corners that drooped like bluebells. Some of the hats were adorned with brilliant feathers like those of Amazon parrots, while others wore tiny caps with veils, pulled over their eyes and intricately woven with small white beads. There was an old English charm in that room, just like from an Agatha Christie novel. Some had laced mitts, and others had fine black leather ones carefully folded to the side on top of clutch purses. They wore solid colours accessorized with scarves, studded broaches, and stoles. It was a treat to just look at them.

"Oh! Did you know Jill's friends are from India...." Edith started the conversation. They all looked up with curiosity and interest.

I felt it was our cue to say something.

"From New Delhi, which is the capital of India," Veer spoke up from behind me.

"Oh really?" John spoke. "Well, dear fellow, it was many years ago that my uncle Ralph, my grandmother's youngest sister's husband, served in the British army and was stationed in the small Indian town of Alipore.... The stories that he brought back!"

Veer was offered a cigar. "You know," John continued, "we Canadians are very fond of Cuban cigars—the best in the world. Did you know, Cuba is one country where we beat the

Americans. We don't need visas to visit, and they respect our dollars more than the American ones."

The girls joined us with flushed faces in spite of the cool afternoon breeze. Bella had my present in her hand. "Grandma, look what I found—is this for me?"she asked Edith.

"Oh dear, I must have forgotten about this. Look what Maya got me!" she exclaimed and then unwrapped the present in her hand.

I was nervous. What if she didn't like it? The box held a large cushion cover with dancing peacocks embroidered in gold thread over silk and tissue and a pearl trim. How awkward. I regretted not selecting something more cosmopolitan.

One by one, Judy, Kate, Jane, Mary, Jeanne, and Rose took the cushion cover between their fingers, smoothened its wrinkles, caressed its fabric, and scrutinized the gold threads, stitches, and pearls. They especially fawned over the peacocks. Judy put on her glasses, and Jeanne trailed the stitches with her pointer finger. Rose bent her nose over the pearls, and Kate pulled up the cushion cover up to her eye level to have a better look. Nothing escaped them. And then the comments came.

"Ahhhh!" and, "It is gorgeous!" and, "What a beautiful fowl!"

"No, silly! It is a peacock! I bet you were thinking of a fancy turkey with a long tail— probably to roast on Thanksgiving!" They all laughed.

"What kind of a thread is it?"

"Are these real pearls?"

"Do you have many peacocks in India?"

I had to speak up. "Yes, these are real pearls, and in India we have gold-plated thread. Many of my family's heirlooms are made of them." They gasped. "And yes, the peacock is the national bird of India. We had a pair of peacocks in our home, and the theme colours of our wedding were those of the peacock." I felt like I was spouting from the latest edition of a travel magazine.

"Ohh!" They were still passing the cushion cover between them.

Edith handed me a mug of hot cocoa. She looked at me with soft eyes and said, "I shall always treasure this, my little peacock—*peacock in the snow.*"

I was grateful for her affection to us strangers. In what she had just said, it was obvious how these people viewed us: distinct, different, and transplanted in this new land. And we would only grow our roots here when we were prepared to shed our doubts and inhibitions, overcome our struggles, and love these new people, and this new land as our own . It was not up to them. It was up to us as to when we made this country our home.

There was a loud holler from the men's corner, and Uncle Andy stood up. Automatically, the other men gathered around him and the women put down their knitting. The girls stopped playing at the pool table and came to join the grownups.

Andy opened a long black leather case, pulled out an elegant maple fiddle, and started turning its pegs for fine-tuning. Then he positioned its lower wooden bout at a certain point on his chest and raised his horsehair bow.

The room came alive from the patterns of his strings. A ribbon of pure music enveloped us, vibrating with the sweet, happy, and warm folk melodies of the highlands.

John brought out a tin whistle and synchronized its tweets with James's rattle. Each new tune was like a vignette, a small window into their life together, their years of friendship, community, and communion in good times and in bad.

The fiddle's notes flowed deep into our hearts and we were glad that we had taken this trip.

***

It was almost dusk when Edith's friends left. The girls were getting hungry, and we had followed Edith to her warm kitchen. She had chosen the largest crock-pots and an old copper boiler engraved, *To my Edith of thirty years* to prepare stew and vegetables. I wondered if *Edith of 30 years* was her age or the number of years someone had loved her. Either way, the message remained alive and warm over the burner every time it was lit. I looked out the full-length kitchen windows into the dark surrounding forest. There was a completely different temper outside. The wind was furiously swaying the branches of the hemlocks and cedars. If it wasn't for the window between the kitchen and the outside, we would be in the middle of this wrath. Brian walked in and headed straight to latch up the shutters.

"There seems to be a storm...." But before he finished his sentence, the lights started flickering.

Edith jumped, 'What was that?'

The room had started blinking repeatedly.

"Let me check the circuit for you, Mom," Jill offered as she picked up the flashlight and her raincoat.

Veer followed Brian to the basement to check for any loose wiring and I followed Jill outside with the girls on our heels, each tucked into oversized mackintoshes.

The torched sky lighted our path to the electric box. The ground trembled with gusts of screeching icy winds that rose up to cut into our face. I could feel a restlessness among the waving trees. Beneath the smell of wet foliage was disguised a deeper stench that I had smelled before. But where?

"Nothing wrong here ..." Jill muttered under her breath. "This is strange," Jill continued, puzzled as her figures checked each fuse.

The sky streaked and roared once again. I had started making my way back to the safety of the house when Jill called out, "Hey, Maya, let me show you something. Follow me."

I didn't want to. I called out for Diya to head back, but she as always was leading the way with Bella through a line of evenly spaced trees deeper into the forest . We had reached a small pond surrounded with shiny stems and sharp red teeth.

"Meet our maple trees," Jill pointed and showed off like a child.

Bella pitched her arm into the pond and pulled out a glossy frog holding one shivering leg. Diya immediately caught the other leg.

Jill laughed, "Oh these tomboys!"

Another flash of lightening ruptured the sky as the rain picked up. "Let's go back, Jill," I pleaded.

I didn't mind the rain but my inner voice of warning had started: *Maya, there is something there ... something waiting....*

"Yes ... yes, but at least have a look at what I came to show you," Jill pulled me in front of a towering maple with mushrooms growing at its base. On one side, was a wooden tap protruding from its trunk. And just below it was a sparkling steel bucket collecting the golden malt from its bark.

"Diya, *come* ... maple sap!" The bucket was almost full. With a long ladle, Jill filled a few glass jars that were stacked besides some fallen cherries. 'We have to do this a couple of times a week before the temperature drops below freezing."

With this treasure in her hands, Jill finally set out towards the house. I turned around to look at the dark forest one last time and heard it summoning me.

As we entered the house, we saw that the flickering had stopped. Brian and Veer were sitting at the kitchen table waiting for us. Edith smiled at the maple jar, the colour of molten lava. "This is going into my maple walnut fudge, but you girls can have a little taste later on. Would you like one, too?"she asked and I politely refused.

***

After the last pot was washed and hung, Diya whispered gently so that no one could hear, "Ma, can you come and tuck me in?" I wondered if she had caught some of my uneasiness in the forest. Our rooms were on the top floor and overlooked the forest like the rest of the house. But unlike the rest of the house, they were small and stuffy. Instinctively I opened the latched windows for ventilation. And then I glanced outside. A thick mist had replaced the storm. I looked around the room. There was an unlit log fireplace in the corner and a large famed mirror hung on pine boards with a jar of potpourri in front. Edith had laid out extra comforters and blankets. Even before my toes warmed up, Diya had slipped into a deep sleep. I was contemplating whether to join the others in the library for a glass of port or remain snuggled next to Diya in the bed, when the room started filling up with mist. Maybe it had not been a good idea to open the windows. As I got up to close them, the lone side table lamp started flickering.

One, two, three. My heart leapt.

Then again, one, two, thee.

I frantically started opening drawers, looking for a flashlight, matches, or anything to cast some light into the room. Finally, in the tall dresser, I found some matches and a candle.

I lit the candle, but again, one, two, three, and it sputtered out. Then pitch darkness.

The mist had brought in the smell of the forest and the underlining odour from earlier that evening. I was glad that Diya was sleeping tightly and completely oblivious.

I saw myself in the mirror moving to the door with the candle in my hand. But I was still in bed and my toes, still cold, were under the comforter.

I looked at my reflection in the mirror again. No, that was not me. She looked like me, but she was not me. The woman in the mirror was calling me and pointing toward the forest.

I opened my eyes. I was sweating. Dream or not, I had to get us all out of this house. Fast .

The clock on the mantle showed one a.m. Where was Veer?

I remembered Edith's offer of an after-dinner drink. Surely they were all still there.

I steadied myself and headed down the staircase, one careful step at a time. The library, where everyone was seated, was made of stone and teak. It looked like the oldest and warmest room in the house. A crackling fireplace cast an amber glow over the room.

Brian was pouring from a crystal decanter and Edith's voice was talking in a loud voice.

"Oh hello, Maya, there you are!" No one mentioned the blackout that had occurred just a few minutes ago. Or, had the electricity only gone out in our room?

Veer looked up and I immediately recognized an excited sparkle in his eyes.

"Have either of you been to the unspoiled part of Nippising County, up north, next to Georgian Bay? It's well-worth visiting. To get there, all you need to do is follow the trans-Canada highway," Edith said.

I sipped some verve back into my tired body and took a seat near the warm fire that was making me drowsy again. But something brought me right back. It wasn't what Edith had said. It was something that I'd caught in Veer's tone, undetected by others.

31.

IT WAS STILL DARK when we dragged a sleeping Diya into the back seat of the car, and drove off after bidding goodbye to a groggy Edith, Jill, and Brian, with a promise to see them again soon.

I wanted to tell Veer about last night, but I was happy that we were finally headed home. "There's nothing like home sweet home," I said, stroking his thigh.

He didn't answer.

"Veer?"

"Maya, we are not returning home. Not just yet...."

My pulse picked up and whatever sleep remained in my eyes vanished in a second. "What do you mean?" I tried to ask calmly.

Veer was concentrating hard on the cold, dark highway but he had fire in his eyes. "I just want to go up North and explore a bit, Don't you?"

"No." The woman in the mirror nudging us toward the forest flashed before my eyes. "Let's not," I said again.

He looked at me sideways and thought I was joking. My mind was bursting with questions. Veer had borrowed a worn-out yellow map from Brian's glove compartment, and I knew that he wouldn't stop now.

"Veer, where are we going?" I asked as a frail morning ray rose on the horizon.

"I don't know."

The sky turned pink and an outline of Northern coniferous trees speckled between mossy green boulders and red earth. Emerald green lochs dotted the roadside. Diya had woken up and sat speechless, mesmerized.

Veer turned in at a sign for Opeongo Lake. Blankets of colourful fungi came passionately alive with fortitude and verve. Spruce, maple, and pines towered above, and the rugged starkness of granite ridges was softened by lavender and yellow wildflowers. I could feel the forest inside me. My earlier fear left me. How could such a place do any harm?

We reached a peninsula overlooking the central portion of the lake. There on the right was the Portage Store, a log house for canoe rentals. Veer steered to a stop, removed his sneakers, walked to the edge of the lake, and sat down heavily, resting his arms on his knees. Diya sprang out after him.

The first rays had not yet pierced the lingering mist, and the air was very crisp. There was not a soul in sight. Veer picked up a flat grey slatestone and skimmed it over the lake's skin in concentric whirlpools. The lake wrinkled one ... two ... three times, at lengthening intervals. Diya filled her pockets with shiny pebbles that she found under the crystal cold water as I sat and watched on a big piece of washed up driftwood.

This beautiful moment in nature had come so unexpectedly. But it was not enough. We wanted more, to breathe and refresh our souls. So we climbed back into the car and headed out to look for signs for lodging.

We had been driving along Oxtongue River, following the signs toward Lake of Bays. After miles of thick forest and wilderness, we reached a ghost town with a few scattered cottages and two churches. On the side was a wooden sign that read *Lodging for Short-Term Lease*. An arrow pointed to the forest ahead.

I hesitated. "Veer, let's not go into the backwoods. Let's stay in this town." But he had already turned the wheels around.

"Mama, is there anything to eat?" Diya asked.

I gave her some oatmeal-cranberry cookies that Edith had packed for us in plastic bags and saved the sandwiches for later. After driving for another half hour, we spotted another sign that was barely visible. A splintered wooden placard with peeling paint read: *Algonquin Outpost: Backcountry Log Cabins for Rent.*

After another fifteen minutes on the rough road, we reached a small stone house. It too had a sign that read: *chalets à louer.*

Veer stepped out to investigate. He returned with an exceptionally large man wearing suspenders on outgrown pants, sorrel boots, and a large grin pinned on his crimson face. He was the first person we had seen in this rough country since we left Edith's house.

"*Bonjour! Je m'appelle Cedric. C'est une si belle journée, madame.*"

He handed Veer a corroded iron key with directions.

"Papa, where are we going?"

"To a place like we have never gone before," Veer smiled, his eyes bright.

Our old Buick, until now, had behaved rather well on these jagged paths. But every time it went over a bump, my heart leapt with fear that a tire might be punctured by the wrath of the sharp-edged stones below.

Veer stopped in front of the last log cabin. It was the last building before a steep chasm ahead. It was made up of round logs stacked one on top of the other. Diya opened the door, and we entered to a fresh, menthol pine scent. There was an animal skin on the floor and two love seats covered with faded fabric, a kettle over a wood stove, and a fireplace with a stack of welcoming logs. We were back in pioneer days.

"Mama, who lived here? Mama, what kind of songs did they sing?" I wondered too.

We sat on one of the love seats, and Veer handed out the sandwiches. "Warm your toes and get ready to look for dinner before dark," I reminded Veer.

We got back into our car and headed back down the same path we had come, with the hope of returning to the small town we'd driven through earlier. It was past noon now, and the sun was smiling kindly in a spotless blue sky. As the car moved ahead, I had the distinct sense that we were going around in circles. Veer seemed to feel the same way.

When I mentioned this to him, he said, "I don't know, Maya. We seem to be moving ahead, but it looks all the same to me too...." This was the first time since we had left that Veer seemed a little shaky. The wind had picked up, but was not as furious as it had been the previous night.

We came to a clearing. It looked like a campground, except there were no trailers. Next to the rusted iron gates were two large dumpsters. The first had *Municipal Property* written on it. And the second's sign was scraped off, but it read something like: Warning. *B ... ar ... Frequ ... ting Area.*

"Maya, let's go a little ahead. We may find some campers...." Veer had just finishing his sentence when he stopped. Behind the second bin overflowing with rotten garbage, not more than a few metres from us, was something black, shiny, and huge. A wild black bear, Algonquin Park's largest predator.

The bear did not look up. But he knew that we were there. He probably knew we were there long before we saw him. Veer brought out the camera, opened the squeaky car door, and placed his foot on the dry gravel to shoot the photo. His foot made a crunching sound.

The bear looked up. Straight at us. It lowered its head, drew its ears back, and started huffing through its nostrils. I stretched across to pull Veer back inside the car, and he slammed the door shut. Then I shouted, "Let's go, Veer! Now ... move ... run!"

Veer jammed on the accelerator and shot ahead. Our old tires kept skidding on the loose gravel. In the rearview mirror, I could see the bear standing on the spot where we had been only a few seconds ago. It could have easily caught up with us, but I guess the garbage dump was more inviting.

"You should have at least let me take a photograph, Maya," Veer said, as we gathered some distance between the bear and us.

"And get killed?"

"Since when are *you* scared, Maya?"

"Since we are lost in this forest at the edge of the earth with no food or directions, and a black bear on our tail, that's when!"

We both laughed, but Diya was irritable. "Mama, you should have let Papa take a photograph at least. Now who will believe me in school?"

The road was getting bumpier with potholes and stones. Veer turned to look at Diya on the back seat, and his hand slipped from the wheel. In a fraction of a second, our car steered to the side, and the tires hit something.

Bang!

We were jolted and came to a grinding stop. The tire had popped. Our car had tilted slightly to one side. Veer got out immediately to assess the situation. "It's a flat tire," he reported. He bent down to inspect the deflated rubber. We were surrounded by thick forest on both sides of this dirt path. The bushy shrubs mixed with dense undergrowth made visibility and access impossible.

Dark shadows filtered down from the torn wings of giant moths that were hovering over our heads. The pungent smell of decomposing leaves seemed to envelope us. The sun disappeared behind the clouds and it suddenly got chilly. A premonition passed over me.

"I will have to change this tire, Maya. Get inside the car with Diya."

I hesitated. "But with both of us inside, won't the car be too heavy?"

"Just sit inside, Maya. It is not safe outside. I will manage."

A light breeze had started blowing through the thick branches, carrying our scent and bringing back smells of the forest to us. Diya was following the swaying leaves, humming her music notes. I was in the middle of pulling her next to me inside the car when she suddenly stopped resisting. She stiffened. Her eyes widened, and she stopped blinking.

I turned to see. There it was. Just behind us. The big black bear had followed us.

I gently nudged Veer with my foot and glided Diya into the car behind me. One look at my face and Veer knew. Very slowly, he turned around to face the bear.

"No jerky movements ... reverse slowly," he murmured.

The bear had started swiping the ground with his forepaw. I had no idea what this meant, but I did not like it. We had to do something fast. Our only way to escape, our old rusted car, was no longer an option. My shaking hand started moving toward the door handle.

Veer lifted his arms and started waving them in the air and walking slowly backward. I knew what he was doing. He was distracting the bear, leading him away from us, and toward him. And the bear had indeed moved a few steps in Veer's direction.

I remembered reading that a bear would retreat if it heard loud noises. I was going to take this chance. With all the air I had left in my lungs, I shouted Veer's name and started banging the loose hubcap from the flat tire on the car's front bumper.

"What are you doing Maya?" Veer turned around in horror. The bear, who was just a few feet away from Veer, stopped dead in his tracks and turned its head to look at me. My heart was in my mouth. I could hear my screams, except they were muffled deep in my chest. Veer started making noise too. So, the bear then turned again toward Veer. And then, as if we had done this before, I made the next very loud noise. By now the bear was either confused or angry. Either way, we knew we could not hold it for long. It would charge at one of us. Which one, we did not know. But I did know, whichever way the bear charged, Diya at least was safe.

Then, out of nowhere, as if God had come to our rescue, we heard some tires behind us. An olive-green jeep pulled up behind us carrying three young men wearing Stetson hats and khaki uniforms. The head of the team carried a long gun. They were park rangers. The first ranger immediately shielded me, while the other two sprinted in Veer's direction. The head ranger flung his gun into the air and fired two shots.

"Please go inside, M'am," the ranger directed me. I jumped into the back seat with Diya who reached out and clutched my arm.

The rangers had reached Veer, and the bear was retreating into the thick forest on the side of the road. I found my breath again. Veer ran back to us, and, when he saw we were okay, he turned to thank the rangers.

"You saved our lives. I cannot thank you enough." He shook their hands for a long time.

The next quarter of an hour was spent changing the punctured tire. One of the rangers helped, the others stayed on guard the whole time.

"It's spring and the bears have come out of hibernation and are starving," one of the park rangers explained. "This year, the hunting season was extended, and the new cubs follow the sound of gun shots as they know it leads to fresh animal carcasses. So when your tire made a loud bang, the bear followed that sound, hoping for a fresh meal." He paused. "And it is anyone's guess how a bear might react to disappointment when it doesn't find the meal it was hoping for."

"Or maybe it did find what it was looking for—a more satisfying meal," I said, pointing to Veer's large size, and we all laughed.

We followed the rangers back to our log cabin. The captain gave Diya a memento. "Young girl, I want you to remember today with bravery and humility. What your parents did there was very foolish, but very brave. It would have saved *your* life. What you learned today was humility in front of nature, to respect our place in the wild." He opened the small leather bag tied at his hip and took out a metal pin, the Canadian red-and-white flag. He pinned it on Diya's jacket. "There. Always carry this when you seek courage and it will come to you."

With that, they tipped their hats and left. So we were back without accomplishing what we had set out for: we were still hungry.

A strong smell of burning coal and something roasting abruptly hit us. With our stomachs rumbling like thunder before a storm, we followed our noses. On the horizon was the outline of a cluster of cabins touching the lake's shore. A number of campers were sitting around an enormous bonfire with some playful dogs dancing around them, and drinks being passed around. One of them was strumming a guitar and the rest were humming along to "Sweet Caroline."

A husky and a Doberman ran over to us, wagging their tails energetically. They walked next to us until we reached the group. The guitar player stopped, and everyone looked up at us. We were pleased to see Cedric, the man who had rented us the cabin.

"Hey, how do you come this way?"

To our surprise it was Diya who answered first. I was amazed by how confident she was in speaking to these strangers. "We ran into a big bear and forgot our way. Then the rangers got us back...."

They had all gathered around. A chubby middle-aged woman sitting on a folding plastic chair, got up, opened her cooler, and offered Diya a popsicle.

"Is there anywhere to grab a bite?" Veer asked, looking at the group.

"Sure, go into the lake and see if you can grab a bite or if the bite grabs you—*ha ha*!" a man under a Toronto Maple Leafs baseball cap sniggered. And the entire group laughed.

"My daughter is hungry," I replied, unruffled by their mockery. "And so are we!" That seemed to thaw the group.

"You can join us if you like," Cedric offered. "We've had a

good day on the water, and there is plenty left to be slapped on the grill."

"But we would like to pay you for it."

"There is no need for payment; it is for the ladies." He pointed his beer bottle at Diya and me.

Three freshly-scaled rainbow trout with diced potatoes and carrots were doused in oil and seasoning and laid on a charcoal grill. The music started again along with the chatter. Once again, we had been welcomed comfortably amongst strangers.

I had never seen Veer and Diya devour a meal with such passion.

After supper, Cedric took Diya for a paddle in his canoe on a silvery rippled lake and told her about the forest.

Veer came and sat next to me on the grass. "One day, Maya, I shall own a patch of land like this and live off it." I remembered he had wished this many years ago, when we were in Delhi.

"And then you will feed the whole village!" I joked.

"Yes, Maya, I shall. You remembered."

"How can I forget, Veer? It was one of the most unexpected things I have ever heard come out of your mouth."

We watched the silhouettes of Cedric and Diya under the moon, in perfect harmony.

"She looks so much like you Maya. The same eyes, the same stubbornness, and the same caring—for everything that does not matter."

And I could not help thinking this meant that Diya also looked like her grandmother, Gayatri. But, of course, I did not say that aloud.

"Teach them young, and they will nourish the earth, my father used to say," Cedric shouted as he pulled the canoe up onto the beach.

That night I settled down next to Veer on the tattered love-seat in front of a warm, amber log fire. The shadows of the flames danced over the wooden walls, crackling and melting the oak logs to ash, destroying all doubts, all negativity. We had been saved and fed by our new countrymen. We had just been granted a second chance of life, a life different from our past. Was I a fool to think this way? Maybe.

32.

THIS TRIP HAD AFFECTED all of us in different ways. Another year had passed since then and Diya wore the maple leaf flag that was given to her by the rangers on her jacket everyday to school. She radiated with a new found confidence and could talk of nothing else but her upcoming choir recital. She spent every waking moment practising her pitch and notes to perfection. I was in awe of her single-minded devotion to music.

But, I was fidgety. I wanted to live again. I wanted some parts of my old life back. I hankered for an anchor, a friend, a distraction, a fulfilling vocation, anything. The emptiness was killing me. One evening I almost called William to find out what had happened to his apprenticeship offer. But then I thought it was best to wait till Diya's big recital downtown was over.

When Diya's rehersal day arrived , she was up, ready, and waiting by the door before I had even finished my coffee. "Come on, Mama, let's go."

I had written directions regarding which streetcar to board and which subway station to get off at on the back of a scrap of paper. Hurriedly, I had stuffed this in my purse along with Diya's one million things—her music sheets, candy, hairbrush, markers, T-shirt.

As we moved toward the downtown core, large Victorian houses gave way to narrow, multi-storeyed buildings, shelters for the homeless, glossy restaurants, and congested streets with countless people dressed in suits and ties. As soon as we reached the auditorium, Diya ran in to greet Bella and her other friends. I waited at the back of the room, and, when she no longer looked up for me, I decided that it was time to leave.

"Mama, don't worry," she reassured me. "The school will bus us home, and I am with Bella." She always knew what was on my mind.

I stepped out on to a side road lined with Japanese red maple trees. It was a windy day, but the sun was making it bearable. I pulled out the piece of scrap paper from my purse and read my directions again. The road led to a row of towering arched metallic canopies, collapsing down into a flight of dark stairs and into the underground subway station. A few people were scattered on lonely benches lining the track. Within minutes, the dark tunnel vibrated and a steel grey monster with large, lighted windows stopped to slit open its belly and throw a bulky crowd out onto the platform. It was the train to Ossington. I hopped on and made my way to a seat, where I could read the signs for the next station well before it arrived.

It was time to look at the scrap of paper for my next landmark. But my coat pockets were empty. Where had it gone? *Don't panic, Maya*, I chanted with deep breaths.

At the next station, without thinking, I got off. It was a deserted platform with only one flight of stairs to the outside, which smelled of stale urine. I was standing on a cobbled street overlooking the entrance of a park.

The ground was a bed of acorns and baby pinecones. The park was full of life. Lots of it. Joggers, dog walkers, mothers with strollers, pigeons scavenging for bread crumbs, toddlers rolling in the grass, and hungry teenagers hovering around a food truck on the curb.

The wind picked up. I fumbled in my bag to get out something to write on. Diya's music papers flew out. I caught them in time. Another gust of wind blew. This time, the loose sheets escaped from between my fingers and flew over the path ahead. With an extended hand, I sprinted after them. From behind me there came another pair of hands. They overtook mine to reach the flying sheets first. A tweed jacket straightened itself up. I was greeted by a mass of cropped blond hair and two deep blue eyes that brightened with recognition. "Well, well, if it isn't the tiniest pistol!"

"William!"

"Hey, Maya!"

"What a surprise!" was all that I could come up with. I never expected to run into him here.

"Always to the rescue, Madam." He tipped his imaginary hat and handed the papers back. We both laughed. He was always debonair and dashing.

"How are you?" we both asked simultaneously and then laughed again.

"What are you doing here?" he asked first.

"Finding my way," and I bit my tongue as soon as I said it.

He chuckled, "Nothing much has changed then." And then, as if to cover up for his amusement, he said, "Have coffee with me?"

I hesitated. It was getting late. But then I remembered how I wanted to know about the apprenticeship. As if reading my thoughts he said, "Maya, it's perfect timing. I am having a meeting with one of the sponsors for the Eastern Line that I spoke to you about ... so let's go meet him together and get a head start.'

Now, I was interested. I needed something to keep me occupied before I went mad.

"Okay, but promise to give me directions home after that?"

"Do I have a choice?"

"No."

I followed him to a tiny table at the back of a red brick café that was inside the park. We sat at a table positioned under a barrel light fixture with vintage bulbs. The last of the sun's rays were blinding us with their reflection from the metal beams off the ledge. The aromas that drifted from the kitchen were heavenly. The menu read: *Pumpkin Spice Latte, Salted Caramel Mocha, Iced Cinnamon Dolce...*

Our sponsor had not yet arrived. So we walked to the self-serve area, picked out the most repugnantly coloured ceramic mugs and started drawing intricate designs in the creamy foam of our lattes. William dipped his little finger and smeared the froth on the tip of my nose.

"That's better," he said, tilting his head.

"Hey, stop!" I raised my fingers to wipe it off, but he caught my hand.

"Leave it, you look nice with a little froth," he teased.

"You are not the boss of me," I retorted. I was pulling my hand free, but he wouldn't let it go. Just then a Sikh gentleman with a beard and a white turban entered.

William instantly stood up and shook hands with him. "So nice of you to come, Mr. Makhani." Then he turned and introduced me.

Mr. Makhani smiled and extended his hand. "*Hella, hella,* Mrs. Mayas, so nice to make your acquaintance, my good self is Mr. Makhani.'

William's face was a picnic of amusement and I could barely suppress my laughter. We both had to stop looking at each other before we lost our sponsor. There was nothing wrong in what he had said. But the way he said it was hilarious.

William and Mr. Makhni engrossed themselves over a spreadsheet for most of the hour. When they had finished, William asked me hesitantly, "Maya, I know that we have not had time to formally talk about this, but would you be able to start next week? For now, it would be simply to take some pictures of samples in Mr. Makhni's storehouse. Then after that we can start your formal training."

I looked at William, somewhat dumbfounded. I hadn't expected to start immediately, and without being trained first. I did not like being surprised this way. But I was bored and desperate for something to do. I placed my cup on the counter and nodded, but William looked at me in a strange way and I knew he sensed that I was a bit miffed. He tilted his head and with slanting eyes, he said, "Stay a little longer, Maya...."

"It is late and I have to go William. Another time..."

"Aha, very good, very good, dear Mrs. Mayas, not you worry, I shall personally come to picks you up ... says Tuesday at very sharp ten in morning?"

"Yes, see you on Tuesday Mr. Makhni," I said and scribbled my address behind one of Diya's music sheets.

William looked at his watch. "Shoot, I am late. I have to meet someone at the subway."

I didn't want William to follow me, but he did. When we were out of Mr. Makhni's hearing range, I confronted him. "I don't know how to do this work. You promised to train me, and now you are just throwing me into the fire!"

"Maya you are working with me, remember. And that means you can do anything ... even a cat walk!" he laughed.

Despite how I felt, I let it go and teased, "Don't tell me you wanted to get away so badly that you left your sponsor back there."

To my surprise, William became serious. "Maya, I am meeting someone special."

I instantly thought it was probably another woman. "So, how beautiful is she this time, William?"

"Actually it is a man, a senior man. I met him on the subway a few months ago. I had just begun conceptualizing the Eastern Line and he came out of nowhere and sat next to me. He was tall, very handsome, with a milk and honey complexion and grey hair. He had a long coat and shoes like I had never seen before. They were made of gold thread and pointed at the toes."

William was quiet, and my mind was screaming with questions. It couldn't be! That would be simply crazy. Then he spoke again: "Maya, there was something very different about him; he had charisma. The moment I saw him I knew that he was my showstopper for the Eastern Line—right there. We started talking, and he told me that he spoke two other languages. Punjabi, like Mr. Makhni, and one more, but I can't remember which...."

"Pushto," I said without looking up.

"Yes. Oh my God, how did you know?" I had to stop walking. My breath was coming in spurts. William held my hand again. "Are you okay?"

I did not answer. I was far away. No, this could not be. It was a mistake.

We had reached the dark subway stairs. We went down slowly, step by step. I realized that William was still holding my hand, and I pulled it back quickly.

He continued to talk once we had sat down on the steel bench to wait for our train.

"Maya, so I thought about it. Our sponsors are now really interested in Canadian multiculturalism and ethnic diversity. They would like us to hire and involve everyday local and diverse people, and thus make the presentation of our clothing lines richer and more authentic. Mr. Makhni agreed to sponsor us when we told him about our interest in the creation of an Eastern Line. So, I also took a chance and asked the gentleman I am meeting if he would walk for me on the runway. After a bit of chatting up, he finally agreed. I am to meet him today to confirm the details."

"What do you mean?" My breath had started escaping me again.

"Well, it means that he has agreed to work with us for the show! In fact, it turns out that he used to be a music teacher in his day."

Now I was certain who we was. I wanted to say that I knew him. But I didn't, of course. I had started to feel faint. A gust of cold air rushed past us, and suddenly the steel monster was standing in front of us with its belly open. William opened my palm and wrote down the name of my station.

"I have to stay here, but you go down a few stations and exit at the one I've written here. After your meeting on Tuesday with Mr. Makhani, I will set up another meeting with just you and me to start your training." Just before I stepped into the train, he gave me a quick peck on the cheek. "Bye, Maya, take good care of yourself."

The subway was more crowded in rush hour. As William walked toward the exit, I waded my way through the cabin to get a better look at the upcoming platforms. There was one vacant seat near the doors and I took it. The train gently glided forward, and an old lady with a basket full of groceries came to stand next to me. I immediately stood up and offered her my seat.

The platform outside was bustling with activity. Everyone seemed to be going somewhere. There was a child holding tight to his mother's finger, a few office people with briefcases and vacant looks, young carefree fashionistas, a women's walking group in track suits, and in the corner, under a lamp, stood a tall, dark, lone figure. Then I saw William approach this figure. I looked again.

Barrel-chested, lean, and towering. The same poise, the same physique, the same idiosyncratic, striking presence. A spirit from the past, from another land. Yes, it was who I had suspected. What I had feared was happening. Our past was catching up with us, seven seas away from India, in Canada.

Had Gayatri's story found a way to continue in our lives in another continent through Sachin? He was greyer, older, but still the same person that I had met a few years ago on that fated night in Delhi when I had handed him Gayatri's peacock bracelets. Then he had disappeared into the darkness.

Was my mind playing tricks? And then he looked up. At me. Directly. He stepped out from under the lamp and into the light. I saw his face.

The train had started moving. I stepped forward toward the big window and put my palm on its glass. My gaze met his. I saw a flicker of recognition as his facial muscles perked up. The train picked up speed as he raised his hand. A wave, an acknowledgement, a blessing. I saw William standing next to him perplexed at who he was waving to.

The train screeched forward. I had just seen Sachin. Veer's grandmother's lover.

33.

ON TUESDAY MORNING, I was dressed, ready, and waiting for Mr. Makhani. Ten o'clock came and went. Then eleven. There was no sign of him.

I sat down on the front porch and decided to wait for thirty more minutes. The thought of his grammatically incorrect English and peculiar Punjabi accent tickled me. In spite of myself, I felt an affinity with him. At twelve noon, when Mr. Makhani had still not come, I took my shoes off and went inside. Just as I was about to hang up my coat, the doorbell rang. There he was, a beaming Mr. Makhani standing on my doorstep, a good two hours late—and unashamedly so. I noticed that he had taken extra care in getting dressed today. He wore pointed waxed moustache tips, a bright orange turban matching his fluorescent shirt, and red patent leather laced-up shoes. He reeked of sweet rose-scented oil, probably from tucking his gelled beard neatly under an invisible beard-net.

"Hello, Mrs. Mayas. How you do?"

"Mr. Mahkani! Are we on time?" My sarcasm was completely lost on him. There was not a shred of realization or remorse for his tardiness.

"Oho yes, yes. You see, I myself got into a very good meetings again in morning. Another one coming up. I think you are my guest, no?'

"No, Mr. Makhani, there is really no need for me to attend your meeting. We can meet another day if you are busy."

"Nonsense, Madam. You see I has applied for some moneys for this new project." He chuckled and continued, "I wear many hats." He pointed to his turban, and, despite my irritation, I laughed.

"I hopefuls to get a very big works with little adjustment. I share all detail in car."

"Mr. Makhani, where is this meeting? What adjustment? We have to finish our work today."

He cut me short: "Not you worry. I explain all."

He tumbled into his electric blue Toyota Camry and proudly showed off its navigation system, stereo, and custom-made leather interior. Then he turned on the Gurbani on his stereo and backed out with a ferocity that only warriors had before going to battle. I buckled up and clutched onto the sides of my seat.

After a few nauseating moments, my body got used to his speed, and my head zoned in on what he was saying.

"You see, Mrs. Mayas, I don't smoke, drink—what is need? I naturally high, *ha ha ha*. He has been kind and given me everything." His hands left the steering wheel to point to the roof of the car. I realized that he was pointing to heaven and that at any moment our car would steer off the road.

Unrelentingly, he carried on. "So I give back to community. On top my business I also director of charity organization. You see, Mrs. Mayas, this great Canada not same when I come to BC, many, many, many years ago from my dear Punjab with nooo moneys. I drive truck and ate *langar* in *gurudwara*. When I told to drive to Toronto, I like north town of Brampton. Very, very nice open space. It remind me of my dear Punjab."

He paused to concentrate for a second on the road. We were at a pedestrian crossing and he had just missed a cyclist by an inch, who was gesturing and shouting profanities at our car.

"Soooo, as I was saying, when Mummyji lettered me to fetch bride from Jalandhar, it no surprise that I got house in Brampton. And then I went for wedding." He became quiet.

At first, I was thankful for the break. But then I saw his face. It was all knotted up.

So I nudged him: "So Mr. Makhani, what happened at your wedding?"

"I sinned." His hands left the wheel again and touched his ears this time.

"What?"

"Yes, yes ... I go under witch spell."

"What?" This was getting more interesting.

"You see, younger sister of bride, Daljit, much pretty in that way. She touch my hand and say bad thing that she like me. So I marry her instead. I break my bride heart. I shamed Mummyji. We come to Brampton."

He was quiet again. We were exiting the Queen Elizabeth Way and heading towards another highway, whose name I could not catch. This time I did not nudge him. I knew he could not resist telling me the rest.

He took a sip from his plastic water bottle and carried on. "Too much new this Brampton, we not know anybody. I volunteer with Punjabi agency but Daljit angry. She say I lie to her, Canada so bad. We fight all time. God feel bad, send divine intervention. Moneys from application for community play program for Sikh children come from government. I teach all our Punjab sports: kabaddi, carom-board, cricket, gulli-danda. I happy, but Daljit want more moneys. She go shopping all day—make-up, tight clothes. My program grow, I hire two staff."

We were passing a landscape dotted with warehouses, churches, and residential complexes. He pulled into a parking lot and turned off the ignition. "Mrs. Mayas, we have reached. Stories will go later."

Before I could ask him where we were and what I was doing there, he had bounced off his seat and was charging inside a pair of sliding glass doors. It was a tall building at the end of a broad intersection with offices on both sides of the adjoining street. We walked into a wide corridor that ended in a set of elevators. The smell of sterile chemical cleaners oozed out of the seams where the polished stone floors met the grey enamel walls. I ran to catch up with him and asked what would happen next.

"*Ya, ya*. Very, very simples, Mrs. Mayas," he replied. "This community meeting. You see, I asks for government moneys for more service, but only one problems. Need small adjustment to get moneys. They want program for all ethnics in Canada, not just Punjabis. Good news, by gods, I like to work for all peoples but have to show, what they say? Aha, they call 'mainstream' team. When I heard you speak that day to Mr. Williams, please don't mind it, Mrs. Mayas, your thoughts in very good English. So I decides to recruit you for my cause." He stopped and smiled. "But you see, Mrs. Mayas, you will have to work very longish hours if you want my job."

I couldn't contain myself anymore. So I laughed out loud, much to Mr. Makhani's surprise.

We passed a set of glass doors on the right, completely ajar. Something made us stop. A young Asian couple with a toddler seemed to be in great distress. The woman was crying hysterically and clinging to her child, and the man behind her was talking to his interpreter, who was interpreting to two blonde women officers standing in front of them.

"This welfare office—poor get government moneys," Mr. Makhani explained.

We continued to watch. The interpreter was pleading with the officials: "Mrs. Chang is apologizing for her earlier actions, and she will obey your rules as long as you don't take away her child." I could not believe what I was hearing.

"Oh, come, we no interfere. I see such case with Children's Aid Society."

But I wanted to know more about the rules that took away a child from his mother.

"Can we not help them, Mr. Makhani?"

He paused then nodded. He walked briskly towards the women officials with a sense of importance emanating from every step he took. With an exaggerated gesture, he dug his hand into his coat pocket and pulled out his business card. I could not hear them, but I saw Mr. Makhani lifting his head to talk and the hesitant women looking at him quizzically. The interpreter had joined them and started explaining something too. Then Mr. Makhani shook their hands multiple times and laughed loudly. He was by my side in an instant with all the news.

"Well?" I asked eagerly.

"You new, so no understand. Our governments very good. When little child not treat well, they take away."

"What do you mean take away?" He did not like being interrupted during his teachings to me.

"Yes, yes, I knows it wrong, so you see, I tolds them that what they think is abuse may be not correct. Different nationality mothers have separate cultures for own children."

"So what happened?" I cut to the chase.

"This Chinese family finish moneys, no job, apply for government helping. Today son fever. Long line waiting. Child crying. Mother scold and then hit. All officer see. Child having fat, fat bruise on little arm. They make report, call officer to take child away from bad mother." He took a deep breath, his chest puffed up and propelled out. "You see, Mrs. Mayas, here my skill very useful. I say them my information on cultural parenting, and I win. They agree child returns to mother. But hard rules and says officer, mandatory Canadian parenting classes." He radiated with childlike bluster.

"Now let's hurry, Mrs. Mayas. I don't likes to become lates," he muttered under his breath.

I repeated the two new terms that I had learnt: *cultural parenting* and *mandatory Canadian parenting*. Were there coaching classes on how to be a good mother?

Our meeting room was on the twelfth floor. Our elevator

opened into a lobby filled with the aroma of Tim Horton's coffee and a lavish spread of sugary cinnamon buns, fresh croissants, truffles, and bonbons. With our coffee cups filled to the brim, Mr. Makhani and I stepped into a large rectangular meeting room, suspended into a bright skyline. All eyes looked up as we entered.

"Hello, Mr. Makhani." An upright brunette with a big bust, square jaw line, and dancing eyes stood up and extended her hand to him. But she was not looking at him, she was looking at me instead, curiously.

"Hallo, very huppy to meet and sorry we late." Mr. Makhani caressed her palm instead of shaking it. Then, remembering me, he continued. "Pleasure to introduce to you ... Mrs. Mayas, very new Canadian, I just picked her up. She speak very wells."

I saw the disappointment in the woman's eyes. Now that it was out that I was freshly arrived, my potential value had immediately diminished. I wanted to correct Mr. Makhani's statement that I had not arrived recently. But I decided to go along with the reaction that I was receiving had I really been a newcomer. The roadside *Immigrant* magazine had featured many articles that I had read on how newcomers were perceived as more needy than useful, except as "gathered participants" or heads to be counted for program funding and other political purposes.

"Hello, I am Sabrina, the President and the Chief Executuve Officer of the largest foundation in Ontario, The Aid World." She shook my hand limply. I wondered why she had two titles, was there a dearth of qualified staff for each job? Then she turned to the rest of the group with a face that was ready to lead the group into combat. "So, ladies and gentlemen, getting back to where we were ... let's start with the agenda for today."

The meeting agenda read like the 24/7 news channels headlines:

1. Sponsored immigrant children under the family

class category: Immediate requirement of a citizenship test—an unfair rule
2. Tolerance of ethnic enclaves now balanced with identifying high-risk areas for resource prioritizing—a positive move?
3. Legalizing medicinal marijuana—what it means for all Canadians

A scrawny South Asian woman in a loose shirt hidden under a large apologizing scarf introduced the first agenda item. Her wiry salt-and-pepper hair was falling all over her tired face. I could instantly sense her pain, as if something was buried deep inside her. There was a guard, a shield of bitterness, which possibly masked feeble remnants of earlier achievements. Her fists were clenched as she started speaking in a low, coiled voice, ready to fight. She introduced herself as Kanchan. "This is an absolute outrage, this kind of racist treatment for minorities. We will just not take it lying down...." For a moment, I felt I was back in India. The same accents and faces, the same issues. She was slowly uncoiling now. "This is against our Human Rights law in Canada. Many immigrant children don't have English or French as their first language, and if they fail the test then..."

Someone else interrupted. It was a black woman wearing a hijab. She had a pleasing demeanour and spoke calmly, with a fixed smiled on her lips. She was choosing her words carefully after mentally weighing the triggers and syntax of each one of them. This kind of impromptu, synchronized perfection was a level of mastery I had not seen before. "Hello, I am Denise, and I just wanted to say that our school boards have limited resources. Decisions on funding priorities will always lead to resentments for recipients who don't need this set of services."

Then someone from the corner of the room spoke up. He had a fancy derby felt hat, a chesterfield overcoat, and an ebony walking stick in one hand. "Service saturation levels need to be balanced with a range of innovative and collaborative partnerships of local grassroot organizations." He was speaking a language of progress, of unity. But no one was listening to him. Some were doodling, others whispering, and some just stared blankly ahead at the skyline. He finished, sat down, and then for some strange reason caught my eye and smiled.

Suddenly Sabrina pointed at me and said, "I agree. Now take, for example, this lady here, she has just arrived, and I can only imagine how marginalized she feels...."

In an instant, all eyes turned to me. The air was full of pressure, as if elbowing me to speak. If I had to be honest, which I did have to, then I was afraid that not only would I defy some of their patronizing ideas of how immigrants *are* treated but also possibly strip myself of their sympathies. I closed my eyes, took a deep breath to dig into a few seconds of foolish courage, and tried to be as diplomatic as I could.

"No, I have not just arrived. It has been a while. And yes, it is tough. But I think integration is a complicated, two-way process. Newcomers are resilient and look for opportunities in everything possible, economic and social. We should not always compare our present life with all the good that we left behind. Instead, we should try to find some of it here. I have found strength in trying hard every day to adapt and to stay hopeful."

Kanchan reacted immediately. "Such big talk. But you cannot hide your reality as a newcomer. What all you must have faced. Tell us, did you face any unfair treatment?"

Before answering, I thought of the episode at Diya's school and then the one downstairs with the Chinese couple. But what also flashed through my mind was the unfairness that I faced in my married household. "Yes, I have faced prejudice. Here and in India. But people are the same all over the world, only the context changes...."

Kanchan was not at all happy with what I was saying. I was not accepting her suggestion that I was a victim. She was not giving up. This time she went straight for the jugular. If I was not on her side then I was to be dismissed as someone who did not count. "Oh, people like Maya here belong to a new profile of newcomers coming into Canada, entitled and privileged. They cannot be bothered with commonplace issues of the integration of less advantaged folk like us."

I resented that. I opened my mouth to react but before I could, the man in the fancy derby felt hat spoke from the corner. "No, I disagree. Too long we have lamented that *one size does not fit all* but do we even know *how many sizes we are*? Maya is one such piece of the larger puzzle. Yes, she represents this new cohort of newcomers. We are so trapped within our filters, in our efforts to place everyone in preconceived boxes that we fail to see the real people that we deal with. It's the immigrant experience that connects Canada to the world. It's sad that your length of stay in Canada defines your closeness to this Canadian identity. The longer you live here, the more passively Canadian you get...."

I could hear the resounding heavy silence in the room.

His ideas were not sexy enough for their liking. I chuckled. I had been called a piece of the puzzle.

Just then Sabrina spoke up, 'Well ... well, on that note, let's break for coffee and just after, we'll take your questions.'

This was my chance to escape. I pulled Mr. Makhani aside. 'I have to go now. Where is the nearest subway, please?'

His fingers crunched around my wrist with urgency. "No, no, Mrs. Mayas, you cannot go. See what riots you creates. Mine very good ideas to bring you here. We talks about my job offer later."

"Yes, Mr. Makhani, later. But I have to go now."

"But our works for Mr. Williams, no, no, we are to leave together." He walked out with me. But Mr. Makhani was restless.

Once we were back on the road, I asked him, "What's up, Mr. Makhani?" I thought he would rant about his job offer again or say something about the meeting.

But, to my surprise, he said, "You naughty, naughty girl, I leave my hot tea on table. So I turn in coffee shop. Take a quick cuppa chai with me?" I could not deny him his chai after I had pulled him out of the meeting.

Once we were seated in the cafeteria, I expected him to plunge into his "work talk" right away. Instead, he sat quietly pondering over his tea, almost pensive.

"All well, Mr. Makhani?" Another surprise.

"As well as one can be in this country." Again, this was not his usual buoyant answer.

"Why? Is something the matter, Mr. Makhani?"

"Oh no, no. I do not bother you." I decided not to ask again, but he could not contain himself, and within a few minutes he plunged into the problem. "You see, Mrs. Mayas, Daljit has left me."

I didn't know what to say. I held his wrist in support. "Oh, I am sorry. You must be devastated!"

"Solely I to blame. My sin catch me. I break heart of pure her elder sister by rejecting her and marrying her younger sister Daljit instead . Now God punish me for temptation to siren."

I was getting angry with the way Mr. Makhani was describing the women in his life. But I held myself back to hear his full story.

He wiped an invisible tear. "Newly to Canada, Daljit so obedient but I too much in work, she be alone. Then one good day from goodness of heart, I encourage to do course in personal support worker. She got good job in old people home. Good mood. Then night shift starts. 'No service in day' she tell me. I allowed because she happy. Then last month it happen. I come to empty house. Note on table. *Thank you for bringing me to Canada. I live my life now. A kind old man promise to take me Florida. Don't bother tell my family back home, I calling them.*" He sighed deeply.

"Well, good riddance then." I tried to make light of it.

"I thought and thought and reached conclusion. I addicted,

not to smoke, not to alcohol, but to woman like that. If I more home, then maybe Daljit still with me. So now I start another charity work for my community."

"Really, what is that?"

"Marriage counselling." I choked over my tea. We had started walking towards the exit doors now.

"This is not your fault, Mr. Makhani. The people who send their daughters to an unknown land through arranged marriages don't do it for love. Always know that. If they find love they are lucky. If anyone finds love they are lucky."

Mr. Makhani was not listening; he was waving excitedly to someone. I turned to see a red Chrysler zoom into the parking lot. In the driver's seat was a woman, a very attractive young woman. "Mrs. Mayas, this is our new marriage counsellor working for our agency now. Meet Miss Saloni."

I could not resist smiling. So he was doing it again, our dear Mr. Makhani, a victim of his own heart. I knew then that Mr. Makhani would be okay.

34.

I ENJOYED WORK. William had kept his promise to train me properly and I was happy with my contribution to the team. But William had not been able to secure the funding he needed to make the Eastern Line of fashion clothes that we were working on with Mr. Makhani a reality. And I was happy that Sachin became a distant memory because of this. I had not wanted to run into him.

Working with William was the most enjoyable part of my day, and I think his too. It was effortless to talk to him and to joke with him. Many times, I caught him gazing at me lazily and many times he made me laugh for no apparent reason.

But we both knew that we lived in different worlds. His was a world where it was easy to live, and to love. He lived for himself, in the present, and nothing else mattered. William was carefree, talented, and self-centred. My craving for William's free, uncomplicated way of life disturbed me.

With Diya keeping longer hours at school, I also started working longer hours with William at his office. It was one of those evenings. With the rest of the staff gone, I too was winding down, when from the corner of my eye I noticed William sitting quietly in the dark at the edge of our settee with a glass of whiskey in his hand. I switched on the light to see his flushed face looking back at me.

"Maya, please shut the light, it hurts. And sit down here, I have to tell you something." He gestured to a spot next to him. "Our next year's line up had no takers. I wasn't able to raise enough funds even for the launch...."

My heart sank for him.

"Don't worry, we can try again next season..."

He didn't let me complete my sentence. "Maayaa ... Maayaa, always the optimist. What would I have done without you?" he said and placed his hand on my knee.

"Done very well..." I joked, but the closeness was making me uncomfortable. I got up to leave.

He tilted his head and looked at me with slanting eyes, like he always did. "Maya, don't go."

His hand reached for my arm and tugged hard at my sleeve. In an instant I fell into his hard lap. He bent over my face with an intensity that I was not prepared for. His lips pressed hard on mine and his tongue tasted of malt inside my mouth. Underneath his cologne, I smelled something else. Pine. Like the forests of Algonquin. He squeezed my shoulders and started stroking the length of my body. His fingers edged towards my blouse.

"William! *No!*" I screamed, gasping for air.

He lifted his head and let go, surprised and a bit shaken.

The walls of that large room had started caving in. I jumped off his lap, stumbled over my bag, and fell in the dark. His lean figure stood over me and he extended a helping hand. But I pulled myself up and heading quickly to the door.

"Maya! Wait, please." I felt another tug, this time it was like that of a child.

I could feel his eyes on my back

In that moment, through my hot tears, for the first time, I realized something that banished all my internal conflicts and gave me strength to do what I had to do next without any regret. I realized that my infatuation for William's life, his lifestyle, and his choices was not a longing for the person who was William. While I found his outlook on life refreshing and while he was easy to be around, this could never have been anything more than friendship. No matter how irrational my complicated bond with Veer was, no one could ever mean to me what Veer meant to me.

I turned to confront William. Even in the dark, his blue eyes sparkled the same way that they had the first day I had met him. I didn't need to say anything. He knew. In that half-lit room, we both knew that this would be the last time we saw each other. He had broken my trust by crossing that sacred line of friendship.

Surprisingly, the imprint of his touch lasted longer than I expected. The next day I sent in my resignation.

PART III

FOREVER, LIFE

35.

I COULD NOT BELIEVE HOW THE YEARS had slipped by. The wind from the lake still blew violently into our garden, banging to be let in through the bedroom window. It screeched, howled, and then lay in wait. Some nights when the moon was bright, and I was not afraid, I sat barefoot on the stone bench under the angel's wings. Those nights the wind dropped to my feet as if thanking me for breaking its solitude.

A few years ago, I had received that phone call that everyone of us who has left their parents behind dreads to receive. "She passed peacefully in her sleep," was Papa's way of breaking the news to me. His voice was too calm for my liking.

Without thinking about what he was saying, I blurted out immediately, "I'm coming, Papa."

"Maya, no, don't come just now. I will call you soon. I am going to be travelling with her ashes to Haridwar to scatter them over the holy Ganga River and then I will be going to our cottage in Kausali. That is where I find the most peace, find her." His composure cracked a little.

"Okay, Papa, but promise to call me as soon as you reach Kausali? I would like to be there with you."

"Yes, I promise my little girl, I will."

I waited for a few days and when his call didn't come I decided to buy my plane ticket.

"I want to go to India, Veer. I have to be there with Papa."

"Yes, that is a good decision, Maya. I will arrange for your ticket," Veer said and left for his office.

That morning I had burnt my toast and its smell was flooding the entire house. For some reason, this smell took me back decades ago to the day we had left India, to a similar hot spring morning when the sun was pouring into a kitchen filled with smell of burnt toast. Why was my mind playing tricks to take me back to India? And the next moment I had my answer. The phone rang.

"Maya, I have some bad news. It is about your father."

Veer didn't have to say more. I knew.

Even though I had lived apart from my parents, they had always been with me. But now I felt like an orphan.

My father's family arranged to have my parents' ashes scattered over the Ganga river as they had both desired. There was no reason for me to now return.

***

Listening to Diya practise her music was one of the few things that calmed me. Then one day as I was watching her practise, she suddenly stopped and said, "Mama, why don't you start playing music again? It is just what you need to revive yourself. Didn't you play a few instruments when you were young?"

And she was right. I regretted not having thought of this earlier. I decided to enrol in a program for beginners. But when I auditioned, they decided to place me in advance level classes. I was told that because of my experience, within a year I could graduate the program and even be ready to tutor if I'd like. I liked the idea of giving back and said I would consider it.

After graduating from high school, Diya had been accepted into one of the top music schools in Canada. It had been a year since she had left for Montreal and I missed her terribly. She was also an active member of the hikers' club, and this gave her an opportunity to explore the great northern regions of Canada. She came home as often as she could and every time she left she said, "Don't worry, Mama, I am only a flight away, and I will call every day."

But when she called last weekend, her voice was pitched differently and I immediately knew that this was not a routine call. '

"What's the matter?" "Oh Mama, you will not believe it. I am so happy! I have an offer to join my university expedition team to travel north, to see the *Aurora Borealis*!"

"The what?"

"The Northern Lights, Mama! We leave tomorrow, and we should be there in a few days. I will keep texting you, don't worry."

"Diya."

"Yes?"

"Be careful."

"Don't worry, Mama, I will. " For some reason I was nervous.

When Veer and I were feeding the doves the next morning, I told him about Diya's trip but didn't mention my anxiety about it. . Veer had continued to pour his life into expanding his father's business even after his father had passed away. His mother now no longer bothered to call home, since she knew he was never here. And even though he continued to come home late, he made an effort to talk most times.

"See, what did I tell you?"

"What, Veer?"

"When Diya was born I said that one day she will go north to the shining light."

"Yes, you did." I remembered now.

"And one day I will have my own patch of green to live by." I also remembered that. I wanted to ask him when that would happen. But just then his phone rang. He answered it and then got up to walk away from me.

I caught a fleeting sentence of his conversation. "...Don't worry Suzy, I am coming." It irked me that she continued to work for him, but I bit my tongue.

After Veer left, the house felt emptier than usual. I started thawing chicken in mushroom sauce and switched on the oven to roast a few vegetables Then I went to switch on the television. It was almost noon. I flipped the channels but could not find anything that grabbed my attention.

Soon it was time for the afternoon news. I got up to get my lunch. But something that the news anchor had just said made me turn around. It was a word, a place ... no, a name. And then I heard it. Every single news channel was blasting this red alert news. There had been an avalanche. Up north. In a small village called Tuktoyaktuk. And a group of students was trapped.

I suddenly felt cold and my mind went blank. What was the TV saying? The screen was filled with scenes of snow-covered mountains, viewed from a the inside of a helicopter, which then panned the Mackenzie River delta. A rescue party was being assembled, a reporter announced.

I picked up my shaking body and reached for the phone. "I want to speak to Veer please." I could barely hear my own voice.

"Sorry, he is not available," the receptionist answered flatly. I did not know what to say next.

But I think "Please, it is an emergency. This is Maya..." I said. I think I was holding on for a long time. The woman had hung up.

Frantically I dialled and redialled Diya's number. It was dead.

I picked up my keys and started my car. I punched Veer's office address into the GPS. Images of the snow and the frozen river flashed in front of my eyes. I called out to Diya from my heart. I knew she was in danger, but I felt she was still alive. And I hung onto that thought.

***

Veer's office was on the twelfth floor inside a glossy high-rise building. It had lofty domes and sparkling granite floors that made me feel like I would slip any moment. There was a gigantic artificial metal tree with bronze petals touching the ceiling in the foyer and a multi-coloured carpet under it that was making me even dizzier.

The twelfth floor opened into a reception area where two pretty ladies smiled plastically through their lipsticked lips.

"I am here to see Veer."

"Do you have an appointment?"

"No, I am his wife." They gasped.

I waited at the edge of a leather couch, holding my breath. A familiar figure walked out. It was Suzy. She looked sharp and not too happy to see me. But I did not care.

"Hello Maya, what brings you to our office?"

"Is Veer there, please?"

"No, he is on a call with Columbia. Can I help you with something?"

"No, I need to see Veer. It is important."

She went through the large maple oak doors again. I could not sit anymore and I started pacing.

Suzy came out again and said, "I was not able to talk to him while he was on the call. Unfortunately, he is booked solid in another conference call after, and then he and I have a lunch appointment with one of our new clients. It will be a while before you can see him. Maybe you should go home. Maybe I will send him home early today." She sniggered.

I had had enough. Who was this woman to stop me from seeing my husband? And nothing was more important than reaching Diya. I brushed passed her and purposefully walked toward the maple doors. Suzy tugged insistently at my sleeve. "No, Maya, you cannot barge in."

"Why not?"

"Because you are disturbing us." There it was. Out in the open. "I am Veer's right-hand person, and I have been appointed by his family to define his day, and who he has time to meet...."

I did not care for this drama right now. But I felt the hot

tears on my cheeks. I immediately wiped them, hoping that no one had seen.

"Our daughter is in danger. She is on a trip, and I have just got news ...." I could no longer speak. I did not want to speak. I picked up my bag and headed for the front door. The two receptionists looked disturbed and smiled weakly as I passed them.

I clutched the handle to open the door and a hand came from behind to stop me. Veer pulled me in his arms I was looking into those hazel eyes.

"The receptionists paged me. I am so sorry...."

"Veer ... it is Diya."

"What about Diya?" His composure cracked a little.

"Have you seen the news?"

We walked to the boardroom and switched on the wall TV. The same pictures flashed, and I closed my eyes.

"Wait here."

He walked out with fire in his eyes. I knew he was angry. When he didn't return for some time I followed him. I heard his deep, low voice, the one he used when he did not shout but was raging with anger.

"... and on your way out, remember to write down all your passwords, and return the office keys please."

"What are you doing? Are you firing me? You have gone mad. I know too much. I will destroy you!" Suzy was shrieking.

"No one can destroy me unless I let them."

"What about all that I have done for you?!"

"It was all work, Suzy, and it has made you a very rich woman too. You did it for the kill."

"I will tell your mother and everyone."

"Tell everyone? Everyone knows. Maya is my wife and no one can or will replace her...."

I collapsed back into the room once again, hidden from this ugly showdown. What a fool I had been to doubt Veer all these years. Only his inner demons could destroy him, and destroy us, not another living person. His occasional frenzy of doubt, his insecurity, his obsession with me and then his break downs and regrets — they were the demons that he had to fight against.

I picked up every ounce of strength and stepped out once again. A shaky receptionist was calling out to Veer with the phone receiver in her hand. "Sir, it is your mother from India."

He came towards me, took my hand and started walking out. The receptionist called after us."Sir, what do I tell her?"

"Tell her that I have gone to find my life."

And, with that, we exited the building in search of Diya, in search of *our* life.

36.

WITHIN AN HOUR we had packed a small bag to catch the train heading out to the Arctic region, the Northwest Territories of Canada, to Nunavut, and a small village called Tuktoyaktuk. I knew in my heart that Diya was alive and waiting. I could think of nothing else but holding her close in my arms again.

As we entered our railway compartment, we found that we were not alone. Across from us was a very tall man with tan skin and high cheekbones, peering at us from under a caribou hat. I noticed his almond-shaped eyes immediately. They were bright green, the colour of the Northern Lights, and they had a distant look, as though he were someone who has seen life in all its starkness, someone who has travelled far. There was a certain restlessness in his eyes, like he was searching for something. He continued to watch us as our train steered and stretched across the cold, rugged Northern landscape. After a while of furtively exchanged glances, he came and sat next to Veer. "Hello, I am Anernerk."

I opened my handbag and pulled out my book at an angle where I could secretly observe Anernerk from behind its covers. His largeness was even more consuming at this proximity. His persona seemed to diminish every object into irrelevance. His angular face dropped into hollowed cheeks that had weathered the severity of seasons. He had an ugly scar down his left cheek. He looked up directly at me and smiled, knowing all this time that I was watching him. I looked away in embarrassment.

Then he turned to Veer and said, "Anernerk is my Inuit name. It means angel. I was given this name by my granduncle when I saved a baby lemming off the cost of Mansel in the Qikiqtaaluk region where I grew up. My parents believed I had healing powers." Why was he telling us this? Was this bizarre introduction leading somewhere?

"Where are you travelling from?" Veer asked.

"I come from Eastern Quebec, and I'm on way to visit my distant blood brothers, my tribe in Nunavut."

"It must be terribly cold in Nunavut right now." Veer commented.

He chuckled at Veer's worry about the weather. "I am on my way to bless the start of a race of seal hunters." He pointed to a very large canvas bag tucked under his seat. "I am carrying their harpoons with me."

Then Anernerk fell silent as a few blocks of isolated tundra boulders flashed past us. He was sitting straight and, at one point, he was staring outside the window without blinking. When he finally spoke, it was as if he were deep in a trance. "After I was honoured with the name Anernerk, I was taught many things by my community. I personally believe that the spirits of the departed respectfully co-exist with the living. Some spirits take masculine and feminine forms and further incarnations of divine father and mother. I see you both in this personification, and now I am obliged to offer you help, the peace that you seek. You should know that this is not something I do normally. As you both entered this compartment, I could feel some chaos, some things unsettled, and some incomplete business in your life. But your spirits are unique, they bring energies from a faraway land."

Veer looked aggravated at what Anernerk was saying. He got up to move away, but I gestured to him to sit down.

Anernerk continued, "Have you travelled far?"

"Just from Toronto," Veer replied dryly.

"Yes, but where did you travel from to reach Toronto?"

"From India," I replied.

Anernerk turned towards me and smiled quietly. A smile that told us that he had found the correct answer now. Then once again he sat in silence. When he emerged, he spoke to me for the first time: "What is your name?"

"Maya."

"Maya ... Maaayaaa ... Maaaya." He toyed with the word on his tongue, playing with its last syllable. "What does that mean?"

"It means an illusion, a spirit."

He smiled that knowing smile again. "Maya, you have a special gift. You need to express it."

I was taken aback. This statement was unconnected to anything he had said before. It was Veer's turn to have fun now, and he returned the same gesture to me as I had to him a few minutes ago—to stay calm.

Anernerk pulled out a large walrus-ivory box engraved with pictures of arctic owls. I remembered seeing those treasures at the Royal Ontario Museum. He brought out a rectangular object and opened its tassels. "This is seal-skin wrapping," he said. "It was given to me by my father to carry special objects like this gift I am about to offer to you."

Wrapped inside was a small turtle-skin rattle, not bigger than his palm. I recognized it instantly. I had read about these. They were used to keep the rhythm with the beating of the drums in Inuit ceremonies.

"Here, take it." He extended it toward me and I heard a pebble-like jingle.

As I took the rattle in my hand and I saw a miniature black etching on its handle. A lone tree blowing in the wind, braving the storm. My finger automatically touched the winding strokes of the branches. I gasped at the similarity, at the symbolism. Oh my God. I remembered something. This was like the stencilled tree in Gayatri's diary. Was this a coincidence? I scolded myself.

No, that was in another country, another time.

"We cannot accept this," Veer said.

Anernerk put up his hand. "The spirit of this object speaks to its owner. I was just the carrier. It has found its owner." Anernerk was watching me closely. "Keep this in a music room. It will bring rhythm and balance to your life."

"I don't have a music room, so what will I use this for?" I asked.

"The use will present itself to you when the time is right. The moment you embraced this, I could see that the spirits were calmer. You will be okay now."

He turned his gaze upwards and held it at an empty space just above my head. The train was slowing down, and we had reached our next stop. He stood up and raised his hand to Veer. "*Son, you will be absolved of the burden , of the curse that you carry. Wait for the white chariot with wheels of faith and true love.*"

Both Veer and I were taken aback at his ramblings.

Anernerk picked up his small backpack and his large, heavy bag of harpoons, and he was about to leave when he stopped and turned around one last time. He looked at both of us now and said, "*The wild love from an ancient land flows in the blood of youth. Let the darkness guide you to revival in a new life.*"

With that, Anernerk disembarked. We sat perplexed and confused. What had he meant? It did not make any sense. We both acknowledged that the encounter had been so unique and powerful, nothing like what we had ever experienced before.

Veer finally spoke. "Maya, make sure that someday you have a music room where the sound of the turtle-rattle destroys all unwelcome spirits. Promise me."

"Yes, Veer, I promise."

He continued, "Maya I am cursed by my family's past. I don't think I can escape it. Everything that I wish for turns out wrong. I wished the Northern Lights for Diya and see where it has landed her. I wished you away from the mansion and see the life we have lived here. But I will not let life be taken away from both of you...."

"Hush, Veer. Don't talk like that. Diya will be with us tomorrow. I just know. And I can find a thousand interpretations of what Anernerk said. Shall I tell you?"

But he was not listening, as usual.

***

Even in the train, there was no escaping the icy, cold draught blowing uninterrupted from the North. The whole night I dreamed of Diya, as a baby in her pink bassinet, standing up for herself with her teacher, catching frogs with Bella in the moon-soaked Algonquin River, and practising her musical notes like a religion. I knew that harm could not touch someone so beautiful. And I knew that before spirits touched my little girl, they would have to pass through me.

When we arrived it was still dark. Wearing our thermal under-layers, we stepped out onto a frigid, barren, and strikingly beautiful landscape. The powder-blue sky was speckled with dusty vapours, and our vision of the earth was seamless. For miles, there was nothing to see except the serene completeness of nature. The biting Arctic wind had started with a low whistle again.

Veer had arranged for a guide, and he greeted us at the station. His snow gear was lined with thick fur, and the only parts of his body that were visible were his swollen red eyes, cheeks, and nose.

"Are you Mr. and Mrs. Raa ... s ing...?

"Yes, we are," Veer answered, relieving him of the agony of pronouncing our foreign name.

"Hello, my name is Aippaq, meaning *companion* in my language. I am your musher."

"This is Veer, which means the brave one, and I am Maya, which means the illusion," I said, a little tickled by my own translation.

Aippaq smirked at Veer, as if sizing him up. Then he said to Veer, "So you are the brave one, eh?"

"I had no choice but to be the brave one, living with her." Veer snorted.

Aippaq let out a loud throaty laugh.

"Dear Aippaq, we are here to find out daughter. She was with a group of students...." I said softly.

"Yes, I know. I will take you to the rescue party. You are just in time. They leave tomorrow morning."

"Have you had any news of the children?" Veer asked what I dreaded to ask myself.

I closed my ears quickly. I did not want to risk hearing anything contrary to my belief. But I did not close my eyes. I was watching Veer's face intently. His eyes expanded and flooded. And then his facial muscles relaxed. His lips stretched with the hint of a smile. I knew that the answer was not what I was dreading. So I slowly opened my ears.

Aippaq was saying, "Yes, yes, the news from the watch tower is very hopeful. A small group of college students has made it to the village at the other end. But nothing has been confirmed yet, and we will only know for sure when we arrive there tomorrow."

Now I closed my eyes and prayed. Again, I called out for Diya in my heart, and I felt her presence inside. Veer held my hand tightly. I was so thankful that we would be able to catch the rescue party in time.

"Come this way, please. Have you ridden in a sleigh before?" he asked.

"You mean a dog sleigh?"

They were the most beautiful blue-eyed, snow-white huskies I had ever seen. Thick furs, muscular bodies, and hefty limbs that could carry you across the world. All twelve were harnessed and ready for take-off. We stepped into a wooden sleigh mounted on large iron skis and it had small brass bells with red ribbons hanging on its rail. The dogs stirred.

Aippaq took the reins in his hands. The bells started jingling. So this is what Santa Claus feels like when he leaves the North Pole on Christmas Eve, I thought. Aippaq was our Santa, and he would deliver us to our gift, our life, our daughter, Diya.

He shouted out loud, "*Muushhhh*!" The huskies stiffened to attention. "*Geegeee*!" and then a hard tug at their leash and a final "*Haaawwww*!"

We were gliding on a glacial terrain, soon whisking through a white spruce wilderness, pulled by the power and grace of these amazing animals. It was as if we had wings.

The spruce eventually emptied out into a clearing. An enormous cloud of mist rose from the ground, and we were going to puncture it. A fog descended and then suddenly cleared. We had passed through an invisible gateway.

Aippaq pointed to a large and crude stone structure on the horizon. It was the shape of a standing man with his hands held out as if it was flying.

The *Inuksuk*!

"This is our Inuit landmark that wards off evil for our village of Tuktoyaktuk and a marker on the travel route for our brothers herding the caribou. It took our villagers twenty moons to build this one. Each rock was personally chosen from a local stone quarry near Monterrey. This Inuksuk has spread its message of unity to guide our people in the harshest of winters and kept us working together, not separately."

"We can learn so much from this place," Veer said, as we continued on.

On the horizon, I could see thick grey smoke from distant chimneys.

The dogs were hushed and stopped. I was still reeling with the movement for some time after we had stopped. With a stiff, frozen body I dragged myself off the sleigh and into knee-deep snow.

We picked up our bags to walk to our huts, but Aippaq stopped dead in his tracks. He pointed to a trail of fresh prints leading towards the huts.

"It is the big grey wolf—he is back," Aippaq said. "Last month a few women saw an Eastern red wolf pack, with the male, female, and eight cubs. It seemed they had travelled from the Algonquin highlands in the heart of Ontario. However, this month we had more trouble. A pack of grey wolves moved in from boreal forests, just north of Lake Superior. Even the Arctic fox and the coyotes that scavenge on our borders don't come close to the might of these red or grey wolves."

My thoughts immediately went to Diya.

Veer read my mind and asked, "What about the lost children? Could the wolf attack them?"

"No, we will make sure of it." I found my breath again.

"How?"

"Tonight is a full moon. Our village's official wolf-howler will lead his team into the woods leading to Skymark point. This is a sacred place where the boulders meet the frozen Mackenzie River that leads to Inuvik-Quebec. He will do a rally cry for the pack to lead them out of our area. I will be accompanying them. If you'd like, you can come too."

Veer held Aippaq's hand in gratitude.

"Don't worry, I am a father too," said Aipaqq. "I know what you are going through. Have faith."

Nestled behind a large spruce, our hut was a single room with a small bed, a kettle, a fireplace, and some eiderdowns. I threw myself onto the cold hard bed and must have dozed off. It was dark outside when Veer nudged me to get up. He pulled me out into the snow. And pointed to the sky.

I looked up. And saw heaven!

The sky was on fire, electrified with bright emerald-green and pale-pink lights that were flashing across the horizon, wrapped around jagged windswept peaks and pulling the earth toward itself with a hidden magnetism. It was a complete collision of all our senses. I could stretch my palms and touch this magical shield. It was as if we had been waiting our whole life for this moment, to see the Aurora Borealis, the Northern Lights! And under the same sky, somewhere, was Diya. She and we were now connected, this heaven stretching between us.

Just then came an unmistakable low howl. The wolves! I looked at Veer, surprised that he had not gone with Aippaq.

As if reading my thoughts, he said to me, "Maya, there is nowhere I would rather be, except under this sky. I am looking at heaven, and I don't care if my life ends now. I have been salvaged. My little girl has fulfilled my wish to see the Northern Lights. I am ready for anything after this."

"Shhhhh, don't say such things, Veer. Be careful what comes out of your mouth. I am not superstitious, but I am not prepared for what you have just said."

"Maya, it is crystal clear. I know what I have to do now."

"What, Veer?"

"Send Diya back to you."

That was a strange choice of words. They stayed in my ears for the rest of the night.

37.

THE NEXT MORNING, Veer and I met the avalanche rescue team. There were several guards from the Royal Canadian Mounted Police on snowmobiles with GPS and other buzzing electronic devices. Each of them carried at least one mountain rescue dog: Saint Bernards, collies, and golden retrievers. Then the local men formed a team with beacons, avalanche cords, Recco reflectors, shovels, and probes. A Blackhawk helicopter with the Canadian Red Cross Flag was on standby.

The lead search commander of the Mounted Police assembled the team. His voice was grave and his face drawn. By the time I reached the group, Veer had already shaken hands with the team and was glued to every word the commander was saying. "In intervals of thirty minutes, my men will scan one hectare at a time. In teams of five, you volunteers will be using avalanche probes and simultaneously combing the same area. The moment you spot anything you will use a smoke signal. Understood?"

He stopped and took a deep, sullen breath. He had been informed that we were the parents of one of the students. He looked directly at Veer and me and said, "I want us to hope for the best but be prepared. Suffocation, injury, hypothermia, and trauma are some of the things these children have been fighting. We are not to lose a single moment more; each minute that we spend here takes away from their chances of survival.

Best of luck everyone." Within a second he had mounted the helicopter with the rescue team, and his guards were buckled up in their snowmobiles with their dogs.

Veer boarded the helicopter. His hazel eyes held mine until they disappeared into the clouds. I collapsed in the snow and prayed.

Aippaq pulled me up and took me into my cabin. "You are not alone," he said. "There are a few families who have come to search for their children. Rest now, you will need your strength later." I obeyed meekly like a child.

The day turned to evening and then night. I walked to the base camp to find out if there was any news. Most of the noise was coming from a mobile home standing on stilts. Aippaq was sitting at a narrow table with a group of local youth, drinking beer and playing darts. A small TV was broadcasting images of snowy places, but its volume was turned down. In a semi-enclosed lounge, the elders were smoking pipes and wearing earth-coloured parkas.

I scanned the room. There was another couple, their faces etched with worry. They looked at me and smiled, no doubt guessing that I was a waiting parent like them. The woman had cropped brown hair. She was fiddling with a handkerchief between her thumbs and using it to wipe her tears frequently. The man, wearing a checked coat and matching hat, had his arm around her shoulder. They were huddled together, clinging to any bit of solace they could provide to each other.

I sat down next to Aippaq, shivering. It must have been minus thirty outside. He immediately called for someone, who came in with a plate heaped with piping hot food for me. "You must eat. This is our dish for the day. We only make one dish and everyone eats the same thing." I looked at the bowl of fresh ginger root and chilli spread over a roast of some kind.

"What is this, Aippaq?"

"Asian barbequed caribou steak. Try it."

The cook was watching me, and I did not want to insult either of them. So I took a bite and controlled the urge to retch. On a good day this food would have tasted so good. But today, the last thing that was on my mind was food.

I wondered what I was doing alone in this godforsaken place. Where was Diya? Where was Veer? That was all I could think about. I felt dizzy. I wanted to go back to my cabin to rest and wait. As I started walking, I heard footsteps. It was Aippaq.

"Maya wait up." He reached me, and stopped to catch his breath. "We have just got news that one of the search parties has found a small group of children who had managed to escape. They survived because of their emergency training…."

"What?" My heart jumped. Diya had emergency training. Yes, she did.

"And the good news is that they are being transported back tonight in the helicopter. The rest of the team is continuing to search for the remaining children and won't be back till later."

I came alive again; I could breathe again under the electric emerald sky. I went back to the caribou steak and took two bites before a smiling chef. Then I sat tight in that stuffy, noisy clubhouse and waited. The other couple waited next to me. None of us had the strength to talk, but we were united in our resolve to get our children back to safety.

***

It was almost midnight before I heard the sound that I had been straining my ears for.

Chop …. Chop … Whirr …. The helicopter was descending vertically, and blowing snow in a whirlpool. Aippaq shouted something to me about moving back, but his voice was taken away by the wind.

The door opened and a beaming commander threw a rope ladder down to the ground. He turned around and faced the inside again. I heard him say, "Ready? Line up."

First, the survivors on stretchers with IV drips attached to their blue arms were sent down. Then their faces emerged.

Bruised, and bloody, but smiling. They had made it. One after the other. I held my breath.

A young boy emerged. He had green eyes and dirty blond hair, but there was something different about him. He stood out from the other faces. I thought I might have seen him somewhere before.

He moved on, and the children kept pouring out. How many could this helicopter carry?

I looked around. The couple that had been waiting with me were still huddled together, just behind me. One of the rescue team members was talking to them with a photograph in his shaking hand. The woman buried her head in her husband's shoulder and started sobbing uncontrollably. Her partner's gaze was frozen on a pile of snow in front of his boots. He had no expression on his face. The rescuer's face was beetroot red with emotion, and his eyes were watering.

Where was Diya? I started praying again, without blinking, without breathing. I called out to her from my heart, and this time I got a response.

Suddenly the sun peeped out from behind the dark clouds. There she was. In front of me. Her face frazzled, crystallized blood on her forehead, blue cheeks, and damp eyes searching with hope. She did not see me when she glided down the rescue rope. But when she stood up, I was there to catch her. Nothing felt more complete in this universe than to have my child back in my arms. We were told to move on the side, and I don't remember where we stood for the next hour. I do remember wiping her tears and mine for a long time. I knew that night that there was a God somewhere and that this God had been kind to us.

38.

"DIYA, WHERE IS PAPA?" After we had become conscious once again of our surroundings, I realized that Veer was not with the group that had just arrived. Diya looked at me blankly.

"Papa? I don't know. Why, was he in the rescue team?"

"Of course. He accompanied the team. He wanted to help find you. Did you not see him?"

"No, Mama. I had no idea."

"Who rescued you?"

"One of the officers in the snowmobile released his golden retriever, who followed the scent of our cardigans all the way to a rough igloo that we had built to survive the night. I saw a few people in the distance, but I was going in and out of consciousness when they pulled me out."

It had to be a mistake. Veer was simply being his usual irresponsible self. I thought he must be busy talking to the rescuers or something. There was no other explanation. I ran to find the chopper, the commander, the rescue team, Aippaq—anyone. Finally, I found the commander who was getting ready to go back.

"Have you seen my husband?" I panted.

"Yes, M'am. He was a great help, considering that he has no formal emergency training."

"Well, where is he?"

"We split into two groups. He wanted to stay back to help

the other missing children. He was the one who spotted your daughter, and then he went with the other group heading north."

"Are you going to pick him up now?"

"Yes, but we will not be back until tomorrow. The winds from the east are very strong tonight, and they will make it impossible to fly back."

As I watched the helicopter fly away, what he had said suddenly sunk in. Why had Veer found Diya and not met her? Diya had no idea that her father was her rescuer. Nothing made sense to me.

I walked back to where I had left Diya. A couple of nurses from the Red Cross were checking her with a stethoscope and handing out steaming cups of hot cocoa.

My head hurt.

I started walking back to our cabin, and from the corner of my eye I saw Diya running to catch up with me.

***

It was a restless night. Images of the couple who'd had to face terrible news kept haunting me. They had heard something that no parent ever wants to hear. And then a familiar voice from the past kept ringing in my ears. A woman's voice. I could not hear the words, but halfway through the message that voiced changed into Veer's voice. Soft, playful. "*Maya ... Maya.*"

I woke up sweating. A blizzard was howling outside. So the commander had been right about not being able to fly that night. Soon it would be the dawn of a new day, and with it would come Veer. We would return home with everything that we needed in this world—each other.

Diya was sleeping next to me like a little girl curled up in a foetal position. I spread my blanket over her and stepped out into the wind. The coldness gave me strength. I thanked it for sustaining my child and my husband within its folds.

Within an hour, the sky had brightened, making it possible

for Diya and me to see the path towards the helipad clearly. I did not see the other couple among the waiting crowd. It seemed like a long wait, but our heartbeats synced with the sound made by each blade of the descending helicopter. The door opened to a beaming commander. My eyes strained once again to concentrate on every surviving face that climbed out of the helicopter to be whisked away by the waiting medical team or their loved ones. One by one they came. One by one my heart beat faster. I knew the belly of the helicopter was large enough to shelter everyone, even Veer, so I tried not to be impatient.

But then the commander announced, "Thank you, everyone, for your support and help. Our operation has been successful and we have brought back almost every student from the avalanche...."

What was he saying? Why was he thanking everyone? No, there was something wrong. Where was Veer?.

I walked up to him and grabbed his hands tightly. "Where is my husband?"

I saw him cringe. He did not speak. I asked again. "Where is my husband? You promised to bring him back. He was helping you."

His face turned white as if he had made a mistake. He looked down on me and almost whispering, he said, "I am sorry. We did not seen him this morning."

"What do you mean? What are you saying?"

"We saw him at our base last night, and he was there. Then this morning the blizzard was coming our way so we called out to everyone, but we didn't have time to do a head count. We presumed that everyone was on board and those who weren't were returning on snowmobiles. But wait, let me ask, I am sure Dylan checked. He called out to one of his fellow officers. "Dylan, this lady is asking about her husband, you remember the big fella who helped us yesterday with tracking the second group? It seems that he has not returned with us on the chopper. Perhaps he decided to come back on a snowmobile instead?"

"Oh yes, the big fella. I remember him from last night. When I took a round of the premises before boarding, he was not there. So I presumed that he had already joined one of the last snowmobile groups that were returning."

"See, there is always a logical explanation," the commander said and exhaled with relief.

"So, *where* is he?" I was on edge.

The commander looked at Dylan and Dylan simply shook his head. "The snowmobiles are all back. And I didn't see him with that group."

There was something very wrong. I just knew.

Dylan started rambling, 'The only way that someone was left behind was if they ventured off in the wilderness ... but..."

"Yes, Dylan?" the commander encouraged him to continue.

"Well, I was just going to say that no one can survive these frigid arctic winds in any case."

The commander flinched again." I am so sorry, M'am," the commander said.

Diya was by my side now. She was holding me up with her hands on my shoulders. The wind had started blowing layers of snow. Diya took over. "Commander, we have to get another team out to look for my father, and to rescue him."

"Of course," the commander said. Within minutes, he had assembled a team. Diya climbed in and the helicopter quickly disappeared into the blue sky.

Aippaq came up to me and asked what had happened.

"Veer has not come back."

"Have faith, sister. You are good people. Have faith, and remember, he is *the brave one.*"

I was grateful for his support. I could no longer feel the tips of my toes, and frost was biting my face. But I waited in the cold in spite of Aippaq's advice. When my shadow became longer, I heard the sound of the helicopter again.

The first thing out of the commander's mouth was the last thing that he had said before leaving. "I am so sorry ...." he repeated.

"Why are you sorry?" I asked again, just as Diya was coming out. Her face was flushed, and tears were streaming down her face. "Mama, we looked everywhere. He is nowhere."

"What do you mean, nowhere? He was everywhere helping everyone, and he was right here with us, with me."

"I am very sorry, Mrs. Rajsinghania. No one could have survived the terrain that we just combed looking for your husband. It seems that there was another avalanche a few hours ago, and there is not a single shelter in sight for miles. The survival rate is almost nil under such circumstances. But I assure you that we will keep looking and inform you personally if anything changes. There is another blizzard expected soon and before it arrives I would urge you to leave with the survivors. Our helicopter will drop you at the nearest base camp."

I looked at Diya and then the commander. My anger was rising. "Veer is a survivor too. You cannot say such things. He is out there somewhere."

"Mama, sit down please. Ma...." I think it was Diya's voice. It was coming from far away. I felt hands on my shoulder pushing me down to sit.

"Nurse, nurse, can you please check her? She is going into shock. Why is she not blinking? Can you give her something?" This time it was a man's voice.

I could hear my breath. It hurt to breathe. I just wanted to lie down. Next to Veer. He would come soon, and we would all leave this wretched place forever. I hated to drive, Veer would have to drive back. Since he had not eaten the whole day, I had kept his dinner on a back burner, warm for when he returned from the snow outside. I had made his favourite, Thai cashew chicken and banana cream pie.

I felt a pinch on my arm. And then the smell of iodine tincture.

"Now, now, she will feel drowsy," I heard another voice say. I felt large cold hands on me. "Yes, she is ready for the stretcher now. Please be gentle...."

I think I was flying. I was next to Veer.... I was okay now. This is where I wanted to be. As numbness took over, the pain subsided to a dark corner deep inside my body.

***

I opened my eyes to a dark room. It was our bedroom. Diya was sleeping on Veer's rocking chair. I looked past our bedroom drapes into the backyard. It was grey outside. But Veer had the Christmas lights on a timer. They were lit but blurry somehow, as if drenched with tears.

Diya woke up and put her arms around me. Then she started sobbing uncontrollably.

"Why are you crying, Diya?" She stopped crying and looked at me with funny eyes.

I had a faint recollection of what had happened. I felt like I was covered with thick black ash from a funeral pyre. I wanted to scrub it off. It was all over my face, my arms. I got up and looked at myself in the mirror. The ash was not there. Could I have imagined it?

I walked to the window. It was twilight. A few winter birds were flitting in our garden, waiting to be fed. Waiting for Veer. I opened the door, and the wind stabbed my face with a cold knife. The sprinkled seeds flew from my palms and fell like black rain. The birds dug in. But there was someone missing. I waited.

Just before my last toe turned blue, the flutter came. Edges of white wings peered from behind the angel's robe. White doves! The colour of pure white peace looking straight at me. I moved towards them. They did not fly, they just pecked. What message did they have for me?

I returned to my dark room. I felt a blanket around me. A faint tingling in the tips of my frozen toes returned. Diya was talking to me in a gentle voice, a voice I had often used on her as a child when I wanted her to understand something important.

"Ma, Papa is not coming back. He is gone. You need to understand that. Ma, whatever it takes. I am here with you.... Ma, Ma...." And then she broke down again. Instinctively, I hugged her.

Her voice was fading again. I wanted her to leave me alone. I needed to be alone. My mind was drifting again. I opened the top drawer of Veer's mahogany desk and found the turtle-skin rattle.

The pain was back, stabbing at my heart, unbearable pain. Veer's words were in my ears, his dancing eyes before mine. "Someday you will play music, Maya.... Make sure you do."

With trembling hands, I reached out for the pile of unopened letters on Veer's desk. He would have gone through his mail on Sunday morning. I had to do this to help him now. There were bills, more bills, and then a few cards wishing Merry Christmas from the various charities we donated to. I was about to give up but there were only three letters left.

"One last try to finish this," Veer would say, "or else they will keep piling up."

Another bill.

I was closing the drawer when something caught my eye. The last letter in the pile. It had a strange stamp from Alliston, Ontario. A large stamp with a smiling Santa Claus, in an unfamiliar handwriting. I opened it mechanically and then pulled out the single sheet of lined paper written in blue ink.

I read it. And then again. And again. Finally, after the fourth try, it registered in my head.

Dear Maya,

You probably don't remember me, or maybe you do. I am Sachin, your husband's grandmother's childhood friend from Peshawar. I have been living in Alliston for many years now. We met briefly many decades ago in your home in Delhi. You gave me her gold bracelets. Then I saw you a few years ago on the subway. You must have wondered, and I apologize, as I should have come forward to talk to you. I recognized you instantly. The same eyes, the same fresh innocence. You remind me a lot of her.

Your conspicuous family name was not difficult to find in the yellow pages. Time has a way of bringing us back to unfinished business, and finally I have something to request of you. It is unfortunate that I am writing to you at a time when I don't have much time left.

Maya, will you come? You will make a dying man very happy.

Here is my address:

1226 Parsons Road, Alliston, Ontario.

Sincerely, Sachin Malik

What did he want? Nothing mattered to me anymore. No, I would not go. It was late; he was correct about that. Too late for me. I did not care about about the past anymore. I would not go.

I took the car keys off the hook in the pantry and drove to Home Depot. I bought two cans of terracotta orange, one can of sunshine yellow, and one can of turquoise wall paint. The beige and grey walls of our home had to go. Veer had always wanted colour on our walls, and I wanted Veer to come home. I opened the paint cans to start immediately. Then I remembered that I had forgotten to buy brushes. I picked up the first thing that came into my hands, my morning teacup. I scooped the cup in paint and shot it high on the wall. It collided, splashed and trickled down. I tried it again, and again. The wall started to come alive. But it did not help, the pain had not been killed. It was still there, in abundance and simmering, the emptiness astounding.

I had to go out again. Anywhere, it did not matter. Immediately. I picked up the car keys again. And grabbed the envelope from the top drawer. I plugged the Alliston address into my GPS and started out.

39.

THE SNOW HAD STARTED falling in sheets as I hit the highway. The radio was broadcasting storm warnings in between Beethoven and Mozart on the Boomers channel, with temperatures dropping below twenty-five degrees with the wind chill. I noticed abandoned vehicles that had skidded into ditches on the side roads, no doubt due to the wrath of the storm.

I exited the main highway into a rural artery facing fields of endless snow. There was not a single thing in sight, dead or alive, moving or stationary. Even the trees were hibernating.

Where was I going? And why? Did I really want to rake up old memories? Memories that did not matter now. What did Sachin have to say after all these years? And why had he come to Canada in the first place?

I entered a small township and drove past a Ford and then a Honda dealership. Then, a wastewater treatment plant, a small hospice, a fire station, a Walmart, a vacant schoolyard, and a cluster of closely-knit houses with sloping snow-covered roofs and oversized backyards fenced with oak and pine trees.

The second last house had the number 1226 painted on its rusted out mailbox. It looked more like a cottage made of stone and wood. I turned into its long winding drive, parked, and stepped out of the car. I hesitated before ringing the doorbell.

After a minute, I heard some noise, and the door was flung open by a young man. He had green eyes and dirty blond hair, a honey olive complexion, a square forehead with high cheekbones, a long face, and cleft chin with a prominent nose. I had seen him before. He looked at me and smiled. A magnetic smile. I couldn't place where I had seen him before, but I knew that I had.

"Hello," he said.

"I am here to meet Sachin," I said and started fumbling with the zip of my handbag to pull out his letter.

"I know who you are," he said matter-of-factly.

"You do?"

"Yes , my father was expecting you. My name is Albert. I am Sachin's son. Do come in. It is freezing out there."

I walked into a tidy, cosy cottage with stained wood cabinets and an exposed stone wall, a backdrop to the rustic interior. There was a bright patchwork quilt draped over the weary upholstery where I took a seat. The windows with wooden frames had thick drapes with lacy fringes. They were pulled back just enough to reveal tiny cobwebs against the dim light. Ornate candles were clustered around vases of fresh flowers on tables in two corners of the room.

"How is Sachin? Where is he?"

"I am afraid you are a little too late. My father passed away three days ago."

I tried to calculate if that had happened at the same time that I had been standing on frozen earth, waiting for Veer to come back and take us home. I was getting jumbled with the days.

"As his last wish, he wanted you to do something for him," the young man added.

I still sat very still. Albert went into the adjoining room. I wanted to leave. Was I to write a note? No, I would just leave. I did not even know these people.

He came out with a shining brass urn and a small wooden box with a peacock feather painted on its lid.

"These are his ashes, Mrs. Rajsinghania. And there is something in this box that he wants you to open when you have left here. His last wishes are in this note."

I opened the note, read it, folded it back along the creases, and took the urn in my hands mechanically. I did not open the box. I was not thinking. I did not know what I was doing or why. I thought the young man looked relieved.

I had turned to leave with the urn when he asked, "Would you like some tea?"

I hesitated and looked at him. I immediately recognized the emptiness in his crystal green eyes.

"Yes, tea would be nice."

He led me into a kitchen that smelled of cinnamon, cloves, and apples. I felt calmer. A tiny mahogany coffee table overlooked a desolate vegetable garden. I automatically gravitated towards the warm fire crackling next to the alcove. The wooden floors shone like honey and struck a perfect balance between refined and casual, traditional and modern. I could feel that peace and love that had resided here once.

I opened Sachin's note. With my mind a little at rest, I could follow it somewhat.

Dear Maya,

Something tells me that you will come. I have faith. And if you do come when I am no longer here, then Albert will hand you my ashes.

This was a life that should have been with Gayatri. Had I not been so careless on that last night in Peshawar when she had come to find me, we would have been united forever.

Once, many years ago, you reunited us through her peacock bracelets. I am returning those to you in the box. They gave me the courage to build what was left of my life. I found a beautiful loving woman, Mary, and Albert is living proof of how God has gifts for us at a time when we least expect them.

I have sheltered Albert from the secrets of my un-

fortunate past, and I would like that to remain so.

I know this is too much to ask of you, after all you don't even know me.

A part of my ashes will be buried with my life in Canada, where I lived, loved my wife Mary, and had Albert. The other part of me you will find in this urn. This part belongs to my previous land and my love, Gayatri.

Maya, there is no one else of whom I can ask this, who knows or who understands. You connected me to her once before; I am requesting you to do so again. It is my last wish that my ashes be scattered next to hers.

I closed the note. It was imposing and intrusive. How dare he, a total stranger, ask such a tall favour of me? I certainly did not owe him anything. But, in spite of myself, I was pulled towards this message.

Albert was pouring piping hot tea in pink bone china cups. He was striking, as his father had been, with classic features and had inherited some of the warmth and charisma of his father.

My mind started drifting away again. My eyes rested on the rustic grain patterns and primitive joinery of the table. Then my gaze moved up to the wall. I saw her. Captured in a silver leaf photo frame, her sunny blonde hair pulled loosely across her rosy plump cheeks, the same emerald green eyes as Albert, and a smile that beat a warm fire on a cold day like this. She glowed with an allure that was rare. Yes, I could see why a steadfast Sachin could not resist her. Albert saw me looking at the picture.

"That is my mother, Mary. She was a student of my father's in her last year at university, where he was teaching Persian poetry and *ghazals*. They spent many hours rehearsing, and, just after she graduated, they were married. I was born a year later. Two years ago, she died of leukaemia." My heart felt heavy at this news.

"I was never close to my father till then, and honestly I was even ashamed of being his son. I did not understand why he had to be different, why he was not from Canada or why my mother had to choose him out of all the men here. I always asked my mother to come alone for parent-teacher meetings. When he accompanied her, it made me uncomfortable. But I promised my dying mother that I would look after him. So when I did come to know him, I was surprised at what I found. I am now ashamed of my earlier limitedness and spite. We started spending many hours together rehearsing the sitar or practising the pitch of a particular note. Then on cold evenings by the fire, he told me stories of a land I have only read about in fairy tales. He taught me about music, love, and life. These past two years have been the most revealing; he helped me find myself. I have discovered an unfathomable urge to pursue art. I have not decided what to do next...." He fell silent.

I was touched by his youthful vulnerability. I became conscious of how alone he was now. The pain inside me was rising fast and I did not realize that I had been weeping as he spoke.

40.

SPEEDING ON THE NARROW treacherous roads felt good. It distracted me. I did not care about skidding while searching for the highway signs to take me home. I could see potato farms buried on the banks of the frozen Nottawasaga River, but he plastic smell of the car seats was nauseating me.

So, at the sign for Simcoe North Western Railway, I crossed the yellow line to stop at the edge of the white countryside. The gaping snowfields called out to me. They had something to tell me. I stepped out and the wind cut into my face, and whipped my legs into an icy numbness. I turned back to see lone footprints in the snow. Just mine. A clump of pine trees seemed to huddle together to brave the onslaught, their branches covered with thick blankets of snow. I moved closer and then in between them. There was a sudden flutter. I looked up at the grey sky, which had started to clear, revealing the occasional patch of a washed-out blue. Snowflakes dropped gently onto my upturned face from the movement of white wings between the branches.

Why had the doves followed me here? Were they hungry? Had Veer not fed them today? Surely, they did not come to complain. Was Veer with them?

I called out, but they flew away toward the strips of blue between the grey. The cold flakes on my nose slithered down to my collarbones and felt surprisingly good. As I wiped them off my face, I saw the last of the white wings vanish from my sight,

I felt a sense of release. As if a heavy weight had been lifted.

I sat down on the ground and buried myself in the snow, up to my chest.

I was freezing, but I did not mind. Something inside me was changing. Was it Veer's way of telling me to let go of this unbearable weight, my grief? And then I knew. Veer was here. Veer was with me. I dusted myself off and waded back to the car.

The slush of melted flakes covered the leather seats. They no longer smelled of plastic. I turned on the heat from the engine to warm me up, but I had no sensation in my body. Where was my body? I had to drive back to Toronto with Sachin's ashes—it was my promise to him, to Albert. The brass urn stared at me from the adjoining seat.

I was going to hit highway any second. I had to stop. I had to call Diya. So I dialled her number. But I started shivering and I suddenly felt extraordinarily tired.

A black cloud had arisen from the fields. Why was it moving towards me? Oh God, I was trapped inside the car. Where was the handle?

I heard Diya's sweet voice: "Mama ... Mama ... are you okay?"

But it was too late. I was already consumed by darkness.

***

I heard Diya's anxious voice again, but could not see her. "Doctor, please tell me. Is she is okay?"

"She is suffering from hypothermia. It's a good thing that you tracked her. It was just in time. Her body temperature was dangerously low. But she is stable now, at least physically."

"What do you mean?"

"Well, she had a panic attack. It is a common occurrence in periods of extreme stress or emotion. It's understandable, considering what your mother is going through. I would like to sedate her and watch her over the next few days."

I was in an unfamiliar room. I strained my neck to see who was on the other side of the room, but could not see anyone. I did not recognize the grey walls, or the three-winged ceiling fan, or the plastic venetian blinds. There was screeching on the tiled floor, probably from something heavy like a janitor's cart being dragged in the corridor. Everything smelled like sanitizer. My hand was sore, and my head was throbbing. I closed my eyes.

Where was I? Had I forgotten to water the potted dahlia in my study? Had the grease stain been cleaned from the garage floor?

Oh, but wait, something else was opening up. I was flying back to a warm and happy place. Running back home from school with Anita by my side, shopping for my peacock-coloured trousseau with Ma, playing Tom and Jerry with Veer in his house. I was back in Veer's mansion, feeding the peacocks under the shimmering moonlight over the lily pond. The wind was moaning through the large leaves of the peepal tree, and then it called me inside to the mirrored room of the west wing. I followed the voice of the woman whispering, and she flew me on her wings, far away, to our frozen garden under the stone angel covered with deep green moss.

I must have walked this path a thousand times before, but today it seemed different. The garden was alive, rasping and whining. I could see the ripples of the lake ahead swelling around the soil that wrapped the boulders. The shore was lined with driftwood and weeds. Despite the frost, our magical garden was still in full bloom. White lilies, orange poppies, crimson snapdragons, lilacs, and wildflowers of all kinds. Passion from the bed of red roses, pride from the geraniums, and undying love from the primrose creepers—all had reflected my moods over the years.

Veer was sitting next to me. He was feeding the white doves. We were happy. The doves were pecking and cooing. But then the wind's whispers became stronger. I turned around, and Veer had vanished. The cobbled stones grew sharp edges under my bare toes. The sky started to change colour.

I felt someone shaking me. I opened my eyes to see a teary-eyed Diya. Behind her was a short, stocky doctor in an oversized starched white gown with a stethoscope around his neck. Behind him was a kind-eyed nurse. The nurse checked my pulse and the doctor scanned the various monitors attached to different parts of my body. He turned to say something to Diya, and they all walked out. "Do you have any family to inform?" I heard the nurse asking Diya.

"No, not here. Just my grandmother in India."

She paused. "I am glad that you were able to talk to someone," the nurse said in a comforting tone.

"Well, not really..." Diya said, shaking her head.

"Why not?"

"At first my grandmother was silent, and then she asked a very strange question."

"What was that?"

"She asked me why Ma was not with Papa when he disappeared."

I did not want to hear more. I could already guess Veer's mother's thoughts, her insinuations, her blame. I felt as though I had not slept in days. So, I gave in to my tiredness, closed my eyes, and was back in my garden.

A cold draft blew in from the lake and brought in the darkness. There was a bolt of lightning, and the sky turned dark with thundering clouds. The tentacles of dandelions and bulrushes sprang out and wrapped violently around my ankles, locking me to the ground. I could not move.

Something was coming. I smelled the rotten carcasses of dead fish floating on the lake's edge. The sky lit up with sparks and then gave way to a piercing blaze. A gaping stillness spread around me. As my eyes acclimatized to the sharpness, I saw her outline. Her long black hair blew over her beautiful ashen face, and her deep brown eyes looked straight at me. She wore a jade green dress with a peacock feather on her sash.

Gayatri Devi Rajsinghania.

I knew it was time to meet her, to ask her, to confront her. She started first.

"*Maya, you are free. I set you free....*" Her voice was an echo, low and silky soft, like the lowest music note of a song. The tentacles that had bound me suddenly vanished.

I stood up slowly, bravely, and asked, "Free ... *of what*?"

She raised her hand and pointed to the sky. It was white as chalk against the expanse of dark slate. "*Free of this cursed family, free of this cursed blood, free of Veer.*"

For the first time, I saw the silver thread woven though her dress. It was reflecting the sparks from the sky like a shield, blinding me. The black ice under my feet was cold and slippery. I inhaled deeply and replied, "Veer's blood is not cursed, and my Diya belongs to that blood. I do not want to be free. I love Veer."

She laughed a slow mocking laugh. Her dress stretched and coiled itself around my waist. I tried to open its knots, to release myself, but she kept coiling it around me, tighter and tighter. I was beginning to suffocate me.

"*Maya, he is gone. He sacrificed himself for your freedom ... for you to live.*"

I tasted lemon on my tongue, and then the sharpness of wasabi.

She suddenly released my waist, and her dress untangled. My feet skidded, and I fell hard on the ice. My knees bled and my hands were scraped.

What had she just said? Veer sacrified himself? I felt my chest fill up. "You are evil...." I whispered from shivering lips.

I didn't want to show her my weakness. I didn't want to cry. But there was such finality in her thoughts. What had she done?

In a flash, she shot up into the sky, above the stone angel's head, above the majestic oaks. Her wild hair knotted up, her face turned livid, the red veins inside her eyes bulged and her nostrils fumed. This was not the beautiful Gayatri from a few seconds ago. She had taken another avatar. Her voice whipped down at me, "*Maya, how can you say that I am evil? Even after how we have both been treated?Ahhhh....*" Her moan slashed against the sky.

Bolts of lightning shot down at me like spears, their light so blinding that I couldn't see where I was running. The clammy mud under my feet had started caving in. Yes, this was my end. I had no where left to run.

I opened my eyes. I was sweating.

Was this the last I had seen of her?

I realized that she wanted to take away my hope, to highjack my spirit and take it with her into the darkness of hatred that consumed her.

I was thankful for returning to the mundane hospital sounds. I welcomed the busyness of the morning around me. The clinking of bedpans, the screeching of trolley wheels, the smell of toast, and the chatter of nurses. I was still groggy. The morning sunlight was streaming in from the open venetian blinds.

A plump matron with a round sweaty face walked in smiling. "Good Morning, Missus. How are you today?"

Diya's armchair was empty. The matron was watching me. "Oh, what a sweet child. You are very lucky, Missus. You know children these days.... The poor girl refused to go home, but then I convinced her that your drugs would not wake you up till later and so she said she was going home only to freshen up...."

The matron was back with a small cupful of dense purple liquid medicine. "Come on, sit up," she ordered. She propped the steel bed up with the lever and wrapped an inflatable cuff around my arm to take my blood pressure.

Diya entered.

I tried to put up some resistance as the nurse came towards me with the cupful of medicine, but I was overpowered by both the nurse and the second-in-command, Diya. "Open up, Ma."

"Oh, so who made you the boss?" I joked feebly.

"You did. When you decided to behave like a child and run in the snow."

She was humouring me. I opened my arms and she ran into them like a child. "You will always be my baby, Diya."

She started weeping. I stroked her hair and then wiped her face with the edge of my hospital gown. The nurse was standing over us, watching. "Now, now," she sniffled, then clapped. "Open wide." She brought the liquid to my lips and then poured it in my mouth with force. "It is time to rest again. Soon you will be out of here," she smiled and clucked.

But I did not want to sleep anymore. I wanted to go home.

I knew what I had to do.

***

Diya brought me home. She carried the brass urn and the peacock box in the trunk with my suitcase. I could see that Diya was curious about the urn and was waiting for the right time to ask some questions. Strangely, my mind was at peace after confronting Gayatri. And, even more strangely, the seed of hope I had for Veer inside my heart grew stronger each moment. Every sunrise the doves would wait under the stone angel statue, and every sunset I would look at the urn on the mantle of our study.

Then one day the doves did not come. I sat on the bench waiting for them to show up, but they didn't. I knew why they had not come to peck. It was their way of telling me to wake up and complete my unfinished business.

I went in and started looking for the last missing piece. If I had to put this story to rest then I had to bury it completely. No part of it could be left behind or remain in our lives any longer.

I emptied my wardrobe and my shoe closet, and looked under my bed, in the storage chest, and finally each box in the attic. It was not there. Where had I put Gayatri's polka-dotted diary? There was only one place left. Veer's study. I looked on the bookshelves, the dresser, even the cocktail hutch and TV cabinet. Where had it vanished? Tired and frustrated, I sat down on the ottoman. A horrible thought crossed my mind. I had shown Veer the diary and the photo. What if Veer had become curious and wanted to read it on his own? Then where would he have kept it? I closed my eyes and thought. Of course, the most predictable place. I opened the last side drawer on his desk and pulled out some files, letters, and bank papers. There it was. So Veer had read the diary!

I opened it carefully and slowly pulled out the small peacock feather that I owed to Sheila. I knew she would be waiting for it. I had promised to return it to her as a token of my well-being. But could I return it? I slipped the feather back into the diary and packed it in my travel bag.

That evening I bought a plane ticket to Delhi.

"Why are you going, Ma? Why do you do this? Who do you have there?" Diya argued relentlessly. I was combing her long hair to calm her down, just as my mother had done for me. And then she finally asked. "Mama, I see you looking at the brass urn. What is in it?"

I had been preparing for her question, but I was not prepared to give her the answer. How could I tell her the story of her doomed ancestors? I wanted the story to die with me. Otherwise Diya would never be free, just like I was never free. But I could not lie either. "Something that needs closure, my child."

She looked at me sideways and opened her mouth to say something else, but thankfully she decided to pursue what was for her a more urgent matter.

"Mama, when you reach Delhi, buy a local cellphone and speak to me every day. And I want you back in a week." She was being the parent again.

Diya came to see me off at the airport. As I walked towards the security check, I turned to look at her one last time. She was waving at me with that same worried look that had been on her face for the past few weeks. I felt like taking her in my arms as I had done when she was a toddler and telling her it would all be okay, that I had much more strength that she could ever fathom. Instead, I waved back and walked through the gates.

41.

THE TRIP BACK TO INDIA was difficult. It was not the same without Veer. It never would be. The journey was long and tedious. The familiar smells hit me as soon as the the doors of the plane opened and allowed us to disembark.

I gave my cab driver the address of my parents' house. Everything seemed different during the ride from the airport. The last I remembered of these streets was the maddening, chaotic traffic. As our taxi moved through the spaghetti junctions and new flyover passes, I was impressed with the infrastructure development and how neatly we glided through the organized intersections.

After about ten minutes on the road, our taxi swirled and honked loudly outside a large iron gate, to wake a sleeping night guard. The taxi driver took out my luggage and placed it on the marble porch entrance of a palatial apartment building. I tipped him an extra three hundred rupees for bringing me safely, but he crinkled his nose. Maybe three hundred rupees was not a good tip anymore, I thought.

Since Ma and Pa passed away, I realized that Delhi was just another empty city for me. Being the only child, they had left their apartment for occasions like these, when one of us decided to visit India. I took off the dusty covers to reveal and relive my childhood with every framed photograph, painting, cushion cover, and teacup. If only I could bring a bit of that abandon, a bit of that carelessness and innocence of childhood back into my life. For the rest of the day, I mourned for my parents, and the fact that I had not been able to come back to see them before they left this world.

The next morning, I opened my phonebook to pick up the threads with the people I had left behind, the people that I remembered often and missed. The first, of course, was my soul sister, Anita. In her last email, she had complained about Ajay's posting in congested Mumbai and how they were hankering to get away from it all. I left a message with her housekeeper, hoping that she would call me back soon.

Then I called Tina, my socialite friend, who had married Rony, Veer's friend and the goal keeper of the school soccer team. A few years ago, I had seen Tina's photograph in one of the Indian newspapers I bought at an ethnic Toronto market. Her hair had turned steel grey, and she looked aged far beyond her years. The article talked about a political rally that she was leading just before the general elections to topple the current government with her renowned politician father. She had changed from being a fashion buff to a self-proclaimed socialist and a politician. Rony was not by her side—instead there was a younger man who had his arm around her shoulder. Again, no response.

I decided to make my last call, to Jiya, who had been in touch over Facebook and was still her ravishing self. Her story had also made headlines in the tabloids, but for a different reason. She had successfully won a celebrated class action lawsuit against her husband Sam, who abused her for not bringing with her a satisfactory dowry when they married. Jiya was one of the millions who faced dowry abuse The tabloids spoke of how Jiya was physically, emotionally, and verbally abused for years because of the inability of her parents to shower her husband and his family with gifts, money, property and other material tokens as payment for his marriage to their daughter. Jiya defied this age-old custom of dowry by winning this court case and she had become a symbol of strength for other women in similar situations. I was so proud of all of my friends.

Jiya picked up the phone. The same voice, a little more poised. "Maya, I cannot believe it! Is that really you?" she cried out with joy, and I felt myself sniffling. "Is Veer with you too?" She did not know. No one knew. "I am so sorry to hang up this way, but I am running late for a meeting and then I am going out of town for a few days. I will call you back first thing when I return. Love you, and so nice to hear from you." We hung up.

I felt an emptiness. How futile this trip was. Diya was right. I was running after shadows. I had nothing in this city except my memories. I did not want to call anyone else.

Instead, I called a taxi, resolving to complete the tasks for which I had come. I gathered all the pieces of my old life that I needed to return to their rightful owners, and then free myself of them forever. I placed these items in my bag, one by one. The brass urn, the peacock bracelets, the black diary, and the peacock feather. Then I placed the bag carefully next to me on the taxi seat.

And, with that, we drove to our old mansion.

My myth about the new and improved state of Indian traffic from the previous night was shattered immediately. I rolled down the window to get away from the synthetic smell of the sandalwood air freshener. Greasy fumes reeking of gasoline mixed with grime hit my face from a platoon of trucks that was blocking the street ahead. There were different volumes of car horns blaring as if in competition with each other. Cars, scooters, stray dogs, pedestrians, rickshaws, cows, buses, cyclists, all moving in different directions on the same road, trying to forge ahead into any inch of space they could seize.

I had never seen such mastery, such skill being exhibited by any driver on the road, except my own taxi driver. He waded through each obstacle as a quarterback would to get a touchdown. I sat up in anticipation of recognizing any landmarks. But nothing looked familiar. Then we turned the corner. And, in a moment, I was back in time. In front of me stood the mansion. The façade was a little faded but essentially the same, with its, arches and domes, east and west wings, and the sprawling gardens.

I paid and thanked the driver, slid out of the taxi, and started out on the long, red gravel pathway to the front entrance. A security guard in a khaki uniform stopped me. "Madam, this is private property."

"I am Mrs. Rajsinghania, the daughter-in-law...."

He frowned, trying to remember a daughter-in-law in this house.

"I live in Canada now; I am just visiting."

He looked at me more intently, as if searching for a passport stamp embossed somewhere on my body.

"I lived in the east wing some time ago." For some strange reason that satisfied him. He saluted and let me pass.

There was not a soul in sight. Only an eerie silence. Even the wind was quiet. The front entrance seemed locked, so I followed the side path that led to the backyard. The hedges were trespassing on the main lawn. The grass was up to my shins and full of rotting weeds, garbage, and plastic bags.

I reached the pond facing the French windows where Veer and I had sat every morning to feed our peacocks. An overwhelming nostalgia filled me, but it left me as soon as it had arrived. The old peepal stood strong but bent, its branches drenched in dry mud, its moth-eaten leaves perforated with the cruelty of neglect. The French windows were bound with rusting black iron grills and peeling paint. The cement pillars of the gazebo were chipped and broken, its roof rotting with the foul smell of green fungus from stagnant water, and our lily pond was nothing but a dry empty hollow.

I reached the west wing, Gayatri's home. The breeze through the soaring gulmohars started whispering. Her tall windows overlooked the spot that I was standing on below. Was she welcoming Sachin and me? Something caught my eye and made me look up at her window on the second floor. I could have sworn that I saw a movement inside, but the glass was stained with the remnants of time and dirt.

I opened the urn with Sachin's ashes. The breeze became stronger. I did not know the exact spot where Gayatri's ashes were scattered I knew that her husband's ashes were scattered somewhere here too.

I found a quiet and clean corner and tilted the urn gently. The wind was waiting to receive the ashes. Another gust blew, and the ashes were scooped up in a gentle whirl and then scattered across the garden. I started chanting the holy mantra under my breath.

I remembered where the garden shed was. It was still there, but it was only a sorry memory of what it used to me. The door was broken and the walls chipped. I found what I was looking for right away. The spade was small but sharp, despite the rust. I started digging a small hole, just big enough for the other two things I had brought with me. These items had to be buried here too. I laid the box with the peacock bracelets inside the small hole and then took out the diary. I gently pulled out the feather and carefully slipped it in my coat pocket. Then I laid the diary next to the box with the bracelets. I was down on my knees, and the wind was growling in circles above my head. But this did not bother me anymore. I was concentrating on the loose mud that I need to cover the hole.

And, so, it was done.

My work here was complete. Three souls tormented in life and united in death. This had to be the end of their suffering and end of ours too.

It was time to leave.

Now I had only two tasks left. The first was to visit Veer's mother. I picked up my bag and traced my way back. Just then, I heard someone calling out. I recognized the voice, but it was weaker, shakier. I turned around.

Wrinkled and bent but with the same eyes, alert as a fiddle. She walked with a cane, her back arched like a bow and her head, tilted and shaking, was still covered with a Pashmina scarf as always.

My heart leapt. Sheila! I had intended to save my visit to her as my last, most important, task.

"Maya-Beti... Maya-Beti .... I knew it was you. I knew you would come," she panted.

I ran and hugged her. Thin tears were running down the deep cuts on her cheeks. "When the guard told me that someone had come from Canada, I ran to the peacock garden. I knew it was you."

I held her hand and led her to the open porch to sit on the broken cane settee. I continued to hold her hand and she stroked my head with affection. "How is my little Diya?"

I opened my wallet and showed her Diya's photograph. She gasped. "Oho, ho, ho ... my little Diya. See how she has grown sooo beautiful!" She kissed the photo many times. And then she looked directly into my eyes. "So, Maya-Beti, I would like it back now."

I pretended I did not understand. I could not return it to her. Had she forgotten the condition that she had placed on it?

"What are you talking about, Sheila?"

"Ohooo, you cannot fool me, Maya-Beti. You cannot."

I kept quiet. She extended her palm as a gesture for me to place the feather on it. I panicked. "Sheila, I don't have it," I lied.

She looked in my pocket right away. She really was a mind reader. But when I looked down, I noticed that in my haste to pull out the wallet with Diya's photo, I had also pulled out the edge of the peacock feather. Its tail was hanging out. No, she was not a mind reader. She was just observant. I bent my head. "Sheila, I cannot give it to you."

She did not ask me why. She did not ask me anything. I knew she understood what that meant. I changed the topic. "Sheila, where does the big Madam live now?"

"After the Master passed away the big Madam moved in with her sisters near the hills." I knew that I would not have time to travel out of the city. I was eager to get back to Diya. She saw my face fall and said, "The big Madam is in Delhi for her niece's birthday. I have also been asked to join them at tomorrow's party."

As always, she knew exactly what I wanted to hear. I wrote down the address.

We sat and spoke about things that had passed. "Bahadur is now the caretaker for the entire estate and lives with his whole family in the quarters at the back. The Master was very kind in his allowance to me."

"Sheila, how are Rosy and Umang? Are they still living in the west wing?"

"Oohooo, so you don't know?"

"Know what, Sheila?"

"Madam Rosy is now married to her friend Ramesh, and they have two children."

"What?"

"It was actually Master Umang's last wish before he too passed away a few years ago. He wanted Madam Rosy to be happy.... He was a kind soul," she said, nodding.

We both sat quietly on the porch of that deserted mansion, silently reliving the life and times, the rise and fall of the Rajsinghanias that the house had stoically witnessed. "So tell me, Sheila, who lives in our east wing?"

"Nobody."

How the tables had turned! The only thing that remained constant was change. I got up to leave. Sheila's gaze was piercing. She stumbled to get up, her knees stiff and painful, and I handed her the cane. She straightened herself slowly. "Maya-Beti, please give me the peacock feather. I have waited for it, and I want to die in peace." It was the most direct thing that Sheila had said to me ever.

"Don't you understand that if I give it to you it will mean that everything is okay? Why don't you understand this, Sheila?" I felt helpless, but I could not tell he what had happened to Veer. To my surprise she remained unmoved and persistent.

"Maya-Beti," she insisted, "please give me the feather."

Annoyed, I slid the feather out of my pocket and placed it in her open palm. Her eyes widened at the brilliance of its colours. Could she see something in it that I could not?

Her figures stroked its eye and slid down to its quill as if releasing a spell. She inhaled deeply, balancing her weight on her stick and started to hobble back inside.

"Sheila!" I called after her, still irritated and now confused by her behaviour.

She turned around and gave me one last look. Her head was bent with the weight of the Rajsighania secrets that she would carry with her to her grave. But under her pashmina scarf, her eyes still glowed with goodwill and hope.

She said, "Maya-Beti, I have your feather now. Whatever reason you had for not giving it to me, will go away."

And as I watched her crouched figure disappear into the house, I realized something. Sheila had inquired about Diya, but not once had she asked me about Veer.

In her own intuitive way, she already knew. She was a mind reader after all. She had been my guardian angel and I hadn't realized it until now.

I wanted to run after her, hold her, and thank her for how she had stood firmly for me like the bent stencilled tree braving the storm, the tree from Gayatri's diary, the tree of the Inuit healer's turtle-skin rattle.

But the wind had started again. With a heavy heart, I left our old mansion, feeling that a piece of me was buried there forever.

***

The next day, with a final gathering of my nerves, I went to pay my last debt. I knocked at Veer's aunt's doorstep, where his mother was staying. My heart pounded harder than the sound of a washer man beating clothes on the banks of a river. The door was opened by a slightly changed, but familiar face. It was Kitty, Veer's elder aunt. She looked older but she was well-groomed as always. Her eyes grew wide, and her mouth gaped at me in astonishment.

"Oh my God, it is Maya! Oh everyone, look who is here!" she shrieked, and her shouts brought out the other aunt, Minnie, and a few toddlers with their maids. It seemed like the entire household was at the door, all except Veer's mother. I was pulled with excited hands into a long corridor and then straight into the living room.

The large room was filled with more screaming children running around in circles, behind the curtains, and around the tables. There were some well-dressed, grey-haired men engrossed in conversations with crystal whiskey glasses pressed between their palms. There were waiters with round trays serving snacks and picking up dirty cutlery.

My eyes searched frantically for her. I imagined that Veer's mother would be the centre of some conversation. I walked to the adjoining dining room, which was just as crowded, but she was not there. Something caught my eye just as I was about to turn back. It was the back of a lone chair facing the window. I walked up to it to see who was in it. And there she was, sitting alone in a corner. I cried out, and, for the first time in my life, I hugged her. And for the first time since I had known her, she held my embrace.

"Mom, how are you?"

She looked at me blankly and said, "I am fine."

I opened my purse and handed her a photograph of our family together—Veer's father, her, Veer, Diya, and me, taken when Diya was born. On the back it was signed, *Happy Times* by Veer. She held it between her fingers and looked at it for a long time.

My tears were falling. I could feel her pain as a mother. I wanted to embrace her again but restrained myself for fear of rejection. Then she opened her lips to say something, but Minnie popped in behind us.

"Oh, Maya dear, meet my son-in-law, Tittoo." She proudly thrust forward a plump man with droopy shoulders and a paunch. He looked bored, but his face lit up when he looked at me.

"Hello ," he hissed suggestively. I had to pull my hand back after the extended handshake.

"You see, my dear daughter Tanya is very busy with her Tupperware business, so she could not come. You see, they both live in Enggglaaand...." Minnie gurgled as Tittoo retreated back into the crowd, and Minnie carried on. "I make sure to visit them every year. I like babysitting my grandchildren. You see, it gets so busy with my daughter and her children that there is no time left for Delhi... *ha ha*," she chuckled affectedly.

I looked at Veer's mother and wondered whether she felt left out by her sisters now that they had their own families. I soon got my answer. Veer's mother called to one of her nieces for a glass of water, but the girls was talking on the phone, and were too engrossed to pay attention to her. In a room full of her relatives and no one could hear her. I poured a glass of water from a nearby pitcher and brought it to her. "Mom, you are always welcome to come and stay with us in Toronto...."

She smiled at me vacantly and then handed the photograph back.

"It is for you, Mom. Keep it."

"Are you sure?"

"Yes, I have Veer with me always."

"And I lost him long ago," she said unexpectedly.

I was taken aback. Today was really a day of firsts with her. It was the first time that she showed me a more vulnerable side of herself, her insecurities, and the demons that haunted her. She was human after all.

"No, Mom, that is not true. You always meant the world

to him, he always hankered for your approval, your blessing ... and so did I," I added revealingly.

"Really? You?"

"Yes, Mom. I never married for anything but love." I found my voice cracking up. She was thinking about what I had said. "Mom, come with me to Toronto," I continued. "We can live together, and I will look after you. I know Veer would have liked that...."

She got up from her chair with great difficulty and asked me to follow her to the adjoining study. Her gait was slower than before, more deliberate. She opened a drawer and pulled out a sheet of legal paper and a pen. She switched on the table lamp and then handed me the pen. "Maya, if it is true what you are saying, if it is true you only married for love, then sign these papers to relinquish your share of Veer's ancestral property."

I was taken aback. I would not have been surprised by this had my heart not softened, hoping for more from her. And this was fate's way of teaching me a lesson, of scolding me for my naivety, for my believing that people change, that things can be different, or better. I started crying.

She looked at me and repeated her request, as if convincing me that she was only being reasonable by asking this of me, based on what I had told her. "Well, you should sign these if you want me to believe that it was not for our wealth that you married my son," she insisted.

I picked up the pen and signed on the dotted line. Then I picked up my bag, wiped my tears, and walked down the corridor and out the main door.

I was numb. But strangely, I felt free. A heavy weight had lifted from my soul. There were no more connections, no more debts, no expectations, and no more hurt. I was free of the mansion and free of its curse.

I held my head high and turned it towards the sky. The sun kissed my upturned face.

The image that flashed across my mind was an image that I knew would stay with me forever: Veer's mother bent over our photograph, searching for something that was long gone.

42.

MY JOURNEY BACK was less painful. The streets were covered with layers of fresh snow. Wind chill warnings were blasting on the taxi radio, and it was threatening to dip down to minus twenty-five. We were officially in a deep freeze. And I was enjoying every moment of it. The taxi driver, an Indian Sikh who was masking his turban under a Toronto Blue Jays cap, tried to make conversation

"So the weather must be great in India these days, right? Maybe it is the wrong time for you to come back?"

I thought about what he had said and replied, calmly, "No, it is not the wrong time. It is the perfect time to come home."

He turned up the radio to mask the awkwardness of the moment, an awkwardness that only he felt. I smiled sweetly at him.

I entered a cold dark house, turned up the heat, and put on a kettle. Then I collapsed in front of my multi-coloured living room wall, basking in the vibrancy of its shades.

I wondered if Veer could hear me? Could he see what I had done to our house? Did he know that I painted this wall with the colours of our life, all the colours of our peacock. Veer?

I woke to the kettle's piercing whistle.

I had to remember to call Diya, who was back at university for a few days. But first, I wanted my tea. There was nothing like a cup of life-saving hibiscus and bamboo tea to help me pick up the pieces and the strength to enter my bedroom again.

It was time to come to terms with the hardest part. My life alone.

But I could not get over the feeling that there was something as yet undiscovered, something remaining, something missing. It was not over yet.

What was it now? I had completed all my obligations, but maybe Veer still had one last challenge hidden for me?

Absent-mindedly, I opened the top drawer of Veer's desk. Then the second and then the third. Frustrated and tired, I sat down to look around me. The room was a mess. As always. Diya's toys had been substituted by her scarves and slacks strewn over the divan. Veer's cardigan was hanging on my side of the closet, and my shawl and a heap of other clothes were dumped in a pile partially hidden by a corner of the window curtains. A draught blew in from under the sill. I would have to fix that tomorrow or the presence of the lake would always be hanging over the bed. I reached for my shawl. And then I saw it. The small luggage that we had carried back from Tuktoyaktuk. Unmindfully, I opened it to take out the rest of my clothes. Jeans, shirt, another sweatshirt, and then something else. On top, lay the turtle-skin rattle from Anernerk, the Inuit man on the train.

I knew then that this was the last missing piece. This was the piece that would lead me to answers. This was what would help me understand why all was not over yet. My finger, traced the etching of the resilient branches braving the storm on its handle.

I grabbed a pen and started jotting down a plan.

43.

"MA, WHY DIDN'T YOU TELL ME that you were back?" Diya screamed with resentment on the other side of the phone line.

It had taken me a week to finalize the details of my plans before I called Diya, and she did not like the fact that I had not called her right away, and the fact that I had a plan that I was keeping to myself.

"Diya, when can you come?"

"I am coming right away. I don't trust what is going on in your head." Diya, the parent, had returned.

"Well, if you are coming, then why don't you meet me at four o'clock at the music studio in Hartville. Here, take down the address."

As I expected, she had a tirade of questions, but thankfully, I was saved by someone calling out her name from behind her, so she quickly noted the address and hung up.

It was an hour's drive to Hartville. I knew I had entered a different world as I approached the wooden bridge over the Spirit Valley River. The bridge opened into a narrow cobbled road with small shops on both sides. At the end of the enclave, there stood an old store, as if it were a gatekeeper, the last bastion before the street dropped into the thick wilderness beyond. It was aptly called The New Chapter. The building had been constructed out of Douglas fir logs, its casement windows propped by hard rocks, and its chimney tossed the warm, burnt smells of coal, ash, and wood into the frosty sky. I opened the door to jingling bells and a warm fire next to a decorated Christmas tree. There were musical instruments everywhere—on the shelves, in the windows, on the rugs, and hanging from the walls. Electric guitars, drums, amplifiers, cymbals, tuba, saxophones. There was a grand piano in the corner and a selection of acoustic guitars were stocked in black leather cases. Diya was already waiting. We hugged and cried for a few moments, then picked up two cups of steaming hot cocoa from the kitchenette that had been sprinkled with powdered cinnamon, whipped cream, and miniature marshmallows. We settled back in front of the fire, for a moment silent, and sipping companionably from our mugs. She was calm but I knew the storm that was brewing underneath that facade.

"Well?" she finally asked pointedly.

"Diya, my trip to Delhi was not as hopeless as you would think. It really made me want to come home, to you. It also reminded me of a promise I made to your father, and I have decided to keep that promise."

"Well?" she repeated, impatiently.

"We saved a little money. Last week I called up the local property agent and made a down payment on a small studio right above this music store." Her eyes widened. She could not contain himself anymore. "For what, mother? Are you moving here? This is bizarre behaviour. I know what you are going through. I know how difficult things have been for you. But to indulge in these random acts? I wish Dad was around to look after you. God, I miss him!" she trailed off, looking miserable.

"Calm down, Diya," I scolded. "This is not a mistake, I am not going insane, nor is this your fault. I have thought this through, and it makes perfect sense. It is like the last piece of a puzzle. Listen to the whole thing, have a little patience. I want to use this creative space for practising and creating music, and I would like to open it to any artist in the community who would like to do the same. I know that there are so many talented people who don't know where to start, or don't have a space that they can use."

There was a long silence. She was digesting what I had just told her. The store assistant came to refill our mugs and offered us a tray of freshly baked chocolate pecan cookies. As we reached for a cookie, I started to tell her the peculiar tale of the turtle-skin rattle and Anernerk's prophecy. "Since that day, the turtle-skin rattle has been tucked away. Until a week ago...."

I pulled out the rattle. Diya jingled it and then her fingers automatically traced the branches braving the storm, the same way I had done.

"Music is a healing process. You revisit the deepest, darkest places of your heart to realize that these places are not so dark after all."

Diya's face brightened. I had finally gotten through to her. She realized that this would take my mind off things. "And there is another reason why you should create music, Ma."

"Why?"

"So that you can give back to your community, for there is no greater satisfaction than that."

I smiled, pleased that Diya was now coming around to this idea.

Diya stood up and beamed. "It is a fantastic idea. Come, Mama, let's go and see this place—your studio. I am already excited." She tugged on my sleeve like a little girl.

We followed the assistant up the winding, squeaky wooden stairs. We landed in a long dark corridor with two doors, one at the beginning of the passage, and one at the end. As we passed the first door, I was suddenly curious. "What is in here?" I asked the assistant.

"Oh, only another studio apartment rented by another tenant."

"Must be another nutcase like you, Mama," Diya joked.

"Actually, he is connected with the arts in some way. Funny you should ask," the assistant mumbled.

"Why?" I asked.

"Because he was asking about your name too. When he came in yesterday, he saw your nameplate being painted for the letterbox outside the door, and he asked me to describe you, but since I had never met you before today, I could not."

I thought of asking the assistant to describe the man, but we had already reached the last door in the corridor. He pulled out a long shiny key and placed it into the keyhole.

It was a large open space split into three levels, with six-foot windows facing north on the cobbled street and south over the river. As the last of the waning sun broke free from behind a cluster of dark clouds and tinted the corners in molten hues, the room smiled back at us. My heart cried. Diya wiped my tears. "Mama?"

"It's nothing."

Without knowing it, I had been waiting for this place all my life. And then, just as suddenly, I knew that there was nothing more I wanted than for Veer to be with me now.

I watched Diya hop from one corner to the other, visualizing and designing each nook and angle. Her eyes were bright and she was breathless with excitement. When she stopped, exhausted, I pressed her hand gently and said, "Diya, if ever you would like to come and join me in this studio, no one would be happier than your mother."

***

It took a month to set up the studio, and in a few hours, I would be ready to inaugurate it for neighbourhood. When I walked in around noon I was surprised to hear "Somewhere Over the Rainbow," from the *Wizard of Oz*, being played on a violin. Who was playing so beautifully and how did they get into the studio? Did the store assistant downstairs open the door a few hours earlier than I had requested? I would have to ask him not to do this in future. But despite myself, I was deeply moved by the music.

The glint from the sun pouring through the windows was blinding me. All I could see was the outline of the person against the light. And then he stopped playing and looked up. His dark shadow on the wall soared as he stood up. I stepped back to get a better look.

It was a face from the past. Sachin. The same jaw line, the same high cheeks bones over a prominent nose. I had just scattered his ashes in another part of the world. I looked at him again. A mop of blond hair had fallen over the young man's smiling green eyes, as he placed his violin down and walked over to me. "Hello Mrs. R!"

Of course it was not Sachin. It was his son Albert!

"Albert what are you doing here?" I asked. "How did you find me?"

I was surprised. I had only advertised in the neighbourhood, and he lived in Alliston, a little town not exactly near by. I had more questions.

He hesitated. "Well, ah..." he stumbled. "Actually, it was through my school."

Just then the door opened and Diya entered with two steaming cups of cocoa. She placed the cups on the counter and ran to hug me. Her lush black hair shimmered like a cascade of fresh water, and her enormous expressive eyes wore a look that I recognized in an instant. She had big news. "Mama!"

"What is it, Diya?"

"I have wanted you to meet Albert, my special friend, for such a long time. I met him when I was at school in Montreal, and he and I went on that expedition in the north, and we were in that first group that got rescued together." Her eyes were big and round and shining with tears and joy and hope that I would welcome him into our family.

Oh my god. Why had I not seen this before?

Of course it made perfect sense.

Diya and Albert. Two saplings from an old seed blossoming on fresh soil. They had known no other soil, and yet their destinies were intertwined with the ghosts of the past.

I wanted to tell Diya that I knew Albert and his father from before she was born. I wanted to tell her how they were connected to our past. But instead I just smiled and shivered and then smiled again. How did the Inuit man know when he prophesized: *The wild love from an ancient land flows in the blood of youth.*

I opened my bag and took out the magical turtle-skin rattle that had waited for this moment of revelation, and to be placed in a room full of music and love as Anernerk had decreed with such certainty.

Fate had brought us a full circle. I could see clearly now. And I was truly bewildered.

44.

AT EXACTLY FIVE O'CLOCK, as the grandfather clock chimed, the studio doors were opened to the neighbourhood. We had been distributing flyers for weeks and the gentleman in the store below had informed us that many people had been inquiring. The owner of the music store had allowed us to borrow a few music instruments and pay for the duration of our studio's open hours. Everything was falling into place it seemed.

The first knock came within five minutes of our opening. Three statuesque, brunette sisters dressed in shades of lavender walked in with their knapsacks. They settled comfortably near the large, glossy fashion magazines. Within minutes, two lanky, hesitant teenagers arrived, their pants pulled down to their hips and trailing baggily at their heels. "Is this where the studio space is?"

"Yes, it is. Come on in. What is your name?"

"Jack, and this is Colin, my friend." They made a beeline to the furthest corner of the reading area.

Then, a young mother with a sleeping toddler strapped to her chest waddled in and sank into the closest chair.

I was just about to start with the introductions when the door opened once again. This time there were twin boys at the door! I was about to ask the twins if they were with an accompanying adult, when the a tall man walked in. "Uncle, come ... come see!"

I recognized the lean physique and confident gait instantly. It was a familiar face, a handsome face that prompted fond memories. He gave me a long hug and peck on my cheek. His spectacular deep blue eyes were creating havoc with the grey on his temples. "Hello, Maya," his voice as warm and welcoming as it had always been

"Hello, William," I said, at a loss for other words. Finally, I managed to sputter, "What are you doing here?"

"Well, I have brought my nephews, Kevin and Kyle, to you."

The two boys were clinging to his legs and pulled him towards the couch in the reading area. "Stay, Uncle Bill," they pleaded He looked at me and I shrugged. And although he stayed with them for a few moments, he did eventually get up and with a wave, he quietly left.

Then I turned my attention to the group that had assembled in the room. "Well, let's start with introductions shall we? A little about why we have to come to this music studio today?"

The next few hours completely rejuvenated me. Some took a musical instrument from our borrowed collection to try out. Others talked about their upcoming music projects or ideas, and the others just did their own thing. At the end of the "open session," when it was time to go, I gave each student something to remember this time by: A poem, an idea, a notepad, a pen, a chocolate, a borrowed book, a wish.

As each of the participants said goodbye, I watched as the twins lingered in the corner waiting for William to take them home, I assumed. But Kevin came to me and said, "We are going down to meet our mother. She is here to pick us up. May we go?"

"Yes, of course, you may."

Relieved that everyone had left, I collapsed happily under my blanket on the couch. But not for long. A deep warm voice was calling my name. I did not want to open my eyes. The sun's warmth was still trapped under my lashes. I heard the voice again and I forced my eyelids open to see William smiling down on me. And behind him was Diya. I propped myself up, still snuggled under the blanket's warmth. "William, what are you doing here again?"

"Is this your pet question to me today?" he joked. "I was catching up with Diya. I had no idea how accomplished she is, and this young man Albert, too." And then he took my hand and clasped it between his own. "Maya, I am so deeply sorry about your husband. Diya just told me."

I looked away quickly before my eyes teared up.

He changed the subject. "And Maya, it may be wise to drop that question about what I am doing here because you will definitely be seeing more of me now."

"*Why*?"

"Because I am your neighbour, Maya. I am the person who lives in the first apartment just down the corridor from you."

So, William was the mysterious stranger next door!

"When I saw your nameplate, I was pretty sure that it was you." He raised his eyebrows as if this was a very frightening thought and we all laughed.

I looked at Diya. I could tell that she liked him. She was bright eyed, just as she usually was whenever she discovered something exciting or intriguing. I wondered what she was thinking now.

Albert brought over a pot of steaming sake on a bamboo mat and four Oshoko cups. As he poured, Diya stirred with a ceramic swizzle. Their movements were perfectly synchronized.

"Who knew you would meet William again, Ma, and this time as a neighbour?" Diya said, her voice almost giddy.

"Yes, life has a way of surprising us," William added.

"Yes ... who could have thought that today...?" I could not complete my sentence. I stood up, forgetting the warmth that was enveloping me. I went to the window and opened it. It was a clear but chilly night. The moon was high in a starless sky. I wished I could have melted into the inviting darkness. I felt a hand on my shoulder. A cold, petite hand. It was Diya.

Somehow, she always knew. "Ma, come away from the window, you will catch a chill."

William had just doused the fireplace logs in oil. Little by little, the flames picked up and the sizzling logs crackled. Albert and Diya had switched on soft music and were swaying in each other's arms. I warmed up next to the burning logs.

I looked around the scattered room and thought of tidying it, but could not muster the strength to get up. William was sitting and reading a magazine in the corner. He caught my eye and came to sit next to me.

"How is work?" I asked. Now was a chance to smoothen out our earlier wrinkles.

A cloud passed over his even features, and then the sun came out. "Oh, long gone."

"Such a pity, you really liked your job."

"Yes, I did."

There was no bitterness in him. Just acceptance. How easy it was for him to weave through life. He had the same ease about him as he had had from the first day I had met him. I suddenly longed for that ease too.

William kept talking for a long time. He made me laugh. Without wanting to, I found myself suspended in his sentences and waiting in between them, eager for his next thought. The flames were now reaching out to every corner of the room.

The grandfather clock chimed again. It was midnight. William stood up to get his jacket, and I started walking him to the door when he stopped abruptly. He looked at me in a way that moved something inside me. "Maya, I know this is bizarre and I am surprised at my own spontaneity. But if I don't ask you now I will regret it for a long time."

I held my breath. I did not want to hear anything that I was not ready for.

"Maya, I leave for Peru next month. I am planning to attend one of the greatest carnivals that takes place once every three years. It is art and entertainment like you have never seen before. It is a wonderful event with dancers, actors, musicians, painters, and artists from all over the world." He paused to take a breath. I was still holding mine.

"Why don't you come with me?"

The silence spoke for me. He turned around and headed for the door. And then once again he turned back and looked at me, probably for the last time.

"Maya, I understand what you are going through. But I think this trip could take you away from your pain for some time. And you don't have to make a decision right now. I will come back in a few days and we can talk. What do you have to lose?"

With that, he left. I was standing with my half sentence of refusal rolling on my tongue.

I switched off the lights and doused the fire. The embers still sizzled as I lay down next to them on the bare floor. The clouds were gathering, but miraculously a full beaming moon poured its light through my window, tucking the room with a cool silver quilt.

Restless, I got up. The pain of Veer's absence always lingered on the edges, in small and big things, in a word, in a sound, in a sign, in my heart. I could not believe that it was happening again. That feeling of something remaining, something unfinished had sprung up again.

45.

I PICKED UP MY KEYS to drive home. My answers lay at home, somehow. I was not afraid of the dark house. I opened all the windows to our wild garden overlooking the lake. An icy cold draft enveloped the house.

I called out to her. *Gayatri!*

I knew that she was responsible for my feeling of incompleteness. I needed to finish this with her. Last time we had faced each she had overpowered me with her aggression. But not today. Today I needed answers. I emptied my lungs again into the darkness like a glassblower on her last breath.

Gayatri!

A low wind had started. A pale moon slithered behind black clouds. I sat on the solitary upholstered chair facing the window, closed my eyes, and waited for the darkness to take me.

I waded toward the edge of the dark garden. Menacing shadows lingered behind me, threatening to catch up. But I kept walking. The wind whimpered, moaned, and then screamed for attention, for allegiance. But I kept walking.

I had reached the mouth of the lake. The lakeside boulders lay awkwardly exposed with webs of green weed. The dark waves submissively obeyed the wind's commands to retreat back into their murky depths.

A heavy blanket of stillness descended from above, and with it came a stench of rotting carcass. I knew Gayatri had arrived. I retched. The wind screeched a battle cry as it charged toward me from across the lake, wrinkling its surface irreversibly. The wind pushed me down with a jolt, tore through my hair, scratched my chest, and then stabbed at my belly. But I ignored the pain and stood up. I called out again.

"Gayatri, show yourself...."

A sharp gust picked me up, and suspended me in the air momentarily. "*Maaayaaa....*"

Was that the sound of the wind? Yes, it was the wind ... it was talking to me. The wind was Gayatri!

I couldn't feel my heart anymore. Her frosty hands were around my chest and an icy cold wind coursed through my body. I turned to go back to the warmth of my room. As the moonlight passed through me, I saw that my shadow was missing. Gayatri was following me.

"*Maaayaaa....*" her words were a fading sigh.

I turned around to face her once again. I had resolved not to break down. "I understood your pain," I cried out. "And I reunited you with Sachin. But what did you do? You took away everything from me!" I was proud that I had the courage to finally speak up.

A surprisingly pleasant musky smell surrounded me. It was a childhood smell of the first rain that kissed a hot parched earth under the mango groves of Ma's house.

A moonbeam escaped from behind a passing black cloud and reflected off the silver thread of her dress, creating small snowy butterflies that fluttered around us. She smiled. The smell of blue hyacinth and lavender sweet pea flooded my senses.

I suddenly understood that forgiveness was the key, not revenge. I had had to learn to forgive Gayatri for all the havoc that she had caused in my life, just as she would have to forgive people who caused her harm. The wind was whispering now, and as it caressed my skin, my body started to feel warm again ... I wanted to reach out to her; she had loved music as I did. As Sachin did. As now my daughter and even Albert did.

Suddenly, Anernerk's words came to me: "*The wild love from an ancient land flows in the blood of youth. Let the darkness guide you to revival in a new life.*"

Perhaps she could be at peace now that she was reunited with Sachin. But how could I be at peace? What good was my life without love, without Veer?

Gayatri read my mind. She entered my head. I started spinning. I knew she intended to empty my mind of all painful questions, all doubt. And I couldn't stop her. I felt light. I was floating. I could see the chipped shingles of my roof. I could see the empty bird nest on the tallest oak. I could see the lake swell on its edges under the summoning of dark clouds. I could remember nothing anymore. I could only feel. I felt her pain and then her joy. And I felt my anger and then my love for Diya. I felt Diya's anxiety and Veer's helplessness and then their love for me.

The grass under my toes was no longer cold. I lay my face on the earth and waited for the giddiness to subside.

Gayatri was circling above me and there was a glow behind her head. She was smiling, the same riveting smile she had in her photograph, the first time I had seen her.

The wind had stopped blowing. I detected the smell of mint and melting chocolate. I tasted something sour and my lips tingled with its fizz. Champagne. And then something crisply sweet. Strawberries. Wild and fresh as they grew at the edge of our garden in summer. Two snowy butterflies landed on my shoulders and followed me as I finally reached the safety of my room.

I slipped under Veer's side of the bed, under the warmth of his eiderdown.

Through the open window, I looked back one last time.

There was a soft white glow behind the rising cold mist where Gayatri had stood.

***

If it wasn't for the open windows that blew in the night storm,

I would have convinced myself that I had imagined it all. Yet, when I woke in the morning, I was in the same position on the sole upholstered chair facing the garden that I had slid into the previous night. I had not moved an inch. Or had I?

I went outside and sat under the stone angel statue with a bag of birdseed, debating with myself about the events of that night. The sun was flirting with the passing clouds and occasionally smiled on our patch below. Winter had passed; spring was almost here.

I looked up at the towering stone angel above my head. His wings were ready for flight, to take me where I wished. His eyes were kind and his face was serene. His long bulky robe tumbled passionately on to the remains of a wildflower bed spouting over green fungi water. Thick green moss had comfortably colonized each crevice, fracturing the angel's joints. I wondered whether after all these years that we had sat under his embrace and reflected on our trials and tribulations, on our passions and our endurance, our little pleasures and big setbacks, whether, through it all, the angel really cared about what happened to us. Or would he just stand there lifeless and for every family and every life that passed under its wings?

I looked behind the angel's robe. And, underneath the dripping water from the angel's robe sat our doves. Dipping their beaks to plump each other's feathers, these love birds were in perfect harmony today.

I dug my fingers into my pockets with the hope of pulling out the leftover stash of seed. I slowly walked over to them with my palm extended. They did not flutter. The first one flew to the edge of my palm and balanced himself on it. Then he bent his head and picked up a red millet speck. I looked over my shoulder for the other dove. Where had she gone? She was here just a moment ago. That was odd. So I walked slowly to the bench and sat down again.

The wind started. It became stronger and gustier. Loose

mud, dry snow, some plastic bags, bits of garbage from the lake's edge, and a few dead leaves started blowing furiously my way. Was this another storm? Surprisingly, the dove did not fly off to look for his mate. I looked up at the sprinting clouds. A newspaper flew my way and crashed onto my face. It was crumpled and smelled of wet earth. I squashed it in my palm to roll it into a ball, but something in bold black ink caught my eye: *Southern man with miracle green thumbs.*

Something stirred inside me. A hint of familiarity, a nostalgic thread. I carefully opened its seams and ironed out the damp, torn page on my lap. But the wind was too strong. It escaped from between my fingers and flew high in a whirl above my head. I jumped to catch it, but it was too high. Another gust of wind blew and hurled the paper under the angel's wing. It was stuck. I ran and grabbed it. I looked up at the angel. He was smiling, and on his other hand was perched the missing dove. She called out to her mate, and he joined her. I ran inside to read it.

> Southern Man with Miracle Green Thumbs.
> In the barren arctic, a Southerner has been able to grow season vegetables to feed himself and the small community of.... Miracles do happen.

I scraped at the smudged ink where the paper had torn. Then I carefully laid it under a table lamp and then under a magnifying glass. Nothing helped. I could not tell what was next.

I looked out into the garden again. The storm had passed. The angel was looking like stone again, and the doves had flown off. But I knew their secret now. No, our angel was not made of stone; he had a heart, and, along with the doves, he had shown me the path.

I got out a pen and a pad and started writing a farewell note to Diya.

46.

THE TRAIN TO TUKTOYAKTUK was cold and fast like the arctic storm. The harsh beauty of the rugged boulders and peaks gave me courage, and the gentle tempo of the glacial rivers gave me much needed solace. Majestic grazing caribou and hulky moose reminded me of how one can be connected even in isolation.

I knew I did the right thing by not calling Diya before leaving. She would never have let me go. So I had left my note on Veer's desk, which would be the first place she would look.

I reflected on its words.

> *Dear Diya,*
>
> *Please don't be upset with me. I have to go back to find out the reason for this incompleteness in my heart. I have to look for him and know for sure. Nourish the studio—it is yours to keep as long as you desire. Let William know that in another world, maybe — but not in this one. He will understand. Take it easy with Albert. He is special, but you are more special. I will see you soon. I know you will forgive me and, more importantly, you will understand.*

The train was slowing down, and I picked up the same small luggage that I had brought with me the first time.

No amount of preparation could have ever acclimatized me

to the sharp knife of frigid coldness that stabbed my face, even though I had been here before, and knew to expect it. With shaking hands, I grabbed the railing of the compartment and stepped onto the slippery platform.

A distant jingle was all that it took for me to know what to expect next. But it was not Aippaq. It was a younger man who led me to the sleigh. He came towards me and shook my hands in a way that brought back some circulation.

Within minutes we were flying on the snow. Just as we passed the Inuksuk and the huts came into view on the horizon, the young man spoke. "Are you from the South too?"

"Yes, south of Algonquin, from Ontario," I said. His eyes widened.

"Just like him. He said the same thing.... How strange..."

"Who?"

There was no reason to raise my hopes just yet. Maybe there were others who had visited after the avalanche. I had read about the increasing amount of research that was happening in this area because of global warming. But he stumped me. "He who has magic green thumbs."

"Who?" I asked again, still forcing myself to be calm, but this time with a racing heart.

"They say that he was carried by the wolves and then left for dead ... but no one really knows. When our elders found him, he was gone. They brought him back to see his spirit circle over his head for several days. My uncle Aippaq looked after him. He was broken from the hip, but my uncle calls him *the brave one*. He learnt so much from the herbs that healed him, that now he lives from the earth and..."

"...And feeds the village." I completed his sentence. He looked up at me surprised.

"Stop!" I shouted. He stopped the sleigh. I grabbed this young boy by his arm. "Take me to him—*now*!"

"What? Now? It is already getting late." He looked up into my eyes, and saw my urgency.

We were back on the sleigh with the cutting wind on my face. But I did not feel anything. We crossed a frozen, treeless zone and then patches of evergreen trees. Scattered muskoxen and a few arctic foxes cautiously watched us from the edges. The young musher was showing me the silky white plumes of arctic cotton and vibrant purple flowers of the arctic saxifrage shrub. But I was not looking.

We had reached the foot of a frozen lake. A bonfire at the entrance of a gated village rose high to spread its warmth. I started running. My foot slipped, but I stood up and started again. I could not stop. A group of men huddled around the fire looked up at me curiously. I recognized one of them. Aippaq!

"Maaayaaa!" His voice was an echo.

"Why did you not tell me?" I cried. He came towards me and steadied my body by holding my arm. "Why?" I screamed, this time livid.

"Because he told me not to...."

"*Why?*"

"Because he said he was repenting for past sins."

"Past sins," I repeated. So Veer was paying for past sins, sins that were not his.

"... And because I knew that true love would follow...." Aippaq said this under his breath, but I heard him clearly.

He walked with me a few steps and then let go of my arm. I raised my head to focus in front. There was a greenhouse of sorts and inside a fiesta of colours, shrubs, edible-looking greens And in front was a silhouette, not so tall and brawny anymore, with shoulders that were much less broad. His back was bent like the stencilled tree that had braved the storm, and the same forehead tapering into a widow's peak peeped through a mass of silver hair falling over smiling hazel eyes.

I came closer. His eyes sparked and then filled with tears.

The sky opened up, its emerald green sheen pulling us with a divine magnetism. All I could hear was quiet sobbing from Aippaq, or maybe it was me. I could not tell.

Veer took a step forward with a crutch under his arm and fumbled. Then he threw away his crutches and opened his arms wide.

My feet carried my soul into his embrace. I did not feel incomplete anymore. The wind had started blowing again. But there was no whisper. We were free.

ACKNOWLEDGEMENTS

This book is dedicated to my childhood friend, my soul mate, with whom I have laughed, cried, lived, and died every day, without whom life would only be a road trip, not a celebration. And to a most beautiful mother who gave me vision, courage, and a lens with magical colours to see the world.

And to all those strong willed wonders of my world: Mama, our matriarch, who introduced me to a world that lay at my feet, one with endless possibilities. She will always live on with me. Daddy, who did everything logistically possible with the undying hope of improving me, who laughed with me even when I laughed at him. The unconventional, eccentric Siddharth, who graduated from following me to showing me what to follow in his own bohemian vernacular.

Arahant, who grounded me relentlessly and eternally to motherhood, who taught me how to love even through extremities of stress, tiredness, tolerance and anger.

Pritha, my gift, who showed me that not everything that floats needed to be pinned down. She has healed me in ways that cannot be fathomed.

Jolly Masi, my alter ego, my escape into alternate reality, a place of serendipity, dichotomy, unpredictability, and wondrous confusion. A place where I run free and wild, in the moment and in my spirit. Khoken Dada, who is the reason I made it to the second draft, we will miss you always.

To my lifelong Canadian friends who enveloped me with warmth on the coldest of snowy nights and granted me space to be myself.

To my loyal childhood friends, my fellow conspirators and bearers of all secrets, who did not give up on me even after I left home.

To Inanna Publications and it's Editor-in-Chief, Luciana Ricciutelli.

And to all the countless unique individuals who have touched this journey, fired my imagination and preserved my faith in humanity when it was the weakest. With you I have walked these pages to make them real. To you I owe each page.

Anubha Mehta is a Canadian writer and artist who was born in India. With a doctorate in Political Science, and two decades of Canadian public service experience, Anubha has won awards for her leadership work with diverse communities. Her book, *The Politics of Nation Building and Art Patronage* (2012), was a culmination of years of her research in late 1990s. Her short stories and poems have been published in several Canadian magazines and journals and reflect her travels and life lived on both sides of the globe. She currently lives in Toronto, Ontario. *Peacock in the Snow* is her debut novel. Read more about Anubha's work on: www.AnubhaMehta.com.